DEADLY
RHYTHM

PETER R. KOWEY MD

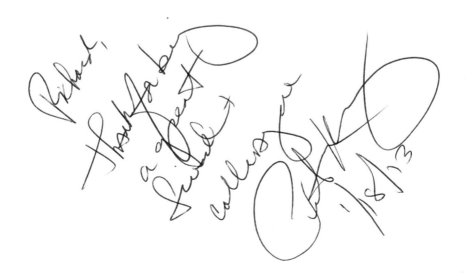

Pavilion Press, Inc.

Philadelphia • New York

Deadly Rhythm
by Peter R. Kowey MD

ISBN:

Paperback	1-4145-0731-3
Hard Cover	1-4145-0732-1

Library of Congress
Cataloging-in-Publication Data
1. Fiction 2. Mystery

Pavilion Press, Inc., Philadelphia, PA
www.pavilionpress.com

Dedication

I dedicate this book to my wife and best friend, Dorothy Freal Kowey, who inspires me daily and in so many ways. In addition, Dorothy has sacrificed an enormous amount of our time together to allow me to be the doctor we both knew I had to be, and to pursue my dream of publishing novels.

To Peter and Edith Kowey, my parents. They didn't need a formal education to learn the most important lessons in life. I was just glad to be around to absorb some of their extraordinary wisdom and goodness.

To my patients. They have provided a treasure trove of stories and experiences that I have used not only to create novels but also to teach other doctors how to take care of people with heart disease. Without these wonderfully brave and forthright souls, none of what I do would be conceivable.

And finally to the remarkable Mitten. Shortly after I completed this novel, our first and most precious dog died at the age of 14. But Mittie will live on forever in this book as well as in the hearts and minds of anyone who ever got down on their knees and gave her a pet.

Disclaimer

Deadly Rhythm is a fictionalized version of a murder case that occurred in the Scranton/Wilkes-Barre area several years ago. I have had the opportunity to meet some amazing people who have inspired the characters I created for this story. However, all of the characters in this book are fictional. Any resemblance to real people, living or dead, is entirely coincidental.

DEADLY
RHYTHM

Acknowledgments

I would like to thank Jim Kaufmann, PhD, my best friend from high school and now a medical editor in Minnesota, for his help with multiple edits. Without Jim, this project would have turned out differently.

I also want to thank Bob Hall, Rob Bokunewicz, Ann Marie Chikowski, Marion Fox, Donna Simonds, and Dorothy Kowey for reading several early drafts and telling me where I went wrong.

My secretaries, Donna Simonds, Roe Wells, and Patricia Basile, have been enormously helpful with the logistics of book distribution and arranging my appearances.

To the "team" of Steve Crane, my publisher, Samantha Lacey, cover designer, Allison Guarino, webmaster, and David Ratner, my publicist, I am deeply indebted for all of their hard work on this novel and its predecessor *Lethal Rhythm*.

I also thank my daughters, Jaime, Olivia, and Susan, for their encouragement, and my six gorgeous grandchildren for being the amazing little people they are.

Chapter One

Although it wasn't obvious to the people who changed his diapers, Alfonzo Romanzo had been a special person. He had grown up in the coal-mining region of northeastern Pennsylvania, the eldest son of poor Italian immigrants. Although his father's brothers had done well in the world of Philadelphia business, Al's father didn't have the aptitude for sales and marketing, and had to take a job as a coal miner to support his young and growing family. His father hated his job, and let his resentment make him a bitter man. He rarely laughed or smiled, and never spent time with his children. His few waking hours at home were usually spent listening to the radio or reading the local scandal sheet, complaining about the politicians who were stealing him blind.

As a young man, Al resolved not to follow his father into the ground as did so many coal miners' sons, including his brothers. Al was determined to make something of himself. He persuaded his parents to allow him to apply to one of the local colleges at a time when few people in his neighborhood finished high school. After earning his college degree, he served honorably in Europe in World War II. When he returned to the States, he paid a visit to the Philadelphia contingent of his extended family. They were impressed with his maturity and energy, and agreed to take him into the family appliance business.

Al responded to their vote of confidence by excelling at his job. He didn't mind putting in long hours, and he had a people-oriented personality that lent itself well to the business world. He enjoyed the vibrant city life in Philadelphia. He wasn't handsome, but he dressed and groomed himself well. His mother had taught him to respect women, and when he was introduced to a new lady, he knew how to make her feel important. It wasn't long before he met Dolly, a cute secretary at the store who convinced him to think about settling down. They married, had two children, and spent the next forty-eight years proving to each other that they had made the right choice.

After a few years in Philadelphia, Alfonzo accepted his family's offer to develop a new branch of the business in his hometown of Scranton. Although Al and Dolly made the transition with ease, his two children inherited Al's sense of independence and love of city life. When they came of age and had the opportunity to escape the cultural desert of northeastern Pennsylvania for the excitement of Southern California, they seized it. As with so many young people before them, they were quickly seduced by the weather and the lifestyle, and never returned to the east.

The next several years were quiet ones for Al and Dolly. When he retired, they traveled to see their children occasionally and enjoyed their elder years together. They were each other's best friends to the exclusion of most others. Al kept up with his former mentors in Philadelphia, but their visits became less frequent. As the years went by, Al and Dolly preferred the quiet solitude of their comfortable home and their precious dogs to the social scene at the local senior center. So when Dolly died rather abruptly of breast cancer, it didn't take long for Al's world to come apart.

Al's children asked him half-heartedly to move to California so they could help him, but he refused. He had lost his wife, and he couldn't bear the idea of losing his nest and his pets, too. But it wasn't long before Alzheimer's disease got him, and Al found himself in a nursing home where his memory loss accelerated and his ability to do things for himself slipped away.

Despite all this, Al still managed some lucid moments. Fortunately, they didn't last very long because they were excruciating. For in those minutes, he realized that his children and grandchildren didn't visit him much. He knew they didn't like the odor of urine that pervaded the nursing home despite the staff's best efforts to keep everyone, including Al, clean and dry. Occasionally, Al would awaken and realize he was lying in his own feces. It would sometimes take hours for an aide to come to his rescue, by which time the stool had encrusted on his bottom and had to be scraped off with wire brushes in the bathtub.

One morning in early spring, Al awoke with his mind as clear as a bell. Suddenly realizing he had to go to the toilet, and knowing he didn't have much time to get there, he found and pushed the call button. He could hear staff in the hallway complaining that two of their colleagues had called out sick so they were even more short-handed than usual. Al's call bell could not be given a high priority. They would get to him after they had taken care of patients with more pressing problems.

Al decided he wasn't going to wait. He tried to slide the side rails down but they were locked from the outside. His next thought was to climb over the bedrail—the bed had been lowered close to the floor so it wouldn't be too hard for him to straddle the rail and get a foot on the floor. But Al forgot to account for his bedclothes. As he stretched his leg over the rail and shifted his weight, his pajama top became caught in the locking mechanism. When he tried to pull it out, he sent himself vaulting over the side of the bed, cracking his head on the thinly carpeted floor.

The aides heard the commotion and quickly ran in to investigate. Alfonzo Romano lay on the carpet, arms and legs akimbo, incontinent of stool and urine, staring at the ceiling, and not responding to their commands.

The nursing supervisor had just arrived on the floor and came in to evaluate the situation. She directed the aides to get

Al into the bathroom and clean him up. She then told the shift director to call an ambulance. Al had stable vital signs and didn't look any different than usual. He didn't seem to have an obvious severe injury, but she wasn't going to take any chances. The nursing home risk managers had instructed the staff to be conservative when a patient might be injured. Some nasty lawsuits had to be settled with greedy relatives, and the facility's insurance payments had skyrocketed. A few more big payouts and they would have to close the place down. Much better to pack the patient off to an acute care hospital for an evaluation that Medicare would pay for.

Al was loaded into an ambulance and taken to the Scranton Memorial Hospital—the closest ER. The ride took only five minutes. Since Al was stable, the attendants were able to focus on their coffee thermos and doughnuts as they lurched around in the back compartment. They offloaded Al quickly, bantering with the cute ER nurse who came out to greet them.

Dr. Jimmy Keith was the emergency physician on duty, and he was inundated that morning. There had been a thin layer of ice on the roads when rush hour started, causing multiple car accidents and minor injuries that the good doctor was triaging and attending to furiously. He was whirling around the ER with decorative blood on his scrubs, stethoscope bouncing around his neck, making good use of his Nikes to save transit time between patients.

Jimmy was an experienced doc and was used to the rush of the ER, but he didn't respond happily when his good buddy, head nurse Martha Rathke (dubbed Nurse Ratchett by her less-than-adoring staff), informed him that he had another nursing home patient. Martha was from the old school. She still wore a starched white uniform dress and a nursing cap, and she didn't mind reminding her nurses that obeying the rules and being respectful to the doctors were the most important parts of being a good nurse. She ran the ER like she ran her MASH unit in Vietnam in the 1970s. When Nurse Ratchett was on duty, patients moved quickly and efficiently through the ER.

"Oh, please tell me, Martha, about my new and fascinating

patient." Jimmy didn't try to hide the sarcasm in his voice.

"New Horizons Nursing Home just sent over a gomer named Romanzo who fell out of bed and smacked his head on the floor."

Keith winced. "I hate that term." *Gomer* is a commonly used acronym in the ER; it stands for "Get Out of My Emergency Room" and was applied to anyone deemed unworthy of medical services because of age or infirmity or anything else the staff found abhorrent. Despite Jimmy's exhortations, the nursing staff loved to use that kind of slang.

Rathke didn't miss a beat. "I'm sorry, Doctor. That's not a proper term, and I shouldn't have used it to describe poor Mr. Romanzo."

Keith brushed off the apology. "Just what I needed. Christ, I have a million minor lacerations to sew up. I don't have time for a nursing home screw-up. Can't they keep these people in their beds?"

Even though Keith meant it as a rhetorical question, Martha felt obliged to answer. "Well, they used to be able to put restraints on the inmates, but the bleeding-heart liberals convinced the legislature that straps are cruel and you need a special order to use them. Most families won't sign an order because it sounds nasty. I guess it's more humane for these old people to splatter themselves all over the floor on a regular basis."

"Well, I can't get to him for a while. Is he OK?"

Keith knew that Martha Rathke was a triaging genius and would be able to tell him what was going on without ambiguity.

"He's OK, as far as I can tell. The floor was carpeted so he has a small lump on the back of his head with only a little bleeding. He isn't with the program but they told me over there when they called report that he rarely is. His vitals are fine and I didn't see anything on the cardiac monitor that knocked my socks off."

Keith felt relieved that he didn't have a sick oldster on his hands. They were the most complicated patients because so many things could go wrong. They couldn't give a good history so they required more tests, and trying to figure out what was normal could be tough. "Great, could you get some labs, an EKG and chest X-ray, and set him up for a CAT scan. By the time they get all of that, I should have these crash cases sewn up."

Martha just shook her head and walked away. She liked Keith because he didn't get rattled easily but he could be a wiseass at times. She suspected he wasn't too much longer for the ER world. Most ER docs burn out after a few years. The pressure to make a correct and swift diagnosis is terrific, and the money isn't good enough to compensate for dealing with the horrors that walk in all shift long. And then there's the constant fear of getting sued for a bad decision made in haste. Martha didn't mind doing what she could to help the poor schmuck out.

Al was stuck, prodded, and probed by assorted personnel for the next two hours as they carried out about five thousand dollars' worth of tests. Keith arrived, examined him for about sixty seconds, and went back to the desk to review the test results. Like many physicians, Jimmy thought that the physical examination was a waste of time, especially in the pandemonium of the ER. He liked to rely on hard test results before making his treatment decisions.

As he suspected, almost everything was in order. The CAT scan didn't indicate cerebral trauma from the fall, the X-rays were negative, and the blood test results all fell within the normal range. The only glitch was the electrocardiogram. Al didn't have a normal electrical system, which meant he was at risk for having his heart stop abruptly.

"I don't like this—he has a left bundle branch block," he told Martha. "I wonder if he went into complete heart block and passed out rather than falling down at the nursing home."

"They told me he tried to get out of bed—it didn't sound like a blackout. Did he have this pattern before?"

"Don't know. They can't find his old chart down in medical records. If this fucking place would spend a little money on their information systems, I could call it up on the computer, but we haven't entered the twenty-first century yet."

Martha hated the whining she got from everybody who worked in her department. No matter what improvements she managed to put into place, it was never enough. But Keith was right about this one. Having to look for paper records in the dungeon that was their medical records department while the rest of the world was converting to electronic record keeping was ludicrous. "I know that it's not optimal, Doctor, but administration tells me that we will have everything on computer soon. I guess I believe them somehow."

"Well, without knowing if this is a new finding, I can't blow this guy out of here. We'll have to admit him to a cardiac telemetry floor to monitor his heart rhythm. And let's have one of the cardiologists see him while he's up there."

"I guess you're right," Rathke agreed reluctantly. "I'll make the calls."

Martha initiated the process that would culminate in Al being sent up to a cardiac monitoring floor. Hospital beds were always in short supply, so Al would have to lie on a stretcher in the ER for hours. Rathke hated having her ER tied up but she had little recourse than to look after Al until a bed was ready upstairs.

By nightfall, and two ER shifts later, the bed was finally ready. Up the elevator he went, accompanied by ER staff, IV poles, and a battery-operated cardiac monitor.

In the meantime, Martha called Al's children, Mike and Linda, in California. She awakened them both and didn't get a warm response from either. Their only question concerned the seriousness of Al's condition. They were relieved to hear he wasn't in immediate danger, which meant they didn't have to interrupt their lives to come east. Mike told her he would call the hospital in a day or so for an update.

"Swell" had been Martha's reply. "We'll be sure to call you if there is any change." She had a hard time keeping her disdain out of her voice.

"What the hell is the matter with children these days?" she

muttered to the ward clerk as she clicked off the call. "Don't answer that," she called over her shoulder as she stood up and walked away.

Al came back to reality again as he was being pulled off the stretcher and transferred into a clean, fresh hospital bed. He surveyed his surroundings and concluded that he had somehow arrived in a hospital, but he couldn't fathom why. He heard nurses buzzing around the room, getting him plugged into the cardiac monitoring system.

A few minutes later, a man in a white coat came in with a chart under his arm. The nurses greeted him as Dr. Wilson. He had gray hair, a wrinkled face, a blue shirt, and military tie that was tied right up to his neck. He stood at Al's bed and asked a few questions. Al could understand Wilson's questions but couldn't fathom an answer. That didn't seem to faze Wilson who held a stethoscope over Al's chest for a few minutes and then patted him on the hand.

Dr. Wilson walked away while the nurses made sure that Al was safely tucked into his bed with the side rails firmly in place. They had heard about Al's acrobatics at the nursing home and didn't want a repeat performance.

Paul Wilson walked back out to the nursing station where he had spent many hours of his life. He was a distinguished member of the Scranton medical community. He had trained in cardiology in Boston many years before specialization was in vogue. He had started the first cardiology practice in Scranton and built it into a twenty-person group that had four offices and membership on four hospital staffs. Wilson had cut back on his practice and didn't take weekend call or work in the invasive laboratories any longer, but he still rounded in the hospital and enjoyed his office practice. He had an excellent reputation in the community for his quiet and competent care. Though he had put in a long day covering the clinical service at Scranton Memorial, he still looked sharp in a clean and pressed long lab coat. He was officially off duty but like the good partner he was, Wilson decided to finish off the consult so his partner taking calls that night would have one less thing to attend to. He would remember his generosity sadly a few months later when the excrement hit the fan.

Wilson didn't think the Romanzo case was going to be difficult. He wasn't expecting a meaningful history from Al, and there wasn't much on the physical examination. And so after a cursory look at the ER record, Wilson sat at a desk, picked up a hospital phone, and dictated his consultation note. "Eighty-three-year-old, frail Caucasian man not responsive to my questions." He hadn't tried too hard to get Al to respond— it would have just slowed him up, and Wilson wanted to get home for dinner before his wife ran out of patience. "Fell or lost consciousness at his nursing home." It would be impossible to figure out which was true from what the ER doc had told him, so why strain? "Negative evaluation in the ER including a CAT scan, chest X-ray, and labs. EKG shows a left bundle branch block. Admitted to exclude heart block and assess the need for a cardiac pacemaker."

Wilson seriously doubted that a pacemaker would be necessary but monitoring the old guy for a few days wasn't going to hurt anything, and daily rounding was a billable service. "Plan to keep on cardiac monitor, check enzymes, and do a cardiac ultrasound. May need an electrophysiology study to exclude conduction system disease." Wilson winced at the thought of sticking catheters in the old geezer, but he had to at least entertain the idea. That way, the hospital was more likely to be paid for the admission instead of having it denied. Insurers loved to conclude that "treatment could have been provided as an outpatient" so they could stiff the hospital for the charges. If an invasive study was in the offing, it would be hard to conclude that the admission was unnecessary. Wilson had learned after years of practice how to massage the chart, to make sure that all parties got what they needed while keeping his butt out of trouble.

Dr. Wilson finished his consult note and talked to the staff nurse, Ginny Falco, who would take care of Mr. Romanzo for the night. "I think he will be fine but keep a close watch on him. We'll be looking for heart block or any heart rate slowing. It might only last a few seconds so keep him on the monitor continuously, please. I'm pretty sure he won't be able to tell you when he has a symptom."

"Sure, Dr. Wilson," Ginny replied. "We'll put him on the full disclosure EKG system so we can go back and look at all of his rhythms."

"Thanks. I'll stop by tomorrow morning early before you go off shift, and you can show me what you pick up."

Wilson was true to his promise. At 6:00 A.M. sharp, he appeared at the nursing station, looking awake, alert, and well rested, wearing another version of his conservative preppy wardrobe. Ginny greeted him, bleary-eyed and more than ready to hit the pillow. "I didn't see anything while I was running around last night, but we were short-staffed and I had to call in an agency nurse to help out. Let me go back and look through all of the telemetry recordings."

"No rush. I have a few patients to see on this floor, anyway. I'll be here for a while."

"Well, I won't be dawdling," Ginny assured him. "I need to get the heck out of here and get some sleep."

Wilson sat at a counter charting. Ginny eventually came over to show him some of the strips from Al's monitor. "Dr. Wilson, what do you make of this?"

Wilson put the strips down in front of him, took out a pair of calipers, and started analyzing the tracings. Wilson had been looking at EKG recordings for years and had seen just about every possible abnormality, but this one was truly bizarre. Al's problem overnight had not been heart block—far from it. Instead, he had a welter of extra beats and they looked chaotic.

"This is very unusual. There seems to be some extra beats coming from a bunch of different places in the ventricle. When did this kick up?"

"Looks like about 5:00 A.M. The patient was sleeping around that time."

"Did he complain of chest pain or shortness of breath

through the night?"

"No, but he was out of it a lot," Ginny admitted. "We did get his labs back, and his enzymes were negative." Wilson knew that this was important because a lack of blood flow to the heart could have precipitated these arrhythmias.

"Is he on any cardiac medicines that I didn't know about?"

"No, Dr. Wilson. He's not getting much of anything."

"Well, he only had a few beats of the stuff and it didn't last long, so I don't think we have to jump on it. Let's just see if he has more of it."

Wilson finished his rounds and stopped by the floor later in the afternoon. The monitor was quiet. The rest of Romanzo's test results had been fine. His echocardiogram had demonstrated good heart function and no problem beyond what one might expect from eighty-three years of wear and tear.

Wilson told the staff on the floor that he would transfer Al back to his nursing home in the morning. "Keep him on the monitor overnight just in case, but I think he'll be fine." Wilson put a call into Al's son. He had to leave a message that Al was doing well and would be discharged soon. Wilson prepared most of the discharge paperwork to save time in the morning.

Dr. Wilson managed to have dinner with his wife that evening, watched some mindless television, and turned in early. He was on call for the night and expected to be awakened at least a few times, so he wanted to grab whatever rest he could.

The first call came in at 2:00 A.M. Ginny Falco was on duty again and wanted Wilson to know that Al Romanzo was having more extra beats. "They seem to be coming in runs instead of one at a time now," Ginny said, trying to keep the panic out of her voice.

"Are his electrolytes and oxygen OK?"

"Yes, Doctor; we checked them earlier this evening and they're all normal."

"Give him a 100-milligram bolus of lidocaine and start a drip. If things don't settle down, give me a call back."

Wilson had barely closed his eyes when the phone rang again. It was Ginny who didn't need to identify herself or the patient. "Doctor, I'm sorry to bother you again, but it is happening more frequently and now the runs are longer. The strips are really bizarre."

"I guess the lidocaine bolus didn't help?"

"Not a bit—in fact things got worse right after the bolus."

"OK, I'm on my way."

Wilson lived in a residential area of older homes about twenty minutes from the hospital. He had made this trek in the middle of the night hundreds of times. This one was routine, and he didn't exactly put the pedal to the metal. The old guy had every right to find a way out after languishing so long in a nursing home. Wilson would do what he could, but it might not make a difference. He had to admit he was intrigued by the arrhythmias, and at least part of the reason he was going in was to satisfy his intellectual curiosity.

By the time he arrived at the hospital, Al Romanzo's room was in chaos. The nurses explained to Wilson that Romanzo's abnormal rhythm had finally become sustained and he had lost consciousness. They hadn't wanted to call a code, but they didn't have a *Do Not Resuscitate* order for the patient. The anesthesiologist on call hadn't tubed his airway or put him on a ventilator yet—he was able to use a bag and mask to breathe for Al. But they had shocked his heart several times and were pumping on his chest. Each time, his arrhythmia stopped and then restarted and accelerated and degenerated until another shock was necessary.

Wilson pushed his way to the bedside, put on some gloves, and took over the code. He analyzed the recordings and called out orders for bicarbonate, intravenous amiodarone, and assorted other drugs, and directed the staff to bag the patient and deliver a few more shocks in between chest compressions.

It turned out to be a *pro forma* resuscitation. After fifteen minutes, Wilson realized that the code was an exercise in futility and he ordered a halt. "Time of death 3:05 A.M." Wilson intoned, just like those TV doctors he hated so much.

Wilson took off his plastic gloves and walked slowly out to the nursing station. He stood at the counter and looked over the arrhythmias that Al had manifested before his heart had gone into its terminal rhythm. Ginny had been correct—they were bizarre. He had what was clearly ventricular tachycardia with multiple morphologies that seemed to alternate with each other in a strangely familiar way. Nevertheless, Wilson couldn't imagine what had happened or what caused them. In the end, as with most bad tachycardias, the rhythm had simply degenerated into ventricular fibrillation during which the heart just sat there and quivered without any meaningful contractions. The shocks hadn't reorganized the heart rhythm, and Al's ancient organs just gave up.

Wilson wrote a code note in the chart in which he summarized in some detail what had happened to Al. He concluded that Al had idiopathic ventricular arrhythmia. Wilson always liked to remind students that *idiopathic* was a term doctors used to describe a problem they didn't understand. How ironic that the term called to mind the word *idiot*.

Now came the worst part of his job. He had to call the family and give them the grim news. He managed to reach Mike Romanzo, who had been watching Jay Leno in his bedroom. The son grunted a few times, asked a few questions about getting the body to a funeral director, and hung up before Wilson could give his condolences or ask if Mike would consent to an autopsy. Wilson put the receiver down and called the nursing home.

"I just want you to know that Mr. Romanzo died here tonight and we notified the family. They will make arrangements to get the body to a funeral home—Mr. Romanzo will not be returning."

The nurse at the other end thanked Wilson and told him she would leave a note in the front office in the morning.

"I guess the family will be coming into town to collect his things but the son didn't say when," Wilson told the nursing home attendant.

"Well, we never really saw much of the family. They live in California, and they don't come east very often. Their kids never liked this place and wouldn't stay very long before getting antsy. A couple of old guys from Philly came to see him once in a while, but I don't know if they were related."

Wilson had heard this story before, many times. Visiting Granddad when he was sick was a burden that everyone wanted to avoid. Well, at least his family wouldn't have to worry about being disgusted by Al's illness. Who knows? Maybe they actually wouldn't mind spending time with the old guy now that he didn't smell so bad.

Chapter Two

Al Romanzo's funeral was a small and quiet affair one morning a few days later. Mike and Linda and their families filled up the first two pews in the local parish church. They stood in line and greeted the handful of friends who were still able to travel to the funeral and walk up the aisle to view Al in his casket. A few of Al's cousins, nieces, and nephews made the trip up from Philly to pay their respects including two elderly gentlemen who stood in the back pews and spoke mainly to each other.

None of the Philly clan had seen Mike or Linda for years, and they had to be re-introduced to the California contingent. Mike and Linda had morphed into West Coast clones complete with hair dyed and blown, assorted plastic surgeries, and linen jackets. They struggled to exchange superficial information about their families while the relatives told stories about Al's life in Philadelphia before he returned to Scranton.

After the short viewing, Mass was said in a traditional format, as Al would have preferred. Mike said a few words to eulogize his father but succeeded only in demonstrating to everyone how much he and his father had grown apart. One cousin was heard to say that a stranger could have done a better job. The graveside service was *pro forma* before the tiny contingent made its way to Angelo and Maria's, a neighborhood Italian restaurant, for the mandatory post-service meal. Mike and Linda had decided on the tavern's economy funeral package to save as much money as possible. They rationalized their decision by pointing out how much their father had loved A&M while telling each other that Poppy would have wanted the grandchildren to have a decent inheritance. In reality, both were trying to figure out if there would be enough left in the bank account to upgrade their digs in Southern California.

Mike and Linda had made plans to return to California the next day—there was no use in hanging around Scranton any longer than necessary. After the luncheon, Mike told Linda they should go by the nursing home to go through their father's things to see if there was anything they wanted to keep. The home had told him they would donate anything they didn't want to the local Goodwill Society.

"I know he must have had some photos of the family that would be nice to keep," Mike speculated. "He may have also had a few pieces of Mom's jewelry, but I doubt there was anything of real value."

Linda was quick to point out, "Well, if there is anything worth money, we should sell it and split the cash."

Linda's lack of sentimentality didn't faze Mike. "Sure, but I wouldn't go out and make a down payment on a Porsche quite yet. He wasn't exactly sitting on a fortune."

Mike was right. They each filled a small cardboard box with mementos from their father's room, finding almost nothing of monetary value. As they left the nursing home and walked out to their rental cars, Linda popped the question that had been on her mind since she learned of her father's death.

"What about the will?"

"Everything left in his accounts gets liquidated and split among the four grandchildren. It should come to about $100,000 for each of us. I'm going over to see Jack this evening at his office to get the paperwork started. You're welcome to come with me, if you want." Jack Oliveri was their cousin and the attorney who had prepared their parents' legal documents, including their wills.

"No, I trust you." Even as the words came out of her mouth, Linda wasn't so sure she believed them herself. They weren't exactly close. Though they lived only fifty miles apart in California, they rarely got together except for Christmas and Easter, and then for only the briefest of visits. Oliveri had helped Mike obtain power of attorney, and Linda had chosen somewhat reluctantly to let him manage their father's money after Al no longer could do it for himself. She was rather pleased with her family's share and elected not to challenge Mike or ask for further information.

Mike knew his sister better than she imagined. He could guess what was going through her mind. "Well, I'm sure you'll eventually get a letter from Jack's office with a full accounting so you can see for yourself. That's only fair."

They parted as they always did, promising to get together soon. They both knew how empty a commitment it was. They hadn't flown in for the funeral together and had made hotel reservations in different places. If this event didn't bring them together, it wasn't likely that a California weenie roast was going to do it.

It didn't take Mike long to drive over to Jack's office that evening. His practice was in the heart of Scranton, near the courthouse, which at that time of evening was dark and quiet. Jack had been at the viewing and greeted Mike at the door, trying to convince him how much he was going to miss Uncle Al.

"He was a real good guy, Mike. Salt of the earth. Worked his butt off. Kept his nose clean." Mike was amused by Jack's rapid-fire assortment of metaphors, but decided to accept graciously Jack's feeble attempt to lionize his father.

"I know. They don't make them like that any more—broke the mold." Mike thought that his own absent-minded platitudes might help Jack get to the task at hand without further delay. Mike was jet-lagged and exhausted after a long day. He still had to get his family packed up and to the airport for an early-morning flight. "So, what is it that I need to do to get the paperwork going, Jack?"

"Well, there isn't that much really. I'll probate the will so I have some papers for you to sign, which basically gets that process going. I also have authorizations for you to sign so I can access Uncle Al's investment accounts. I'll liquidate all of that, and once the will process is finalized, I'll cut checks to the grandchildren."

Mike was wary of having the money go directly to the grandchildren, but he didn't know the tax consequences of taking the money himself, and he didn't want to ask Jack. After thinking about it, he decided it was better to get the money into his hands as soon as possible.

"Linda and I thought it might be simpler if you just made the checks out to us. We will make sure the money goes to the right place."

"Sure, Mike, that's fine. Whatever you want is OK with me. It'll take several weeks for all of this to go through. I'll check with the accountant to make sure that any final income and inheritance taxes are paid out, and I'll deduct my fee— don't worry, it'll be nominal—and then I'll send each of you half of the rest. The figure I gave you at the funeral should be pretty accurate, give or take a few thousand."

Jack's cavalier attitude about the "few thousand" difference irked Mike. It was easy for a big-shot lawyer like Jack to dismiss that amount of money. Mike decided to let it go. He watched Jack as he pushed the Romanzo file to the side, put his elbows on his desk, and leaned forward. He clearly had something else on his mind.

"Mike, how much do you know about the details of your father's death?"

"I don't understand."

"Well, I talked to Linda a little bit at the viewing, and she told me your father fell out of bed at the nursing home and ended up dying of a heart rhythm problem at the hospital."

"Yeah, that was the deal, I think. Why is that important?" The look on Jack's face suggested to Mike what was coming next.

"Wait a minute, you aren't implying we should go after the nursing home for my father's injury are you?"

"No, Michael, that is not my suggestion at all," Jack replied defensively. "These things happen at nursing homes all the time. It's hard to prove negligence, and it sounds like your father's head injury had nothing to do with why he died. Besides, nursing homes don't carry that much insurance. Juries don't react well to people suing nursing homes. It looks bad, and the awards usually suck."

"Then what's on your mind?"

"The hospital, Mike. Now, I'm not a malpractice attorney, but I do know that people who go into the hospital because of a head injury shouldn't die of a bad heart rhythm. At least, I don't know how those two things could be connected. And if they aren't related, I have to wonder if your father died because the hospital or doctor made some kind of mistake."

Jack now had Mike's attention. "What kind of mistake?"

"I don't know—maybe a medication mistake. You read the papers, don't you? They're always talking about patients in hospitals dying because of medical mistakes, and apparently medication errors are the most common. And if there wasn't an actual mistake, don't you want to know that the people who took care of your father didn't miss a chance to save him from dying the way he did? For all we know, it might have been completely avoidable."

"I don't know, Jack. The guy was eighty-three years old, crapping himself in a nursing home. Do you really think it's worth trying to blame somebody for his death?"

"Like I said, I'm no malpractice attorney, but we have plenty of them in this state. They all work on contingency, which means it won't cost you and Linda a nickel to have someone reputable take a look at the records."

Mike wondered if "reputable" and "malpractice attorney" belonged together, but what Jack was proposing was not as outrageous as it had sounded at first. "So, what would Linda and I have to do if we wanted to pursue this?"

"That's the beauty of it, Mike. You don't have to do anything. I'll make the referral to one of the firms I know, and they'll take the ball and run with it. If they think there's merit to the case, they'll tell us and you can decide if you want to go forward with a lawsuit. You won't even have to come back here unless there's a trial. That's unlikely, and even if it happened, it'd be years away."

Mike couldn't resist the obvious question. "So how much money do you think a case like this might be worth, Jack?"

Jack suppressed a smile. He knew that he had Mike hooked. "Hard to say, cuz. Could be anything from a hundred grand to a million. It all depends on how good the case really is, how much the hospital and doctor want it to go away, or how hard the jury wants to slap their wrists for being careless or stupid."

"If you don't mind me asking, what's your angle?"

"Well, if I make the referral and the case either settles or we win a verdict, the firm that prevails will pay me a part of their fee. How much depends on what we negotiate. It won't come out of your share."

"That sounds like fee splitting—I thought it is illegal."

"It is for doctors but not for us lawyers. That's the value of being the people who make the laws, Michael!" Jack started to chuckle but caught himself when he saw that Mike was not smiling.

"Let me talk to Linda and my wife, and I'll let you know. Right now I don't see much harm in taking a look."

"Right. At the very least you'll find out exactly what happened to your dad."

It was this conversation that started the investigation of Al Romanzo's death. The next day, as soon as Jack Oliveri got to his office, he told his secretary to call Chip Markley. Markley was one of the best-known malpractice attorneys in the country. His main office was a palatial affair in a high-rise building in downtown Philadelphia, but his firm's tentacles reached to Pittsburgh, Erie, Harrisburg (the state's capital), and of course Scranton and Wilkes-Barre.

Jack had sent cases to Markley before and had reaped the rewards. Chip could afford to be generous with referring lawyers since his standard commission on most cases was over forty percent. Pennsylvania had no limits on lawyers' contingency fees. Chip figured that if a client wanted the best chance to win a lot of money, they had to be willing to pay for the privilege of Markley's representation.

Jack didn't waste time on pleasantries when he got Markley on the phone. "Chip, I have one for you. I don't think that it will bring a ton of money, but I think you should be able to turn it over without a lot of effort."

Markley listened as Jack told him what he knew about the case. As usual, Jack's knowledge was superficial and inadequate. Markley used his standard line: "Sounds real interesting; I'll get one of my people on it right away and let you know in a few weeks."

"That's perfect, Chip. Should we do the customary split on this one if it makes anything?"

"Sure, Jack. That's fine." Markley couldn't remember off the top of his head what that number was but he never agreed to give away more than 15% of his earnings. Jack should be happy about that. After all, it could be a pile of money for doing nothing more than making a phone call.

Markley looked out his office window at his panoramic view of Philadelphia and considered which of his junior associates would be best for this case. He smiled as a vision of Pamela Brady popped into his head.

Pamela was a young lawyer Markley had recruited out of Villanova Law School. She was a good Catholic girl who had gone through the parochial school system before entering Villanova Nursing School. She worked for a few years as a floor nurse before she came to hate it and decided to go to law school. When she graduated, malpractice law was a natural. She applied to Chip Markley's firm.

Chip interviewed all of the associate applicants, and Pamela made an instant impression. Besides being very bright, Pamela was a knockout. She had long blond hair that she wore tied back, a great rack, and killer legs. Markley, lascivious man that he was, had an eye for good lawyers but really appreciated great-looking young women. He hired Pamela on the spot and spent the next several months trying to score. Pamela never succumbed to his clumsy advances and finally asked to be transferred to the Scranton office, mainly to get out of Markley's way. She used the excuse that she had an elderly aunt who needed help, but the aunt she moved in with was as healthy as a horse.

Well, missy, thought Markley, now you'll have to deal with me on your turf.

Markley sent Pamela an email with the information she would need to start her investigation of the Romanzo case. He instructed her to call him after she knew the story. "I'll take a drive up there, and we'll set up dinner or something to go over the file when you're ready." When Pamela read the email, she winced. She knew she was being manipulated but had no choice. "Sure, that will be fine," she wrote back, but as she did, she resolved that there was no way that lecherous prick was going to find his way into her pants.

Pamela dove into the case with her customary zeal. She had always been a hard worker and enjoyed the challenge of discovering the facts in a new case. For starters, she wrote a letter to the hospital requesting Al Romanzo's records.

She smiled as she dictated the letter. She knew damn well the letter would send the minions at Scranton Memorial scurrying around, wringing their hands, and muttering epithets. A letter from Markley's firm would send shivers down the spine of hospital administrators who would assume that the letter was a prelude to a potentially messy and costly malpractice action. Pamela hated hospital administrators. Based on her nursing experience, she thought they were petty and stupid bean counters who deserved to have their balls in a vice. Too bad for them.

The records arrived within a few days, certified by the hospital attorney to be up to date and complete. Pamela brought the files home and spent the next weekend poring through them. She read every page and every line, looking for inconsistencies in care or any clue that someone had done anything that could be interpreted as substandard care. She was immediately drawn to the issue of the cardiac arrhythmias. Pamela had worked in a coronary care unit after graduation and was familiar with rhythm problems. She looked over the recordings and was as mystified as Dr. Wilson had been. She wondered why he hadn't done something about the abnormalities when he first saw them. Could this be the breach in care that would allow the case to go forward?

Pamela made copious notes as she reviewed the file and tried to look for other evidence of malpractice, but she kept coming back to Romanzo's arrhythmias. She was pleased to see that Wilson had been given plenty of opportunity by the nursing staff to act, and he clearly had not. That the nurses had noted the arrhythmias in their notes and clearly documented inaction was even juicier. They would be able to drag the hospital and its deeper pockets into the case along with the hapless doctor.

Pamela prepared a brief on Monday morning and called Markley. "I think we have something in the Romanzo case. I can send you the brief that I prepared if you want to look it over."

"Sure, Pamela, send it to me as soon as you can. I'll have my secretary set up a time to meet to review it later this week if that's OK with you?"

"Sure, Mr. Markley, whenever it's convenient for you." Pamela knew that convenience had nothing to do with it. Exploitation was the gambit.

Markley had his secretary make a dinner reservation at the Ipanema Grille, one of the nicest eateries in Scranton specializing in Brazilian cuisine. Although it was a few notches below what Philly could offer, the place had a Latin atmosphere, and romance was what Chip was after.

Pamela arrived attired as much like a nun as possible. Her hemline was well below her knees, and perfume and cleavage were nowhere to be found. Chip didn't seem to mind. He expected that those dowdy clothes would be on the floor of his hotel room before midnight anyway. He was deferential as they met in the bar and prepared to be seated. "Pamela, you look wonderful. Thanks for meeting with me this evening. I'm looking forward to hearing your theory in this case."

Pamela knew that her appearance had nothing to do with the purpose of the meeting and ignored the compliment. "This is a very interesting case, Mr. Markley, from the medical point of view."

"How so, Pamela? Tell me why we should pursue it."

"Well, after he fell at the nursing home, Mr. Romanzo was taken to the ER and from there admitted to the hospital because he had an abnormal EKG. The ER staff was worried but didn't know what it meant so they admitted him and called a consult. A Dr. Wilson was the cardiologist who saw the patient. He knew about the arrhythmias Mr. Romanzo was having. On the monitor, they looked terrible, but Wilson told the nurses to just keep an eye on Mr. Romanzo and not to treat him. Sure enough, Mr. Romanzo had more of the arrhythmias the night he died, and he finally had a cardiac arrest from which he couldn't be resuscitated."

"So you're saying that the nurses informed Dr. Wilson that Al Romanzo was having arrhythmia problems and Wilson ignored them?"

"That's how it looks."

Markley was intrigued with the case almost as much as he was with Pamela's blue eyes. "And those arrhythmias culminated in Romanzo's cardiac arrest?"

"Yes, there's no question about it."

"Well, it sounds to me that we can go ahead and file a lawsuit against Wilson and the hospital for wrongful death. Do you agree?"

"I do. However, you need to know that the arrhythmias were pretty bizarre. I suspect that Wilson was as mystified as I was, and that he really didn't know what was causing them. I guess he didn't treat because he couldn't figure out the etiology. Sorry, that means the cause, Mr. Markley."

"I know what *etiology* means, Pamela," Markley scornfully reminded her. "But not knowing the cause isn't an excuse for ignoring the problem is it?"

"I guess not, but you need to know that Wilson is a good

cardiologist with a solid reputation. He didn't treat for a reason, and I can't believe it was simply negligence."

"Well, his motive is an issue for a jury to decide, don't you think?"

Pamela felt like a defendant herself. "If you say so, Mr. Markley."

"I do, Pamela. So we'll proceed with the suit this week, if that's OK with you. My office will help your secretary with any of the particulars." Markley paused, deliberately putting aside the legal matters. "Now we have to deal with more relevant matters this evening. Do you have a preference for wine, and what entrée on the menu entices you the most?"

The rest of dinner was a mix of polite small talk from Pamela, playful bantering by Markley, and a bit of discussion about other active legal cases. Pamela used a variety of non-verbal clues to make it clear that she was not interested in her boss, but Markley either chose to ignore the hints or was oblivious to them. He stared longingly into her eyes whenever she looked his way and even grabbed her hand across the table a few times, not to mention knocking knees under the table. By the time Markley had finished the second bottle of wine, he was bold enough to brush his hand across Pamela's butt as he helped her on with her coat. Pamela twisted around and faked a smile while shifting away from any further contact.

As they left the restaurant, Markley made the inevitable overture. "Pamela, I have a wonderful suite at the old Scranton Hotel for the night. They have done a terrific job of restoring it. Would you like to come back with me for a nightcap and see the place?"

When Pamela declined, Markley tried to convince her. After she declined for the second and third time, he finally snapped, "Pamela, I hope you know that your future in the Scranton office is not exactly a lock. I have some tough personnel decisions to make, and I would dearly like to keep you on the team."

Pamela feigned indifference. "I really don't care about being on your team, Mr. Markley. There are plenty of jobs out there."

"You know, it's the damndest thing. People who are asked to leave my firm always seem to have a hard time finding a new position. Isn't that strange? I wonder why."

"Are you threatening me, Mr. Markley, because a sexual harassment case wouldn't be something that your 'team' would like to have brought against them, would they?"

That seemed to shock Markley back to reality. He decided to try one more time to convince Pamela with a little more sugar. "You're a talented girl, Pamela. I think that you could do very well with our firm. Why not just come on over for a quick drink, and we can go over your qualifications for advancement?"

"Mr. Markley, I think we both know what you want to 'advance' and it just isn't going to happen. So, you'll have to be satisfied with the quality of my work or you'll have to let me go. I don't intend to keep running away from you, and I'm certainly not going to spread my legs for you, either. Figure out what you want to do with me, and let me know tomorrow. I'm going home."

With that, Markley was left standing alone in the nearly empty restaurant parking lot, asking himself if he should fire the bitch and lose a valuable employee, or swallow his pride and accept a rare defeat in the interest of keeping a highly qualified attorney in the firm. He got into his monstrous Mercedes sedan, turned on the ignition, and made his decision before he pulled into the street.

The next morning, Pamela Brady was told by the managing partner in the Scranton office to clean out her desk.

Chapter Three

After Pamela Brady's sudden sacking, Chip Markley didn't miss a beat. He assigned another attorney to the case and picked Helga Podolinsky, a homely woman who had grown up poor in the Scranton area. Helga had no medical training and was far less intelligent than Pamela. Markley's major motivation for giving her the case was that she presented no temptation for him. He didn't want to be humiliated by another young lawyer, and it was time to get down to business. He would be able to strategize after Helga did the remainder of the grunt work. Brilliance wasn't a priority.

Markley was particularly motivated to win this case. He liked a challenge, and this one certainly presented that opportunity. Also, he especially didn't like the people in the Scranton medical community. They were smug and liked to boast that lawsuits didn't mean much to them. They assumed that the nice people of Scranton and Wilkes-Barre wouldn't sue their doctors, and if they did, any jury picked from the local citizenry would inevitably side with the doctor. It was in fact more difficult to get a plaintiff's verdict in the coal mining regions of Pennsylvania, but that just motivated Markley all the more. It was time to stick it to those straw-in-the-teeth assholes. And this was just the kind of case that would make the local yokels sit up and take notice.

Pamela had suggested that Dr. Wilson did not react quickly

or appropriately to Al Romanzo's arrhythmias so Markley had a theory of liability he could exploit. He was sure he could get somebody from his herd of experts to say that Wilson had dropped the ball on making an accurate diagnosis and hadn't treated Romanzo correctly or expeditiously. The next step for Markley was to see what he could do to maximize the payment for damages.

Markley conceded to his staff that the usual economic damages, like loss of wages or support, were not an issue in this case. Fortunately for plaintiffs, Pennsylvania had not enacted legislation to cap the amount of money that could be recovered for "pain and suffering." Consequently, if Markley could portray Wilson and the hospital staff as callous and uncaring, as he knew they were, a jury just might decide to slap them hard with a big verdict for all of the agony they had inflicted on poor Mr. Romanzo. After all, the old guy had gone to the hospital for a relatively minor problem. He was put on a cardiac telemetry unit because the ER physician was worried about him. And yet when he had the very arrhythmias that the doctors and nurses were supposed to be looking for, they went untreated and culminated in Romanzo's death. Had Al been fifty or sixty years old, the case would be a slam-dunk. Markley didn't see why Al's age should interfere with getting a juicy award.

Markley held case conferences at least twice a week with the lawyers in his firm. None of his associates, no matter how much they contributed to the bottom line or to the prestige of the organization, could rise to partner in the truest sense of the word. They were employees indefinitely. Markley treated the more senior associates with respect, and he certainly paid them well. However, he had made up his mind that his sole-proprietor operation would be passed on to his family intact when he died. Since Markley never planned to retire, and since he considered himself immortal, the family parasites were going to have to wait a while to get their mitts on his baby.

Markley regarded his case conferences as a forum in which he could teach his underlings the law while the firm was conducting business. After some housekeeping details, they reviewed the status of the firm's active cases. Chip loved to lecture his young associates. These conferences gave him the opportunity to play the law professor he had always wanted to be. He dressed up special for the event. Cufflinks and tie tacks were a must to highlight his impeccable pin-striped suit and silk tie. With hair parted low on the left to cover his bald spot, his mustache impeccably trimmed, Markley paced in front of the audience as he made his most eloquent points.

This week, the Romanzo case was the featured event. "Remember that we have two big priorities in this case," Markley declared. "First, we have to emphasize that this sad old guy died needlessly. They basically ignored him to death. They sat there and let him have arrhythmias that eventually became sustained and killed him. The doctor was home sleeping in his nice warm bed when things went sour, and he didn't come in until the nurse called him twice. Maybe if he had responded to the first call, Al Romanzo would have made it. As it was, the nurses had to resuscitate the patient while the doctor dressed, got in his car, and drove in."

Markley surveyed the boardroom in which the meeting was being held. His junior partners and associates were sitting forward in black leather swivel chairs around the massive table, listening to Markley deliver his treatise on the Romanzo case. Many took notes, but none diverted their attention, even for a second.

"Even more importantly, we have to do everything to keep the hospital in the case. If this thing is going to settle, and I suspect it will, it'll be the hospital that kicks in the money to make it go away. They're self-insured, so they have more to lose with a big verdict. This doctor won't care as much. It won't be money out of his pocket. Besides, Wilson is over the hill and getting ready to retire. A verdict against him won't carry much weight as far as his future goes."

Markley was launching into his next point when one of the young interns sitting in the back of the room had the temerity to raise his hand and interrupt. The other lawyers in the room whirled around, mouths agape. A few people sitting nearby tried to warn the guy not to break in with a question. It was simply not done, and they were certain that Markley would crush him. It was too late.

"But, Mr. Markley, this was a very old person who had lots of medical problems. Why wouldn't the jury figure he didn't have long to live? And isn't dying suddenly at that age better than dying slowly?"

There was silence in the room as everyone waited to see how Markley would react. He managed a whimsical smile that was more like a smirk, stopped pacing, folded his arms, and stared down at the neophyte.

"Mr. Jones, isn't it? You're a student at Penn Law, if I remember correctly?" He fixed his gaze on the young man who grinned and nodded, oblivious to the fury that might be unleashed upon him at any moment. "Well, Mr. Jones, you have asked a very good question and I will tell you it is this very thing that makes me want to take this case to verdict and win it for our clients. Just because someone is old doesn't mean they're worthless. In fact, I know quite a few young people, some of whom are in this very room, who aren't worth a shit." If Jones didn't know he was one of them, everybody else in the room did.

Markley walked over to the young man. The spectators nearly gasped in anticipation of what could be physical violence. Instead, he put his hand on Jones' shoulder. "Mr. Jones, every life is sacred, and sometimes we have to remind our distinguished medical colleagues of that. Poor Mr. Romanzo didn't want to die that night. He wanted to go back to his nursing home to be with his friends and watch sports on TV. Is that so unreasonable?"

Markley was obviously warming up his courtroom shtick. The question was rhetorical but Jones, in his naïveté, thought Markley wanted an answer. "I guess not, Mr. Markley, but I've been helping Helga with this case, and I don't think that Mr. Romanzo had the ability to watch television. He was pretty much out of it most of the time."

Markley stared down at Jones, his face reddening. Several in the room feared that Markley was going to re-enact DeNiro's baseball-bat clubbing of an upstart in the movie *The Untouchables*. But Markely answered Jones in an even voice.

"Well, Mr. Jones, I will remind you that assessing anyone's ability to think and to enjoy their surroundings is tricky business indeed. I would be careful about inferring what Mr. Romanzo was actually thinking as he sat in that infernal nursing facility. In fact, it will be our job to make the jury disbelieve that he was completely unconscious and unaware. That is precisely what we are getting paid to do."

To the relief of all in the room, Jones chose not to reply but simply looked up at Markley, nodded, and sat back in his chair. He would live to work another day. But Jones had crystallized the arguments that would be made for the defense, which is probably why Markley had not torched him.

At the same time, in a considerably less well-appointed law office upstate, Dr. Wilson was discussing the same issues with the attorney whom the insurance company had assigned to the case. Sean Gracey worked for a reputable law firm that contracted with a large medical malpractice insurance company to defend doctors. Sean was a local boy who worked his way through the University of Scranton, a good Catholic college in the area, and then had attended Dickinson Law School, only about two hours away in Carlisle, Pennsylvania. Sean's mother had been a nurse, so he had been around the medical profession all of his life.

As a student, Sean hadn't particularly liked science, and so he had not entertained medicine as a career choice. However, he found he had an aptitude for understanding medical issues when studying cases in law school. He did well at Dickinson and decided to apply to medical malpractice firms for a job after graduation. He didn't tell his mother that he had considered working for a plaintiff's firm. That would have broken her heart and was one of the prime reasons he ended up at Oakley, Kendall, and Kramer, working the defense side of the bar.

Sean was one of the firm's favorite young guns. He was bright and articulate, and didn't mind working hard. Even better, he was good looking, in an Ivy League kind of way, played a decent round of golf, and the senior partners liked to hang out with him. Sean had cut his teeth on some pretty difficult malpractice cases since starting with the firm five years earlier. Nevertheless, going up against Markley, with his vast experience and army of lawyers, was daunting. He fully intended to work hard on this case to at least manage a reasonable outcome for Dr. Wilson and to make his bones with the firm.

The meeting with Dr. Wilson today was their second. The first had not gone well at all. Wilson had come in as mad as a hornet, fuming over the fact that he had been sued over the death of an ancient man who had a million reasons to die, and for whom death was a blessing. It took Sean over an hour to get Wilson to calm down enough to begin to go over the facts of the case. In the end, Sean basically gave up and told Wilson to cool off and return in a week. Today, Wilson was more lucid and could respond in a civil tone to the questions Sean had to ask.

"All right, Dr. Wilson, let's review your initial assessment of Mr. Romanzo. What did you think of his overall cardiac condition?"

"I thought he was fine when I examined him. His vital signs were stable, his heart and lungs sounded normal, he was not in heart failure—that is, he didn't have extra fluid in his body—and he had good circulation."

"What about his EKG?"

"What about it? It was fine for an old man."

Sean was concerned that Wilson was being overly dismissive. "But wasn't there something on the EKG that prompted the doctor in the ER to admit Mr. Romanzo?"

"Yeah, he had a left bundle branch block. A lot of old people have that. You can live a long time with one bundle branch blocked—that's why you have more than one. The problem was that the guy in the ER couldn't determine if this was something that had been there for a while or not. If the damn hospital did a better job of storing old medical records, he would have seen that it had been there for years. Then he would have sent the old guy back to the nursing home, and my ass wouldn't be in a sling. So I have our wonderful hospital to thank for this mess."

"But wouldn't Mr. Romanzo have died at the nursing home, anyway?"

"Look, this guy was going to die sometime soon—at the nursing home, in the hospital, or anywhere else his damn family parked him. The problem is that he died on my watch, so the family is trying to cash in."

Sean saw he was going to have to be patient with Wilson to get the information he needed. "I understand, but what about all of the arrhythmias? What did you make of them?"

"I saw them, I was worried about them, but I didn't know what was causing them. In retrospect, I guess he was having ischemia—you know, reduced blood flow to his heart. Left bundle branch block can mask ischemia, so the only way I could have proven that was to do a catheterization, and the guy was too old and sick for that."

"Did you discuss that option with Mr. Romanzo and offer it to him?"

Wilson was incredulous. "He was flashing the Q sign— there was no way he was going to discuss anything about his care."

Sean decided to allow Wilson to emote. He made a note on his pad to remind Wilson not to use jargon like "Q sign" in a deposition or courtroom. Sean understood that medical personnel did this all the time. They probably thought that "Q sign" sounded a lot cooler than describing a patient with his mouth hanging open and his tongue draped off to the side. Nevertheless, the jury was unlikely to be sympathetic to someone who made fun of his patients.

"How about his family?"

"You must be joking. They weren't around. I called out there and didn't exactly get a warm greeting. The son—

Michael, I think his name is—seemed more concerned about not having to come to see his father than what was actually going on."

Sean was concerned. "So you never really spoke with anybody about leaving Romanzo alone and not treating his arrhythmias aggressively and not finding the root cause?"

Wilson sensed Gracey's criticism and went on the defensive. "This happens all the time with nursing home patients. They can't communicate and the family doesn't give a shit, so we have to make tough decisions. If they happen to die, nobody gets bent out of shape. Hell, the families are usually thankful that mom or dad didn't suffer too much. Who would have expected this piece of shit son to come after me?"

Sean tried to help Wilson understand. "I think the problem here is that the old guy came in for an unrelated problem, one doctor flagged a cardiac problem, the thing he was worried about seemed to happen, and you didn't do anything about it. Can you understand why they might be angry about that?"

"I would, but you and they have to understand that we're limited in what we can do. Sure, he was having arrhythmias, but he was stable overall. I suspected those arrhythmias had been there forever and we discovered them only because the ER doc was stupid enough to put him on a cardiac monitor. Giving him potent drugs to suppress the arrhythmia or taking him to the lab to go into his coronaries looking for blockages would have been very risky, and *that* could have killed him, too. I made a decision to be conservative and given a similar set of circumstances, I would do the same thing again."

Sean could see that Wilson was a good doctor, but like a lot of senior clinicians, he had a patriarchal attitude about patient care. He knew what was best and didn't believe he had to get anybody's permission to make decisions. Wilson had approached the Romanzo case conservatively, and was convinced he had acted appropriately. If Mr. Romanzo's family didn't agree, too bad for them.

"So in retrospect, Dr. Wilson, do you have any idea what caused Mr. Romanzo's arrhythmias to get so much worse?"

"I've gone over those strips dozens of times and I'm stuck. In the beginning, they weren't so bad. He had a few skipped beats and there were times when impulses were blocked and the heart rate slowed. But the night he died, the arrhythmias became much more frequent and ugly. When Ginny Falco called me the first time, the arrhythmias were starting and stopping. But then they became incessant, and it didn't take long for them to degenerate into ventricular fibrillation."

"What does that mean?"

"Well, after a period of fast beating from the bottom chamber or ventricle, the electrical activity becomes completely disorganized and we call that fibrillation. If VF is not shocked back to normal right away, the patient dies. What's unusual in this case is that they managed to get Romanzo out of the arrhythmia several times by shocking him, but he immediately lapsed back into it. There were even a few times that the shock accelerated the arrhythmia and things got worse quickly. That's truly bizarre, and I have no explanation for it."

"So, Doctor, think along with me for a minute. If this were something very unusual and something you had never seen before, it would be difficult to come to the conclusion that you somehow violated the standard of care by not caring for it appropriately. Is that a correct statement?"

"I think so. Treatment, other than doing nonspecific things like shocking the heart, would be impossible unless one knew the etiology—I'm sorry, I mean the cause of the condition."

Unlike Markley, Gracey chose to overlook the unnecessary word definition. "Why didn't you call a consult with an arrhythmia expert?"

"I was the cardiology consultant. We don't have an arrhythmia expert at that hospital."

"Why not transfer him to some place that did have an electrophysiologist?"

"We do that all the time, but this patient got real sick real fast. There just wasn't enough time."

"Sorry to be asking so many questions, Dr. Wilson, but these are the things that will be asked of you in deposition or at trial, so we have to be clear on the answers."

"You think this will go to trial?" Wilson asked nervously.

"I hope not, but one never knows. We have to play it out and see."

Wilson lowered his head into his hands, obviously worried. "Sean, I have given this case a lot of thought. I know I didn't do anything wrong and yet I'm being raked over the coals. I discussed things with my wife and I'm going to retire from medicine now."

"Dr. Wilson, are you sure? You're a relatively young man and you enjoy practice. You certainly have a nice reputation hereabouts."

"That's true, but this is the second time I've been sued. The first one was as absurd as this case. It involved a young man with blackouts who had a mildly abnormal electrocardiogram. I was in the middle of working him up when he had a cardiac arrest and suffered severe brain damage. The plaintiff brought in some hotshot all the way from Europe who claimed that my patient had a rare syndrome that I should have recognized. I had three local doctors testify that they would have done the same thing I did, and that I conformed to the published guide-lines, but we still lost. There was a five million dollar verdict against me. I thought they were going to go after our assets and my salary, and they probably would have except that after another two years of agony, an appellate judge adjusted the verdict to something reasonable and my insurance company paid it all off."

Sean of course knew about the case, but didn't interrupt Wilson, who obviously needed to ventilate. The insurance company that paid off the first case wasn't happy about a second. They had already informed Sean that Wilson's policy might not be renewed, and if it were, his premiums would be going up substantially. So retirement at this point might be a good thing.

Sean decided to move on from the case discussion. His client was distraught and he wanted to talk about things that might make Wilson feel better. "I can see why you don't want to continue practicing here. Would you think about relocating?"

"I might, but at this point it would be hard to start over. My wife and I are inclined to spend time with the grandchildren and hope that the money we've put away will be enough to see us through."

There was one more detail to discuss. "Dr. Wilson, would it be safe to say that we need to have somebody review this case and offer an opinion about the nature of the problem and what might have been causing it?"

The tension drained from Wilson's face. "Yes, that would be a great idea. I'd really like to get somebody else's opinion about what happened. My partners have tried to be supportive, but this thing is way over their heads, too."

Sean was happy to get Wilson back on a positive track. "OK, Dr. Wilson. We have to find somebody who's known to be an expert in this field and also lives in this part of the state. The courts don't like it when we bring in somebody from far away—the juries sometimes assume outsiders don't know the local standard of care."

Wilson couldn't resist the temptation to comment. "Like somehow, medicine around here is different from everywhere else?"

"I know it's dumb, but, like I told you, we have to play the game. Now do you have anyone in mind that I can recommend to the insurance carrier?"

"There are lots of hot shots in arrhythmia around Philly, but most of them are young or might not handle themselves real well in the courtroom. There was a guy we had up here to give a lecture a few years ago who really knew his stuff and was a great public speaker. I heard that he left academia and is practicing general cardiology in the Poconos somewhere."

"If he's in practice in the area and is credible, he'd be perfect. Do you know his name? I can have my office track him down."

"Yeah, his name is Philip Sarkis. Lebanese guy, as I recall. You shouldn't have much trouble finding him."

Chapter Four

It took Sean Gracey a fair amount of time to locate Philip Sarkis. When he called Gladwyne Memorial Hospital, Sarkis' most recent address on a Google search, no one seemed to know who he was or where his office was located. When he called the medical staff office, Gracey was told that Sarkis had resigned from the hospital staff four years earlier, and left no forwarding address. About to give up, Gracey decided to call the cardiology office. When he asked for Dr. Sarkis, he was immediately placed on hold. A few seconds later, a pleasant woman asked Gracey why he was looking for Philip Sarkis.

"I'm a lawyer defending a doctor in Scranton in a medical malpractice case. My client asked me to see if Dr. Sarkis would take a look at the records. We want to know if he could help as a defense expert. Dr. Sarkis did work at GMH, didn't he? Nobody seems to know who or where he is."

"Yes, Dr. Sarkis worked here for a long time and left GMH over three years ago. My name is Rhonda Simons. I used to be his private secretary when he was chief of cardiology."

"Can you tell me where he is and if he might be interested in looking at a legal case?"

"I can contact him, but I don't know if he'll look at your case. I know he still does some outside work, but I would have to ask him and get back to you."

Sean gave Rhonda his contact information and made his last plea. "Dr. Paul Wilson is my client, and he's very anxious about the case. I know he'd feel much better about things if Dr. Sarkis could see his way clear to help him out."

Rhonda promised an answer as soon as possible. She understood what Gracey meant about the stress associated with malpractice cases. After all, it had been that very thing that shoved Dr. Sarkis over the edge and led to his dismissal from the GMH staff years earlier. Rhonda had been Philip's secretary for many years and missed having him around. Although she spoke with him on the phone once in a while, she hadn't seen him since he'd left. The new chief had brought along his own secretary when he took over the department. That also made Rhonda unhappy because it removed her from the inner circle, which she so enjoyed. Times had changed, Rhonda regretted, but she had pleasant memories of Philip's tenure.

Rhonda flicked through her Rolodex looking for Philip's home phone number. The area code reminded Rhonda that Philip had moved to the Pocono Mountains. Rhonda couldn't fathom why Philip would want to live in that godforsaken place. Philip had been a city guy, in Rhonda's estimation. The legal hassles must have really gotten to him to force such a radical move.

Even though Rhonda had lived through the Sarkis implosion, she wasn't sure she was privy to everything that had transpired. She remembered that Philip and his friend Dorothy Deaver had been questioned after the mysterious deaths of two rich Main Line people, but she had lost touch with the story, and never had the nerve or the chance to ask Philip about it directly.

Rhonda dialed the phone number and was surprised when Philip answered in the middle of a work day.

"Philip, how are you?"

"Rhonda, is that you? It's great to hear your voice."

"I'm sorry it's been so long since we've talked. What have you been up to since then?"

"Well, I can tell you that my life is still very different from what it was when we worked together."

Philip wasn't exaggerating. He had never recovered from the malpractice case brought against him by Hugh Hamlin after his wife Moira died suddenly and unexpectedly. Philip had lost the case, and his career and family in the process. He and his newfound friend, Dorothy Deaver, had worked hard to discover that Moira's death had not been his fault but rather the evildoing of Hugh and his mistress Bonnie Romano. Two days after the murderers found a legal loophole and extricated themselves from the criminal proceedings against them, Hugh and Bonnie were found dead in the trunk of a limousine fished out of the Schuylkill River. Philip and Dorothy were questioned by the police, but they had been out of town when Hugh and Bonnie met their end, and, despite their suspicions, the authorities were unable to implicate Philip and Dorothy in any way. The murderers had never been caught.

After the dust had settled, Dorothy and Philip decided to leave Philadelphia. Neither of them wanted to be too far from their families. Philip, in particular, wanted to be able to see his children, who were living with his estranged wife Nancy in the Philadelphia suburbs. After much negotiation and soul-searching, they settled on the Pocono area. It was less than two hours from Philadelphia, but the community couldn't have been more different.

Natives of the Pocono area were easygoing and gentle people. Even though many new families had moved there from New York and Philadelphia, the ambience of the region had been preserved. Most people had simple lives and simple values. There was a strong demand for doctors in the Poconos, so Philip had no trouble finding a job. There were also several good law firms in the Scranton/Wilkes-Barre area. Dorothy found work as counsel for a large firm that was happy to have her general law expertise, not to mention her personal surveillance experience.

Philip was well acquainted with the area. With his first wife, he had kept a vacation home in the Poconos that had been sold to pay damages from his malpractice case. This time he decided to buy a lot on a lake and build a small home that was just large enough, with a nice guest bedroom for his children when they came to visit.

Philip had a part-time job in a nearby cardiology clinic and spent the rest of his time puttering around their new home. He enjoyed the physical labor that cleared his mind after listening to patients' complaints in the clinic.

And now Philip had dogs. He had resisted the idea, but Dorothy thought that a pet would be therapeutic for him. She had been right, except that Philip wasn't satisfied with one. Their two Portuguese Water Dogs, Mitten and Buffy, became Philip's constant companions. In addition to supplying comfort and safety, they stimulated Philip and Dorothy to take long walks in the woods, and they demanded petting and stroking that clearly made them both happy and engaged. Philip talked to them constantly and became convinced that they answered his questions with a wag of the tail or a tilt of the head. Philip found his hounds to be endlessly interesting, and was happy to tell anybody inclined to solicit his opinion that dogs were superior to almost any human he knew.

Philip filled Rhonda in on a few of the details of his new life, but generally, he didn't enjoy his occasional contacts with people he had known at Gladwyne Memorial. He found it painful and embarrassing, especially when the person he was speaking to was privy to his disgraced exit from the Philadelphia medical scene. Rhonda understood this; she had always been able to sense Philip's moods when she worked for him, so she came to the point of her call promptly.

"Philip, I need to know if I can give your phone number to an attorney who wants you to review a medical malpractice case. Are you still interested in doing legal case review?"

Philip hesitated several seconds before responding.

"I've been avoiding anything having to do with malpractice, but I guess it wouldn't hurt to talk to the guy. Did he say what the case was about?"

"No, he didn't get into that. It sounded like the doctor in the case wanted you specifically, if you could manage."

"OK, give him my number. Do me a favor, though. Don't call him back until tomorrow afternoon. I want to talk to Dorothy about this first. If you don't hear from me by noon tomorrow, assume you can go ahead."

Rhonda had never heard such uncertainty from Philip. He had been a very decisive person when she worked for him. And she really couldn't remember any time in the past when he thought he needed advice from another person about a work issue. Yes, this man was different.

"Very good, Philip," Rhonda said, trying not to sound judgmental. "The lawyer's name is Sean Gracey if he calls, and he's representing a Dr. Paul Wilson in Scranton."

Rhonda didn't lose any time closing the conversation. "By the way, I hope we have a chance to see each other soon. Give your kids a hug for me, would you?"

"Sure, Rhonda—I will definitely do that. And do the same for your family."

Philip hung up and stared at the phone. Although he liked the idea of some outside activity to generate income, he was intimidated by the fact that this work involved malpractice litigation. The case that had been brought against him by Hugh Hamlin had been specious, and yet it had turned his life upside down. He knew that any doctor who is sued goes through a tremendous emotional ordeal that includes an almost pathological dependence on the expert who renders an opinion on his or her behalf. Philip wasn't sure he wanted that responsibility. But before he decided, he wanted Dorothy's perspective.

Philip's relationship with Dorothy had come a long way since their romantic tryst years before. They had gone through the crucible of the Hamlin case, an experience that Philip believed had brought them closer together. But when Dorothy accused Philip of conspiring with the Philadelphia mafia to kill Hugh and Bonnie, Philip had been shocked. He told Dorothy he was disappointed that she believed he could do such a thing. With his repeated assurances, Dorothy had come around. They had eventually bought the Pocono house together. Philip told Dorothy he wanted to marry her. Dorothy's response was that they needed more time to learn about each other. The refusal only fed Philip's fear that Dorothy didn't trust him entirely.

Dorothy had her own life adjustments to make. Her new job was not very different from the position she had vacated in Philadelphia. Most of her time was spent in general law practice, but occasionally she was able to use her talents as a private investigator. Dorothy had worked on several cases, including Philip's ordeal with the Hamlins, in which a bit of information about personal habits or indiscretions gave her a distinct advantage in resolving a case. Dorothy still worked long hours but now could look forward to an evening cocktail with Philip on the dock with their two Portuguese water dogs at their feet as they watched the sun set over the lake.

On this particular evening, Philip used their cocktail hour to tell Dorothy about the phone call from Rhonda and to sound her out about the malpractice case review. After reviewing the usual mundane events of the day, Philip eventually got around to it.

"I'm kind of inclined to do it," Philip said after explaining the details.

"Then what's the problem?"

"You know how I am with these things. Once I get started, I tend to get emotionally involved. I feel like the white knight charging in to rescue the helpless doctor from the evil plaintiff lawyers. And when I do, I get pretty wound up. I'm worried about the stress. Do you think I'm ready for all that?"

"Gosh, Philip, I don't know. I guess it would be a good idea for you to get back to some of the stuff you were doing before. You used to like the challenge of reviewing legal cases. And you were good at it. You helped a lot of doctors. You can at least find out what the case is about and then decide if you want to do it."

"So you wouldn't reject the idea out of hand?"

"No. Talk to the lawyer tomorrow and go from there. I can ask around to see if anybody knows him."

As usual, Dorothy had rendered sound advice with a good game plan, and Philip was relaxed and confident the next day as he waited for Gracey's call. After a brief introduction,

Gracey described the case to Philip and then explained what he needed.

"Dr. Sarkis, Dr. Wilson truly believes he had no reason to expect that Mr. Romanzo would die an arrhythmic death shortly after his admission. I need to know if you agree. I also need your idea about the reason for Mr. Romanzo's death. What caused that ugly arrhythmia, and was there anything that Dr. Wilson could have done to prevent it or treat it?"

"First of all, when people get to that age, things happen. So I'm blown away by the idea that his family is looking for money. In the end, I may not be able to provide much on causality. But the key will be a thorough analysis of the rhythm records. I need to go through them page by page."

"Of course. We'll send you a copy of all of Mr. Romanzo's medical records. After you look at them, let me know if there is anything else you need. In the meantime, I'll put together an agreement. What's your hourly fee?"

"Five hundred dollars an hour for case review and testimony," Philip half asked and half stated.

"That should be no problem, Doctor." Gracey was relieved that Sarkis didn't want more. Some experts had the audacity to demand twice that much. But before he could agree to use Philip as a defense expert, he had a few more delicate questions.

"Dr. Sarkis, I'm sorry to ask, but I have to get a little more information about your current situation. I assume that you're licensed to practice cardiology?"

"I am. Was there reason to doubt it?"

"No, but I did have occasion to go on the federal databank, and there was a mention of the Hamlin case. I understand you went through some tough times after the verdict."

Philip didn't know how to respond. The two years after the verdict had been a roller coaster ride that ended with the Hamlins' deaths. "Yeah, I was on the outs with the profession for a while, but I'm back as a member in good standing. I never had my license revoked or suspended. I just chose not to practice medicine for a while."

"That's great. I just didn't want anybody to be embarrassed when we get into the case." What Gracey really meant was that he didn't want the case to blow up in his face because his chief witness had a skeleton in his closet. Gracey knew that a plaintiff's attorney might not bring up Philip's malpractice record in front of a jury directly, but there were ways to intimidate a witness who had something to be ashamed of. Given his client's confidence in Sarkis, and because of Sarkis' acknowledged expertise in the field, Gracey figured he would take a chance.

"And you're currently seeing patients in Pennsylvania, right?"

"Yes, I work in an outpatient clinic nearby. I don't see patients or round in the hospital, but I refer many of them to colleagues who assume their care."

"I see no problem with using you as an expert, Dr. Sarkis. I'll ask my office to get all the paperwork processed. We'll inform the malpractice insurance carrier, and the records will be sent to you with a retainer check in a week or so."

"That's fine. The material should be delivered to my home address, not my office."

"We'll do that. Remember, keep all this confidential. In fact, you'll need to sign a form that says you won't divulge patient information."

Philip wasn't surprised. Patient confidentiality was now the mantra of everyone in the healthcare industry. Philip couldn't figure out why this had been such a big deal. Did doctors really need to be admonished and threatened to keep patient issues secret?

"Give me a call after you look things over," Gracely continued. "Don't write a report until we talk." As expected, he didn't want a negative opinion in the file should Philip arrive at a conclusion that did not favor Dr. Wilson.

The medical records arrived in a cardboard box a week later. Philip waited for one of his days off to begin. After waving goodbye to Dorothy and taking Mitten and Buffy out for their morning stroll, he poured himself another cup of coffee, wiped the dining room table clean, and began to dig through the pile of documents. He organized them in chronological order, starting with Romanzo's outpatient and nursing home records, continuing through previous hospitalizations, and ending with the final admission.

Although the records were copious, Philip had no problem picking his way through them, knowing from experience and instinct what he wanted to see in each pile. He was particularly interested in Romanzo's cardiovascular history. He was somewhat surprised to see that Al didn't have as much heart disease as he had assumed. In fact, except for the tracings with the left bundle branch block, it looked as if Al's heart had been pretty darn healthy. When he had been examined, he didn't have any murmurs. His blood pressure and blood sugars had been normal, and Philip couldn't find any reason for Al to have had coronary artery disease. This made the fact that Al had developed a lethal arrhythmia even more difficult to understand.

Philip had been trying to refrain from looking at the dramatic arrhythmias until he had gotten through all of the appropriate background information. But despite his orderly approach, he was totally unprepared for what he saw when he turned to the telemetry recordings. Al Romanzo had started out in the unit with a completely normal heart rhythm, and nary a blip. However, within a few hours of his admission, he was having isolated premature beats. The arrhythmia that was brought to Wilson's attention on morning rounds was nonsustained ventricular tachycardia. In essence, Al was having runs of abnormal beats coming from the lower chamber of the heart. Some of the runs were rather long, up to ten beats in duration, but they weren't particularly fast and there was nothing about them that was peculiar or diagnostic of anything.

Wilson's reaction had been appropriate. He had decided to check some routine tests like electrolytes but didn't see any reason to treat or be overly concerned. But he did keep Al in the hospital for further observation.

Most of the test results had been fine, with the exception

of the electrocardiogram on the second hospital day. The bundle branch block pattern had resolved, but the ST segment, the part of the electrocardiogram, or EKG, that reflected the heart's recovery of excitability, was well below the baseline. The pattern of depression looked like the effect of a particular drug called digitalis. Digitalis is a drug that is used frequently in cardiac patients to improve the force of heart muscle contraction, or to keep the heart rate from accelerating in those with upper heart chamber rhythm abnormalities. Al didn't have heart failure or an atrial arrhythmia to warrant the use of digitalis, so Philip dismissed the possibility that he was receiving it. ST segment depression can also be caused by many other things or just be a nonspecific finding.

But, as it turned out, the digitalis idea couldn't be so easily dismissed. As Philip flipped through the pages of recordings from the second hospital day, he observed a pattern of quiescence during the daytime hours followed by progressive arrhythmias in the afternoon and evening. However, the nighttime events, those that had prompted the nursing staff to rouse Wilson from his bed, were more bizarre and serious. Instead of a monotonous run of ventricular beats like the night before, the arrhythmias seemed to be coming from two different foci in the ventricle. The morphologies alternated perfectly, with one beat having a positive and the next a negative configuration.

"Damn. He was having bidirectional ventricular tachycardia." The only beings in earshot were Mitten and Buffy, napping on the sofa next to the table. The pups tilted their heads and looked at Philip as if they understood the significance of Philip's observation but had no strong opinion themselves.

Philip, on the other hand, believed that he had a possible reason for Al Romanzo's arrhythmic death. "I bet you the son of a bitch had digitalis toxicity." Philip's dogs had already returned to their late morning snooze, and so he had nobody to share this revelation with, nor his next observation. "Now I just have to figure out why they were giving him the drug and why he got more than he needed."

For the next two hours, Philip scoured the records looking for any mention of digoxin, the most common formulation of digitalis used clinically. He found it nowhere. It was on none of Al's medication lists, it was not mentioned in the orders, and it was not in the nurses' notes. Philip next checked the laboratory data. Doctors who prescribed digoxin frequently ordered blood levels of the drug to determine whether the patient was getting too much or too little. Digoxin levels were not listed anywhere.   Finally, Philip went back to Al's office records. There was nothing about digoxin there, either, and the ST segments on those tracings looked nothing like Romanzo's EKG the morning before he died.

Philip pushed his chair back from the table, took off his glasses, rubbed his eyes, and tried to make sense of what he had discovered so far. He was reasonably sure that Romanzo's death had been due to arrhythmias associated with digitalis excess, but he couldn't find evidence that it had been prescribed by anyone caring for Al in the several months to years before his death. Could Al have been taking it on his own? Given his altered mental state, that didn't seem likely.

That left the possibility that someone was giving him the drug without a prescription or order. From what Philip could see, it was most likely administered in the hospital since Al had progressed from fine to bad very quickly. According to the nurses' notes, Al had no visitors, so it probably was given by somebody on the hospital staff. But by whom, and why so much? There was an obvious but sinister answer to that question.

Philip looked over at Mitten, the older and more contemplative of his precious pets. Maybe he could entice her to opine on the big issue.

"So, girl, do you think that somebody maybe was trying to off the old dude?"

Mitten cocked her head to the side and her ears perked up. Clearly she agreed that something truly weird had happened to poor Al Romanzo. Her demeanor however indicated that she didn't have enough data to conclude there had been a murder. She put her head back on her pillow and closed her eyes. "You're on your own, pal," she seemed to say.

And as he himself had feared, Philip was getting entangled in another complicated malpractice case. But he was hooked and he knew it. And he also knew he wouldn't be able to give up until he had a plausible explanation for what had happened to poor Mr. Alfonzo Romanzo.

CHAPTER FIVE

That evening at sunset, Philip and Dorothy sat in the Adirondack chairs on their dock and sipped vodkas diluted in lots of tonic, topped off with fresh limes. The lake glistened as the sun began its descent to the horizon. The water reflected the evergreens from the opposite bank; it was a scene from a postcard.

Philip was anxious to discuss his suspicions with Dorothy. He liked the idea of having Dorothy as a sounding board. If there was a glaring hole in his thinking, she would point it out. Dorothy turned out to be as surprised as he was about the potential for foul play.

"Philip, are you sure that nobody prescribed the drug for the patient? Maybe he brought his medicine to the hospital and took it on his own."

"Unlikely. He was at a nursing facility before he was admitted and was given all of his medicine by the staff. There is nothing in the hospital nursing notes about digoxin when he was admitted or when he was on the telemetry unit. And there was no good reason for him to get the drug."

"And you went through all of the records carefully?"

"Yes, and I came up snake eyes."

"Well, you're going to have to tell Gracey what you suspect and see how he wants to handle it."

"That's what I thought—I just wanted to make sure I wasn't missing something before I called him."

Philip placed a call to Gracey the next morning after Dorothy left for her office. He wasn't in but returned the call after lunch. Philip was in the middle of his domestic chores, folding laundry and emptying the dishwasher, when the phone rang. Gracey waited while Philip took out his notes.

"Doctor, can you give me your overall impression of the case before we get into the specifics?"

"Mr. Gracey, this is a strange case for many reasons. I had a hard time understanding why the family was bringing the lawsuit in the first place. It shouldn't have been surprising to anyone that a guy this old died from an arrhythmia. So I wasn't expecting to find much. On the surface, it looks like Mr. Romanzo had an arrhythmia related to heart disease. But the rhythm strips tell an interesting story and are the key to the case."

"How so?"

"Well, they show a peculiar form of ventricular tachycardia; that's an arrhythmia from the bottom heart chamber. That isn't particularly surprising because it is what most people with heart disease manifest. What's remarkable is that the arrhythmia traveled in two different directions from different locations in the heart. We call that bidirectional tachycardia."

"I don't understand. Why is that important?"

"The thing that usually causes arrhythmias that look like that is toxic amounts of a cardiac drug called digitalis."

"I've heard of that drug. Isn't it a pretty commonly used drug for cardiac patients?"

Philip was happy to hear that Gracey had at least minimal familiarity with drugs and arrhythmia treatments. Working with knowledgeable lawyers could make his job easier, unless the lawyer was a know-it-all. That ilk took forever to re-educate.

"Yes. It's used a lot in heart failure patients to improve pump function. It's also used to treat upper chamber, or atrial arrhythmias. But when given in large amounts, it actually causes lower chamber arrhythmias in a characteristic pattern, which is what Mr. Romanzo clearly had."

"But why did he get that medicine? Did he have heart failure?"

"Like I said, he didn't have any reason to get the drug. And I can't find any evidence that anyone ordered it for him either at the nursing home or at the hospital."

"I don't understand," Gracey answered. "Are you telling me that he got a drug in the hospital that nobody ordered?"

"Yep, that is exactly what I'm telling you."

"Doctor, I have a lot of respect for your opinion, but is there a chance you're wrong and the arrhythmia was caused by something else?"

"Nothing is a hundred percent in medicine, so your question is a good one. The reason I think it was digitalis in Mr. Romanzo's case is that he also had some findings on his EKGs that were consistent."

"Consistent how, Doctor?"

"Digitalis has an effect on several ion channels in the heart, some of which govern how the heart recovers its ability to re-excite. The waveforms on Mr. Romanzo's EKGs were altered, also in a pattern characteristic of digitalis."

"So having both of those would have to be an amazing coincidence if digitalis were not the culprit?"

"Precisely," Philip concluded. "And the icing on the cake is that Mr.Romanzo also had a few periods of AV block, when impulses from the top chamber of the heart don't make it to the bottom chamber."

"And digitalis does that, too?"

"Yes, and here again the pattern of the block is highly compatible with digitalis excess."

"It sounds like awfully good evidence, Doctor. So how do you think this happened? Do you think the drug was a mistake or was somebody trying to poison him?"

"I would say he got a lot of the drug and judging from the pattern of the arrhythmias, it may have been administered multiple times. That would be one heck of a mistake."

"Do you think he was intentionally overdosed?"

"I can't rule that out but before we can get into that question, we need hard evidence that he had digitalis toxicity, not just an interpretation of the EKGs."

"How are we going to get that?" Gracey asked, not sure he wanted to hear the answer.

"As far as I can determine, we have two ways, one easy and one not so simple. The easy thing to do is see if the hospital stores serum on patients for later analyses. A lot of places do that in case a doctor forgets to order something and remembers it later. If the hospital provides that service, and they still have the specimen, it would be easy to see how high the level was. I'm not optimistic about that one; they don't keep specimens forever."

"I'm afraid to ask what the hard thing would be."

"Digitalis binds avidly to muscle tissue, including the heart muscle, and it stays there for a long time, even after death. The other thing we could do is assay the amount of drug in Mr. Romanzo's tissues."

"And since we don't have any of his tissues lying around, that would require..."

"Exhumation," Philip finished the sentence emphatically.

"I don't think that the family is going to be real happy about that," Gracey countered.

"It is pretty grisly."

"Not only that, but they are trying to prove that Dr. Wilson acted negligently. I doubt they'll want to help us prove their father died through no fault of Wilson, but because of a mysterious drug overdose. On the other hand, it would put the hospital on the hook and maybe help Dr. Wilson. I never met the family, so I don't know how they'd react."

"Well, what do you suggest?"

"I'll see if there are blood samples left over. If not, I'll talk to opposing counsel and see what the reaction might be to exhumation. I doubt it will be a congenial conversation."

Philip was apologetic. "Sorry for putting you through this. I've racked my brain and can't come up with any other explanation. The pattern of the tachycardia and the look of the EKG are just too much to ignore."

"That's OK, Dr. Sarkis. I understand. I'm just going to have to do my job, as unpleasant as that sometimes is. I'll let you know how this sorts out."

Philip put the medical records aside and didn't think about the case for a few weeks. He immersed himself in the simple life of a primary cardiologist in a rural outpatient setting, and spent the rest of his time working around the house and playing with the dogs while Dorothy worked full time at her law practice.

Philip's kids visited for long weekends once a month. Their trips to Chuck E. Cheese and kid movies were about the extent of their social life. Dorothy occasionally joked about their isolation, but Philip liked the simple existence and the solitude that their lake home afforded.

Sean Gracey's phone call two months later jolted Philip's memory of the case. "Doctor, I'm sorry it's taken so long to get back to you, but I've been working hard to answer the questions you raised. First of all, you were right about the hospital saving serum samples on patients. They only keep the stuff for ninety days after somebody is discharged or dies so Mr. Romanzo's samples are long gone."

"Yeah, that sounds about right. It was worth a try."

"It sure was, especially since our request for an autopsy went over like a lead balloon. Opposing counsel scoffed at the idea even before they asked the family, and the family was downright hostile. I'm sure counsel didn't present a balanced opinion to Mr. Romanzo's children. In any case, they turned us down flat."

Philip shook his head. "Not surprised. Do you have legal recourse?"

"Well, I ran it by a judge informally, just to get an opinion. Her attitude was that it would be hard to compel an exhumation over the family's objections unless there was a strong suspicion of foul play. That would require a criminal investigation, and that is way past my interest in the case. I'm just trying to help Dr. Wilson."

"Wouldn't proving that Mr. Romanzo got a lethal dose of medicine that Dr. Wilson never ordered help your client?"

There was a pause as Gracey considered his answer. "Yeah, it would. But how would I ever be able to convince a jury? Proving a homicide is a little outside the bounds of usual malpractice defense work."

"So what are you going to do?"

Gracey was prepared with the answer. "I already spoke with Dr. Wilson. We're going to make an offer to settle the case. Mr. Romanzo was old and the economic damages will be small. If Wilson apologizes to the family and throws himself on their mercy, he'll get out of it pretty cheaply."

Philip was outraged. "That just sounds wrong to me. Wilson shouldn't take the rap for this. There's no way he could have suspected digitalis poisoning."

"Really, Dr. Sarkis? You did. No matter how Mr. Romanzo got so much of the drug, if Dr. Wilson had recognized the problem, he could have given an antidote, right?"

"Yes, he could have given antibodies that bind to digitalis, and that would have reduced the level of the drug in the heart."

"And saved Mr. Romanzo's life?"

"Most likely, yes," Philip admitted. "The arrhythmias would have been suppressed."

"So, no matter how you look at it, a smart plaintiff's attorney like Chip Markley should be able to prove that Dr. Wilson missed the diagnosis, and in doing so, lost an opportunity to save the patient."

"I can't argue the point, except to say that making the diagnosis is not as easy as you think. If you and Dr. Wilson settle this case, somebody could literally get away with murder."

"Not my problem, Dr. Sarkis. My firm and I are paid by the malpractice carrier to look out for Dr. Wilson, not to be the caped crusader who brings murderers to justice. In this case, if I pursue your idea, I could put Dr. Wilson in an even worse position. After all, Dr. Wilson would have to be considered a suspect if we assume that Al Romanzo was murdered.

Dr. Wilson is almost certainly going to retire, and he doesn't want to have this case on his mind when he's bouncing his grandchildren on his knee."

"Don't you have some kind of ethical duty to report a case of murder, even if it endangers your client?"

"I do, Dr. Sarkis, and attorney-client privilege can't be used to protect Dr. Wilson in that scenario. But I would have to possess credible data to support my suspicions, and we are far from that."

Philip was impressed that Gracey had so thoroughly considered all of the angles, especially how best to protect his client.

"So," Gracey continued, "I'm going to take a pass on this one. As far as I'm concerned, Al Romanzo's death was natural and due to his underlying heart disease, just as the death certificate states. Now, if you give me your preferred address, I'll be sure to send payment for your time on the case. We won't need your services further. On behalf of Dr. Wilson, we do thank you for all you've done. And if you wouldn't mind, please send the records back to my office—we'll pay the shipping charges."

Philip ended the conversation with Gracey and tried to force himself to believe that he was through with the case. Maybe so, but he made a mental note to copy key parts of the medical records, just in case.

Philip couldn't wait for Dorothy to come home that evening. He held the front door open for her as she got of her car in the driveway. "Something on your mind, big boy? Or are you just happy to see me?"

"You aren't going to believe the conversation I had this afternoon with Gracey."

"Oh, he finally called back?"

"He sure did. The hospital didn't keep blood, of course, and the family refused to consider an exhumation. But the mind blower is that Gracey is throwing in the towel. He told me he's going to try to settle the case for Wilson rather than try to find out what really happened!"

Dorothy walked into the house with Philip back-pedaling in front of her. He was speaking rapidly, and Dorothy could see that Philip was incensed. This was the same behavior she had seen when the Hamlins had nearly gotten away with murder in their last life. It made her worry that Philip might do something rash.

"Hold on, Philip. Remember, Gracey is not a criminal attorney and there is no proof that a crime was committed. And also keep in mind that Wilson may not be willing to take the case to the mat. As I recall, you said he had been sued previously and was thinking about leaving medicine. So before you get angry about this, remember that Gracey has a client to protect and all you have is a theory without much to support it—except your reading of an EKG, of course."

"Several EKGs, and I'm telling you I am right on this one. This guy got too much digitalis somehow, and Gracey isn't going to push to find out why or how."

Dorothy knew that Philip wasn't going to let this go. The best thing to do might be to channel his energy so he wouldn't get himself and others into trouble. "OK, let's think this through. To prove your theory that digitalis poisoning killed Al Romanzo, the body has to be exhumed. Correct?"

"Correct."

"Now, if you can't get permission from the family, what you need to do is convince someone in a position of authority that there's a good chance Al Romanzo was the victim of foul play, so the exhumation becomes part of a criminal investigation."

"I guess so."

"So, we have to find someone in law enforcement who will listen to your story, buy into it, and be willing to get a court order."

"That sounds exactly right. But where do you find such a person?"

"Beats the heck out of me. We're pretty new to the neighborhood. Let me ask around at work to see if we can find someone who'd be willing to handle this discreetly."

The next day, Dorothy spoke to a few of her senior law partners who had practiced in the area for a long time. She was careful to omit any details about the Romanzo case, and kept her request as generic as possible. Although none of them worked in criminal law, the community of Wilkes-Barre was small enough for reputations to spread beyond strict legal disciplines. Every cop knew the best divorce and bankruptcy attorneys, and every attorney knew which policemen could be trusted, and which couldn't.

Many of her associates came up with similar suggestions, and one name was mentioned by nearly all. Chief Detective Steven Detweiler had established a reputation in Wilkes-Barre for honesty that all agreed was beyond reproach. His good work had earned him the admiration not only of his peers, but also those in authority who had recommended him for the top investigative job in the city. If Dorothy needed an advocate, there could be no one better than Detweiler. "But you need to know," warned one of her close friends in the firm, "you'll have to work hard to convince him. Detweiler's definitely a tough sell and has a low tolerance for bullshit."

And for good reason. Detweiler had grown up in Wilkes-Barre, the son of German immigrants who believed in the value of hard work. They were poor but proud people who taught their only son to be honest and to expect the truth in return. Steve had never appreciated being lied to or fooled with.

Becoming a policeman seemed a logical choice. Enforcing the law was another way to keep people honest for everyone's benefit, and he excelled. He was physically gifted, and his imposing stature and athleticism were inducements for would-be criminals to do the right thing.

His ascent in the force had been predictable and rapid. He progressed from cop on the beat to detective in record time. His work on some highly publicized murder cases early in his career earned attention from his superiors. When the Chief Detective job became available, no one quibbled with his appointment.

When Dorothy suggested to Philip that he talk to Detweiler, he was wary. "Are you sure this is the right guy? He's pretty far up in the police force. Do you really think he'd take my opinions seriously?"

"Oh come on, Philip. You're the one who came up with the idea of going to the police. Are you having second thoughts now that you have someone you can call?"

"No, I just don't know who this guy is, and I don't want to look foolish."

"Well, take it or leave it. To tell you the truth, I don't care one way or the other." Dorothy walked away shaking her head, secretly hoping that Philip would grow tired of his amateur sleuthing.

But Philip was determined and screwed up the nerve to call Detweiler's office. "Detective Detweiler, my name is Dr. Philip Sarkis. I live in Pocono Pines. I recently had the chance to review a legal case, and I came across some disturbing information that makes me think that somebody might have intentionally harmed a nursing home resident in Scranton."

Detweiler responded in an even tone. "Well, Doctor, I don't have much to do for the next few minutes, so why don't you just fill me in. For the sake of the legal case, don't mention any names for now until I get the gist of things, and then we can decide how to proceed."

"OK."

Philip went on to explain the case, careful to omit names of people and places. At the end, there was silence on the other end. Philip was concerned that Detweiler had cut him off or fallen asleep. "Detective, are you still there?"

"Oh, I'm here all right. Just taking some notes. So the way you figure it, this old man might have been poisoned by someone at the hospital?"

"Possibly, but I am by no means certain."

"So the logical question, of course, is what do you want from me?"

"Well, if I'm right, the only way to know if there was foul play is to see if the patient's heart has a high concentration of digitalis, and the only way to know that is to exhume the body and do an autopsy."

"Hmm, that's a pretty big deal, Doctor, as I am sure you know, especially if the family is opposed."

"I understand, but the family has a reason to keep the information buried, so to speak. If there's no evidence of foul play, they'll have a better case against the hospital and doctor, but then somebody might get away with murder."

"All right, Doctor, tell you what. Let me call one of the assistant DAs up here to see if she thinks we have enough of a reason to pursue this, and I'll get back to you." Detweiler took Philip's number and promised a call back in a few days.

But Detweiler went one better. Two evenings later, Philip answered the door to find a well-dressed, tall, handsome man in business attire and raincoat standing on his front porch. Detweiler introduced himself. "Sorry to barge in," he said, "but I was in the neighborhood and thought we should talk in person. Actually, I was anxious to meet you."

Philip took his coat and ushered Detweiler into the living room and sat across from him on the sofa. Dorothy joined them and introduced herself.

"Detective Detweiler just told me that he was looking forward to meeting us," Philip said.

"Really, Detective? Why is that?" Dorothy asked.

"Well, after we spoke, I talked to an assistant DA, as I promised. I also took the time to find out a little about you two. Your names came up on the computer with the Hamlin murder case in Philly, so I called Detective Scotti, whom I happen to know. He had some interesting things to tell me about you. Sounds like you and Dr. Sarkis here were pretty involved with that case. Funny how it turned out, wouldn't you say?"

"Yes, tragic really," Philip answered, oblivious to Detweiler's implication. But Dorothy didn't miss it.

"Lieutenant, I'm sure Detective Scotti made it clear that we were out of town when Hugh and Bonnie were murdered. We were never accused of any crime."

Detweiler thought that Dorothy sounded defensive but decided to let it go. Scotti had already assured him that Philip and Dorothy were never serious suspects in the gangland-style murders of the Main Line couple, even though Philip had a clear motive.

"Understood, but you did good detective work yourselves in that case, so I guess that gives you some credibility. Anyway, after going over everything, I think there is a reason to get a court order for exhumation of the remains of the victim. But now comes the tough part. You have to give me some names. Did you sign a confidentiality agreement before you reviewed the legal case?"

"I did," Philip said

"That's too bad."

"You should be able to get an exception, Lieutenant, since this is a potential murder case," Dorothy reminded him.

"I can and I will. It will just take a few calls but I hate spending time on that nonsense. Would going ahead with this jeopardize the case for the defendant doctor?"

"No, he agreed to settle the case so this shouldn't have any impact on him."

"That remains to be seen," the Lieutenant answered disdainfully. "I just don't want the doctor to come after us if we violate your confidentiality agreement and put him in harm's way."

"Do you really think he would do that?"

"Don't worry, Doctor, I'll make sure that's all squared away. So why don't you tell me the patient's and doctor's name and what hospital he died in?"

Philip filled in the gaps for Detective Detweiler who took notes, asked a few questions before leaving, and promised to get back to Philip shortly.

After Detweiler departed, Dorothy had a worried look.

"What's wrong?" Philip asked.

71

"I hope you did the right thing. If Romanzo was poisoned with a drug he was never prescribed, there's going to be a big investigation, and you're going to get dragged into it."

"I know, and I am not looking forward to that—but what choice do I have?"

Dorothy didn't answer, but only shook her head as she returned to the book she was reading.

Detweiler was a man of his word. Early the next week, he phoned Philip to let him know that his office had obtained a written order from Judge Klatsky to exhume the body of Al Romanzo immediately.

"It wasn't easy. The family's attorney filed for an injunction but the judge put a lot of weight on your certainty that the EKGs were indicative of drug poisoning. So he went out on a limb and denied the motion."

"I'm impressed—I hope I don't let him down."

"Me too. Judge Klatsky is a good guy, but he doesn't like getting bushwhacked. The gravediggers have already started on the hole, and we should have the remains at the Medical Examiner's office in the next few hours."

"That was fast."

"Well, once the decision is made, it's best to do things quickly. If there is a perpetrator, we don't want to give him or her any opportunity to tamper with the evidence."

"Makes sense."

"And I was told by the ME office that they'll be able to run the digitalis samples from the heart tissue within forty-eight hours, so we should know by mid-week."

"They need to check other organs for their drug concentration to get a good idea about total body exposure. And while they're at it, they need to examine the heart to see if there was any evidence of severe underlying heart disease, or just the normal aging process."

"I'm sure they'll do a thorough job. The ME is a careful person."

"You'll call us when you know something?"

"Doctor, that's something you can depend on. You will literally be the first to know."

Chapter Six

Philip and Dorothy didn't discuss the case for the next few days. That is not to say that the matter didn't weigh heavily on Philip's mind. This was the second time that a malpractice issue he was involved in had morphed into a murder case. Was this a coincidence? Was Philip unlucky, or was the Romanzo matter a product of his overactive imagination?

Detweiler's call came when Philip and Dorothy were shopping for groceries on a Wednesday evening. The detective left a message suggesting a lunch appointment the next day near his office. He wanted to show Philip the report from the Medical Examiner and didn't want to discuss it on the phone. He proposed the Sunshine Café, a popular sandwich shop in downtown Wilkes-Barre, near the river. Philip returned the call but also got a message machine. "Certainly," he replied in his voice mail. "I will be there at noon."

Like many old cities in the Northeast, Wilkes-Barre had undergone an urban renewal, trying hard to shed its stodgy reputation as a dirty coal mining city. The major problem it faced was attracting new businesses, so the town leaders provided economic incentives. The owners of the Sunshine Café were New York natives who welcomed the chance to escape the city and launch a new enterprise: a deli-style restaurant serving big sandwiches at reasonable prices. The site was also a draw since it provided a scenic view of the river from tables placed on an outdoor deck for good weather munching.

Philip arrived five minutes late and saw that Detweiler was

already seated on the deck, waiting for him. They both went for the house specialty, a club sandwich on rye with enough turkey, bacon, lettuce, and tomato to choke a Clydesdale. Armed with an ample supply of napkins, they dove in, washing it all down with iced tea. Between gulps, Detweiler began the briefing by carefully laying the five-page report from the ME on one of the few clean spots on the table.

"Well, Doctor, all I can say is that my hat is off to you. You nailed this one. As you suspected, Mr. Romanzo didn't have much heart disease. He had pretty good-looking arteries and no evidence of a heart attack or stroke."

"So he didn't just die of plain old-fashioned cardiovascular disease. Now the big question: was there excess digitalis in Mr. Romanzo's heart?"

"The ME pulled samples from the heart, leg muscle, intestine, and kidney. Everywhere he looked, he found huge concentrations. He said they were pretty much off the chart, and set new records for the reference laboratory."

"It's unusual to find that much in tissues other than the heart."

"The ME said the same thing. Highly unusual."

"So he must have gotten a shitload of the drug."

"Yeah. Not exactly the term the ME used, but the same general idea. And that is important from my perspective because..."

Philip cut in, "...because nobody gets that much drug by mistake?"

"Yep. And the ME was pretty certain from its distribution that the drug was given intravenously, and not taken by mouth. That means somebody literally pumped it into the guy's veins."

Philip shook his head. "I guess that it could have been a dosing error—the problem is that nobody ordered it."

Detweiler was pleased that Philip was willing to consider as many alternatives as possible. "Could they have gotten mixed up and just given him the wrong drug? He was getting a few other things by vein. You read about nurses making mistakes with drugs frequently. Didn't I just read about something like that in the papers? An Institute of Medicine study of some kind?"

"Yeah, and medication errors do happen all the time. But here's the problem, Detective. To give him that much digitalis would have required opening several vials and injecting all of them. So you would have had to repeat the mistake over and over again."

"You're the expert. If you can't conceive of a good reason as to why this happened, I doubt I'm going to come up with a reasonable explanation either."

Philip paged through the ME report as he finished his iced tea. "From the chemical constitution of the digitalis they pulled out of Mr. Romanzo, the ME was pretty sure that this was generic and not brand digitalis."

Detweiler smiled. "Doc, you have to give that to me again. What does that mean?"

"I'm sorry, Detective. I didn't mean to get technical. When a drug first becomes available, it is marketed exclusively by one pharmaceutical company while they have patent protection. When the patent runs out, usually in a few years, other companies can copy the drug and sell it more cheaply. From its composition, the stuff they found in this case was definitely the generic stuff. That means it was purchased by the hospital from a drug wholesaler at the best price they could get. Those wholesalers usually have contracts with several hospitals for a specialty drug like this."

"Does that make a difference in this case?"

"I doubt it. Even if this hospital somehow got hold of a bad batch of medicine, it would be hard to account for such a massive overdose."

"So where does that leave us, Doc?"

"I was going to ask you the same question. Do you have enough reason to pursue a murder investigation at this point?"

Detweiler sat back in his chair and put his chin on his hand. "Let me put it to you this way, Doctor. I have maybe fifteen homicide cases on my desk right now—I mean real cases where we are sure that somebody deliberately offed somebody else. We have a body, and in many cases we even have a murder weapon and a motive. I don't have a big staff, so fifteen cases already spreads us pretty thin." Detweiler crossed his arms. "Don't get me wrong, I have every intention of following up on this. I just don't have any idea how much time and staff I can commit right now."

Philip was visibly disappointed. "Detective Detweiler, unless you come up with a suspect, somebody is going to get away with killing poor defenseless hospital patients who..."

"Very old and very sick hospital patients," Detweiler interrupted. "I don't want to argue with you about this—you're right, no matter who the victim is, we need to pursue a possible murderer and we will. I'm just telling you that it's not going to get a high priority from my office, at least not right now."

Detweiler could see that Philip was not assuaged. "If it makes you feel any better Doctor, I did call the attorney who represented Dr. Wilson and I gave him the ME information. He's going to pass it on to the other lawyers on the case. Hopefully that will get the malpractice mess settled faster."

"As I told you, Wilson wanted out of the case anyway and planned to take a settlement offer no matter what. I don't know how much it helps or hurts the hospital, but at least the family will know what really happened to their father—that is, if they care."

"Tell you what, Doc. Let's stay in touch. I'll call you if I hear anything more, and you can let me know if you have any other thoughts about the case. I know you aren't happy, but it's the best I can do for the time being."

"OK, Detective. I understand your position. Let me think about the case and see if I can come up with any other angles. I'd like to hear from you from time to time."

Even as he said it, Philip knew he was going to have a hard time putting the case aside. At the very least, he and Dorothy were going to have yet another soul-searching discussion during cocktails that evening.

Soon after Detweiler and Philip met at the Sunshine Café, news about how Al Romanzo died reached Chip Markley's law office. Helga Podolinsky had just rung off with Detweiler when Sean Gracey called her to discuss the results of the exhumation. "I know we're on opposite sides of this case, but this puts a whole new spin on things, don't you think?" Gracey asked.

Helga had been surprised by the information but could do little more than agree on general principles. She knew that any official opinion would have to come from Markley himself. "Sean, I haven't had a chance to think about this. I'll call you back after I go over it with my partners and staff."

"You mean you have to find out what Chip wants to do, right?" Gracey laughed. Without waiting for an answer, "Yeah, just call me back after you confer with the big cheese and we'll see what's what."

Helga knew that Markley was not going to be happy with this new development. Rather than wait, she decided it would be better to get it over with. She interrupted Markley during a meeting with some prospective clients. Markley politely excused himself, his face darkening the instant he turned away and left the conference room to see what she wanted.

"Damn it, Helga, what's so damn important?" Markley hissed as soon as they were out of earshot. "I'm trying to convince this family they should go after their general practitioner for missing their mother's breast lump. They're just about ready to sign the papers."

"I thought you would want to know that we got a call from the police and Sean Gracey. They had some very interesting information about Al Romanzo's death."

"You mean that old guy who died at Memorial? I thought Gracey was throwing in the towel on that one and wanted to settle for his client—what was his name?"

"Wilson. Yes, he told us that, and he's getting out of the case, but now he thinks we have even a better reason to settle it."

Markley was still not particularly interested. "Can you cut

the drama and just tell me what the fuck happened?"

"Remember that whole thing about exhuming the body that Gracey had been harping on?"

"Yeah, we told Linda and Mike to oppose it and they did."

"Well, somehow the defense expert got Steven Detweiler involved, and he managed to convince Judge Klatsky to issue a court order to have the body exhumed and autopsied."

"What? Why wasn't I told about this?"

Helga knew that Markley would have this reaction. "You were out of town at the time. It didn't seem like a big deal, and there wasn't anything we could do about it. I figured that opposing it further would make it look like the children had something to hide, which they didn't—at least I didn't think they did."

"So why didn't you tell me when I got back?"

Helga blushed. "To tell you the truth, I just forgot about it. The whole thing seemed so stupid. I thought that the defense expert was just showing off and that nothing would come of it. So I just entered a notation in the file and put it away."

Markley bit his lip while Helga looked at the floor. They both knew that she was going to pay for this mistake later. But now Markley just wanted the information. "So... are you going to tell me what the damn autopsy showed?"

"Mr. Romanzo somehow received a massive dose of digitalis that caused his heart to go out of rhythm, just as Wilson's expert had suspected. I can't believe he was right. And even worse, nobody knows how he got it or who gave it to him. Nothing in the hospital or nursing home records gives a clue."

"Holy shit! That is news." Markley leaned against the wall, deep in thought. "Let me finish with this client and we can figure out where this leaves us. And we will deal with your behavioral lapses later."

In fact, the Medical Examiner's report generated several meetings and conversations in the Markley office over the next few days. It was clear that Romanzo had not died of natural causes. Indeed, it was possible that someone at the hospital had murdered him. The attorneys for Scranton Memorial told Markely that the hospital intended to conduct a complete investigation of the matter and would cooperate fully with the police. At the same time, they were anxious to keep the matter confidential. They said they didn't want to alarm their patients and staff, but their main fear was the impact that negative publicity would have on their business.

Markley's other concern was how to handle Linda and Mike. He had led them to believe that the case would be fairly straightforward and would yield a small to moderate sized settlement to add to their meager inheritance. Now the case was a monstrosity, the outcome of which was far from clear.

Although the hospital was culpable for not protecting Romanzo, they could hardly be blamed for the actions of some lunatic who poisoned the patient, especially if the nutcase was a visitor or family member. For all he knew, Mike or Linda might have had something to do with it. No matter, the case would now be tied up for a long time and there would be no easy resolution.

Markley rehearsed what he would say before placing the call to Mike. Then he related the story as succinctly as possible, leaving out many of the details.

"So, you're telling me that they got a court order and dug up my Dad?"

Markley had no answer.

"And that my father died of digitalis poisoning, and nobody there knows how it happened?"

"Correct," Markley managed.

"Well, how does this affect your approach to the malpractice case?"

Even the cold-hearted Markley was surprised at how quickly Mike Romanzo moved on to the monetary implications. "Well, it has a big impact. The whole case has been thrown up in the air. It puts the hospital and Wilson on the defensive because your father didn't die naturally. But now there's probably going to be a detailed investigation to redevelop the theory of the case."

"You must have a recommendation."

"In my experience, the best thing to do when things get this complicated is take the money and run. I'll negotiate settlements with Wilson and the hospital separately. If they want to continue the investigation into what happened, or the police decide to get more aggressive, that will not be our concern. You'll get what you're entitled to as soon as possible and walk away."

"How much can we expect?"

"I would say $800,000 total should be no problem. That will be within the limits of their coverage and will make them happy. Believe me, they don't want the negative publicity as much as you don't want to get dragged back here for endless fact finding. It will be the best for everybody."

Except Al Romanzo, of course, but his rights weren't even in Markley's rear-view mirror.

Mike and Linda readily agreed, as did Sean Gracey, the attorneys for the hospital, and the malpractice insurance carriers. Within a few weeks, checks were cut and sent westward. The children were pleased that grandpa had come through with a decent inheritance—enough money to buy a sports car or a boat, with a little left over for the kids' education.

Fifteen percent of Markley's $300,000 commission was mailed out promptly to Jack Oliveri with a thank-you note for the referral. Markley knew that keeping the flow of referrals coming in was worth every penny of the fee split.

A few evenings later, Philip sat on his rocking chair on the dock and stared out at the lake, disturbed by what he had learned from Detweiler. Dorothy sat across from him, reading through the newspaper, absentmindedly petting Buffy, who had her head on Dorothy's lap. It had been a long day at the office, with several client meetings and teleconferences, and she had been looking forward to some diversion this evening. The last thing she wanted was to plunge back into the details of the Romanzo case. But Philip was having trouble putting the shocking news into perspective.

Finally, Dorothy laid the paper on the deck and took a long sip from her vodka tonic. "Philip, you're obviously distracted. Do you want to talk about it?"

"Well, yes and no."

Dorothy smiled. She understood Philip's approach/avoidance attitude. "It might be better just to talk it out a little. It is pretty extraordinary news."

"Yes, it's complicated. On one hand, I'm distressed that a terrible crime was committed and that the perpetrator may get away with it. I also have to admit that some of my discomfort is because of my own curiosity. I always like to know the cause of things."

"And it bothers you that you might not find the reason for Al Romanzo's death."

"Yes. And I'm irked that the people who should care the most about it will look for ways to get off the hook. The hospital doesn't want its reputation damaged. Wilson had no loyalty to the patient. He hardly knew the guy, so why should he take responsibility? The kids are more interested in the money they'll get from the settlement, and they will get plenty."

"So who speaks for Al Romanzo?"

"Precisely!"

"Sound familiar?"

Philip turned to see Dorothy grinning. "I think this was the same conversation we had about Moira Hamlin. Weren't you concerned that nobody spoke for her? And that some poor slob of a doctor was made to take the fall in her case?"

Philip didn't need to be reminded of the analogies. The Moira Hamlin case had many disturbing similarities. "I knew that would come up—and you're absolutely correct. I guess I was raised to believe that people should be held accountable for what they do, especially if they harm someone."

Dorothy quietly shook her head. She understood that it was this quality that had attracted her to Philip in the first place. His willingness to push for the truth and for what was right was compelling. And yet Dorothy had seen Philip become consumed by the Hamlin case. He had been transformed by his obsession into someone she didn't know, or want to know. And she still had not resolved in her mind how far Philip might have gone to exact justice.

"So what do you propose to do?" Dorothy asked.

Philip put his face in his hand and looked across at her. "You're not going to like the answer, but I think that I need to figure out what happened to Al Romanzo."

Before Dorothy had a chance to react, Philip raised his hand in a stop sign. "I know what you're going to say—we almost got ourselves killed or arrested the last time we did this, so I propose strict limits this time. Remember, in the Hamlin case, it was all about the drug, and this case has the same feel to it. I really think that if we follow the drug, we can learn a lot fairly quickly. If our initial probe doesn't yield anything, we simply put the case away."

"Suppose we *do* come up with something?" Dorothy asked.

"The advantage we have now that we didn't have in the Hamlin case is Steve Detweiler. He's a good guy and I believed him when he told me that he wants to see justice done. The poor guy is just bogged down in his other work and can't give this case the attention it deserves. Besides, I don't think a lay detective would know how to track down something this crazy. We have a major advantage in that way."

"And if we break the law a little, that's OK, too?"

"You know better than I do that bending the rules can sometimes get you exactly what you need."

"Or land you exactly in jail," Dorothy retorted. "All right, Philip. I can tell I won't be able to talk you out of this. And I also know that you're going to suck me into it no matter how much I protest. So we'll set up a few ground rules. As you said, we will 'follow the drug' to see if that gets us anywhere. If it does, we call Detweiler. If it doesn't, we call it quits and lay some roses at Al Romanzo's grave. Is that satisfactory?"

"Perfectly. We'll definitely take no for an answer this time."

Dorothy remembered that Philip had made the same promise in the Hamlin matter, and it hadn't prevented them from getting mired in a murder case that had changed their lives.

Deep in her heart, Dorothy knew that the Al Romanzo case had the potential to do the same thing. But for some reason, she could not find words to express her fears, to either Philip or to herself.

Chapter Seven

Early morning found Philip seated at his desk in his loft office, cradling his coffee cup and staring out past the trees to the placid lake. Mitten and Buffy snored loudly on the sofa almost in rhythm while Philip tried to concentrate. *Follow the drug.* It had worked so well in the Hamlin case that Dorothy had argued it was the best way to get started. Philip quickly ticked off the established facts.

The medical examiner had pointed out that the chemical constitution of the drug was consistent with a generic version. Generic drugs typically are manufactured and distributed by smaller companies in bulk. Those companies don't market or sell to hospitals directly, but rather distribute through wholesalers. The intermediaries buy drugs in large quantities and then fill specific orders from hospital pharmacies.

This arrangement is good for hospitals for two reasons. First, they have to make drugs available quickly for the physicians who order them, and they can get deliveries from local wholesalers within hours. Second, most drugs can't be left on the shelf indefinitely, so the hospitals generally have a consignment agreement with the wholesale houses. If they order more of the drug than they need, they can send back what they don't use and get partial credit for unused product.

To provide these services, wholesale houses place a hefty markup on their products. So, even though generic drugs always cost less than trade-name drugs, the difference in price is much less than consumers and payers assume.

It was relatively easy for Philip to identify the drug wholesale houses in the Scranton/Wilkes-Barre area. Although they didn't advertise, they all had offices within twenty miles of the metropolitan area with findable Internet sites. They positioned themselves to make fast deliveries and keep their distribution costs as low as possible. Hospitals and pharmacies renegotiated contracts with these distributors frequently. If any of the competitors couldn't control their overhead, they were quickly outbid. Even with this strong competition, there were still five wholesale companies that did business with local healthcare providers to provide drugs, in both intravenous and oral formulations.

Preparing for bed that evening after a long day fact-finding on the computer, Philip wondered out loud, "Who was selling intravenous digoxin to Scranton Memorial in the weeks before Al Romanzo's death, and what formulation did SMH actually purchase?"

"You mean the chemical mixture?" Dorothy asked. They stood side by side at their matching bathroom sinks, brushing their teeth and washing up.

"Right. Each generic imitation of the original drug will have a unique chemical profile. Sort of like a fingerprint. They change the fillers and the solvent as little as possible, to mimic the effect of the brand drug, but you can always detect a difference. If we could match the solution that killed Al Romanzo to the stuff the warehouse sold to the hospital, it would mean that whoever gave him the drug got it from the hospital pharmacy. That will narrow the number of possible perpetrators to the people who had access to drug that was stored in the hospital itself."

Dorothy nodded. "I see, and if we can't make the match, it would mean that somebody from the outside gave him the drug."

"Presumably. It still could have been somebody on the staff, but we would have to consider outsiders, like the family, for example."

"Sounds like a good plan."

"A plan that probably won't work very easily," Philip frowned.

"What do you mean?"

"Well, we can get the chemical structure of the generic digoxin the drug houses sell, but we will never get the detail I need from the exhumation report. They didn't precisely quantify the fillers and preservatives they found in the heart. But there may be another way."

"What?" Dorothy was holding her toothbrush in front of her face, now absorbed in the discussion.

"Volume, my dear. If someone at the hospital used large amounts of digoxin for murder, it might be reflected in the amounts the hospital purchased from the wholesaler. And if we're lucky, we will even be able to time match the extra orders to Romanzo's death."

Dorothy asked the obvious question. "So how are we going to get all of that information?"

"Getting it from the hospital would be very difficult. I have another idea how we might do it."

"Why do I have the feeling that the *we* you're talking about is actually *me*?" Dorothy asked gritting her teeth.

Philip smiled. "Only because you're such a good actress, and so experienced with this kind of thing."

"Stop buttering me up and tell me what you want me to do, and I'll tell you if I'm willing to do it."

"Actually, it's reasonably simple. All you have to do is visit the drug wholesalers and somehow get a look at their hospital sales records."

"And how am I going to get them to show me their records, Dr. Sarkis?"

"Do I have to think of everything? Actually, I'm sure these places get inspected by government agencies all the time. You look like an official kind of person. How hard would it be for you to create some FDA credentials?"

"You want me to impersonate a government person? I think that's called a felony, mister."

"Come on, Dorothy. How will anyone find out? You're just

going to be dealing with clerks and they won't care enough to check you out."

Dorothy wasn't happy but she had to admit that Philip's request wasn't too outlandish. "I can ask my dad to help, but it shouldn't be too difficult." Dorothy's father, Dick Deaver, ran a private detective agency and had been a help to Dorothy during the Hamlin investigation.

Philip went on with his instructions as they positioned themselves in bed, being careful not to disturb Mitten and Buffy, spread out and sleeping peacefully. "I can give you an outline of what you want to get out of the distribution records. Basically, we need to know how much drug the hospital purchased in the few months before and after Al Romanzo died compared to the same period the year before. And how much of the drug was returned on consignment."

When Dorothy called her father to ask about fake credentials, he was not receptive.

"I thought you two learned your lesson. Amateur sleuthing is not a good idea, Dorothy. And impersonating a federal officer is a serious offense. If you get caught, you could get a significant dose of hard time."

"I know, Dad, but the chances of getting caught in a situation like this are pretty slim, don't you think? I'm not violating anyone's privacy. Besides, Philip and I are concerned that somebody hurt a patient intentionally."

"Maybe the police should be doing the investigating?"

"The local police detective admitted that he doesn't have the manpower to do an intensive investigation of the case. He all but told Philip that the death of one ancient patient in a hospital isn't important enough to commit police manpower. I think he expects Philip to do some checking on his own."

"That's what your boyfriend wants you to think. When did you ever hear of a police detective asking a cardiologist to help out in a murder investigation?"

"Dad, you're oversimplifying. This is not a routine murder case—in fact, there's very little evidence that anyone attempted murder. We're just trying to find out what happened to poor Mr. Romanzo. And to get to the bottom of things will take a good deal of medical knowledge that the police simply don't have."

As he had so many times before, Dick Deaver finally gave in to his daughter. "All right, I'll look into getting the ID for you. But for Christ's sake, be careful."

After only a couple of discreet phone calls, Deaver had the requested credentials on his desk and on their way to his daughter's office the next day.

Dorothy called the five drug wholesale companies and set up appointments with each. She stipulated that she planned to inspect all of the wholesale houses in the area, in case they happened to speak with each other. She also reminded them that the inspections were confidential hoping to minimize the chances they would discover that no one at the FDA had authorized the visits.

At each of her stops, Dorothy was greeted by a secretary who had pulled the information she requested. Dorothy was given a vacant desk or office and allowed to plow through the records at her own pace. At her first three, it had taken Dorothy only a few minutes to see that the firm had not sold any form of digoxin to Scranton Memorial during the time period in question. Dorothy did notice that wholesalers and hospitals moved their business around quite a bit, obviously trying to get the best price at every opportunity. There were literally dozens of generic drug houses, vying with each other for a share of the lucrative drug market.

Philip had told her that the potency of each formulation could vary by as much as twenty percent and still be deemed "equivalent" by the FDA. "I doubt that the public has any idea how much the strength of the drugs they are taking may vary," Philip had mused during their breakfast conversation. "A patient can get any of several generics, each with a different potency, and never really know what to expect. It's pretty obvious that the hospitals don't care as much about drug potency as they do about their bottom line."

"So there isn't much quality control."

"Correct," Philip replied. "And that is a big part of the reason why we are seeing so many shortages of common drugs. If a generic house can make it cheaply, they corner the market. But if their manufacturing process goes whacko, they have to shut down and supplies plummet."

"A lot of cancer drugs have been scarce from what I read."

"Old tried and true drugs like methotrexate are no longer made by big pharma companies because the drugs went off patent. We are at the mercy of much less reputable manufacturers and you have seen the results. Pretty scary."

Dorothy reflected on that conversation as she went through the company records. She was finished so quickly at the first few places that she had to sit for an hour or two and pretend to make notes before declaring she was finished with the inspection. While leafing through the information, Dorothy noticed that several of the other local hospitals had been purchasing more digoxin in recent years. Letters from hospital administrators in the file posited a resurgence of the drug because it had been proven effective as a comparator agent in trials of newer, fancier drugs. It didn't hurt that the drug cost only a fraction of other drugs used for the same indications. But Dorothy noticed that some of the orders from other hospitals were very large and most of the uptick had occurred in the last several months.

As she departed each of the distributors, Dorothy assured the medical directors that the inspection was fine and that she had found no deficiencies. She promised a follow-up letter she knew they would never receive, but it seemed to make each one happy. They would be able to tell their supervisors about the good performance of their department and hope to parlay that into a raise or bonus.

Dorothy discovered what she needed at the fourth distributor, Peerless Pharmaceutical Exchange. Peerless had sold large amounts of all kinds of cardiac drugs to Scranton Memorial, including generic intravenous digoxin. They did so mainly because of an aggressive pricing strategy. Dorothy found that Peerless had sold one hundred and fifty one-milligram vials to the hospital in the three months before Al Romanzo's death. The number from the year before had been similar, but each of those counts was nearly five times the quarterly average in years past. So there had been a dramatic increase that had not been anticipated by the hospital or the wholesaler. The uptick had been so abrupt two years before that the hospital had almost run out of drug and had needed emergency deliveries before increasing their monthly allotment.

"Do you know of any reason for the sharp increase in use?" Dorothy asked the Peerless medical director at the exit interview she had arranged with the clerk.

Dr. Marcia Rosensweig didn't know much about the drug distribution business. In fact, she knew precious little about pharmacology. She was a pediatrician by trade. She had moved into the area with her husband and looked for part-time employment. Peerless was advertising for a medical director to sign papers and provide minimal oversight for medical issues. The job would allow Marcia to spend time with her three small children. The best thing about Marcia was that she was willing to admit what she didn't know and, in this realm, that was a lot.

"I can't explain it. In fact, this is the first time it was brought to my attention. Sometimes when this happens, it's because the hospital adds a new doctor or a new service that uses a particular drug more than anybody else. But that's only a guess."

"From what I could see, Scranton Memorial didn't send back much unused drug during those months."

"No, you're right. They used all that they ordered and that isn't usual either."

"Why doesn't your company keep track of these trends?"

"Well, we do for controlled substances. Those requirements are very stringent and your office will tell you that we've been squeaky clean with narcotics and drugs with abuse potential. We don't view cardiac drugs like digoxin in the same way.

They don't have any abuse potential, so why would anyone want to stockpile them?"

Dorothy had to agree with Marcia's logic, but since she was in the middle of a fake inspection, she had to be quick on her feet. "You have a point, but the agency does spot inspections like this to make sure that companies like yours can account for the drugs they receive and sell. It looks like you delivered appropriate drug to the hospital. Now I need to see your patient logs."

Marcia looked perplexed. "I don't know what you mean."

Dorothy had done her homework before going on her fake interviews. Philip had told her and she had confirmed that the hospital was expected to return logs to the drug distributor on which they were to list the patients who had received drug. It was a way to assure that drugs were used appropriately. Concerns about patient confidentiality had changed the regulations. The hospitals now had only to list the patients by a coded number and were not supposed to identify patients by name, age or any other characteristic.

"I had no idea those listings existed for uncontrolled drugs like digitalis," Marcia confessed. "I'll have to ask the staff if we have them. Of course, we will get them for you as soon as we can."

"I need to see them while I'm here and preferably this morning. I'll tell you what, why don't I just concentrate on cardiac drugs from Scranton Memorial, since that seems to be an outlier for volume. I can come back another time and go through drugs that were sent to the other hospitals in the area."

Marcia scurried off to find the requested logs while Dorothy pretended to outline her report. Marcia returned an hour later with a large stack of documents. "I'm afraid they aren't in very good order, but my staff told me that these are all of the records from Scranton Memorial for the last two years. You'll find cardiac drugs in there someplace."

It took Dorothy hours to sort through the pile of documents that Marcia had dumped on her desk. She had to match patient logs from Scranton Memorial with the drug delivery notices.

Things seemed to line up for the first of the two years. However, for the second year, starting about twelve months before Al Romanzo died and during the period when Scranton Memorial was quintupling its digoxin orders, she could not account for even a fraction of the drug that had been delivered to the hospital. The number of patients who received the drug and the amount administered to each had not changed. The unaccountable drug had not been returned to the wholesaler, nor was there any record of where it had gone.

When Dorothy pointed this discrepancy out to Marcia Rosensweig, she was not worried. "That isn't our responsibility. It's up to the hospital to do the drug accounting, not us. You would think they'd be on top of something like this. If those logs are correct, they paid for a lot of wasted drug."

Somehow Dorothy wasn't surprised that Marcia's first thought concerned the financial implications. "Doesn't it bother you to know that a massive amount of a potentially dangerous drug is not accounted for, and this has been going on for months?"

Marcia attempted to look worried. "Sure. But there's little we can do if the hospitals don't keep good records. My staff told me we did what we were supposed to do, which is send your agency a copy of those forms."

"You could have sent a cover letter to the FDA pointing out that the amount of drug dispensed was not consistent with the use documented by individual patient logs," Dorothy noted.

"I guess so, but you guys also had a chance to respond to the discrepancy. We send in forms like that all the time, and we rarely hear a thing."

Marcia had a point. As required by law, copies of the forms probably had been sent to the FDA, where they were duly filed and promptly forgotten. The agency just didn't have enough staff to review the reams of information they received from all over the country. The best it could do was random audits, like the fake inspection Dorothy was carrying out at Peerless. FDA administrators had no easy way to direct their investigations to maximize the chance of finding wrongdoing or bad practices.

Dorothy decided not to push her luck any further. She would excuse herself before Marcia could become suspicious of the audit's authenticity.

"I think we're finished here. You've been very cooperative; thank you. I'll review our records to make sure the forms were properly filed. I don't think Peerless has anything to worry about. Your records are in order, and we'll try on our end to reconcile what we learned here with the hospital records when we do their pharmacy inspection."

Marcia seemed satisfied with this outcome. Her biggest worry was her own neck. She didn't want the Peerless CEO getting on her about FDA matters. Regulatory agencies have the power to shut places down, sometimes permanently, if inspections show significant deficiencies.

Dorothy packed up her things and drove home. Philip was down by the lake tossing dog treats into the water from the dock. Buffy and Mitten leaped into the water after them, swimming out to the snacks, gobbling them up while still paddling, and then returning to shore. There they fixed their gaze on Philip until he produced more goodies and tensed up with anticipation as he reared back to heave a few more out into the water. Bisecting the ripples, they paddled out to the treats, scarfed them up happily, and swam back eager for more. It was a game they would play as long as Philip's shoulder and supplies held out.

"Doggies do need their exercise," Philip explained.

Dorothy nodded. "Especially those scoundrels. Otherwise, they prowl the house keeping me awake all night. Of course, you don't have that problem, do you?"

Since the end of the Hamlin case, Philip was able to sleep soundly through the night. It was as if he were making up for all the hours of sleep lost when the case had been active and his life had fallen apart.

"I love to sleep up here," Philip admitted. "It is so quiet and cool, and the doggies keep my feet nice and warm until they decide it's time to get up to play. But enough of that. How did your inspections go?"

"Well, I was able to answer a number of questions. Scranton Memorial bought most of their intravenous digoxin from Peerless. I bet that when you take a look, the chemical composition of the Peerless diluent will at least be consistent with the drug Al Romanzo received."

"I'll go on the FDA site tonight and pull up their application to see what they have in their digoxin formulation. Did you reach your conclusion based on the quantity of drug that Scranton Memorial bought from Peerless?"

"Yep. The hospital received large shipments of the drug in the year preceding Romanzo's death, much more than they had used the year before. Even more importantly, the drug accountability logs didn't match up with the quantity shipped."

Philip asked the obvious question. "Did the hospital send what they didn't use back to Peerless?"

"No, and that's remarkable because that means that they didn't get the refund they were entitled to. From what I could see, hospitals are usually pretty careful about getting their credit for unused drugs. So somebody at the hospital may have administered the drug, but the records don't indicate which patient received it."

Philip paused. Dorothy could tell he was excited but didn't want to jump to the natural conclusion. Instead, he surprised her with another idea.

"When you were looking at the records, did you happen to notice if other hospitals in the area had any upticks in digoxin use?"

"Now that you mention it, yes, I did see the total sales of digoxin for the region, and it looked like all four distributors saw a large increase in usage that would not have been completely accounted for by the rise in SMH volume alone. Why did you ask?"

"I was just wondering if Al Romanzo's case is unique. He was a pretty ordinary guy and he was a stranger to the staff at the hospital. Why would someone have chosen to kill him with digoxin?"

Dorothy saw Philip's point immediately. "Oh my God! You think that maybe somebody has been killing patients randomly?"

"Maybe not completely at random, but in quantity. You pointed out that the volume of digoxin use at SMH had been up for over a year before Romanzo's death. And if other hospitals were buying more of the drug, it might be because the same thing was happening somewhere else. A bunch of sick old people dying wouldn't attract too much attention. The only reason we know about Al is the lawsuit."

"It's an interesting theory, Philip, but you'll have a hard time proving it, and good luck trying to figure out why."

"I know it would be difficult."

But, Philip mused, I might be able to figure it out with some help from an old buddy of mine.

Chapter Eight

The more he thought about it, the more Philip was convinced that Al Romanzo's death was not an isolated incident. But as Dorothy had pointed out, a key element in the case was motive. Why would somebody use digoxin to kill patients at other hospitals as well as Scranton Memorial? To begin to answer that question, Philip had to find out if there really were other victims, who they were, and if they had any common characteristics.

That weekend morning, Dorothy and Philip sat at their kitchen table sharing morning coffee. They watched as the sun peeked over the trees and rose to warm their lake. The dogs lounged around the table, waiting for a crust of bread or a treat. Dorothy admonished Philip constantly about spoiling the hounds by feeding them from the table, but he just ignored her or argued that the dogs had few joys in their lives, of which eating was the most important.

Philip thought it would be a good time to outline the issues, but before he got very far, Dorothy quickly cut to the crux of the issue.

"I can spend all the time you want with the wholesalers. If their records are as bad as Peerless, we won't be able to identify specific cases. And even if they had all the forms they're supposed to keep, they're de-identified for privacy reasons, so you couldn't trace them to individual patients anyway."

"You're right. Trying to do it that way won't work. Besides,

I doubt that our killer would have been nice enough to fill out logs for the drug she used to off her victims."

"Wait a minute," Dorothy protested. "Why is the villain necessarily a woman? What is it with you?"

"Don't be so touchy," Philip answered defensively. "I was assuming the perpetrator would likely be a nurse and nurses are more likely to be women."

"Yeah, well, before you impugn an entire profession, not to mention gender, maybe you should get your facts straight. And that's the challenge in this case, don't you agree?"

Philip nodded and then bit his lip. That gesture, Dorothy knew, meant that he had already thought the problem through and had a possible solution. "Let me ask you a question. After hearing about the Romanzo case, are you convinced that digoxin produces a characteristic arrhythmia pattern?"

"I'm not an expert by any stretch of the imagination," Dorothy replied. "But I was impressed by your ability to predict that Romanzo had a high level of digoxin in his heart just by the pattern of the ventricular tachycardia. Are there any other arrhythmias that are characteristic of digoxin overdose?"

Philip smiled knowingly. "That's exactly the right question. In fact, there are a host of other heart rhythms that are characteristic of digoxin overdose."

"Why is the drug so toxic? And why do doctors still use it?"

"Good questions again. Digitalis is a really old drug. It's been around for hundreds of years. It works well to improve cardiac function in patients with heart failure. Even though it can provoke some nasty rhythm problems, it's also used to treat certain cardiac arrhythmias, and it does an efficient job. It's cheap, once-a-day, and doctors are accustomed to using it."

"And now the down side?"

"I'm getting there. Turns out it's a complicated drug. It's eliminated from the body through the kidneys so when renal function is reduced, as it frequently is in old cardiac patients, the stuff tends to accumulate. And it doesn't take much of a build-up before it starts to have toxic effects. Folks in the pharmacology world call that a narrow toxic-therapeutic ratio."

"So why not just use other drugs? There must be more modern options."

"Well, docs frequently do use alternatives these days. But when digoxin is studied in clinical trials and it has been compared directly to newer therapies, it actually looks pretty good. So it's hung around a long time."

"Is that why I saw an increased utilization of digoxin for the region when I visited the wholesaler?" Dorothy asked.

"I doubt it. In clinical practice, we've seen a leveling off or even a slight decline in digitalis use. A big regional increase like you saw at the wholesalers is pretty bizarre."

"So you think the increase may have a sinister explanation."

"That would be logical, don't you think? Why else are hospitals using so much more? It might be a clue. But let me get back to your other question. You asked if digoxin could cause other characteristic arrhythmias, and it can. It can sensitize either the top or the bottom chambers of the heart to beat faster, or it can slow the heart rate in some circumstances. And the elderly are the most susceptible to these effects."

"OK, so where does that get us?"

Philip smiled. "I have to try to identify deaths at our regional hospitals in the last few years in which there is a high likelihood that digoxin was the culprit. Some of those might be poisoning cases."

Dorothy was skeptical. "Even if we assume you have a Carnac-like ability to identify those cases, it seems to me you have two pretty big hurdles. First, you need access to patient records, and two, you have to go through thousands of charts to find the cases you're interested in."

"I thought of that, and there is a work-around. If there are other victims, they died like Mr. Romanzo, suddenly and unexpectedly in the hospital. Those cases get kicked into what is called 'peer review.' In essence, the case is scrutinized by a panel of doctors and nurses and administrators to see if there is an identifiable cause for an unexplained death. The reviews are pretty superficial and rarely come to much—docs don't like criticizing other docs unless there's a strong reason."

"But isn't unanticipated drug toxicity a good reason to thoroughly investigate a case?"

"Of course, if they knew it was a drug effect. But digitalis toxicity is the great imitator. Toxic rhythms can look like common arrhythmias that occur in patients all the time. The docs who sit on the peer review committees are not arrhythmia super-specialists. They wouldn't know the problem was related to digitalis unless they had some clue, like a high blood level or an incorrect dose. In the case of an intentional overdose, there would be no dose in the chart, and no blood levels."

Dorothy was intrigued but tried to maintain her objectivity. "Let's assume that the relevant cases got kicked into peer review. My recollection is that quality information is carefully protected and can't be discovered by attorneys or by the public."

"Correct. The courts have been very clear about that. But in Pennsylvania, each peer review committee is required to keep detailed minutes and to store them so they can be accessed during licensing inspections. The committees are also expected to police their staff, so if a particular doc has a lot of cases, they can be notified, sanctioned, or even suspended."

"Store them where, in their computer system? Uh-oh, I think I know what's coming!" Dorothy exclaimed.

"Yep, it's José time," Philip replied.

José was the shady character Philip had used in the Hamlin case. He was a gifted computer hacker who didn't seem to like Philip, but who, for a price, claimed he could find his way into any data base.

"And let me guess, you're going to ask me to ask my dad to get in touch with José for you again, right?"

"You bet. And like he did before, your dad is going to read us the riot act, and tell us how dangerous José is."

In the Hamlin case, Dick Deaver found José through one of his detective firm's contacts, and had put him in touch with Philip. Dick and Dorothy hadn't been happy about the illegality of hacking in that case, and had warned Philip about the consequences. Dorothy was especially displeased with Philip's new plan.

"There's a good reason why my father demurred in the Hamlin case. He has a lot of experience, and he knows what happens when neophytes like you get in over your head."

"I know there's risk, but either we go to José or we accept the fact that someone is getting away with murder. What's your preference?"

Dorothy shook her head, expecting full well that Philip would play that trump card. "I'll talk with my father about getting the contact information. But get ready because he's going to warn you about taking this on—and then he'll probably help as long as you keep him out of it."

Dorothy was right about her father's reaction. Dick Deaver raised his usual fuss and then caved in. A call to his source brought him a number for Philip. When Philip called, an elderly woman answered in an inappropriate sing-song voice that to Philip sounded like a television commercial. "Please don't call this number again. A Sunday afternoon visit to the Franklin Institute would be nice. At 1:00 P.M., go to the heart exhibit." And the phone went dead.

The heart model at the Franklin Institute in Philadelphia is one of the most popular science exhibits in the country. It attracts thousands of visitors who walk through the gigantic heart. They move through the model like a giant red blood cell progressing from the body, through the lungs, and back into the left ventricle before exiting through the aortic valve and propelling into the aorta. The site selection made sense; José was a Philly native. Sunday afternoon was a busy time at the exhibit so José and Philip could converse without attracting attention.

Philip made the drive to Philadelphia from his Pocono

house feeling anxious, but not nearly as nervous as he had been before his previous meetings with José. It was almost as if he was going to see an old friend, a weird perspective since José was anything but amiable.

José was leaning against a wall in a corner of the room directly behind the heart model entrance. He was working a toothpick in his mouth. Philip figured the toothpick was a poor substitute for a cigarette, what José really wanted but couldn't have. José amazingly looked pleased to see Philip.

"Well, if it isn't my favorite home boy from the Main Line. I didn't think I would see your white ass again. You don't have some kind of thing for your friend José, do you, Slim? You don't look like somebody who swings both ways—could I be wrong?"

Philip had braced himself for José's abuse and was determined not to react. Not only would it not get him anywhere, it might jeopardize getting the information he needed.

"José, I can't say I was looking forward to seeing you, but I need information. Do you think you could help me out?"

"Sure, white trash. Why the hell else would I be wasting my time at this fucking joke of a place? I told you before that José is just like an expensive whore. Pay him enough and he'll do anything you want. So tell me what you need and I'll give you the price."

"There are five acute care hospitals in the Wilkes-Barre/Scranton area. Each one has a thing called a peer review committee. This is a group that evaluates all unexpected deaths and severe complications that occur in their hospital. The information they generate at each of their monthly meetings is confidential. They wouldn't want the public to know about these things because they don't want to invite a lawsuit. The law protects their proceedings, but they do generate minutes. I want you to get those minutes. The records will include a list of patients they reviewed and what their complications were."

"Ain't done something like that before. That'll mean having to figure out how to get into five different computer systems. And probably they'll be extra careful to block hackers out of the files you want."

"So is it possible to get the data?" Philip asked anxiously.

"Like I said before, whitebread, José can do anything. I'm just letting you know that this one is going to be expensive."

Philip steeled himself. He and Dorothy were just beginning to get back to some fiscal balance. It would be hard to justify spending a lot of money to investigate a case just to satisfy Philip's curiosity.

"How much are we talking about, José?"

"Five large—a grand per hospital."

Philip shook his head. "That's too much—I can't afford it."

As he had before, José erupted. Through clenched teeth, "Look, asshole, this ain't no flea market. You don't get to negotiate a price. You'll pay what I want, or you can go fuck off."

"Don't go off on me here, José," Philip hissed. "People will notice and neither of us wants that. I know what you do is dangerous. I just don't have the money. The best I can do is $3,000, and even that will be a stretch."

José worked his toothpick from one side of his mouth to the other as they watched a fat lady trying to enter the heart model while her husband pushed her through the entry portal. Getting her out through the aortic valve was going to be interesting, Philip surmised, as he waited for the reply.

"OK, $3,500 cash on delivery as long as this thing doesn't take me forever to do."

Philip was relieved. He would be able to scrape that much together from his private account without alerting Dorothy, who would go ballistic if she knew how much money he was spending. It would also mean blowing most of the money he had made on the Wilson case review.

After he agreed, José set the timeline. "Give me about ten days. I don't want to meet in Philly again. You got any suggestions about where we could exchange shit without anybody caring?"

Philip thought for a moment. "There's a bar near where I live in the Poconos called Leon's. The place is pretty empty during the week in the afternoon. I could meet you there and nobody would care."

José smirked. "So you live up in the fucking mountains now, huh dickhead? OK. Just don't think it's a date, homo boy. José is a whore but not the kind who bends over and takes it up the Hershey Highway."

The image was a little overwhelming, but Philip wouldn't be provoked. "Don't worry; we won't be there very long. Just meet me next Wednesday at 3:00 P.M."

Philip spent the next week anxiously awaiting José's report. He tried to imagine how someone like José, with no medical training, would be able to access highly restricted minutes. He admitted to Dorothy that José was an enigma. "I think this guy is a lot smarter than he lets on. And I also suspect he has some kind of medical background. Why would he try to make himself look dumb and bigoted?"

"Maybe it's kind of a disguise. But it also sounds like he's an angry man. I wonder if he got screwed by someone in authority who happened to be a white guy."

Philip nodded. "At the risk of sounding like a profiler, I thought the same thing. And 'screwed' may be the correct term. He makes constant sexual references. Makes me suspect there was some kind of harassment, maybe by a superior male?"

"Who knows? We're amateurs making this stuff up. The only thing you have to remember is that José has hot buttons that you don't want to push too often. This guy is a complete unknown to us and could have a history of violence as well."

"Yeah, I think about that, especially when he goes off. That's why I like meeting him in public places."

And these things were very much on Philip's mind as he parked his car at Leon's bar the following week. Dorothy and he came here for dinner and a brew on occasion. Leon was a retired Italian chef from New York who knew that a bar with good food would be popular in the Poconos. In fact, it had become a favorite of the year-round inhabitants, who particularly liked the idea that the uppity vacationers from New York and Philadelphia didn't know about the place. The locals had the bar to themselves most of the time.

Leon greeted Philip warmly as he did all of his regular patrons. "Hey, my friend, it's great to see you. How's your beautiful bride, Dorothy, doing?"

Philip was impressed with Leon's name recall, and he wasn't about to clarify his marital status for the bar patrons. In fact, Philip and Dorothy had chosen not to broadcast to their friends and neighbors that they weren't married. It was just too hard to explain. And it wasn't that they hadn't considered it. Philip's divorce had been the original impediment, but that was long done.

Philip had proposed dozens of times and Dorothy declined every time. Her latest refrain had been, "If we get to the point of deciding to have children, we'll do it. I'm not ready for that yet, so I prefer to defer." Her decision disappointed Philip but not enough to make him insist. He didn't want to lose Dorothy, who was the most important thing that had ever happened to him.

"She's fine, Leon," Philip summoned up. "Thanks for asking."

"What brings you in this time of day?" Leon asked casually.

"I have someone from Philly bringing me papers to sign. I told him I would buy him a beer before he turns around and goes back. I couldn't think of a better place to do that."

Philip picked out a corner table, ordered a couple of Pocono Lagers, and Leon brought over a basket of pretzels and chips. José arrived exactly on time, wearing low riders and a tee shirt. He took off his shades and looked around as he entered, found Philip, and sauntered over.

"You were right about this place being empty. This is the middle of fucking nowhere, man."

"People who own vacation homes come up on weekends, especially in the summer. They don't come to places like this too often in the middle of the week."

"Well, thanks for the beer, whitebread," José said, holding the beer bottle in the air for inspection. "Never heard of this fucking brand before. Hope you're not trying to have your way with me, man. You already got lucky."

"What does that mean?"

"Turns out I was able to get into all five hospital computer systems. It was a lot easier than I thought. Man, I hope people don't stop using familiar words as passwords. That would make my job a lot harder."

"So it was easier than you thought?"

"Not that easy, asswipe, but José is smarter than the hicks in those hospitals. All I had to do was find out who the chief medical officer was and then try to guess what that mother-fucker used as a password for the hospital computer system. Four of the five used one of their kids' names. The other idiot used his dog's. And the relevant emails were in their regular list without any kind of encryption. Morons. Anyhow, I got you thirty-six months' worth of data for all five places."

"How did you know that those hospitals even had a chief medical officer who was responsible for things like peer review? I didn't tell you that."

Even before he finished the question, Philip knew he had made a mistake. There followed another classic José eruption. "Do you think I'm an idiot? And who the fuck are you to question how I do my work? It's none of your motherfucking business, cocksucker."

Philip hung his head and decided not to apologize. It would just make things worse. José took a swig of his beer and nearly spit it out. "This shit sucks. Can't you get anything decent to drink up here?"

Finally, José calmed down enough to hand Philip a CD. "OK, asshole, here it is. When you open it, it has a password. Do you want to guess what it is?"

Philip thought it might be best to play along with José's little game. "Asshole?"

"Close. I thought 'cocksucker' would be more appropriate. Anyhow, you'll see there's a lot of data so use a computer with a bunch of memory and not a piece-of-shit laptop. It has to have Adobe 6.0 and Excel upgrades, too."

"Understood." Philip handed José an envelope with the cash. "The $3,500 is in there in fifty-dollar bills. Is that OK?"

"Perfect, douchebag." José took another gulp of his beer and stood to leave. "Hate to drink and run but this place is fucking depressing. I need to get back to where people are actually alive."

Philip was happy to see José leave. The guy was an enigma but also a pain in the ass, and Philip wanted to start going through the data. He said goodbye to Leon and promised he would come back with Dorothy soon. Leon obviously admired Dorothy's looks, so why not humor the old goat?

It took Philip about ten minutes to drive home. Mitten and Buffy met him at the door and reminded him with melancholy eyes that he owed them a romp in the woods. "OK, you two. Let's go take a run in the woods before it gets dark." He loaded them into the back of the car and drove them to the entrance of a nature trail where dogs were allowed to be off leash (or at least no one made a fuss over it).

Mitten and Buffy sniffed their way around the trail, urinating as if they had each just consumed a gallon of beer. They were careful to pee on the same spots, an instinct dogs had to distract their predators. What a joke, Philip thought. These pampered hounds wouldn't survive more than an hour in the wild by themselves unless they somehow found a supermarket that had processed turkey breast, kibble, Mother Hubbard treats, and Greenies of course.

By the time Philip returned, Dorothy was home and beginning to prepare dinner. They exchanged a light kiss as Philip cleaned the mud off the dogs and got out of his sweatshirt. "I have a CD from José. If you don't mind, let me take a preliminary look."

"Fine, but brief me over dinner. Pasta OK?"

"Comfort food always makes me happy."

Philip went up to his loft study, put the CD into his computer, typed in José's suggestive password, and saw that José, in usual fashion, had carefully organized the data. Each hospital had its own file, and in each file was a listing for every peer review meeting. For each, Philip found a full set of minutes and a listing of the cases the committee had considered. In all, there were more than a thousand cases distributed among the five hospitals over the thirty-six months.

Philip started his own Excel file of cases in which an elderly patient with no obvious cardiac problem died precipitously of a cardiac arrhythmia. There were about two hundred, but in only a handful of cases was there a detailed description of the arrhythmia. Most narratives commented on the presence of ventricular tachycardia like Mr. Romanzo's, but some described complete heart block in which the heart rate had slowed almost to a complete stop followed by cardiac arrest.

Philip was in the middle of his tally when Dorothy called him to dinner. She had prepared a ravioli dinner complete with sausage and meatballs, a healthy green salad, and warm Italian bread they used to sponge up the gravy. They opened a nice Chianti and happily munched away as they watched a re-run of *King of Queens*. When they finished, they sat at their kitchen table and sipped a second glass of wine. Philip turned off the TV and summarized what he had found on José's CD so far.

"There were a lot more suspicious arrhythmias than I would have expected. And there appears to have been a distinct uptick in the last two years."

"So, does this substantiate your theory?" Dorothy asked.

"Well, yes and no. It does, because of the number of arrhythmias, but the detail just isn't there. One striking point is that there were a lot of men and just a handful of women. And I can't find any reference to digoxin in any of the case narratives, even when the arrhythmias were consistent with digoxin overdose."

"Even the heart block cases?"

"Yeah. Like I told you, digoxin can kill you in many different ways, including slowing your heart to a stop. Depends on what it's being used for and how susceptible people might be because of prior disease of their electrical system—which many of them had. So those cases are as important as the fast heart rhythms. I just don't have enough detail to say more than that."

Before Philip had a chance to make a suggestion she wouldn't like, Dorothy interjected, "Well, why don't you finish going through all of the things José gave you. Be careful and take your time, and we'll see where it takes you."

Philip agreed. He had a lot more to look at, and he didn't want to ruin the mood of the evening with a long argument about subsequent steps that Dorothy didn't want to take. What he really didn't want to do was tell Dorothy how her unique skills might be needed yet again.

Chapter Nine

Philip had the next afternoon off. He sat in his den, elbows propped on his desk, looking out his second floor window as shadows spread across the lake. The temperature was dropping; Philip knew it was going to be a chilly evening, despite the rapid approach of summer. It was one of the things Dorothy and he loved about the mountains—you could justify a little fire in the fireplace and a hot cup of tea in the late afternoon almost any time of year.

Mitten and Buffy were lying next to his desk chair, snoozing. Philip had an hour or two until he would have to get dinner started. He decided to try a couple of ideas on his canine friends.

"All right, girls, here's the scoop." Mitten and Buffy raised their heads off the floor and looked at Philip askance. Didn't he know better than to interrupt their late afternoon nap?

Philip saw their consternation but decided to press on. "Come on, girls, this is important. We have this long list of patients who died with unexpected cardiac arrhythmias in this area over the last few years. It looks like the deaths were pretty evenly spread out among the hospitals. Do you think that was on purpose to avoid attracting attention?"

Buffy, the younger dog, wagged her tail so hard she made a slapping sound on the floor. "That's what I thought. But if that's true, it means someone was planning this out carefully and coordinating what happened across several institutions. Now that really sounds diabolical, doesn't it?"

Buffy stood up and put her paw on Philip's knees. Philip stroked her head. "That scared you, didn't it? OK, so the $64,000 question is what to do next. We could go back to the authorities with what we know, we could try to go underground to get more information, or we could go to the families of the dead people to see if we can get their cooperation. Now for this one, we'll need a unanimous opinion."

Buffy was uniformly believed to be the less intelligent of the two Portuguese water dogs, although Philip sometimes suspected she played dumb to get what she wanted without a lot of work. Mitten, the older and craftier of the two, found her way into trouble much more frequently by trying to out-smart her owners. "So, Mitten, you sly dog, how would you play this one?"

Mitten raised her head at the sound of her name but was not forthcoming with an answer. Philip knew he would have to use his customary enticement. "All right, I have a treat for the doggie who gives me an opinion."

Mitten leapt to her feet and stood in front of Philip. "Let's shake. Right paw is we go to authorities, left is we go to families, no paw means we go underground." Philip extended his hand and Mitten immediately offered her left paw. "Just as I suspected. You're worried about getting us into more trouble but you don't think the cops will get off their butts and help us."

By this time, Buffy was jumping up and down, beside herself with the possibility of a treat. "So, Buff, can I assume your behavior means you're in agreement? If so, we have reached a consensus."

The dogs chewed noisily on their treats and then went back to their naps. Philip pondered his next moves as he started his housework.

Dorothy returned from work, almost on cue. By that time, Philip had the tea ready, the fire stoked, leftover turkey soup on the stove, and he was sitting in the living room scribbling a "to do" list. Dorothy paused at the door to take in the idyllic scene: the dogs sleeping contentedly on the sofas and Philip scribbling away on a legal pad seated in front of a cozy fire. "Well, you guys certainly look comfortable," Dorothy observed. "How was your afternoon off?"

"It was sublime. We had a nice lunch and then I took the doggies out for a romp on the cross-country trail. They chased a herd of deer a long time before giving up."

"Philip, you have to be careful when you take them out. There are some busy roads around there, and we don't want them to get hit by a truck."

"I know and I try to be careful. But I did get them nice and tired. We came back here and I got a little work done."

"Great. Did you make any progress on your consulting projects?"

Philip had only recently heard from a few companies that were interested in his opinions about new drugs in development and had cardiac safety issues. After Philip's three-year suspension by the FDA, it had taken a long time to get anybody to use him again. Dorothy knew he had to do a good job with these first opportunities if he was going to make a comeback.

"I did that work for a little while, but then we had a canine conference about the Romanzo case. I'm trying hard to make a decision about what to do."

As she had in the Hamlin case, Dorothy felt compelled to be Philip's compass. "I would hope that man's best friend would have advised you to drop this thing altogether and get back to something that makes sense and money for your family. You will remember that your kids are going to want to go to college someday?"

Philip's children lived with his ex-wife Nancy, who had left him at the height of the Hamlin case. He dutifully paid child support, even though Nancy was remarried to an accountant and doing well financially. Their divorce agreement put Philip on the hook for college tuition, and Dorothy knew Philip wanted to honor that agreement, especially since default would mean loss of his treasured every-other-weekend visits with his children.

"I know, and I should be more responsible, but the case seems to be on my mind."

Dorothy wanted to bring Philip back to reality. "If you pursue this, you're going to have to pump many more hours into the case, and we both know you're going to drag me into it, too. And the chances for success are vanishingly small, aren't they?"

Philip wondered what Dorothy would say if she knew how much money he had paid his computer hacker. So far she hadn't asked him directly.

"Yes, the odds are small, but it isn't hopeless. I know this is going to be difficult, which is why I did a doggie survey."

Dorothy couldn't help but smile. This wasn't the first time Philip had used the dogs to help make a difficult decision. She decided to play along. "And what did our trusty canine buddies come up with?"

"They agreed we should do this on the up and up and try to get more information from the families of the victims. But the truth is that I would feel much better if your father would be willing to weigh in."

"He already told you we're crazy, but if that would help you decide what to do, sure, we can give him a call."

Dick Deaver was a confirmed bachelor after the death of Dorothy's mother years before, but that didn't mean he was a homebody. Dorothy figured he would be sitting at a Center City Philadelphia bar chatting up the most attractive woman he could find. He was not inclined to pay attention to his cell phone after hours but would answer for his beloved daughter. He picked up after two rings.

"Hi, honeybunch. What can your dad do for you?" Dick answered in a cheery voice.

"Hi, Dad. Sorry to bother you, but Philip is in the middle of trying to make a decision about the case we told you about earlier—you know, the old guy who died in the hospital under mysterious circumstances?"

"Yeah, he wanted a computer person again. Did José get the job done?"

"That he did. As a matter of fact, we're in the middle of deciding what to do with José's information. Let me put Philip on, and he'll explain it to you."

Dorothy handed the receiver to Philip who grimaced. Talking to Dick Deaver was always difficult for him. He felt resentment from Dick for embroiling his daughter in the Hamlin case and almost getting her killed or jailed. And for taking her away to live two hours from Deaver, in the godforsaken Poconos, a place Deaver would always consider a two-bit honeymoon refuge and not a place to live your life. And he disliked the fact that his little girl was not married to an upstanding gentleman who would help her produce the grandchildren he so richly deserved.

"Dick, sorry to bother you but I just wanted to get your professional opinion on the case Dorothy and I have been working on."

"You mean, you've been working on and dragging Dorothy into. OK, make it snappy, I have someone waiting for me. And she's a hell of a lot better looking than you."

Philip quickly summarized the case, ending with the list José had managed to accumulate for him.

"So, you have a list of about two hundred men who died of a particular cardiac cause that you think might have been related to getting too much of a drug they weren't supposed to get in the first place?"

"That about sums it up. And now I would really like to find out more about each case, and I want some advice about the best way to do that."

Philip went on to list what he thought his alternatives were, much as he had for Mitten and Buffy, but this time with no offers of a treat for the right answer.

Dick did not hesitate. "You need to take this to the families of the dead people. If you find there was a crime, they can help you put some pressure on the police and prosecutor to get off their asses and do something. In the meantime, they can legally get you copies of the medical records you need."

"That's what the doggies thought," Philip blurted out.

"Huh? What did you say?"

"Oh, I said, that's what Dorothy thought," Philip recovered.

"That's because she has good horse sense. Trying to get those records any other way would be a nightmare. They are not available electronically, which means you would have to get somebody to copy them for you. And I assume that just getting part of the chart, like the discharge summary, wouldn't help much?"

Philip was surprised at how savvy Dick was about hospital matters. He hadn't learned that many of the cases Dick's firm took on and solved had a medical twist. Like the junior hospital administrator who used stolen medical records to coerce a young student nurse into a sexual affair.

"You're right," Philip agreed. "I have to see all of the orders, the EKG recordings, nurses' notes, everything."

"OK, now think about trying to infiltrate a hospital medical records department to access those charts, and somehow taking them to a copying machine, and standing there and making copies for hours on end."

"It would be challenging."

"You're damned right," Dick emphasized. "And dangerous, too. Your chance of being caught would be multiplied several-fold. The government now has a special place in hell for people caught invading patients' privacy. It's called HIPAA—remember that?"

Philip was well aware of the law passed during the Clinton administration that had greatly increased the penalties for tampering with or invading patients' medical records.

"Yes, I remember. We had to deal with that in the Hamlin case."

"But that was one case. The penalties are for each infraction. Multiply a few years in prison and several hundred thousand dollars times two hundred and you have a first-class mess on your hands. This is a no-brainer. Give the families the chance to help you or forget the whole thing."

"I have no problem speaking with the families. There are just so many of them, and I have so little experience with this kind of thing." Even Philip had to think that he sounded like a whiney child, and Dorothy's facial expression made it clear that she agreed.

There was a prolonged silence on the phone, then, "I don't believe I'm saying this, but I might be able to lend you a couple of young associates to help with the canvassing. I suspect you're going to have trouble finding some of the families, and my people can assist with that, too. And I suggest you let Dorothy mentor you on the approach before you visit any families on your own."

Philip was delighted by Deaver's offer of assistance. "Dick, that's just terrific. Any help you and your firm can give to this is welcome."

Deaver didn't want Philip to think he had gone soft on him. "This is for my daughter, friend. And I am not happy about the possibility that some nutcase up there is offing old guys who weren't bothering anybody. Nobody deserves that kind of treatment."

Philip understood Dick Deaver's need to be a gruff and accepted it. "I feel the same way, which is why I have committed so much time to the project."

Philip knew Dick's help would be particularly valuable in locating family members. When he hung up and told Dorothy what her father had said, she was relieved.

"Getting help from my father is huge. There is going to be a lot of leg work to do, and you and I don't have that kind of time. Plus he knows how to keep out of trouble."

"He sounded interested in the case."

"Well, he probably feels for the dead guys, and doesn't like the idea that somebody could be getting away with murder."

"That's exactly what he said. But if he's willing to help us out, I think we ought to make it easy for him and his detectives. How about if I put together a standard questionnaire they can use when they visit the families of the victims."

"If you think you can make it simple enough—and let's be careful not to assume that these dead people were 'victims.' You really don't know that yet, and we shouldn't bias our canvassers out of the gate. We don't want them to spook the families either."

Philip loved Dorothy's common sense. "You're spot on about that—better to send them in with an open mind."

They chatted a little more about the case as they ate their soup. Philip used some fresh Italian bread to mop up the dregs and they finished their comfort food dinner with an arugula salad. They cleaned up the dishes together and then went their separate ways, Dorothy to the sofa in front of the fire to review some briefs from work, and Philip to the loft office to work on the questionnaire.

Philip wanted to gather reliable information, but didn't want to take advantage of Dick Deaver's generosity. He ended up with a list of about ten questions, enough to get a general profile of each patient, ending with a request to sign a release to get the hospital records they needed. It wasn't an hour before Philip asked Dorothy to look over the form and make a few minor changes.

"It's going to be a fine line between getting these people upset, and being truthful with them about why we're doing this," she said.

"Do you think they'll call the police after our visit?"

"That's a possibility. I think you should alert Detweiler to what you're doing, just in case. Tell him you're working on the case, but don't get into specifics. And for God's sake, don't tell him how you came up with the names you're canvassing."

"Duh! You must think I'm an idiot. Of course I wouldn't blab about that, but I will let him know that we're pursuing the case."

When Philip called him the next day, Detweiler's reaction was a pleasant surprise. "Wow, you guys have really stayed on this thing. Are you sure about the two hundred cases you came up with? How did you find them?"

Philip had expected Detweiler's logical question and had rehearsed the answer. "It's probably not a good idea to go into the details right now, Detective. Let's just say that no laws were broken and the information is pretty reliable. I suspect at least some of the cases will be bogus, but I won't know until I see the medical records. That's why we're going to the families. I just wanted to warn you because they might call the police if they suspect foul play."

Detweiler didn't pursue his question, perhaps afraid to know the real answer. "Understood. I'll make sure the calls are routed to me. Is there anything else I can do to help you at this point?"

"No, Dorothy's father's private detective firm is on board and will be helping with the canvassing."

Detweiler paused. He was obviously thinking about the propriety of letting Philip and Dorothy go about doing detective work in his backyard. "Look, I'm sure you know this is unconventional. Having you guys out and about trying to determine if a whole bunch of people have been murdered in my town is not something I want to advertise to the media or my bosses. So keep a low profile, please, and report back to me as soon as you have something definitive."

Philip agreed readily. "You bet we will. If there is a bad person out there, I don't want her putting digoxin in my beer. I'll keep in touch, believe me."

Philip and Dorothy decided to use the next Saturday afternoon to try out the questionnaire on the families of a few of the alleged victims in the case. Dorothy said, "I just want to make sure the instrument works before I unleash Dad's dicks on the populace of Wilkes-Barre and Scranton."

Philip seemed pleased by the suggestion. He was anxious to move ahead, and this would be a good way to kick start the process. "I'll make a few phone calls on Friday and try to line up a couple of folks."

By the time Dorothy came home that evening, Philip was

prepared. "I have an elderly widow and a daughter to interview. They don't live far from each other, so it shouldn't take
long to visit both of them. They were very nice on the phone.
I told them we had some questions about the final hospitalization."

Dorothy prepped Philip on their way to their first stop. "Let
me set this up after we get there. Remember that we're impar-
tial surveyors. Don't do or say anything to bias these folks.
And don't let them know you have an axe to grind."

Mrs. Frieda Bernsteil resided in a neat row home in a blue-
collar section of Scranton. Her husband Joseph had been admitted to St. Paul Hospital in Scranton a year before with what
appeared to be pneumonia and died within a few days of admission of a heart arrhythmia. Mrs. Bernsteil greeted Philip
and Dorothy politely, welcomed them into her living room,
and offered them coffee. Her housedress and apron were clean
and pressed, and though now old and without make-up or lip-
stick, it was clear that she had been a beauty in her youth. The
house was immaculate, although the furnishings had obviously
been purchased decades before.

"I spend at least a half of every day on housework, even
though I'm by myself," Mrs. Bernsteil explained. "I just can't
stand having the place a mess."

"I wish we could keep our home this nice," Dorothy commented.

"Well, as a matter of fact, I used to clean houses for people
up until ten years ago. I liked doing it and it helped bring in a
little extra money. Joe was a good man but he never made
much of a salary in the mines."

"How long ago did he retire," Philip asked.

"Let's see, he quit when he was seventy, so that was fifteen
years ago."

"Was he pretty healthy before he got his pneumonia?"

"Oh yes, like a horse. Almost never had to go to the doctor,
and didn't take much medicine, either. For some reason, he
never got the black lung like a lot of his friends. He had a little
bit of a problem with his knee—it was shot up in World War

119

II—but that didn't stop him from working hard. He started having problems breathing a few months ago, and when it got bad, I took him to the hospital. He was such a good man. He kept telling the doctors he had to come home because he didn't want me to be alone."

Philip could see that Mrs. Bernsteil was on the verge of tears, but had to probe further. "Mrs. Bernsteil, I don't want to upset you but we need to ask you a few questions about your husband's hospitalization at St. Paul's. As I told you on the phone, we're consultants who are following up on a few cases of people who died there as part of a quality assessment the hospital needs to do for its accreditation." Philip and Dorothy decided that this ruse would arouse the least suspicion among their targets.

Mrs. Bernsteil nodded. "That's fine. I understand and I'll help you as much as I can. My memory sometimes isn't as good as it used to be."

"That's OK," Dorothy reassured her. "We don't need great detail, just some general facts." Dorothy proceeded to ask a few questions about Joe Bernsteil's medical history, some of which they already knew.

Mrs. Bernsteil emphasized that Joe responded well initially. "After the first day in the hospital, Joe started doing better. His fever went away, and he said his breathing was much easier."

Then the big question: "Mrs. Bernsteil, did your husband ever use a drug called digoxin or digitalis for his heart?"

"No. Joe never had any heart problems until he went into the hospital."

"But he died from a heart rhythm problem, correct?"

"Yes, he did," Mrs. Bernsteil affirmed. "They told me that the pneumonia had weakened his heart and caused it to go out of rhythm. It was a big surprise to me because, like I said, he seemed to be getting better. Was it true about his heart going bad?"

"Yes, he did die from a heart problem," Philip answered. "Our understanding is that no autopsy was done, is that also correct?"

"I didn't see the point, and neither did his doctors at the time," Mrs. Bernsteil answered defensively. "Was that the wrong thing to do?"

Philip rushed to reassure her. "No, no, that's fine. Just checking our records."

Dorothy went on to their most important request, using the line she had rehearsed in the car. "Mrs. Bernsteil, as an outside auditing agency, we don't have access to your husband's medical records. Would you have any objection to signing a release to have copies of those records sent to us so we can extract the data we need? We'll pay for all of the copying charges. When we're finished, we can either send the copy to you, or have them properly destroyed—whichever you prefer."

"I can't see any harm in that, and I would like to have a copy. There isn't anything in there that's secret. Do you think this will help someone in the future?"

Philip nodded. "That's possible. Knowing the details of your husband's care will allow the hospital to put measures into place to take even better care of elderly patients."

Frieda Bernsteil signed the papers Dorothy gave her, and handed them back over. She had tears in her eyes as she walked Dorothy and Philip to the door. "I have to tell you I miss Joe so much. We were married for sixty-four years, and the only time we were apart was when he was in the service. I don't think I ever got enough of him. I wish you could bring him back to me."

Dorothy's eyes welled up and Philip left the house with a lump in his throat. As they walked to their car Philip said, "I didn't think this would be so hard."

Dorothy shot him an evil look. "Why? Because they were just some old guys who died when their time was up? Shame on you, Philip!"

Philip hung his head. He couldn't argue with Dorothy. He tended to have a cavalier attitude about the death of old folks, just as he had when he was in practice. He knew many doctors had the same idea, but now he felt guilty as he sat in silent rebuke on the ride to the apartment house where the family of their second patient, Bernard Luderitz, lived.

They were greeted warmly at the threshold of the garden apartment by Nina and Sophie Luderitz, the spinster daughters of Bernard. Both were in their late sixties, with gray hair and stooped postures but lively eyes and pleasant smiles. Neither had married, and both had lived with their elderly parents until eighteen months before.

Nina explained, "After Daddy died in the hospital, Mom went downhill so quickly. She just lost her will to live."

This was something Philip had often observed in practice, and had been proven in many surveys. Spouses who had been together for many years tended to die soon after each other, and frequently from similar illnesses. No one had a good explanation aside from the obvious—deep depression made caring for oneself seem like a waste of time.

Philip wanted to turn the conversation to the positive. "You have each other—that must be a comfort."

"Of course," Sophie agreed. "Except, we often wonder what will happen to the survivor when one of us dies—we don't have anybody else in the world."

Despite his best efforts, Philip had managed to blacken the conversation. Dorothy stepped in quickly.

"We really don't want to take too much of your time, ladies. We just have a few questions as part of the survey Philip told you about on the phone."

"Well, Nina is the person you need to talk to," Sophie exclaimed. "She was a nurse, you know, at Scranton Memorial Hospital. Worked on the same floor Daddy was on when he died."

"I retired five years ago," Nina chimed in. "But I know a lot of the people who work there. They were as surprised by what happened to Daddy as we were."

"You mean they didn't expect a cardiac arrhythmia?" Philip asked.

"No, they didn't," Nina answered. "He was admitted with a urinary tract infection. He had prostate problems the last few years of his life that seemed to be handled pretty well with medicines. But he got obstructed and started having fevers and chills, so we took him to Memorial right away. Within twenty-four hours, he was much better. His temperature had come down, and he was eating well. The doctors told us he would be able to come home soon, and then the heart problems started out of the blue."

"And he was dead two days later," Sophie added.

"The doctors did everything they could," Nina observed, "but the arrhythmias were just terrible and his heart finally stopped. When they tried to shock him, his rhythm degenerated further. I was outside the room when he arrested and I could hear the doctors and nurses cursing because they couldn't get his heart to stop fibrillating."

Philip and Dorothy took notes, and asked the sisters a few more questions about Mr. Luderitz's cardiac history.

"He told me once that he had a heart murmur when he enlisted in the army in 1941," Nina recalled. "It was right after Pearl Harbor, so the military wasn't being too picky. They signed him up and shipped him off to Europe lickity split. Truth be told, he was always healthy until he got that darn prostate problem. Anyhow, he never had anything else wrong with his heart, as far as I knew."

Philip and Dorothy exchanged a glance during that last piece of history. Dorothy then asked Nina and Sophie if they would grant permission to access and copy the medical records. They wanted to cooperate, just as Mrs. Bernsteil had, but Nina had a surprise. "We don't have to sign a release."

Philip immediately objected. "No, if you don't sign a release, we won't get to see your father's records."

Nina smiled. "You don't understand. I have all of Daddy's records right here in the house. We had copies made right after he died. I went through them with a fine tooth comb to see if I could figure out why his heart went bad. Couldn't make any sense of it myself, but I can give them to you if you promise to return them."

Philip and Dorothy thanked the sisters for their help, and

took the large box of records with them to the car. Nina and Sophie followed them to the curb.

"We'll have them back to you in a week," Philip reassured Nina. "Thanks for being so nice. We'll also get you the results of our survey when it's completed. In the meantime, if you can sort of keep this under your hat, we'd appreciate it. Some of the information could be sensitive for patients and families in the survey, and we don't want to upset anybody."

The sisters agreed and said their goodbyes. As soon as they pulled away, Philip looked over at Dorothy. "So, you obviously picked up on the World War II thing. Bernsteil's wife said he was in the service, and if I recollect, Al Romanzo was a World War II vet."

"You need to find out what service he was in and where he served," Dorothy suggested.

Philip nodded. "We have another intriguing question to add to the data form your father's staff is going to use."

Chapter Ten

Philip and Dorothy decided to have the files sent to Dorothy's law office in Scranton. Dorothy reasoned that this would raise less suspicion since medical records departments in hospitals frequently field requests for records from legal offices. Dorothy hoped that having the cases sent to a legal office wouldn't cause them to be flagged by the risk management department of the hospitals.

"Risk management" is a hospital euphemism for the systematic review of cases in which patients have allegedly been harmed. Each hospital has a team of nurses, clerks, and attorneys who keep track of problem cases, hoping to limit the damages they might cause the hospital. Many hospitals, particularly the larger ones, insure themselves against malpractice litigation. A few large verdicts could deplete their reserves quickly, so better not to let cases get out of control, especially if the hospitals can establish that the blame resides elsewhere, with a private practice physician, for example.

Some risk management cases originate with so-called incident reports, in which a hospital employee points out a deviation from good medical practice, regardless of whether a patient had an adverse outcome. Also included are instances in which case records are requested or subpoenaed by an attorney's office, the presumption being that malpractice is the reason for the summons.

"I think we're going to have to bite the bullet and have the records sent to my office," Dorothy told Philip when they had been putting their plan together. "Otherwise the medical records departments might call the families for verification, and that will just get them all stirred up."

"I agree. But the hospitals will notice that a bunch of their records are going to one particular law firm. Is that a problem?"

"I doubt it," Dorothy answered lost in thought. "If they're paying that much attention, they'll also know that my firm is not one of the usual malpractice factories." Dorothy's firm had gone out of its way not to take on many plaintiff malpractice cases. There were far too many hacks who advertised on the backs of buses or on television during soap operas. "Our firm never wanted to get that reputation. We take malpractice cases once in a while, but only if there is a special reason or the case is really blatant."

"Are you sure you're OK with transporting them back to me at home?" Philip asked. "Some of those guys were resuscitated and were in the hospital on ventilators and in units for a long time before they actually died. Their files will be gigantic."

Dorothy smiled. "That's why I lift weights when I work out. Any self-respecting lawyer expects to heft some big cases during her career."

"I can't wait to start looking at them," Philip remarked, and as soon as he did, he regretted it. Dorothy's response was swift and stern.

"And how much are you getting paid to put in all that time? Oh, let me guess—nothing?"

Philip lowered his head. They were back to their usual argument about Philip's legal dabbling. "I know you want me to do things that make money, and I promise to do that as much as I can."

"I understand and I'm sympathetic, but I am begging you not to let this become your sole occupation for the next several weeks. You have a family to provide for."

Philip agreed and was determined to make his case review as efficient as possible. "I don't think this'll take long. I know exactly what I need to look for in each case, and either I find it or I don't."

Dorothy bit her lip and smiled. "We'll see, Mr. Sherlock Holmes. Just do me a favor, and make sure you come up with something that convinces us to drop this thing. I hate to think how much work we'll have to do if you actually discover that these people were being murdered."

Every day for the next several weeks, Dorothy brought home at least three or four cases. Philip went at the project in the same organized way that he had conducted his research during his now-ruined academic career. Mitten and Buffy watched carefully and with concern from the doorway of his den, as he made room on one side of the loft and stacked the cases against the wall in alphabetical order. "Don't worry, girls," he reassured them. "There'll still be plenty of room for you to stretch out on the sofa."

Philip entered each case into an Excel spreadsheet on his computer, logging in critical information, including the hospital, dates of admission and death, and index arrhythmia as described in the discharge summary. He made a column for "actual arrhythmia" that he would add after his own thorough review of the records, and "treatment" that had been administered to try to bring the arrhythmias under control.

Philip was immediately struck by the case patterns. Almost all the deaths had occurred in men within a three-year period, and they were fairly evenly distributed among the five regional hospitals. The admitting diagnoses were diverse, ranging from falls to infections to abdominal pain. The patients were usually admitted to a general internist or hospitalist service and were cared for by a variety of specialists, depending on the admitting diagnoses.

The similarities were striking. In most cases, the patient had been admitted from the emergency department to a telemetry floor, where their rhythms could be continuously monitored. Each appeared to respond favorably to whatever treatment was prescribed. Appropriate diagnostic studies were ordered. Although several laboratory abnormalities were uncovered, in no case were the patients found to be at a high risk of dying from the problems that had brought them into the hospital.

After carefully examining the timelines, Philip discovered that cardiac problems almost never surfaced until the admission issue had been addressed and the patients were improving. Then, with remarkable consistency, cardiac arrhythmias began to emerge. The vast majority of these started out as short runs of an abnormal rhythm that were picked up incidentally on a routine electrocardiogram or were seen on the telemetry monitors, usually at night. A few were identified when the patient began to complain of palpitations or dizziness. A handful of patients, those not on a cardiac monitor, had passed out in their rooms before anyone suspected they were having an arrhythmia. In a few, the very first manifestation was a cardiac arrest from which the patient couldn't be resuscitated.

Philip eagerly reviewed the arrhythmias themselves. Fortunately, in most of the cases, there was EKG documentation before the patients died. The arrhythmias were as varied as Philip had imagined. Some were rapid rhythms originating from the atrium, or top heart chamber; others, from the ventricle, the lower or main pumping chamber of the heart. Still others were extreme bradycardias, or slow heart rhythms, in which the entire electrical system of the heart seemed depressed. When they started, they tended to be paroxysmal, meaning they came in short or long bursts, punctuated by periods of normal rhythm. And they were clearly episodic: after having arrhythmia storms lasting minutes to hours, the patients would have quiescent periods, rarely longer than hours, when everything was normal. Eventually, however, in every case, the arrhythmias became more frequent and persistent, until they were sustained and required emergency resuscitation.

In most of the cases, the attending doctors, seeing that the patient had some kind of cardiac problem that they didn't understand but looked serious, consulted cardiologists who usually saw the patient promptly. The five hospitals in question were relatively small, so the cardiologists who were called in consultation were general cardiologists and not electrophysiologists like Philip, with special expertise in cardiac rhythm disorders.

Philip explained all of this to Mitten and Buffy, who were sitting on the sunny side of the sofa. "That's important, girls. If these patients had been in a big city hospital and had been seen by an arrhythmia specialist, they might have suspected that digitalis was the cause, even though the drug hadn't been ordered."

The dogs raised and cocked their heads to the side to indicate their agreement, and then went back to their midday sleep, leaving Philip to ponder the implications.

The diagnoses made by the cardiologists in their consultation notes were all over the map. In many cases, the arrhythmias were blamed on cardiac conditions that the patients didn't have. A myriad of tests were ordered to try to establish the root cause of the arrhythmias. Many things were uncovered, as expected in an elderly population, but rarely anything definitive. In dozens of cases, patients underwent cardiac catheterizations on the presumption that coronary artery disease was responsible for the bizarre arrhythmias. But in cases where coronary artery blockages were found and relieved with a balloon or stent, the arrhythmias continued unabated.

Other treatments recommended by the cardiologists were as varied as the arrhythmias, reflecting their inability to make a correct diagnosis. Philip was disappointed but not surprised. Doctors didn't have time to read and study as they should, so their skills were not always the best. Rather than taking the time and energy to make a solid diagnosis, frustrated doctors tend to shoot from the hip, using therapies that themselves have the potential to cause problems.

And that clearly had happened. In many cases, it was hard for Philip to know how much of the bad outcomes had been caused by the arrhythmias and how much had been caused by the faulty measures used to treat them. In fact, many of the patients seemed to be holding their own until their blood pressure plummeted after they were given intravenous drugs meant to quell the arrhythmias. And a few patients had succumbed from the complications of procedures carried out to treat the arrhythmias. Two had heart perforations and bled to death during insertion of temporary pacemaker catheters to keep the heart from beating too slow. A few had been referred to another hospital's electrophysiology laboratory, where their tired old hearts had been endlessly stimulated with electrical energy until they failed. In not one single case had the patient received digoxin antibodies, developed as a specific antidote for digitalis toxicity.

The cardiac arrests themselves were especially painful to review. Applying electrical energy to a heart that has been poisoned with digitalis is analogous to throwing gasoline on a fire. And yet, in every case of ventricular tachycardia, the unwitting cardiologist had presided over a resuscitation in which the heart was shocked multiple times until the doctor finally gave up, or the aged heart muscle simply stopped beating.

"Whoever was behind this was very smart," Philip explained to his dogs. "Once they got the arrhythmias going, they knew the docs wouldn't just sit back. They would feel compelled to do something, and what they did helped get the job done." Buffy slapped her tail twice and rolled over hoping for a belly rub, but Philip was too distracted to notice.

Despite his own expertise in arrhythmia, Philip came across some truly strange arrhythmias that even he couldn't explain fully. "I need to know if these cases were also due to digitalis toxicity," Philip explained to Buffy who wagged her tail in agreement. Philip prepared a file of the dozen or so most complex recordings, and prepared to share them with the smartest arrhythmia person he knew, Win Chung.

Recounting Win's story to colleagues always put a smile on Philip's face. The only son of poor farmers in China, Win fought his way through the arcane and highly selective Chinese educational system to emerge as one of the brightest graduates in the history of his Beijing secondary school. He studied medicine and physiology on scholarship at Beijing University, obtaining an MD and a PhD in five years. He became fascinated with cardiac electrophysiology, a field totally unknown in China at the time. He realized that he would have to go to the United States if he wanted to pursue his dream of being a clinical and research electrophysiologist.

Win's first step was to apply for and obtain a postdoctoral fellowship in a prestigious electrophysiology laboratory in New York. He impressed his mentor there with his knowledge and energy. Win then decided to advance his clinical training. He applied to several programs, including Philip's at GMH. A phone call to Philip from Win's mentor sealed the deal, and he joined the GMH clinical cardiology fellowship, while at the same time assuming the directorship of the basic electrophysiology laboratory in Philip's department.

Win and Philip worked together closely, publishing seminal papers in basic electrophysiology. Win finished his clinical training and stayed on the faculty. When Philip left GMH, Win was devastated. But Win was accustomed to adversity and had continued to prosper, becoming a prized senior member of the GMH cardiology staff. He developed a rich clinical practice but remained devoted to his bench research as well.

Philip and Win had spent many hours discussing the mechanisms by which digitalis excess could contribute to cardiac arrhythmia. Win's insights complemented Philip's extensive clinical experience. If anyone could confirm that an arrhythmia was related to digitalis poisoning, it would be Win. Philip decided to call the division, and was pleased to be greeted by Rhonda's Philly accent.

"Rhonda, this is Philip. How are you?"

"Philip, it's great to hear your voice again and so soon. I was just thinking about you last weekend. I was running an errand and went through your old neighborhood. How are things in the Poconos?"

"I'm sure some people would find this boring, but we're very happy up here. The pace is much slower, for sure."

"I'm glad to hear you're well. What can I do for you?"

"Is Win around? I need to ask him a question."

Rhonda paged Win and connected Philip, saying goodbye as she got off the line.

"Win, this is Philip."

Win sounded genuinely happy to hear from Philip. "We've missed you, Philip. How have you been?"

"Just fine, Win. I see your name on a lot of things, so I guess you've been keeping busy with your research?"

"Just improving on the stuff you started." Win had a true appreciation for Philip's early mentoring. Philip had a tendency to be aloof and neglected to give enough credit to people like Win, who carried out much of the actual research work. But Win knew that Philip had clearly put him onto some important lines of research that Win was still mining.

"Win, I have a favor to ask. Could you please look at a few rhythm recordings for me and tell me what you think they are and what caused them?"

Win was surprised. "Are you kidding? You want me to tell *you* what they are?"

"I just want another opinion—I have a bias and I want to get an objective read."

Win agreed readily. "Sure, send them to me. If you aren't sure what they are, they must be pretty interesting."

Philip knew that Win didn't have to be prodded to finish a task quickly. Philip made photocopies of the tracings from a few of the cases and sent them to Win by express delivery.

Two days later, Win emailed Philip a three-page single-spaced document. Win thought that each of the arrhythmias Philip had sent him were consistent with digitalis excess, although there were a number of other possibilities.

"I think that each of these arrhythmias was initiated by DADs," Win wrote. DADs or delayed afterdepolarizations are caused by an excess of calcium inside the cardiac cell. Many things cause calcium overload, including digitalis that poisons the pump responsible for emptying the cell of calcium. In therapeutic concentrations, trapping excess calcium inside the cell strengthens the force of cardiac contraction, one of the principal uses of the drug. In toxic amounts, extra calcium causes premature beats and tachycardias in both the top and bottom heart chambers.

"It is clear that that the arrhythmias were caused by calcium overload," Win continued, "and unless there are other reasons, digoxin overdose has to be the most likely culprit."

Philip answered Win's email with a heartfelt thanks and a pledge to keep in touch, realizing even as he wrote it that the message was an empty promise. But Philip now had the extra ammunition he needed.

It took all of Philip's spare time over the next three weeks to review the cases. He cancelled one of his weekends with his kids to give himself extra time, a decision that infuriated not only Dorothy but also his ex-wife, Nancy, who had made plans with her new husband that she had to scrap.

"I really can't keep interrupting myself," Philip tried to explain to Dorothy. "I finally have some momentum, and I want to keep my review going." Dorothy doubted the momentum argument. It was more likely another example of his singlemindedness taking over their lives. "There are many reasons why I love you, Philip, but this damned obsession of yours is not one of them."

But when Philip was finally able to compile the results of his chart review, Dorothy had to admit she was anxious to hear his conclusions. They decided on a midweek evening briefing. Their dinner that evening had been hamburgers on the grill. The weather was finally warm enough to permit grilling on the back deck, and they enjoyed their burgers on soft rolls, with all of the fixings, accompanied by a good bottle of California merlot. They cleaned up quickly, and Philip gave Dorothy a copy of the spreadsheet he had put together, with some summary tables.

"You can look at all this yourself, but let me summarize it,"

Philip said. "As you can see, I reviewed 190 cases. We identified another ten—hopefully they'll come in soon. Of the 190, I can say with certainty that digitalis was the responsible agent in 160. For another 22, I'm fairly sure it was digoxin—12 of those went to Win Chung, who agreed with me that digoxin is in the equation, if not the definite cause. That leaves eight in which the documentation is so poor that I can't make a statement at all. But there is nothing, even in those cases, that's inconsistent with my theory."

"Wow, this sounds pretty definitive."

"In each case, the men were admitted for a non-cardiac reason, had no active cardiac disease, and were getting better when their arrhythmias hit."

Dorothy was intrigued. "So somebody waited until they were improving and were likely to survive when they stepped in to do their dirty work?"

"That's what it looks like. Which means there were other men who were 'evaluated' by the angel of death, but in whom nature took its course."

"You mean they likely died of whatever hospitalized them in the first place?"

Philip nodded before Dorothy took the next logical step. "And you have no idea how many more cases you didn't pick up because the arrhythmias didn't stick out."

"That's right. There could have been many more victims who just needed a little nudge to get to the other side. I would be surprised if there weren't several who went down that way. And what is really scary is that most of the beds in these small hospitals don't have monitors."

"Which means what?" Dorothy asked.

"Given enough drug, some victims might have gone into a lethal arrhythmia in the middle of the night and no one would have detected it. Nurses can be out of the room for hours."

"So the person would have been found dead in the morning."

"And who would care? It's just some old man from a nursing home."

Dorothy shook her head. "I'm beginning to understand why you've been working so hard the past few weeks. Whoever did this could be the most accomplished mass murderer since Adolf Eichmann."

"Funny you should say that. I picked up a few other interesting tidbits. All of the guys in my review were in their eighties and nineties. According to the information gathered from their families in the surveys we used, they served in the army in World War II, and were in the European or North African theaters."

"And that held up in all of the cases?"

"Yep, and there was one amazing thing they all had in common."

Dorothy braced herself. "And that was?"

"Every one of them had a name that sounds like their families came from Italy or Germany."

It took only a few seconds for the message to register before Dorothy muttered, "Oh my God."

Chapter Eleven

Dorothy and Philip now agreed they had something sub-stantive to share with Lieutenant Detweiler. Philip called Detweiler's office and suggested they meet soon.

"Let's do it at your office, if you don't mind, Lieutenant. I can come down there late one afternoon after I get out of the clinic."

Detweiler agreed and they met the following week on a gloomy Thursday afternoon in Scranton Police Headquarters. Though he was the "chief detective," to say that Detweiler had an "office" was being generous. His desk was in the middle of the squad room with only a flimsy partition to give him any privacy. Detweiler's cubicle was by far the most cluttered, with files piled high all around, except for the smallest area where he kept his phone and a small blotter. Paper files over-flowed onto the chair he kept next to his desk. He hurriedly cleared the chair so Philip could sit down.

"Detective, is this your way of impressing me with how busy you and your staff are? If so, then I'm entirely sold."

"No, Dr. Sarkis," Detweiler answered with a sigh. "It's like this all the time. Detectives like me have a choice—work the cases and discover something important, or keep up with the paperwork and let the cases go to hell."

"Looks like you chose the former?"

"Highly observant of you, Dr. Sarkis. And I have the feeling you're here to burden our case load even further."

"Good observation yourself, Lieutenant. Dorothy Deaver and I have made some progress on the Romanzo case, but I have to tell you that we had some professional help."

"Can't say that surprises me," Detweiler replied. "Your task was pretty complicated. Where did the help come from?"

"Dick Deaver. He's Dorothy's father and he had some people from his private investigation firm help us with canvasing."

"Canvassing? Now this is starting to sound interesting. Who is it that you happened to canvas?"

Philip went on to explain their visits to the families of the patients who appeared to have suffered a cardiac arrhythmia without explanation. Although he tried to gloss over just how Dorothy and he had come upon the patient list they used, Detweiler wouldn't allow it.

"I think I understand how you might have selected the cases you chose to review, but where did the master list come from?"

Philip hesitated. If he told Detweiler the truth, he would be admitting a violation of patient privacy that could land Dorothy and him in jail. But he couldn't dodge the question altogether. He decided to be coy.

"Lieutenant, can we just stipulate that we obtained all of the information from the families of the deceased with their full permission?"

Detweiler cocked his head and stared at Philip. He realized immediately that something underhanded had been done to get the list, and he was smart enough not to dig too deeply, at least for the time being.

"I think we can make that assumption for now, Doctor. But the case is going to have to hold water if and when I take it up the ladder. If knowing how you obtained your patient list becomes a critical part of the case, and you did something illegal to get it, we're going to part ways very quickly, do you understand?"

In fact, Philip understood the problem precisely, and he admired how adroitly Detweiler had found a way to make a decision to plumb the case further but not cross a legal line.

"That makes perfect sense to me, and I concur," Philip replied. "I think the case won't hinge on that in the end so why don't we just move on."

"OK, that's fair," Detweiler said, obviously relieved that he didn't have to arrest Philip on the spot or abandon the case. "Now tell me what it is you found out in this canvassing of yours."

While Philip spoke, Detweiler alternated between taking notes and doodling on the side of his note pad. He used an old-fashioned lead pencil that was extensively decorated with teeth marks. Philip leaned forward in his chair and reported his principal findings, trying hard not to use overly technical language to describe the patient cases and the arrhythmias he uncovered. He emphasized the clinical similarities among the alleged victims, noting in particular that none had ever received digitalis at any time in his life, and that the drug had not been ordered during the hospitalization.

"So it's the Romanzo story multiplied and scattered among our five area hospitals. Is that what you're telling me, Doctor?"

"It's even more interesting than that, Lieutenant. All of the victims had several other things in common. First of all, they all served in the European theater in World War II."

Detweiler immediately stopped doodling and put his gnawed pencil down. "Why on earth?" he began, and then paused in thought.

"I can't begin to guess, Lieutenant. If there was a murderer or murderers, they seemed to have singled out men who had served in the armed forces. But it gets better."

"Or worse. What else?" Detweiler asked.

"The other thing we found was that all of them were of either German or Italian descent," Philip answered.

"Couldn't that be a coincidence? This area is packed with German and Italian families."

Philip countered, "And Irish and Polish and Greek. With a

sample size so big, I can't believe this finding can be the play of chance."

Detweiler went silent, lost in thought. When he finally spoke, he said exactly what Philip hoped he would not. "Sounds like we're going to need more information, and that you and Ms. Deaver have more work to do, Doctor."

Philip lowered his head. Dorothy had already warned him about further immersion in the case without active support from the authorities. He braced himself while Detweiler went on.

"Let's say you're right and there is a pattern. What can I possibly do with this information? Wilkes-Barre and Scranton have enormous Italian and German populations. Most of those families have been up here for years, since the old coal mining days. So you can expect there'll be thousands of old men hospitalized for a variety of medical problems, and old guys die in the hospital. Furthermore, you're telling me that all of this happened at five different hospitals. Some of those places are not in my jurisdiction. To conduct a full-scale investigation when I don't have the authority to do so is impossible."

"So you're saying you can't do anything with the information?"

"I didn't say that, but I will need more detail before I can ask my department to get involved officially."

"And what is it you'll require, Lieutenant?"

"A suspect."

Philip was incredulous. "Are you serious? You want us to find the friggin' murderer?"

"Or murderers. From what you've told me, there may have been more than one, right?"

Philip and Dorothy had discussed that possibility, and once again, Detweiler had proven to be a quick study. Detweiler could see that Philip was dumbfounded and hurried to make his point.

"Look, Doctor, I don't expect you to crack the case, but I bet there's more you can glean from the records that'll help us focus our investigation."

"Geez, Lieutenant, we've already put a major effort into the case. We were really hoping to lateral it to you at this point. Besides, I went through the records pretty carefully. I don't think there's a lot more to learn."

Detweiler put the eraser end of his pencil against his chin and grinned. "Doctor, you'll be amazed how much more you can get out of documents you think you've plumbed completely. There's always something else to uncover."

Philip suspected that Detweiler was dragging his feet. He wondered if Detweiler really believed what he was saying, or was simply sending Philip and Dorothy on a fool's errand. "It would be enormously helpful if you could give me some clue as to what the hell you want us to look for."

Detweiler sat forward in his creaky swivel chair and put his elbows on his desk. "Think about it, Doc. You suspect that somebody was going around giving patients lethal doses of digitalis, right? You further suspect that the victims in these cases had a strong commonality. So who had ready access to these patients day in and day out, and who spent the most time with them? And who is expected to administer medications by pill or by vein?"

"The nursing staff, of course," Philip answered instantly. "Dorothy and I thought of that, but the nursing staff is different at each hospital. How would a nurse at one place gain access to patients at other places?"

"I don't know, but it brings me back to the multiple perpetrator idea. I'm not smart enough to figure out how all this ties together. That's why I need your help to find something in the charts that does it for us."

Philip nodded. "I can do a little more digging, but I have to tell you this is going to provoke a lot of unhappiness on the home front."

"I realize that, and I understand. Just tell Ms. Deaver that I'm being a jerk."

Which is exactly what Philip did over drinks that evening on their dock, when he reported to Dorothy on his meeting with Detweiler. Mitten and Buffy lay quietly at their feet, drying out after an hour of hell raising, ripping in and out of the lake, chasing each other and any creature in sight. Philip and Dorothy turned their chairs to admire the sun as it set on the western side of the lake. Faint clouds provided the canvas as the sun painted the sky pink and orange. Philip sensed it was the right time to deliver Detweiler's message.

"I'm going to have to get those charts out again and do some more dredging," Philip offered while be sipped his beer.

Dorothy turned to answer. "What on earth for? What did Detweiler have to say?"

"He wants us to find the evildoer, as they say in those cheap murder mysteries."

"You can't be serious. How are you supposed to do that?"

Philip noted that Dorothy had said *you* and not *we*, which he took as a sure sign that Dorothy was not eager to stay involved in the case.

"Detweiler suspects that a nurse is the culprit. He wants me to go through the charts to see who was taking care of the victims."

"You've got to be kidding. There are dozens of cases and they came from several hospitals. How on earth are you going to tie them together?"

Philip could only nod. "That was Detweiler's exact position. He pointed out that if I have trouble with it, he sure as heck wouldn't be able to make much headway, either."

"Well, it sounds incredibly difficult, but if you're willing to go back through those tomes, help yourself." Dorothy delivered the message curtly, obviously annoyed.

Philip tried to hide his disappointment; he had been hoping that Dorothy would be willing to assist. "It'll be incredibly boring but I promise to be as quick as possible."

Dorothy smiled knowingly. "Yes, so you can then get back to the business of supporting this little family unit, such as it is."

"Glad to see you're thinking of us as a family."

In fact, Dorothy had found it difficult to relate to Philip's children in a meaningful way. She continued to try to be their friend and stepmother but realized she ran a poor second to Nancy. It was a sore point that neither Philip nor Dorothy chose to broach very often.

Later that evening, Dorothy plopped on the sofa and immersed herself in a recently purchased historical novel. Philip used her repose as an opportunity to begin culling through the charts. Now the focus was the nurses' notes, specifically, trying to identify nurses who were on duty when the problem arrhythmias had developed.

After only a few charts, Philip was discouraged. "I can't identify a common person or anything that links the nursing staff," Philip explained to Dorothy as they prepared for bed later that evening.

Dorothy took the dental floss out of her mouth. "I wouldn't expect an easy answer. You're going to have to be patient and go through a lot more charts. Don't be discouraged, and make sure you look carefully. What you're searching for may be very subtle."

Dorothy's admonitions made Philip want her help even more. As if she'd read his mind, Dorothy added, "But you're on your own, buddy, at least until you get something we can chew on. I am not plowing through those charts with you."

Over the next several days, Philip did as Dorothy had instructed. He went through the charts looking for a link among the alleged victim's caregivers. There were men and women, some with good and some with poor handwriting, some meticulous in detail, others more cursory, and some downright sloppy. In cases that occurred on telemetry units, where the electrocardiogram could be monitored, the nurses appended rhythm strips. Their bland notes uniformly failed to transmit the true drama as single premature beats escalated to life-threatening arrhythmias. They detailed physician notifications and the multiple phone calls and verbal orders that became more complicated as the patients deteriorated. They did so without editorial commentary, as they had been trained.

Philip made a list of the nurses and nurse's aides who had entered notations in the charts. As he listed their degrees, he came across a few who had signed their name followed by multiple letters. In most cases, the nurses were showing off the fact that they had advanced degrees or were members of nursing societies that admitted individuals who had passed some kind of qualifying examination. Philip had his usual negative reaction. He had once told a colleague, "There is an inverse relationship between how good somebody is and how many letters they choose to put after their names." Philip rarely listed anything more than "MD" though he was a member or fellow of several professional organizations. But here were nurses making routine chart notations and filling the signature line with all kinds of letters.

"I can figure out what most of these mean," Philip explained to Mitten, one afternoon as his faithful pup lay under his desk during a gusty rainstorm. She hated thunder and lightning and shivered at his feet. "A lot of the nurses took and passed board examinations in critical care nursing so I know what *CCRN* means. But there are a few I never heard of and some were used by a lot of the nurses. Do you think it might be worth trying to find out what they mean?"

Mitten lifted her head and tilted it to the side, cocking her floppy ears to agree with the idea. Philip Googled a few nursing societies, and sure enough found that nurses in telemetry units had the opportunity to join a myriad of organizations, mostly based on seniority and subspecialty experience. Using the lists he found on line, Philip was able to identify nearly all of the suffixes.

Again, he sought Mitten's wisdom. "OK, girl, you were right and I was able to decipher most of them. But I still have one or two left. At least four nurses used *ANA*. At first I thought it meant Association of Nurse Anesthetists, but none of those nurses were responsible for giving anesthesia to patients, and even if they were, the abbreviation for the American Association of Nurse Anesthetists is *AANA*."

This time, Mitten didn't flinch. "So you're out of ideas too?" Philip asked the hound. "But don't you think I should pursue this? Maybe it's a clue?"

Mitten chose that moment to sit forward and use her hind paw to scratch her neck, after which she sat up and looked searchingly at Philip.

"I don't know, either, old girl, but I think it's time to go to the source and add just a little deception. This is going to be tricky, but I think I know how to get what I need. We'll appeal to the hospital's collective ego."

Philip knew that all hospitals love to brag whenever they are cited by any organization for being good at anything. And there are many for-profit companies willing to rank hospitals for any one of a hundred "quality indicators." These companies know that hospitals are desperate to gain an edge over their competition and what better way than a designation as a "top hospital" for an important service like cardiovascular surgery? Hospitals are happy to subject their staff to an endless array of audits to identify one or a few service lines about which they might successfully advertise.

Philip selected the smallest of the five hospitals, likely to be most eager to have some honor conferred out of the blue that it didn't deserve. He decided to call the nursing office to give them the "good news." Communication among departments, even within small hospitals, is frequently poor. Philip figured that notification of an award wouldn't be challenged. The chief medical officer was supposed to pass along information to all departments in a timely way but frequently dropped the ball.

Philip tried to sound official but friendly when he called the nursing office at Montage General Hospital. "Hello, this is James Derrick at *Health Report Card* magazine. I'm the person in charge of your audit. To whom am I speaking?"

"This is Caroline Dunphy, assistant to the vice-president of nursing."

Great, Philip thought. Another mid-level hospital administrator with a "staff" to support her, and people wondered why health care was so expensive.

"Ms. Dunphy, I need some information to complete our survey."

Ms. Dunphy had a sweet young voice. "I didn't know that *Health Report Card* was doing a survey at Montage."

"You bet," Philip answered, using his most pleasant and optimistic tone. "*Health Report Card* is considering designating Montage one of its Top 100 Cardiovascular Programs. I'm auditing a random sample of patient charts and I have some questions. I want to make sure I can place your institution in the best possible light."

The secretary was so excited she was practically breathless. "That's quite an honor. I'll make sure I let my boss know this afternoon."

"That would be great," Philip acknowledged.

"But I didn't think our hospital was big enough for that award."

"Size doesn't matter," Philip said, almost laughing at his own ridiculous comment. "Really, we care much more about quality, and Montage has been doing a bang-up job for a long time. We're going to have a separate category for some of the really excellent small programs in the country, and yours is certainly on our radar screen."

Philip wondered if he was laying it on too thick, but the reaction at the other end seemed enthusiastic. "Well, just tell me what you need and I'll do my best to get it for you."

"I really appreciate that," Philip countered. "I just have a few things." To prevent suspicion, Philip asked for some meaningless data about unit census that the woman assured him would be easy to find. Philip gave her a fake number and asked her to fax the information to him at her earliest convenience. He then pretended to wind down the conversation.

"Ms. Dunphy, you have been most kind. The *Health Report Card* staff likes to give extra points to hospitals that cooperate with us. I'll make sure your supervisor is aware of how helpful you've been. Let me just make sure I got everything on my list. Yep, it looks fine. Oh, wait a minute, just one more thing.

I noticed that many of the nurses at your place have advanced degrees and are members of some very prestigious organizations. There was one I didn't recognize. A few of your nurses put 'ANA' after their name. That one has me stumped. Can you find out what that is for us?"

Ms. Dunphy didn't hesitate. "Oh, I don't have to look that one up. I see it all the time."

"You do?" said Philip, pretending to be surprised by her answer.

"Sure. It means that the nurse came to us through a nursing agency, the Adolphus Nursing Agency, to be exact."

Philip nodded and smiled at Mitten, who looked back up at him with her usual soulful stare. "Right. A nursing agency. Of course. Thanks so much, Ms. Dunphy, you've been very helpful."

"That's the thread, old girl," he said to Mitten after he hung up. "A friggin' nursing agency. How the hell do you like that?"

Chapter Twelve

Philip and Dorothy enjoyed their home in the Poconos for many reasons. It afforded them the opportunity to enjoy the outdoors, something they didn't have when they had lived in Philadelphia. They particularly liked the summers, and took advantage of the convenience of their lakefront property as often as possible.

Lake Naomi was a wonderful place, ringed mainly by vacation homes but with a smattering of people who, like Philip and Dorothy, lived there full time as refugees from a hectic urban existence. The lake was man-made and fairly shallow, designed and built in the late 19th century to produce ice, which was transported to and sold in New York and Philadelphia for use in "ice boxes," the forerunners of refrigerators. The lake had been abandoned in the early twentieth century, only to be rediscovered by entrepreneurs in the 1970s as the centerpiece of a resort community, now populated by several hundred fortunate people who could afford a second home to which they escaped regularly.

One of their favorite activities was an evening canoe ride with Mitten and Buffy. The dogs would readily vault into the boat and wait for their owners to take up their paddles. The ride offered wonderful views of the sunset, underscored by the stately trees that lined the tranquil water. Their journey would take them past neighbors' homes, carefully hidden in the woods, with a boat dock that marked their property. It was a gentle place and time. Dorothy could see that living there helped Philip heal after his terrible ordeal, and for that she was grateful.

Philip chose one of their lake excursions to bring Dorothy up to speed on the Romanzo case. As they pulled away from the dock, he poured two glasses of Prosecco from a bottle he had brought on the boat, and put them in home-made cup holders.

"It should have been obvious. Detweiler himself told me to focus on the nurses, and if they were the suspects, I should have guessed they would have had to come from a common source."

"Don't feel bad. Here I am an investigator for god's sake, and I missed it, too. An agency makes sense. But you're a long way from hanging this on the Adolphus Agency. From what I've heard, it's a pretty solid firm that's been in business in this area for a long time. Their nurses have a reputation for giving great care."

"I know. I went on their website last night after I got off the phone with the nursing office, and checked them out. They've been supplying nurses to all of the regional hospitals for about ten years and have built their business the right way. But there were a few interesting things that made me suspicious."

"Like what?" Dorothy wanted to know.

"Well, they work mostly in cardiology. In fact, they staff cardiac intensive care units and cardiac telemetry units almost exclusively."

"So why is that significant," Dorothy asked.

"It means they understand heart disease and therapies. They have to know a lot about the drugs doctors typically order on those units, and that, of course, would include digitalis."

"Lots of nurses know about digitalis," Dorothy countered. "And how much do you need to know to poison somebody with a drug? I think that's a stretch. What else got your attention?"

"Well, if that one didn't impress you, this one won't either."

Dorothy persisted, "Come on, spit it out."

"Lots of men," Philip mumbled.

"Did you say, 'lots of men?'"

Philip nodded.

"You mean the agency has a lot of male nurses?"

Philip nodded again, embarrassed by the meagerness of his evidence. He tried to recoup. "Over eighty percent of the nurses at Adolphus are men. That's way above the average for agencies or hospitals, where it runs at least eighty percent women."

"And somehow you think that men are more likely to be killers than women? That sounds like inside-out chauvinism."

"I knew you were going to think I was a sexist for that observation, but I guess I have this stereotype of a wonderfully helpful female nurse taking care of patients, and never placing them in jeopardy. Male nurses, on the other hand... well, you know what people think about them."

"Yeah, everybody assumes they're gay. But how would that make them more likely to harm patients? If you want to keep stereotyping, wouldn't that make them too prissy to be killers?"

"OK, I have to concede that much of what is coming out of my mouth right now is not all that well thought out. For whatever reason, it just got my hackles up."

"Well, lower your hackles, whatever the hell they are. It's time to get some real data about this agency, more than what you might be able to infer from their stupid website."

"I know. We need to get in there and find out what the story is."

Dorothy stopped paddling, and from the front of the canoe turned around to face Philip. "What do you mean *we*, white man?"

Philip started mumbling again, something he did when confronted by Dorothy's strong reaction to one of his ill-conceived ideas. "I don't think I can pull this off myself. I need someone who looks like a nurse."

"So we'll preserve yet another stereotype and send me, a

woman, to do a fact-finding mission? I thought you said they hired mostly men."

"Think about it, Dorothy—you're the perfect foil. You know something about medicine, you look like a nurse, and you know how to get information out of people who wouldn't ordinarily offer it up. It wouldn't take long, and it would really help us get this case resolved."

"You did a good deal of thinking before asking me this, didn't you? So this leisurely boat ride was a set-up all along. You knew what you wanted, so you figured you would get me out here on the lake, soften me up with some small talk and sparkling wine, and then hit me with your request. Philip, you are so devious and calculating, it's frightening."

Philip didn't see the point in denying Dorothy's accusation. In fact, he had played this request out in his mind several times earlier in the day, and knew this would be a good time and place to spring the question. "OK, you got me."

Dorothy shook her head. "Well, it so happens that one of the cases I'm working on just got settled. The greedy plaintiff finally understood that the miserable schlep I've been representing doesn't have enough money to make his frivolous lawsuit worth his time."

Philip pounced. "Does that mean you'll go talk with the agency director?"

"I'll do you one better. I'll do a background search of the agency through my father's firm first, and confirm what you did with your little web search. Then I'll set up an appointment to talk to the person who runs the place. I need an edge. I'm afraid if I just go barging in there, no one will talk to me, and I won't learn much."

"I love having you on my side. You always know exactly what to do."

Dorothy looked askance. "You don't have to butter me up any more, buster," she said. "I'll help you, but I'll do it my way so I don't get embarrassed or worse. Remember, if you're right, these may be dangerous people who could come after us if they're implicated. Or if they're falsely accused."

Philip nodded. "Can't argue with you there."

"That's the smartest thing you've said since we got into the boat."

"And that's the last thing I will say about the case," Philip said softly. "Let's try to enjoy the rest of our ride." Dorothy grunted an approval, petted Buffy who was sitting next to her, and resumed paddling.

Dorothy called her dad the next morning. She knew he had clients in the coal mining regions of Pennsylvania, and would be able to help gather some general information she needed about the Adolphus Agency.

"Dorothy, it's great to hear your voice. I miss you."

"Dad," Dorothy answered, "it's only been three weeks since we had dinner. You make it sound like months."

"Well, damn it, I used to see you a lot more when you lived down here."

This had become her father's favorite refrain since she moved to the Poconos with Philip. Dorothy knew her father wanted her closer to him, but he wasn't exactly the lonely old man living in Philadelphia.

"Come on, Dad, I know you aren't sitting around pining away for me. How many new women have you met and dated this month?"

Dick was highly active on the city's social scene and had several interesting ways to meet new women friends, with whom he enjoyed spending what he liked to call "quality time."

"Those people don't matter to me," Dick protested. "You're the only one I truly love. But I bet you didn't call to chat with me about my social life. Judging from your tone, and the time of day you're calling, you want something."

Dorothy paused. "Let's just say I need a little information. If you agree to get it for me, I'll come down there, and I'll let you take me out to lunch and brief me. What do you say?"

Dick Deaver was wary. "I say it depends on what you want me to find out. One lunch may not be an adequate payback."

"Why you greedy old man! I don't think this one will tax you at all. But I'll throw in a dinner later, which you will also pay for by the way, just to keep you happy."

"I can't believe I'm making this deal, but go ahead and tell me what you want."

"There's a nursing agency in Wilkes-Barre called Adolphus. They supply nurses to intensive care units for hospitals in their region."

"I don't understand. Why do hospitals need agency nurses? Why don't they just hire their own nurses?"

"Good question," Dorothy replied. "Hospitals are constantly shuffling personnel, including nurses. It's hard to keep a full staff, because nurses in particular come and go pretty quickly. So it's common for hospitals to need nurses to fill in, especially during vacation season, or when people get sick. Agency nurses are accessible on fairly short notice, but they cost more and aren't as familiar with the work routine."

"Are they any good?" Dick asked.

"It's pretty spotty. Some are terrific, and some not so hot. Agencies earn a reputation based on how well their nurses perform. The better the skill set, the more money the agency can demand."

"So what do you want to know about Adolphus?"

"Just general stuff," Dorothy answered. "Nothing complicated, or necessarily secret. Like who are their nurses, where do they come from, who runs the place, who does business with them, that kind of thing."

"And what, my dear, do you plan to do with this newfound knowledge?"

"I want to set up an interview with the administrative director, and I thought having background information would be useful."

Dick Deaver was not naïve. "You side-stepped my question. Let me rephrase. You and I both know that you aren't doing this for the hell of it. So what is it about the Adolphus Agency that has attracted your interest?"

Dorothy was torn. She wanted to be honest with her father,

but Philip's ideas were so preliminary that she didn't want to get the old man excited for nothing. She decided to compromise. "Tell you what, if you can find out what I need to know, I promise to brief you when we meet for lunch."

"All right—I'll get Al Kenworthy to do a standard sweep for us. He's a good computer guy, and I suspect that we can get you most of what you want to know that way. Cuts down on the expense and the fuss. Now who did you say was going to pay for this?" he teased.

"Just pick a nice place for lunch, and that will have to make you happy," Dorothy reminded him. "Can you make it for about a week from now? I have a few new cases that should be set up by then, and that should give you and big Al a chance to get some juicy intel for me."

Dick was ready a lot sooner. Within two days, Al had found out about the history of the agency and its leadership. Dick made a few discreet phone calls to some of his counterparts in northeast Pennsylvania to fill in the gaps.

Al, a single guy, had a crush on Dorothy and dropped several not-so-subtle hints about coming along to meet with her— an idea squelched immediately by Dick, who didn't need some lovesick geek making eyes at his daughter during their lunch. Al took it fairly well; Dorothy was living with someone, Dick pointed out to him, but as long as she was not married, Al could hope.

Dick made reservations at the Fountain Restaurant in the Four Seasons Hotel on the Ben Franklin Parkway. It had the advantages of elegance, good food, and accessibility for Dorothy, who had to drive down from the Poconos.

Dick walked to the hotel a little early and had a Bloody Mary at the bar. Dorothy valet-parked her car and came in a few minutes later. They gave each other a casual peck and hug. A stranger might have wondered if this was a case of an old guy with money getting lucky with a young, attractive woman, unless of course he or she was close enough to hear the cheerful greeting Dorothy gave her father.

"Hey, Dad. Thanks for setting this up."

"Been looking forward to it all week, my girl," Dick replied quickly. "Couldn't wait to see you."

They were seated by one of the windows that overlooked the Parkway, with a great view of the famous swan fountain and the Cathedral-Basilica of Saints Peter and Paul across the street. It was a favorite people-watching location, especially at lunchtime, when many office workers were out and about.

It took little time to order, a salad for Dorothy and a sirloin sandwich for Dad. Dick wanted small talk, Dorothy wanted information, so they compromised and interspersed the topics as they ate their lunch. As it turned out, what Dick had to tell Dorothy was more helpful than she had anticipated.

"I guess you know Adolpus has been in business for about ten years. They aren't very big, only have about thirty nurses all told, but they've all been with the agency for a long time— most since the beginning."

"What keeps them there?" Dorothy asked. "Do they get paid really well?"

"Not as far as we could see. Al was able to get their pay scale, and it's lower than most of the other places in town. And their benefit package is nothing to write home about, either. So I can't explain this loyalty."

"And their specialty is intensive care medicine?"

"Even more specialized than that," Dick pulled his notes out of his breast pocket as he spoke. "From what we could tell, it's all about cardiology. Their nurses only work in cardiac and cardiac surgery ICUs and telemetry units. Whenever they've been offered other gigs, they've declined. Their website now makes it clear that they're exclusively cardiac."

"That's pretty unusual, right?"

"To some extent, although perfectly understandable. Things are so amazingly specialized in medicine these days. I can see why someone would like to narrow the aperture a little. But that's not the most unusual part of the agency."

Dorothy was prepared. "I know, most of the nurses are male."

"Not just most. How about nearly all? Only three women work in the place. One nurse, a secretary, and Brenda."

"Who's Brenda?"

"The person who started the business and runs the place. And from what Al was able to learn, with an iron fist."

"This sounds interesting. Tell me more about the boss."

"Brenda Straub is in her mid-forties. She was an army nurse back in the late eighties and left the service after fifteen years. Came back to work at Wilkes-Barre General for a few years before starting Adolphus with some guys she knew from the army and a few locals. Took out a small loan to do it, but used her own money for most of it. Built the agency from nothing but did it steadily and with good results. Hospitals now consider Adolphus the go-to firm for excellent cardiology nurses—so if a unit is in trouble for quality or personnel reasons, Adolphus is immediately called in from the bullpen. They don't stay long; they fill in and help out as long as necessary and then are on their way."

"And Brenda has accomplished this by keeping experienced people, but we don't know how she manages to retain them?" Dorothy asked.

"Right. We did find out that she runs a tight ship. She has a reputation among her employees for being above board and honest. Everybody talks about her fairness, and her work ethic. Wouldn't ask any of her employees to do something she wouldn't do. And she proves it by filling in for people during vacations. Rolls up her sleeves and pitches in. The staff likes that."

"Any staff would like to have a boss like that. It sounds like Brenda has good people skills. And she likes to throw herself into her work. Does that mean Brenda doesn't have a private life?"

"You can say that again," Dick smirked. "Absolutely zero. She has a modest home in a residential area of town, nice but not extravagantly furnished, small backyard, no pets, and rarely seen by the neighbors. Lives like a hermit."

"No gentlemen callers?"

"Or ladies, for that matter. And the weirdest part is that 'her package is well wrapped.'"

"Huh? What does that mean, Dad?"

"I mean that Brenda is to die for. Drop-dead gorgeous, and a great bod to go with it. She should be fighting them off with a stick, but this pretty piece of bait is being ignored by the local fish. As I'm sure you can imagine, once he got a load of Brenda, your buddy Al Kenworthy spent a good amount of time trying to figure that one out."

"Without much success, I bet."

"But not for lack of trying. Al loves that part of his work. Brenda was never married or engaged. Doesn't hit the bars or social clubs in the area. Dated one of the male nurses a few years ago for a couple of months but that ended when the nurse left the agency—rather abruptly, as we found out. One of the few defectors. Anyhow, that's Brenda."

Dorothy was pleased to get details about Brenda. It was a bonus from her dad that would help her a great deal at her planned meeting. She sipped her after-meal cappuccino patiently, waiting for her father to ask the expected question.

"So are you going to tell me what this is all about, or are you going to leave me in the dark?"

"Well, Dad, I have to admit you've been really helpful, so I'll tell you what I can."

Dorothy went on to give Dick a few details about the case, leaving out patient and hospital names, and trying to minimize her own involvement. She knew her father would not be pleased to see her deeply involved in another one of Philip's "follies," and she didn't want another lecture from him. What she got was a mini-tirade.

"The last time you two novices started sneaking around, you damn near got yourselves arrested for murder, or blown away by some well-connected Italian gentlemen. I'm sure you remember that. If you suspect these people have been killing patients in hospitals, what makes you think they won't kill a couple of snoops who are trying to expose them?"

"Granted, this is dangerous," Dorothy admitted. "But remember, if these nurses murdered anybody, it was defenseless old men and they didn't do it with a gun or a knife. Anyhow, what would you have us do? Let them keep killing innocent people?"

"Those men were in the service, my darling. I suspect that they learned something about weapons and how to use them to kill people. How about turning the case over to the police? Tell the detective up there to get off his fat ass and do his job instead of sending amateurs out to do it for him."

"Dad, I think you're right on this one. After I talk to this Straub person, we'll go back to Detweiler and give him what we've got. Hopefully at that point, Philip will be assuaged, and he can get back to what he's supposed to be doing."

"Just be careful. If you corner those rats, they may be a lot more dangerous than you think, and you don't have any way to protect yourself. Plus you're isolated out there, so far away from civilization. Hell, killing you guys would be a lot easier than offing patients right in front of several hundred healthcare professionals."

Dorothy was anxious to end the conversation. Her father didn't understand how much he scared her when he cautioned her like this. Her sleep at their mountain house for the next several weeks would now be fitful at best.

As they walked out to the curb and waited for her car, Dick sensed her distress and offered to travel up and stay at their house for a few days. "I think we'll be OK, but thanks for the offer, Dad. I'll use a good alias when I meet with Brenda Straub so they won't be able to trace me. In fact, do you think you could get me a fake nursing license in the next day or so? The name would be Dorothy Breur. I already have a resume I sent into the Adolphus Agency with a request for an interview."

Dick laughed. "Well, you won't have to worry about getting hired. I doubt they're going to take a woman seriously. But the interview ought to be interesting. You'll have to fill me in afterward. I'll get the license this afternoon and express-mail it to your office. You'll have it by tomorrow afternoon."

157

Dorothy was always surprised how readily her father could assent to an illegal request, and how fast he could secure documents. Getting caught doing that kind of thing didn't seem to bother him in the least. It was all about protecting his precious daughter. On that principle, he was bullish. And even though she hated the lectures her father seemed compelled to deliver when he sensed she was in danger, she knew she would be bitterly disappointed if he didn't care enough to roar at her, at least once in a while.

Chapter Thirteen

A few days later, Dorothy left the house and headed north in her Lexus to Wilkes-Barre. If not so intent on her mission, she would have been able to appreciate the delicious weather. The sky was crystal clear, the humidity, usually an issue in the Poconos, was low, and there was a cool breeze from the north. The drive to the Wilkes-Barre business district would take her through large expanses of greenbelt, those forests protected, at least for now, from greedy developers.

The Poconos were evolving yet again. For years, Philadelphia and New York residents saw no point in venturing there and ignored them. The mountains did not have enough vertical to afford world class skiing, and the few resorts in the area were seedy, designed to attract low-income honeymooners with gimmicks like heart-shaped beds and whirlpools. Scranton and Wilkes-Barre, the nearest cities, were prime examples of urban blight, hopelessly polluted, home to underpaid coal miners who were destined to die lingering deaths from black lung. People of means in New York and Philadelphia vacationed at the Jersey shore or on Long Island, and for those who wanted the mountains, the Catskills and Berkshires had much more to offer.

The Pocono renaissance began in the 1970s, when some clever developers took advantage of the cheap land and the wooded lakes to set up a few vacation communities. With disposable income and the baby boomers came an increased de-

159

mand for vacation properties. The slow trickle of young families looking for a bargain retreat turned into a substantial flow when Interstate 80 opened access from the highly populated New York and North Jersey cities and suburbs. And that flow became a torrent with the arrival of legalized gambling in Pennsylvania. Shopping centers, restaurants, hotels, casinos, and every facet of "civilization" sprouted up along the main avenues of the Pocono cities.

Philip and Dorothy had managed to find a home off the beaten path to maintain their privacy, but driving and shopping in the area was a lot like being in the New York or Philly suburbs. In the meantime, Wilkes-Barre and Scranton managed to change their identity. While environmentalists cleaned up the air and water, new businesses came into the area, bringing an economic resurgence in which the citizenry took great pride. With more workers came more demand for health care.

Not only was the population growing apace, but patients were no longer willing to drive hundreds of miles to access high quality care, so hospitals in the region developed tertiary care programs like open heart surgery and joint replacement. The facilities began to outstrip the supply of medical personnel who were willing to settle in the region. Hospitals and practices grew quickly and began to entice medical graduates from the big cities. The small hospitals became large medical complexes that effectively choked off referrals to the Philadelphia and New York medical centers. Pennsylvania even decided to fund a new medical school in Scranton to ensure a supply of new physicians for years to come.

All this growth created a nursing crisis. Experienced nurses were at a premium, and hospitals were willing to pay handsomely for skilled staff. It became clear that the hospitals would never be able to hire enough of their own nurses, so a number of agencies opened businesses in the area. They supplied hospitals with nurses in specialty areas, like intensive care and pediatrics. Agency nurses were paid better than regular staff in exchange for moving from place to place and doing shift work. The model worked well, but even with all of this activity, there were never enough nurses to go around.

Into this void stepped the Adolphus Nursing Agency. The office was housed in a single-occupancy bungalow set back off the main drag in Wilkes-Barre on a nicely sized tree-lined lot that afforded privacy. The place looked a lot like the description of Brenda's home, modest and neat with some nice landscaping.

Dorothy pulled into the small parking lot next to a late-model white Subaru station wagon parked near the entrance that Dorothy assumed was Brenda's. The antiquated bumper sticker, "Nurse on Board" provided a clue.

Dorothy had prepared herself well, and felt she could pull off her masquerade. But she wasn't taking anything lightly. If Brenda and her band of merry men were murderers, they would be wary of anyone who came seeking information. Dorothy made sure to arrive a little early, just as she assumed a nice girl like Dorothy Breur would. Breur was the name of a classmate from law school. Dorothy had been careful to select a name that sounded German. And she liked to keep her own first name when she used an alias—it cut down on the chances that she would slip.

Dorothy introduced herself to the male receptionist who asked to see her identification and then to be seated. Ms. Straub would be with her in just a moment. Dorothy wondered how this nice-looking young guy fit into the agency. Her musing didn't last long because, true to his word, Brenda Straub emerged just a few minutes later to greet Dorothy.

"Ms. Breur, hello, I'm Brenda Straub. Nice to meet you."

Dorothy sized Brenda up quickly. Her dad had been right: attractive, petite, but forceful and confident. Long hair pulled back into a bun, casual clothes, neat and professional. Nice smile, good dental hygiene. More like a successful businessperson than a nurse.

Big smile. "Hi, Ms. Straub. Thanks so much for taking the time to meet with me."

"Not at all. Thank you for your interest in our agency. Come on back to my office. Can I offer you a beverage?"

Good manners, disarming personality. All the hallmarks of an experienced interviewer. This was going to be a tough cookie. "No, but thanks for offering."

Brenda's office was modest but had room for an oblong table at the far end for conferences and interviews, to which she beckoned Dorothy. Spartan furnishings. No photos. Pretty generic, again not much to help the profiling.

"May I call you Dorothy?" Brenda asked. Before Dorothy could answer, Brenda added, "and please call me Brenda—everybody does. Ms. Straub is much too formal."

"Sure," Dorothy agreed. So far, Brenda was manipulating the meeting. Dorothy knew that she would have to reverse that if she was going to walk out with any useful information. "I'm really anxious to learn more about Adolphus," she said trying to sound eager.

"Of course, that's why you're here. After our chat, I'll make sure you have some of our literature. I've been over your resumé and it's very impressive. I see you went to school and have worked in the Midwest. What brings you to this area?"

Dorothy knew this was coming and regurgitated her pre-fabricated story about returning to be near her elderly family, who lived in the area. "They're getting to an age where I really want to be nearby to help out."

"How did you hear about us?" Brenda asked innocently. "We haven't been advertising in nursing journals recently."

"A woman I went to school with worked with one of your nurses and mentioned how expert he was in cardiac. I'm interested in learning and doing more in cardiology, so I thought I'd give you a call." Dorothy wondered how well she was reciting her rehearsed answers, and how convincing she sounded.

"How much experience do you have in cardiac nursing, Dorothy?" Brenda asked.

"I spent two years working on a telemetry floor in a small hospital in Michigan. We saw some pretty sick heart patients there because we didn't have a dedicated cardiac ICU. I really loved it. It felt like we were really doing some good for the patients, unlike a lot of other areas of medicine."

"I see," said Brenda pensively, chin on hand, supposedly pondering how Dorothy might fit into a job with Adolphus. Dorothy knew Brenda was not going to offer her a position, and that the interview was a courtesy. On the other hand, Dorothy wasn't going to submit an application and give Brenda a chance to check references that didn't exist.

After a few more cursory background questions, Brenda asked, "And what can I tell you about Adolphus?"

This was Dorothy's opportunity. She had to learn as much as possible without appearing overly anxious. She needed a can-opener question.

"Well, one thing I noticed was that most of your nurses are male—that's pretty unusual in this field."

"It is," Brenda responded without a pause. "Is that a problem from your perspective?"

"Only if it makes it harder to get a job with your agency," Dorothy answered.

Brenda smiled reassuringly. "That is a common concern. I always find it ironic that qualified women worry about getting a nursing job because of gender bias. I can promise you that isn't a problem here at Adolphus. We are always looking for new talent, regardless of sex."

Dorothy pretended relief. "Well, that's good to hear. You have to admit that most nursing agencies are not so heavily male. How did that come about?"

"It's a long story," Brenda began. Dorothy was afraid the explanation would stop there, but Brenda continued. "I met many of the nurses who work for me when we were together in the service."

"That's interesting—you were in the military?"

"Yes, I was a colonel in the Army Nurse Corps, and many of the nurses in my company came to work for me when I set up Adolphus. And my Army company at the time happened to be mostly men."

Dorothy was far from satisfied with this explanation. She knew about Brenda's military background and wanted more, but she was afraid to push Brenda too hard lest the conversation end. She probed a bit further.

"So how did you choose this area for your agency?"

"That's easy. It's home. Most of my family is still here. I know the area, and I thought that I understood the healthcare market well enough to set up a successful nursing operation. And I knew there was a dearth of good cardiovascular nurses in the area, despite the fact that there was a dramatic increase in the CV market here."

"Because so many people have cardiovascular disease?"

"Yes, and because it's lucrative. Hospitals that have big cardiac programs do well financially. Naturally, the area hospitals decided to open large CV programs but seemed to forget that they didn't have the nursing infrastructure to support their units."

"And how did you come up with the name Adolphus?"

"My father's name was Adolph. He encouraged me to open the business and helped me get started. I wanted to honor his memory."

Dorothy could see that Brenda was getting into the discussion, and was enjoying the chance to show off what she had accomplished. This was the perfect way to draw out some important information, but so far Dorothy wasn't getting much she didn't already have.

"So you were able to fill a niche with your agency?" Dorothy asked.

"Yes, and that was gratifying. But I also love the field. It's so interesting. Cardiology has come a long way in the last twenty years, and it will continue to move quickly, I think. The new technology gives us so many new and important ways to benefit our patients."

Dorothy had turned the tide of the conversation so that Brenda was now being interviewed. She wondered if Brenda realized it and was just going with the flow, or had she been successful in turning the tables without Brenda's being aware? Dorothy could see little down-side to continuing her questions.

"What else attracted you to cardiology?"

"I was also impressed with how many new ways there are to treat patients with cardiac conditions. Drugs and devices in particular, and we've tried to make pharmacology a point of emphasis for our agency."

"That sounds like an important idea given how complicated some of the new drugs can be—not like the old days."

Brenda bit on Dorothy's bait. "Well, it isn't just the new drugs that are complicated and can create trouble. We have a lot of people in hospitals who don't know enough about the drugs we've been using for years."

"That's pretty scary. You hear all of the time about medical mistakes and patients dying because of them. I'm sure a lot of those are medication errors."

"No doubt," Brenda nodded. "And the only way to prevent them from happening is rigorous education. We have regular classes for all of our nurses on cardiac pharmacology. We review all of the drugs and make sure they understand dosing and toxicity. They really need to know side effects of commonly used drugs and how to deal with them quickly. It's costly and we pay for it out of our profits, but we think it's worth it."

"I remember the doctors at my last hospital complaining about how hard it was to treat congestive heart failure. Has that been your experience at the hospitals Adolphus serves?"

Dorothy was hoping that a discussion of congestive heart failure would segue into digitalis, a drug used for years to treat patients with cardiac decompensation. She wanted to know Brenda's views and hoped that discussing digitalis would elicit something important.

"Yes, heart failure is a terrible disease and hard to treat. Patients really suffer and can be so terribly crippled. People don't realize that it has a worse prognosis than most cancers. And I really hate to see patients not able to breathe or do even simple tasks."

Dorothy nodded. "It seems like it would be better to die suddenly than to have to sit around and be so miserable for so long."

Brenda shifted in her chair and re-crossed her legs. Dorothy couldn't tell if she was uncomfortable with the last observation, but she continued her musings. "I have noticed that patients with heart failure are brittle. Almost anything you give them can hurt them if not administered carefully and at the correct dose."

Dorothy took advantage of the turn in the conversation. "I remember that my professor in nursing school used digoxin as her example of a drug that has that kind of problem. A good drug, but dangerous if given in excess or to the wrong patient."

Brenda pursed her lips. Otherwise, she registered no reaction. "That's a good example. Older patients with kidney problems are particularly vulnerable."

Dorothy pushed harder. "My professor showed us some wicked cardiac arrhythmias that resulted from digoxin toxicity. I know that they can be very hard to treat and can be lethal."

"Fortunately, our doctors don't use that drug as much as they used to, and when they do, they know to use low doses. But we've trained our nurses to be vigilant and to make sure that patients on digoxin have their electrolytes carefully balanced."

"That's always a good idea," Dorothy said. "It must be a terrible thing to see a patient die because of a medical mistake."

She tried to lean on her legal experience to draw Brenda out with an actual case she had reviewed for her law firm. "I saw it happen once, and the staff really never got over it. A nursing student transported a patient for a test on a stretcher and took him off the pump that controlled the amount of drug he was getting IV. She thought it would be easier to move him. Well, the poor old guy got a full bag of lidocaine and went asystolic—heart rate went to ten and there was nothing we could do to get his heart restarted. When the family found out, they sued everybody and won a big verdict."

Dorothy regretted the last sentence. It made her sound more like a lawyer than a nurse. Brenda didn't seem to notice.

"Unfortunately, medical mistakes are pretty common, especially with drugs like lidocaine. I've seen it myself. Now hospitals have a responsibility to report them to the state in Pennsylvania. When families find out, they inevitably sue no matter what the situation is. Even when the patients are old, like your example, and are bound to die from their disease anyway. It's a bad situation all around."

"I know the nursing student took it very hard," Dorothy observed. "I'm not sure she ever got over it."

Brenda nodded and changed the subject. "What else can I tell you about the job, Dorothy? I'm sure you will want to know about salary, benefits, shift assignments, and things like that. Most of it will be in the paperwork my secretary will give you before you leave, but if you have any questions, call me and we can go over it."

Brenda paused, and seemed to make a decision to go a bit further.

"You need to know that I run a very tight ship here. I take responsibility for just about every aspect of management and personally supervise everything. I guess you can call me a control freak, but I believe this agency has prospered because of the way I have managed it over the years. I'm really proud of how successful we've been."

Dorothy nodded. She could have guessed that Brenda didn't do a lot of delegating. There weren't many desks in the small administrative area, and Brenda's was cluttered with schedules and phone messages.

"And one other thing to get out front is that we pay our nurses adequately, but none of us makes a fortune. We believe that by keeping our salaries relatively low, we can be attractive to the hospitals that need us to take care of sick patients. Nobody here expects or gets a high salary for the work we do."

Dorothy took note of Brenda's candor. She wasn't sure why Brenda had made the last speech since the interview was *pro forma*. Maybe she wanted to bring the interview to a close. Dorothy had not learned as much as she had hoped about Brenda or the agency, but she was beginning to doubt Philip's theory that Adolphus was responsible for disposing of a bunch of old, sick people. She decided to probe one last time.

"My parents wanted me to get your opinion about medical care at the various hospitals in the area. They're traditional Germans who prefer to be among their own. Is there a place you can recommend that has good medical care that focuses on the needs of elderly ethnic patients?"

"I know what you mean. My parents were German too and they felt the same way. Scranton Memorial probably has the most elderly ethnic patients. There are several established Italian and German communities right around the hospital. Most of the kids, like you, have moved away, but the old folks have stayed behind. The quality of the homes is not what it used to be; they really can't afford to keep the places up. Most of the older men used to work on the homes themselves. Now they're too infirm, and they can't afford outside help. It's sad to watch the neighborhoods fall apart."

"I know. Thanks for recommending Memorial. My father fought in Korea and could go to the Veterans Hospital, but he wouldn't like it there. And my mom wants both of them to go to the same place. You know how stubborn old folks can be about things like that."

"Yes, we have to handle our ancestors gently. They gave us many opportunities, and we owe them a lot. I can certainly understand your father's attitude about the VA. It's a depressing place, especially when you consider what those old soldiers went through in the wars."

If Brenda had anything to hide, she wasn't going to give it away. Dorothy decided it was time to leave.

"Well, thanks for taking the time to speak with me. If it's OK with you, I'll take an application form and information about the agency with me, and get back to you. I have a few other jobs to look at before I decide what I want to do."

"That's fine," Brenda replied amicably. "Take your time. We don't have many positions, but if you apply, we will consider you carefully and let you know what we might be able to offer. I think you'll find our people friendly and fun to work with if you do come on board. Our top priority is to give the best care we can to our cardiac patients. It's hard but rewarding to work at a high level."

Dorothy collected papers from Brenda's secretary, said goodbye to Brenda, and walked to her car. She tried to organize her thoughts on the way home. She kept coming back to the same conclusion. Brenda Straub came across as a dedicated nurse who had set up an agency in her hometown to take care of cardiac patients. She had recruited some good people and appeared to be dedicated to her job and her employees.

When Dorothy explained her impression to Philip that evening, he went through the roof. "You were sucked in! I can't believe a small-town operator could sell my sophisticated companion a bill of goods. Wasn't there *anything* that made you suspicious?" Philip paced back and forth in the living room, obviously agitated and unhappy with Dorothy's report.

"I tried to be objective, and not assume anything. All I can tell you is that she's articulate, seems to be rightly motivated, and had all the correct answers about medical issues. I'll admit I'm not as sophisticated in medicine as you, but I didn't detect any racial or ethnic bias. In fact, she told me that she has sacrificed her own income to keep the agency competitive. She seems motivated to improve the quality of cardiac care in her old hometown."

"Sounds like a bunch of happy horseshit to me. How do you think she convinced her old army buddies to throw in on that deal and work for lower pay?"

"Do you have to be so damned cynical? Isn't it possible that these people really want to do the right thing? Does everybody have to have some evil motive for what they do?"

Philip hung his head. "Not everybody. But we have pretty impressive evidence that nurses from Mother Theresa's agency were taking care of some old men who just happened to check out from arrhythmias they shouldn't have had. Brenda must be an incredible actress to put this one over on you."

"I'm just telling you what I think."

"Well, I think I won't let this go so easily."

"What do you have in mind?" Dorothy asked warily.

"Something simple that your dear old dad can help with."

"It better not take a lot of time, cost a lot of money, or get us into trouble! I have just about had it with your amateur sleuthing, Philip. It got us into a lot of hot water in Philly, and I don't want it to happen again."

"Somehow I thought that would be your reaction. Don't worry, it won't."

Philip stormed out of the room, went to his den, and slammed the door so loudly that Mitten and Buffy jumped off the sofa. Judging from his reaction, Dorothy was sure that Philip wasn't finished with the Adolphus case. And he wasn't, not by a long shot.

Chapter Fourteen

Philip really didn't want to go back to Dorothy's father. He tried hard to like Dick Deaver, but it didn't take a genius to figure out that Dick wasn't going to accept any man who had the audacity to pursue a romantic relationship with his daughter.

Dick's wife had died shortly after Dorothy's birth. Reeling with grief, his first thought had been to pawn Dorothy off on one of his many female relatives. It hurt him just to look at his new daughter—it brought back too many memories of his wife, the only woman he had ever loved. It was only after numerous polite but firm rebuffs from his family that Dick concluded he had no recourse but to raise his child his own way.

Gradually but relentlessly, young Dorothy worked her way into his hard heart. Dick surprised everybody, including himself, by becoming a doting father. He made time for her school activities and even coached some of Dorothy's sports teams, and did so with unbridled enthusiasm.

The two became inseparable. They spent all of Dorothy's school vacations traveling or hanging out at their vacation home at the Jersey shore. Dorothy became an avid Philadelphia sports fan, rooting for (and booing) the Eagles and Phillies at the many games she and her father attended. Dick sat with Dorothy every night after dinner to make sure that all her homework was completed. He was a single parent and intended to stay that way, but he decided no one was going to accuse him of doing a lousy job of raising his daughter.

Dorothy went on to establish an outstanding record in grade and high school. Dick worried that she would choose to go away to college, and was relieved when she selected Penn, not only for undergraduate work, but also for law school. Dorothy lived in apartments in town those seven years, and Dick made sure they saw each other frequently. He had hoped that Dorothy would bring her legal expertise to his private detective firm.

After working in the office in the summers during college, Dorothy and Dick both realized that she would never join his firm. Nevertheless, she learned a good deal about surveillance and interrogation that she used frequently in her law practice. It was the thing that distinguished her from other personal injury attorneys. Knowing something about the habits of her adversary's clients had turned many cases to her advantage.

Dorothy dated occasionally in college and law school. But despite her good looks and outgoing personality, she never developed a long-term relationship with anyone. Dick liked to think that Dorothy would never find a man who could measure up to the standard he had set. There had been one period a few years back when Dorothy had someone on her mind. Dick never found out who it was, and would have been furious to know it had been Philip.

Dorothy and Philip had been attracted to each other when Philip was married, and although they only had a one-night stand, each had been obsessed with the other for months before and after. Philip and Dorothy rekindled their relationship during the Hamlin case. And now, Philip was the "other man" in Dorothy's life. Dick tried to get used to it, but he didn't have to like it.

Consequently, each exchange between Philip and Dick had an edge. Dick treated Philip like a retarded cousin. He knew he had to be civil, but intentionally dumbed down everything he said, even when he didn't have to. Philip didn't mind the simplicity when Dick talked about his detective work. But it drove Philip nuts when Dick oversimplified common knowledge, or, even worse, medical matters. Philip had managed to reduce most of his conversations with Dick to sports and weather, but still had to restrain himself when Dick delivered a valedictory on the state of the Sixers or the latest Caribbean hurricane threatening Florida.

This time Philip had no choice. He had a specific request to make of Dick, and there was no one else who could provide the service. He called Dick and suggested that he come up to the Poconos for a Saturday evening dinner and sleepover. Dick accepted. He wanted to see his daughter and spend some time with her, and this wasn't a painful way to do it.

"I do have a few questions for you when you're here, if you don't mind. I need your professional opinion."

"Sure," Dick replied warily. "As long as I have some time with Dorothy. Don't get much of a chance to see her since you moved her up there."

Dick insisted on blaming Philip for the move to the mountains though it had clearly been their joint decision to venture out of Philadelphia. Dorothy and he had both agreed it would be good to get away from the places that generated so many bad memories for both of them. Dorothy had an old law school buddy in Scranton who jumped at the chance to add an experienced lawyer to his firm, especially one who had experience in personal injury and surveillance. Philip had several choices of jobs in private medicine in the area. In the end, he took the simplest, seeing cardiology patients in a clinic in the small town of Mount Pocono.

Philip had no inpatient responsibility; he referred patients who had complicated problems to a grateful private practice in Stroudsburg. That meant he didn't have to take night or weekend call. He could set his own clinic hours, usually nine to five during the week with a few afternoons off. It was the kind of job he would have scoffed at earlier in his career. He had no respect for "docs in a box" back then, but now he understood the importance of private medicine and a job that allowed him to maintain quality in his life.

Philip thought Dick should respect his decision to seek a simpler life so he would have more time to spend with

Dorothy. Instead, Dick used it as another way of harassing Philip.

"See any interesting patients at your place this week?" Dick would ask when he ventured to the Poconos for a visit. "I guess they're pretty few and far between," he would muse as Philip seethed.

Dick knew the nature of Philip's practice. Philip saw many patients with atypical chest pain and palpitations that were not serious problems but manifestations of anxiety and depression that seemed to be ubiquitous. Trying to explain that these people needed help just like patients who had severe cardiac disease was futile, so Philip tried to ignore the barbs. Dorothy watched the interchanges, irritated by her father's orneriness, and appreciative of Philip's restraint.

"He's just a cranky old guy who hates the idea that I'm in love with another man," she would explain to Philip after her father departed.

"Yeah, I just wish he would get the hell over it. He wears me out with that stuff."

This visit with Dick started off pleasantly enough. He arrived in mid-afternoon, with enough time left to enjoy the end of a beautiful late spring day. They decided to take the dogs for a walk. They picked a trail the dogs knew well and where the hounds could be let off the leash.

Buffy and Mitten ran in and out of the woods that bordered the trail, chasing whatever wildlife they could find. They were particularly fond of squirrels that would taunt them and then dart up the nearest tree, leaving them barking in frustration. Though the water temperature was still in the fifties, the dogs didn't hesitate to swim after the treats that Philip generously tossed into the lake. They warmed themselves in the sun on the trail, intermittently sprinting and sniffing their way along. Philip and Dorothy agreed that when the dogs wagged their tails, they were "smiling" to show their pleasure—an opinion that Dick, who could care less about dogs and pets, considered rubbish.

Philip decided to hold off on the subject he wanted to discuss with Dick until cocktail hour. They bundled up in sweatshirts and settled themselves on the dock to watch the sunset. Philip asked Dick what he knew about nursing agencies.

"Not a whole hell of a lot. I recollect that Dorothy's mother had a few friends who were nurses at big hospitals in the city. From what I remember, they weren't too enthusiastic about the agency concept. I seem to remember hearing them say that the agency nurses weren't as good as the regular nurses but they got paid a hell of a lot more. Past that, I know little."

"That's a good start," Philip replied, trying to engage Dick. "Agency nurses have become an important part of the medical establishment around the country. They have filled a void for hospitals that have put in large clinical programs but don't have enough good nurses to go around."

"Especially up in this area," Dorothy chimed in. "Hospitals have tried to grow quickly to keep pace with the population growth."

"Damn if I can understand why anyone would want to live in this godforsaken place," Dick observed. "I assume you're going to get to the point of what you wanted to talk to me about?"

Philip expected this from Dick and replied calmly. "I went through the records your men helped collect, and I came across some very interesting information in the nursing notes. Dorothy and I have reason to believe that a specific nursing agency up here has been killing off old men in hospitals where they've been working."

Dick sat looking down into his drink. "I know you suspect Adolphus, but are you sure a nursing agency set out to kill a bunch of defenseless old men?"

Philip spent the next few minutes reviewing what he had learned, asking Dorothy to fill in the blanks with details about Brenda and the agency. Dick didn't interrupt but at the end of the story, his doubt had obviously turned into concern.

"I don't have any way of refuting what you have to say about the medical aspects of the case, but if what you say is true, this is a major deal. A scandal like this could have a huge impact on medical care for this entire region."

"We know," Dorothy replied. "That's why we're trying to be careful with it."

"What do the police up here have to say about all of this? Have you talked to them recently?"

"There's a Lieutenant Detweiler who's interested but doesn't think he can take what he has to his superiors. He asked us to do more to develop the case."

"That sounds pretty nuts to me," Dick observed. "You guys are amateurs. If these people are as dangerous as you say, like I told Dorothy, I don't think they would hesitate to come after you to defend themselves."

Philip appreciated Dick's reaction, and in fact was pleased that he was concerned about their safety. "We don't like it very much, either. But what choice do we have? We don't want people to get away with murder, but if we just let it go, that's exactly what is going to happen."

Dick hesitated, weighing the issues in his mind. Finally, he said, "So what do you want from me?"

Philip had his opening and didn't hesitate. "We want to know if you might be willing to assign a few of your investigators to this case. We think that all of their nurses might be involved so surveillance might get us somewhere. If they don't suspect that anyone is on to them, they'll eventually do something to expose their motive and maybe even their methods."

Dick shook his head. "Invasion of someone's privacy without cause is a serious matter, Philip. You, more than anyone, should know that. It almost landed you in jail a few years ago, as I recollect."

Dick's reference to the Hamlin case didn't surprise Philip or Dorothy. It was a vivid memory for both of them. Philip had used a unique method to eavesdrop on Hugh and Bonnie Hamlin to extract a murder confession. After the Hamlins were murdered, Philip and Dorothy had been interrogated by the police in Philadelphia and were considered important suspects.

"Not to mention that it didn't work anyway," Dick added

correctly. The confession had been rejected in court shortly before Hugh and Bonnie were drowned in the trunk of a limousine.

"Yes, we did learn something from that," Dorothy interjected. "We don't expect to get evidence that will hold up in a court of law. We just want to provide Detweiler with ammunition to take to his superiors. At that point, we're out of the case for sure."

Dick didn't respond but only shook his head.

"Dick, you can't tell me you haven't done a little gentle surveillance in situations where you knew you weren't going to get anything conclusive," Philip cajoled. "We just want to develop the case a little further before backing out. Do you really think that's so dangerous?"

"Not if it's done carefully. But the more gentle the investigation, the more likely you'll come up snake eyes," Dick answered. "I'm sure you understand that."

"We're willing to accept that as an outcome," Dorothy replied firmly. "We don't want to push the envelope by any means."

"I have a feeling that you two jokers are not going to let this go no matter what I tell you, so maybe I should provide a little help to protect you from yourselves. Tell me what you have in mind."

Philip was ready with his plan. "If your people can tail a few of the nurses, we might be able to get some idea of how they're organized. If that doesn't yield anything, maybe a little electronic eavesdropping as well, but I'm hoping that won't be necessary."

"You and me both, because wire tapping or planting a microphone is something I really don't want to do up here. My people aren't familiar with the area, and they could easily stub their toe." Dick paused. "How about if we compromise on this? I'll agree to low-level surveillance for a few days to see what we can find. I have a couple of pretty experienced guys in between cases right now, so I'll send them up. Just get me the names of a few of the nurses—we should be able to locate their residences and begin the tail there."

"Thanks, Dick," Philip said. "We really appreciate whatever you can do."

"But I'm warning you," Dick replied sternly, "If we come up with nothing, it's highly unlikely I'm going to go along with anything electronic."

Dorothy and Philip nodded and agreed. Neither wanted to push Dick further, at least for now, and jeopardize the concession he had just made. Nothing more about the case was discussed that evening. But the first thing Philip did the next morning was to call Dick's office and leave a voice mail with the names of the three male nurses he and Dorothy picked off of the Adolphus list for surveillance.

When Dick returned to his office, he prepared to send two of his middle-level investigators north. Alex Underwood and Chris Youngblood, both in their mid-thirties, had been with Dick for a few years. Chris was a retired cop who had gotten tired of the routine. He had never married, lived alone, and Dick and his firm was the only "family" he had. Alex had a degree in criminology from Penn State and had struggled to get an FBI job, never quite making the grade. He doted on his wife and kids and looked for every excuse to spend time with them.

Dick considered Alex and Chris reliable if not brilliant. More importantly, they were neither senior nor stupid enough to go beyond exactly what he asked them to do. His orders were explicit and clear: keep a close watch on the marks and try to get some information, but don't get aggressive. He would be perfectly happy to come up with nothing so he could extricate himself from his agreement with Philip and Dorothy as quickly as possible.

It turned out that the three nurses they decided to follow lived reasonably close to the agency. Alex and Chris made some preliminary observations. They discovered each was male and fairly young, and no one was married nor had children. Two rented apartments and the third owned a house on the outskirts of Scranton. Their lifestyles were modest—economy cars, conservative dress, and nothing extravagant about their residences.

All three had the same pattern of activity. When they weren't working their shifts, they stayed at home or exercised. Each liked to run or bike and used the extensive trails in the public parks on a regular basis. Alex and Chris were forced to buy some athletic wear so they could watch the nurses without looking out of place. Alex tried to keep up but Chris refused to do the fitness thing. Although he was concerned that his mark might be outside of his immediate observation for relatively long periods, Chris, an inveterate cigarette smoker with a poor diet and a sedentary lifestyle, wasn't about to chase the fitness fanatics through the woods.

Alex and Chris devised a simple method to keep the three nurses under observation as much as possible, making heavy use of their cell phones to coordinate their surveillance. They kept a motel room in the area with a king-sized bed that they shared but rarely occupied at the same time. And they decided to double-team when the nurses weren't working or sleeping, since that would be the obvious time for clandestine activity.

After three weekdays of fruitless observation, they called Dick to deliver a report. "So far, we got nothing," Alex reported. "They're about as bland a threesome as I've ever seen."

"I'm not surprised," Dick replied. "Anybody who wants a social life wouldn't bury themselves in coal country. It's where boring people go to die, I guess."

"It's dull all right," Alex agreed. "In fact, we were wondering how much longer we have to put up with this."

"Well, it's Friday. Their pattern might change for the weekend. I would say, give it till Sunday, and then we'll stop. I'll give my daughter the bad news but I'll be able to keep peace in the family, if you know what I mean."

"Anything for your family, boss," Alex spit out sarcastically. "It would be nice to get home for at least part of the weekend. My wife isn't real happy about my being away. I think the kids are getting to her."

"I understand, but ya gotta pay the light bill," Dick said and rang off.

Alex and Chris decided to intensify their weekend surveillance, but Friday night and Saturday afternoon were just as unremarkable as the week had been. Their marks worked their shifts, did some grocery shopping, and went for their usual exercise. On Saturday evening, Alex parked himself outside the residence of one of the nurses and waited. Chris was doing the same a few miles away.

The night was a little chilly, so Chris sat in his car and let the engine run to keep warm. He smoked a few cigarettes, grateful that this infernal surveillance was almost over. Shortly before 8:00 P.M., dressed in jeans and sneakers, his nurse got in his car and drove off. He took an unfamiliar route, away from the cities, traveling south toward the Poconos. Chris was careful to keep his distance, not hard to do since the nurse's taillights were easily discernible from a distance on the long stretches of vacant road.

The nurse finally drove off the main road, down a long unpaved driveway into a wooded area. Chris turned off his headlights and followed his mark into the parking lot of what appeared to be an old campsite. The nurse got out of his car and headed toward a barn across from the lot. The lighting was terrible, the only illumination coming from spotlights affixed haphazardly to the exterior of the barn, but Chris could make out a few other parked cars.

Chris drove into the woods, turned off his engine and watched as more people arrived. He got out of his car and carefully circled around the lot intending to sneak up on the building and peek through one of the barn's windows. Unfortunately, the large windows were several feet off the ground. He looked about in the dark and found some old milk crates that he piled up to use as a stool.

He edged his way up the wall and looked in. Over a large stage that had been set up in the barn, a bright red, white, and black banner had been placed. The insignia was immediately recognizable to Alex and to anyone who knew anything about Nazi Germany.

His shock was so severe that Chris lost his balance and fell backward into the underbrush around the barn. He would have injured himself if his fall had not been broken. In fact, someone had seen Chris climbing up to his precarious perch, anticipated his fall, and tried to catch him. Chris was surprised once again to see his partner Alex lying spread-eagle beneath him.

"Friend, am I glad to see you," Chris whispered breathlessly as he rolled off of Alex. "And man, you are not going to fucking believe what I just saw in there!"

Chapter Fifteen

Chris' fall knocked the wind out of Alex. All he could manage to whisper after he recovered was, "You have *got* to be kidding me."

"No shit," Chris replied breathlessly. "They have a huge fucking swastika up on the wall with a stage underneath, and there are people strutting around on the stage in Nazi uniforms!"

"Un-fucking-believable. Could you get a look at any of them?"

"No. They all had hats or helmets, and some of the fuckers even had those little shitty fake mustaches."

"What do you think we should do?" Alex asked.

"Well, I don't think those assholes in there would be real happy about us spying on their meeting, so I ain't looking in another window. I think we should book."

"Not so fast," Alex cautioned, his criminology instincts kicking in. "Isn't this what we came up here for? Don't you want to know who's in there and what they're up to?"

"I know what they're up to. They're neo-Nazi shitheads, and I don't think they're organizing a cookie sale. They're probably trying to figure out how to murder more people they don't like or don't like them. People like us who are spying on them, for example."

"We should at least call Dick and get his opinion before we bail."

"That's fine but we can't do that under this window."

They backed into the woods. Chris took out his cell phone and cursed under his breath. "No fucking coverage. Try yours."

Alex opened his flip phone. "Same damn problem—I knew I should have listened to that broad on TV and changed phone companies."

"Wouldn't have mattered. We're in the middle of fucking nowhere, buddy, and on our own. I'm telling you, those assholes scare me. There's a lot more going on up here in the sticks than we were told. I say it is time to get on the road."

Alex reluctantly agreed. "All right, we'll get out of here but can't we at least get some license plate numbers before we do?"

"I have a penlight in my car," Chris said. "I'll get it."

"Let's just wait another few minutes to make sure there are no latecomers," Alex cautioned. "You can cover me while I write down some numbers."

Ten minutes later, holding the penlight in his mouth, Alex crawled around in the dark parking lot scribbling the license numbers from about twenty cars, SUVs, and pick-up trucks. He worked quietly and quickly. They got back to their own cars and, without slamming their doors or putting on their headlights, made their way out to the road, each anxiously eyeing the rear view mirror to see if anyone followed them.

As soon as they got back to the motel room, Alex called Dick to fill him in on what they had seen and done.

"Son of a bitch!" Dick hissed into the phone. He had been sleeping soundly but it didn't take him long to wake up. "You mean to tell me that both of the nurses you were following ended up at a neo-Nazi rally in the middle of nowhere in the Poconos? What the hell is that all about?"

"Fuck if I know," Alex answered, as if he had to.

"Well, you guys did good getting those plate numbers. We will run them through our source first thing in the morning. Give them to me now so I can get started early."

"Will do boss. And if it is all the same to you, I think we will get on our horse and come home now. This place is creeping us out, and we'd both like to sleep in our own beds."

"Sure. No reason for you two to hang around."

"Great. One of the cars we've been using up here is a rental. We'll drop it off and get home before dawn."

Alex read the numbers to Dick, who wrote them down before he rang off. "Be careful getting out of there, and don't stop anywhere," he warned them before he hung up.

The last thing Alex said to Dick was, "Don't worry, we'll be on the road in a minute or two."

It took Dick a long time to settle down after the call. Once again, his daughter and her boyfriend may have unearthed major criminal behavior and were placing themselves in jeopardy. Except this time they were dragging two of his employees into it. Thank God they were on their way home.

Dick lay in bed ruminating about what to do next. First he had to find out to whom those vehicles belonged. He would run the numbers as soon as he got into the office in the morning. Then he would make sure his daughter and her idiot boyfriend went to the cops with the information. Amateur hour was over.

He finally fell asleep for what seemed like a few minutes before the phone rang again. Dick looked at the clock—it was 5:00 A.M., four hours since he had spoken with his men. He picked up the receiver, and this time it was his answering service.

"Mr. Deaver, I have a call from Mrs. Alex Underwood, who said it was urgent that you call her at home." Dick had met Darlene Underwood at a few of the firm's functions but didn't know her well. He remembered a plain and pleasant woman who couldn't stop talking about her kids. He figured this wasn't a social call, and knew he was right as soon as she came on the line.

"Mr. Deaver, I'm sorry to wake you up, but I just got a call from the Pennsylvania State Police," Darlene sobbed into the phone. "They said Alex's car was involved in an accident on the turnpike just south of the Lehigh Tunnel."

"Are the guys OK?"

"They wouldn't tell me. They said they were still sorting things out. They told me to call somebody to stay with me, and they would call me back when they know more."

Dick had an ominous feeling and didn't hesitate. "Do you have somebody in your family nearby who can come over now?"

"I called my sister who lives down the street. She's on her way over. Is there some way you can find out what happened to Alex?"

"You bet," Dick answered quickly. It was exactly what he was intending. "Let me phone some people I know at the State Police barracks in Allentown and I'll call you back as soon as I can."

Dick crawled out of bed and limped into his office. Damn arthritis, he thought. Getting old sucks, especially when you have to go zero to fifty in seconds. He rummaged through the top drawer of his desk and pulled out his phone directory.

Dick had done a favor for two Allentown State Police troopers when they had been accused of sexually assaulting a prostitute they had pulled over for speeding a few years ago. He was able to establish that they had been entrapped by a spiteful pimp, and cleared the guys without a penalty. He refused to take a fee for his work because he knew it gave him *carte blanche* to call the State Police for information if and when he really needed it. It was time to call in the chit.

His call was redirected a few times until he got to the shift director in Allentown, Fred Beans. Fred happened to be a close friend of the troopers who were falsely accused, and was more than happy to help Dick find out what had happened to Chris and Alex.

Dick explained that he needed some information about the crash on the Northeast Extension of the turnpike. "Yep, pretty messy from what I heard," Beans said. "Let me see if I can get some specifics for you. I need to put you on hold for a minute or two."

When he came back on the line, Fred didn't have good

news. "As best we can tell, Mr. Deaver, a car owned by Alex Underwood with two front seat passengers was smashed up against the median strip just south of the Lehigh Tunnel."

"How did it happen?"

"A tractor-trailer swerved into their lane. Their car had nowhere to go apparently. They got pushed into the concrete barrier. The car turned over a couple of times and caught fire. Your guys never had a chance."

"They're both dead?"

"I'm afraid so. Sorry to be the one to tell you."

Dick paused to absorb this confirmation of his fears.

"Underwoods's wife was told that the State Police didn't know what happened."

"We didn't tell Underwood's family because at that point the guys at the scene couldn't make a positive identification on the burned bodies. That will still take a while. But since there wasn't anybody else in the car, we have to assume Mr. Underwood was involved. I am giving you this information as a favor, Mr. Deaver."

"I know, Fred, and I appreciate that. You will probably find that the passenger was a guy named Chris Youngblood. Do you know who was driving the truck?"

"I don't. The truck had been stolen from a rest stop a few minutes before the accident. It jackknifed after the crash and the driver got away on foot. The police are scouring the area but they haven't found him yet. There's an access road nearby, so they're afraid somebody might have picked the driver up and gotten away clean."

"So you think this was a planned hit?"

"Certainly looks that way. There didn't appear to be any reason for the accident. A witness said that the truck just came over and nailed the car. The precision of the hit and the use of a stolen truck make it look like they were set up."

Dick agreed—he just didn't want to admit it to himself. He had sent two of his nicest guys upstate, and they weren't coming home.

Dick called Darlene and told her that she would be getting

a call from the State Police but that it didn't look particularly good. "Darlene, I don't think they survived the accident. And I'm afraid it might have been murder."

By the time he finished, Darlene was nearly hysterical. "Who would want to kill my Alex?"

"I don't know, but it could have something to do with the matter they were investigating. They might have run into some dangerous people up north. But I promise you this: I will make it my business to find out who did this, and I will make them pay."

A promise of revenge was of no particular comfort to Darlene Youngblood at that moment. Dick told her that he would keep in touch with her and offer whatever financial help she needed. After he finished his call with Darlene, he figured it was time for Philip to get up.

The phone call jolted Philip awake. At first, he thought his alarm had gone off, but repeatedly hitting the alarm button didn't make the noise stop. When he finally realized it was the phone, he wondered if the hospital might be calling, but then remembered that his on-call days were long over.

After a few more rings, Dorothy nudged him. "Answer the phone, Philip. It's disturbing the dogs."

He pulled the wireless receiver to his ear. "Philip, this is Dick Deaver. I have some bad news for you."

Philip sat upright on the side of the bed, surprised to hear Dick's voice so early in the morning. "What is it?"

Dick told Philip about the Nazi rally attended by at least two of the nurses who worked at the Adolphus agency. With a lump in his throat, he went on to tell Philip about the turnpike crash that had killed two of his men.

Philip was struck dumb but Dick was just getting started. "I am really unhappy about this, Philip. Let's say, I am royally pissed off. This has now become personal. I want to crucify the motherfuckers who murdered my guys."

"I understand, Dick," Philip finally managed. He walked out of the bedroom so as not to disturb Dorothy or the dogs, and paced the kitchen, his feet slapping the cold hardwood floor. "You have every right to be pissed off, but we have to stay focused. What your guys found is major. It may give us a motive for what those nurses have been doing up here."

"Don't you think I know that?" Dick replied impatiently. "But to tell you the truth, I don't give a shit about motives."

"So what should we do next?"

"First of all, there is no *we* to worry about anymore, friend. This case is now way past amateur level."

"I don't understand."

"I didn't expect you to. Shake off the cobwebs and think about what this means. If the skinheads fingered my guys, it won't take them long to connect them to me and you—and my daughter, of course. So you guys are out of it. I'll be taking over from here."

"I see your point. But can you please tell me what you plan to do?"

"I have to run those plates. I expect that will take us to several more of the agency nurses. And then your Lieutenant Detweiler and I are going to have a come-to-Jesus meeting."

"And what do you think he'll do?"

"The right thing, I hope. For all of our sakes. Because if that SOB keeps dragging his feet, I'll have to do something about this myself."

Dick hung up, promising Philip that he would call back later in the day when he had more information. Dick tried to go back to sleep but after tossing and turning for an hour, he decided to get busy. He drove to his office and emailed the license plate numbers to his friends at the DMV. Within minutes, Dick had the names of the car owners. A quick visit to the Adolphus website proved that his men had been correct. Of the twenty-three license plates, sixteen belonged to Adolphus nurses. He also wasn't surprised to find that Brenda Straub was the only woman among the attendees.

Next he called Lieutenant Detweiler's office and left a message on his voicemail. The return call came within minutes.

"What can I do for you, Mr. Deaver?"

"You don't know me, Lieutenant, but you know my daughter, Dorothy."

"I thought the name sounded familiar."

"Well then you will remember that my daughter and Philip Sarkis talked to you about some deaths that occurred in hospitals in your region."

"Of course I remember. My recollection is that they had some preliminary information but nothing definitive."

"Right, and you encouraged them to go ahead and develop the case further?"

Detweiler paused before answering defensively. "I really didn't have a choice. Nothing they had amounted to much."

"Well, because of your advice, some really awful things have happened, and now I fear for my daughter's safety."

"Awful things? I have no idea what you are talking about."

"Look, Lieutenant, this isn't going to play too well on the telephone. I'm willing to drive up there this afternoon and meet with you."

"That would be fine, Mr. Deaver. I can meet you in my office, say about three o'clock?"

"I'll be there."

Dick's anger over Detweiler's empowerment of his daughter and her idiot partner was overflowing as he drove out of Philly and made it to the turnpike. As he headed north, he alternated between paranoia whenever he saw a tractor-trailer and uncertainty about Detweiler's passive behavior. Why had Detweiler chosen to let amateurs stay involved with such a difficult case? Why had he encouraged them to ask questions and expose themselves to the danger of confronting an organized group of criminals? It didn't make sense. Maybe that was the way they did things in the boonies, but it sure didn't sound like something a good policeman would countenance. Was Detweiler lazy or moronic, or did he have another agenda?

Dick gulped hard as he approached the tunnel and could see where crews had already completed emergency repairs to the median barrier. When he finally arrived in Scranton, he parked his car in the municipal lot, and walked to Detweiler's office while he steeled himself for the meeting. He tried to remember to stay under control. Detweiler was a veteran who undoubtedly had good reasons for what he had recommended. Besides, if Dick lost his temper, Detweiler would clam up and Dick wouldn't get what he needed.

Detweiler greeted him in the vestibule and took him back to his cluttered office, once again removing files from the chair so Dick could sit down.

"Before we start," Detweiler began, "I want you to know that I heard about your men who died on the turnpike this morning. I assume that's why you're here."

Dick was impressed with Detweiler's homework, but his anger was not assuaged. "You're damn right. I'm very upset about what happened to them."

"And I assume this has something to do with the case your daughter and her friend told me about a few weeks ago."

"You bet it does. As you know, they suspect that the Adolphus Agency is behind the death of those poor old people in the hospital. They asked me to do some informal surveillance of a few of the nurses to see if we could learn anything. It was all completely legal, of course."

Detweiler merely nodded and let Dick go on.

"My men found a bunch of nurses from that agency attending a neo-Nazi rally at a barn in the middle of nowhere near Blakeslee. They called me with the license plate numbers of the cars in the parking lot, and then started home."

"And never made it," Detweiler concluded.

"Right. I ran those numbers this morning and almost every one matched to nurses who work for Adolphus, including the bitch who runs the place, Brenda Straub."

"Did your guys ID any of the people at the meeting?"

"No. They were afraid to hang around once they figured out what they were dealing with. I think they did the right thing, and there can't be any argument about who attended, unless you're going to tell me that all of the nurses lent their cars to bad guys while they were home knitting."

"I was just hoping they actually fingered a few of them."

"Well, they obviously hit a nerve, or they wouldn't have been roasted in their car on the turnpike. I'm sure you heard that the truck that hit them was stolen and that the State Police can't find the driver, who was probably picked up by his accomplices. Looks like a professional hit to me."

"But not easily traceable to the nurses, I'm afraid," Detweiler said, leaning back in his desk chair.

"Lieutenant, what do you want? A confession from Straub?" Dick asked. "Shortly after my men identified a group of killer skinheads at a rally, they get rubbed out on the turnpike. I would say you have something to bring to your superiors. Maybe even enough to arrest the SOBs?"

"Mr. Deaver, you are an experienced investigator. I think you are reacting emotionally. I don't disagree that I need to put this all together and vet it with my superiors. I just don't know if they're going to want to run with it yet. They might want more evidence before we arrest anybody."

"More evidence? Well, good luck. It seems to me that this is a very well organized and successful group of killers. I doubt they have been sprinkling breadcrumbs along the path for you to follow."

"Well, Mr. Deaver, you have dealt with scumbags like this. What would you suggest we do?"

"First of all, this is a brand of bad guy I haven't had to deal with very often. However, I would bring Ms. Straub in for a little sit-down. I doubt that she has had much experience with police interrogation, and I bet that a good sweating would get some information out of her."

"I'm reluctant to do that until I can actually charge her with something. Otherwise, she'll just call an attorney and walk."

"Look, Lieutenant, I have a lot of skin in this game. First of all, I sent two of my men up here on a low-level stakeout. I told them they were probably dealing with a bunch of fairies who may have convinced themselves it was OK to play God and kill some defenseless old people. They walked into a hornet's nest and were murdered. And it won't take long for that witch Straub and her band of merry men to figure out that my daughter and her naïve partner are involved in this damn case. We have already seen what they like to do to people who get in their way. So, I want you to do something, and I want it done now."

It was clear from Dick's expression that he wasn't going to take no for an answer. "I understand, Mr. Deaver, and you have my word that I will take this to my captain today. In the meantime, I recommend police protection for your daughter. I suspect that would make you feel better. And I'll get back to you as soon as I can to let you know what is going on here."

"Yeah, if you can send a cruiser by her house in Lake Naomi, that would be good," Dick said, partially assuaged. "But I don't want to tell her she is being guarded. She would probably refuse, and it would just scare the hell out of her and Sarkis."

"Consider it done."

"I'm willing to give you a little time to figure out what to do, but I don't want this to drag out. Those pricks know someone is on to them, and I doubt they're going to sit around and wait for our next move."

"Look, Mr. Deaver, I don't doubt you. Your firm has a mighty fine reputation in Philly for working closely and well with law enforcement. Obviously, you know that we have to take this through channels if we want to have a prayer of nailing the bad guys, and making it stick."

As he walked back to his car after his frustrating meeting with Detweiler, Dick tried to place the case in perspective. First of all, Detweiler had already checked on Deaver and his firm and was favorably impressed. Dick knew when he was being placated, but he also tried to put himself in Detweiler's shoes. This was a police lieutenant who worked in a pretty sleepy town in northeastern Pennsylvania. He was being told of a massive conspiracy to kill dozens or even hundreds of people, based on little hard evidence. The fact that some of the nurses happened to be right-wing fascists didn't necessarily make them guilty of murder.

Dick understood that Detweiler was going to have to handle the case carefully. It was a political bomb and if it went off, it could destroy not just the case, but Detweiler and Deaver as well, not to mention his daughter and her idiot boyfriend. The reputations of the local hospitals would be damaged and since they were the leading employers in the area, the economic implications were vast.

But Dick's paternal instinct was such that he couldn't let Detweiler just go through channels at the usual snail's pace. And he had little confidence that police surveillance at his daughter's home would be adequate to protect her and her dimwitted live-in. He decided to go ahead with the other appointment he had set up in Wilkes-Barre, and all he could do was hope that the meeting wouldn't lead to another turnpike fatality.

Chapter Sixteen

Dick really didn't know what to expect from his meeting with Brenda. He didn't have a lot of medical knowledge or experience. His late wife, Jane, had worked in a doctor's office and taught him a few things, but when she was alive, she didn't bring her work home with her much. He knew that she had been concerned about the patients, so the idea of nurses who were inclined to murder their patients just pissed him off even more. On the other hand, if he wanted to learn anything important from Brenda, he knew he had to go into the interview without an attitude.

Dick had decided to pose as an official from Wilkes-Barre General who was interested in expanding the business of the Adolphus Agency at his institution. He knew that any self-respecting manager, no matter how successful his or her business, would have a tough time saying no to a new opportunity. Since most hospitals had dozens of administrators, he didn't have to worry about a complicated alias. Brenda would just assume that he was another middle-level manager carrying out a task about which he knew less than she.

Dick also wanted to look the part of an administrator so he could get in the door. His customary jeans and corduroy jacket was not the dress of a hospital employee with aspirations. Fortunately, he had one blue serge suit, bought in a department store, and poorly tailored. He hauled it out when he couldn't get out of going to somebody's funeral or when he had to testify in court, a task he avoided assiduously. With a cheap white shirt and a striped necktie, he would look like the dozens of drones who worked at dead-end hospital jobs to pay the rent. Sure, he had gray hair and a beard, but Dick kept himself in good shape for the ladies and looked at least ten years younger than he was. And Dick would be damned if he was going to shave his beard like some damn method actor.

Dick changed clothes at a rest stop and arrived on time for the appointment he had made with Brenda's secretary. Brenda greeted Dick cordially at the door to her inner office. "Mr. Dickson, is it? Hi, I'm Brenda Straub. Nice to meet you—come on back. May I offer you a beverage?"

As he sat in the chair in front of Brenda's desk, Dick offered Brenda a hospital business card, something it had taken precisely five minutes for Al Kenworthy, his office guy, to shoot off the printer. "No thanks, Ms. Straub. I do appreciate your willingness to meet with me. Perhaps I should clarify why I'm here and taking your time?"

Brenda interrupted, "No need to apologize. I'm always open to the idea of expanding our business opportunities at area hospitals." Brenda seated herself at her desk.

Dick started by probing the Adolphus business plan. "Our hospital has been very impressed with the quality of your nurses over the years, Ms. Straub. How have you managed to recruit such a stellar group and keep them on the job?"

"The pay is fair, the benefits are excellent, and we share a common philosophy of patient care."

"Interesting," Dick answered. "And what might that philosophy be?"

"Simple, really. High technical skill combined with a real feeling for the patients as people."

"That's important, I will agree."

Brenda seemed willing to chat about her successful enterprise. Dick felt like he was making some progress. "We feel strongly about nurses spending time with patients and their families. And doing the things that nurses don't seem to want to do anymore, like giving baths and massages, changing beds, and just sitting and talking to the patients and families."

"That's laudable, Ms. Straub, and I'm sure it makes a big

difference. It sounds like you have a good close-knit group of nurses here."

"I like to think so."

"Do they do things together outside of the hospital as well?"

"You mean like going to sporting events, or having parties? Yes, I think some of them do hang out together. They all work different shifts, at different places, so it is hard to organize outings, but I have heard about a few gatherings."

"That's terrific. It has to help morale to share experiences outside of the workplace."

Brenda paused. Her facial expression changed from friendly to wary in a microsecond. "Is this going somewhere, Mr. Dickson?"

Dick had to handle the next conversation turn carefully or risk being exposed. "I don't know. Maybe. Just trying to get a handle on what your nurses are like outside of the workplace."

"Why is that an issue, Mr. Dickson? That is your name, is it not? Maybe you should show me an ID from your hospital before we go any further."

Dick didn't have a hospital badge but didn't see much of a point in continuing the charade. "Well, Ms. Straub, I'm afraid you got me. No, that's not my name. Fact is, my name is Dick Deaver and I'm a private investigator from Philadelphia. Two of my employees were recently killed in a crash on the northeast extension, and I'm up here trying to find out if it was an accident or murder."

Brenda looked incredulous. "Why on earth are you talking to me about that, and why did you use an alias to get in here?"

Dick smiled. "I didn't think you would let me in here if you knew what I was really interested in. My men weren't up here to ski Camelback, Ms. Straub. They were working a case, and I think that's what got them killed."

"You still haven't explained what that has to do with me and my agency," Brenda hissed.

"I'm getting there, Ms. Straub. They were investigating a clandestine meeting of neo-Nazis up here. From the license plate numbers in the parking lot, a number of your male nurses were in attendance. I assume they weren't there to provide first aid to the membership."

"I still don't understand why you're here. You can't believe I have any control over my employees' politics. They're big boys and girls and can do what they wish with their free time."

"And I'm sure you know there are good reasons why the political orientation of your staff might be important to a murder investigation. I would also like to know what you thought about the meeting yourself and where you went afterwards."

"I think we're done, Mr. Deaver, or whatever your name is. Our meeting is over."

"That's fine, Ms. Straub, but I hope you don't think you've heard the last of this. I suspect some other people might want to ask you questions."

"And they will get the same answers. I have nothing to hide, and you're not going to intimidate me with this nonsense."

Brenda rose from her chair and leaned forward on her desk. "And if the reputation of this firm is harmed by your unfounded allegations, I will come after you and any other warped people you work with, of that you can be sure."

"As you wish, Ms. Straub. And you're absolutely right, this investigation may go nowhere—and I will have no problem with that. I know there will always be sickos in the world, and I'm not going to play the caped crusader. But I do have one caution for you, Ms. Straub, one line you will not cross."

Brenda stood up and crossed her arms. "And what might that be, Mr. Deaver?"

It was Dick's turn to rise from his chair, but he moved around it, holding the back casually, fixing Brenda in his stare.

"My daughter is named Dorothy Deaver. She is an attorney here in Scranton. Let's just say that she has been involved peripherally in the investigation of this case. Regardless of the outcome of anybody's investigation of you or your little operation, I can assure you, Ms. Straub, that if Dorothy were to be harmed in any way, I will come after you, and what I do to you will make your skinhead shenanigans look like a walk in the park. You got that?"

"Like I said, Mr. Deaver, I have absolutely no idea what you are talking about. I never heard of your daughter and this interview is over. It is time for you to leave."

"It's been a real pleasure, Ms. Straub. No need to show me out."

As Dick left the building and drove out of the agency parking lot, he called Dorothy and suggested a meeting at her house. Dorothy was just leaving her office and knew Philip would be back from walking the dogs shortly.

"That sounds good, Dad. Philip has been keeping me current through the day by email. I can't believe what happened to your men on the turnpike."

Dick decided not to get into the details. He didn't know how much Philip had told his daughter.

Dorothy continued, "I have some extra fish in the fridge so maybe you can stick around and have an early dinner while we sort everything out."

When Philip walked into the house from the late-afternoon chill, he was surprised to see Dick sitting on the sofa. "Dick, I thought that was your car out in the driveway. What are you doing up here in the middle of the work week?"

"I wanted to tell you about my meetings today with Detweiler and the ice queen, Brenda Straub."

"Why did you go to see Straub?" Philip asked as he took a seat across from Dick. Mitten and Buffy jumped onto the sofa and put their paws on Dick's lap, expecting new information. They were also happy when anybody gave them pets or treats, and Dick was happy to oblige. The doggies sat upright with tails and ears cocked, ready for the details.

"After my chat with Detweiler, I realized that I needed to talk to the bitch. Let's just say I wanted to warn her," Dick explained.

"About what?" Dorothy asked from the kitchen, suddenly very engaged in the conversation.

"Detweiler is still dragging his feet, even with the murder of my two men, and I wanted Straub to know what would happen if she went after anybody else I care about."

"Was that a good idea, Dick?" Philip asked.

"She's already onto us, so what's the difference? I think all of those assholes need to know there will be repercussions if they continue their terrorist attacks."

Dorothy could sense that her father and Philip were heading for an argument, so she chimed in, "Philip, before we start dissecting the case and going off on all these tangents, we have some chores. Dad is staying for dinner, so I need you to fire up the grill while I marinate some salmon."

Fortunately, Philip picked up on Dorothy's intentional stall. "OK, we obviously need time to sort things out. Dick, how about a beer? I have some good Mexican stuff out in the garage refrigerator."

Dinner as well as its preparation went smoothly, as all three steered clear of the obvious issues. When coffee was served around the dining room table, Philip started back in. "I think it would be a good idea to summarize where we are with the case. I'll take notes and put it into a brief for our use only."

"For God's sake, Philip, be careful with any documents you draft," Dick warned. "If they get into the wrong hands, we'll all be in hot water."

Philip suppressed his typical reaction to Dick's instructions. "Correct. We'll be careful with anything we write down. Now, Dorothy, do you want to start?"

After a heavy sigh, Dorothy began. "We now have several elderly men who died of an unexpected and previously undiagnosed cardiac arrhythmia in one of the area hospitals over the last four years. There may be more cases, but we elected to discount all of the questionable ones."

"And what ties these cases together?" Dick asked rhetorically.

"In addition to their advanced age, all of them were second-generation German or Italian, and all had fought for the

Allies in World War II."

Philip added, "And each of them had arrhythmias that could have been caused by digitalis."

"How sure are you about that, Philip?" Dick challenged. "How do you know the heart stuff wasn't caused by something else? Weren't they all old enough to have a lot of clogged arteries?"

"That's where the chart reviews were so important. In each case, the victims were poisoned gradually, which means they had arrhythmias for several hours to a few days before the terminal event. In most cases, the nursing staff was able to get recordings of the arrhythmias."

"I still don't understand how you can be certain."

"It's the constellation of arrhythmias, not any one single strip. So I would expect that digitalis poisoning, especially if done slowly, would cause the heart rate to slow a lot and to cause some nasty upper-chamber arrhythmias before the lower chambers would go crazy."

"And that's clearly the pattern you saw in the records?"

Philip stirred his coffee, trying to be patient with Dick. "Yes, there were periods of what we call advanced heart block, followed by some wild rhythms from the bottom chamber. The genius of the plan was that shocking the heart with paddles on the chest is futile."

"So there is no effective treatment for this?"

"There are some great treatments if you've made the diagnosis. For example, one of my mentors in Boston developed antibodies that can be given to people intravenously that bind to the digoxin and take it out of the circulation quickly. They work great, but again, you would have to be certain of the diagnosis before you gave the antibodies. They cost a ton and cause some hellacious side effects. The poor people taking care of these patients didn't have a clue about what they were dealing with so the antibody idea never came up."

"What about other treatments?" Dick asked.

"There are a few other drugs that might work, like lidocaine, but when you get to massive levels of digoxin, giving those drugs is like pissing in the ocean."

Dick sat back in his chair, and pushed his hand through his hair. "The more I hear about this case, the more these people frighten me. They put a lot of time and energy into this plan, and they are scary smart."

"What do you think is going to happen next?" Dorothy asked her father.

"Straub knows we are on to her and her crew, so I'm pretty sure they will lay low and not go after any more veterans, at least not for a while."

"They've already done a lot of damage," Philip said. "I have no idea how many people they actually killed in the last few years. The cases we identified may just be the tip of the iceberg."

"I don't think they believe their work is done," Dick reasoned. "They might have reached their quota here, but there are lots of other places to go in this country, and many more veterans who have to pay the price for their treason against the Fatherland."

Dorothy nodded her agreement. "That's why we have to try to stop them here. How do we know there aren't sister organizations set up in other cities with big Italian and German neighborhoods? There are still thousands of World War II vets alive and at risk, and the old guys can't protect themselves."

Dick sat forward, elbows on the table with a look of deep concern. "This is a real tough one for all of us. None of us want Brenda and her band of merry men to get away with murder, but so far, we don't have any firm evidence. On the other hand, they now know who we are and where we live, and I doubt they're going to let anybody stand in the way of their mission."

"But doesn't the fact that we have told the police about our suspicions protect us to some extent?" Philip asked. "If anything happened to us, wouldn't they be the first people to go after?"

"Of course," Dick answered. "My problem is that I haven't been overly impressed with the authorities up here. I think Detweiler is a decent guy, but his superiors look like a bunch of wimps. And I suspect they're under a good deal of pressure."

"From whom?" asked Dorothy as she rose to clear the table.

"Think about it," Dick answered quickly. "This is an economically depressed area of the country with an aging population. Jobs are at a premium. What industry up here employs the most people?"

"Health care," said Dorothy.

"Bingo. And working people pay taxes, and taxes keep the government and the police employed."

"So the last thing the politicians want is a black mark on the hospitals," Philip concluded.

"Correct. Remember that Lehigh Valley, Lancaster, Hershey, even Philly hospitals, are not that far away. That's where people used to go before the hospitals up here started doing a better job. So if the local populace loses faith in their institutions, they would leave in droves to see doctors elsewhere."

"And you think the arrest of these crackpots would cause the community to lose faith?" Dorothy wondered.

"Who knows?" Dick replied. "The politicians can't take a chance. If this thing gets out, it will make the national news and then anything could happen. I'm sure the feds would come in and start asking questions, and it would take a long time to clean up the mess."

"And hospitals compete real hard for patients," Philip pointed out. "I'm sure the competition would go out of their way to advertise to the public how good their safety record has been. People don't want second-rate health care, even if they have to drive a couple of hours to get the best."

"Do you think Detweiler is aware of the political issues?" Dorothy asked.

"He isn't a moron. He understands the issues and knows the pressures his superiors are under. Even if he wanted to do the right thing, he's too far down the chain of command, and his job is probably on the line as well."

"What can Detweiler do for us?"

"I don't really know," Dick said. "It depends on who he answers to and how much access he has to people who might want to pursue the truth. At this point, I haven't seen any evidence that there are any enlightened people in his department, but I could be wrong."

Dorothy shuffled to the kitchen and began to stack the dishwasher. "What's our next move?"

"I told Detweiler that I wanted to hear from him real soon, and I think we will hold him to that. In fact, if he doesn't get back to us tonight, we should call him from here in the morning. I want information in the next day or so."

"Does that mean you might stay with us for a few days, Dad" Dorothy asked expectantly.

Dick was conflicted. He didn't want to worry his daughter, but he wanted to do all he could to keep her safe. "I think that would be a good idea under the circumstances. I'm a little worried about you being alone, and I can't trust Detweiler to get people over here to keep an eye on you. So, yes, make the bed in the guest room, and tell those crazy dogs of yours not to keep me awake all night."

"They love you, Dad."

"They love being warm at night, and there's more room in my bed than yours."

"Something tells me you like the company, but we'll keep the door closed if you want, and we'll have a nice breakfast for you in the morning."

Dick helped Dorothy clean up the kitchen while Philip took the dogs out to the back for their evening constitutional. Philip made sure all of the lights were on in the yard and for the first time since he bought the house, looked over his shoulder and flinched at every odd sound, and there seemed to be many.

Philip loved the Poconos because of the peace it had always brought him, even in the middle of the terrible malpractice case that had cost him his career, his marriage, and his kids. Now that tranquility was threatened by a group of thugs who didn't understand that the war was over a long time ago, and that the world had moved on.

Walking along with the dogs on the leash, Philip tried to play out the myriad of possibilities. If the Adolphus Nursing Agency was in fact the front for a neo-Nazi extermination unit, and if Dick had raised an alarm during his meeting with Brenda Straub, how would the bad guys react? And to what lengths might they go to preserve their dark secret? Would they simply choose to move on to another place, or would they try to intimidate the people who suspected them? And if the latter, to what lengths might they go to protect themselves and their dirty business? And how long would it be until Philip would again feel safe with Dorothy and his dogs in his own backyard?

Philip was uneasy and he didn't like that feeling. Not one little bit.

Chapter Seventeen

The ringing of the phone jolted Philip and the dogs awake. The dogs had sniffed at Dick's door and then resigned themselves to their usual sleep venue. They were out cold—Buffy on the bed and Mitten on the floor, on her back, legs sticking straight up in the air. They had been restless through the night and had bugged him to go out a couple of times. Philip was fairly used to their routine, but last night he had stood at the door and watched the woods carefully as the dogs made their way through the trees to find just the right spot. And it had taken him much longer to get back to sleep. When the phone rang, it took him a few seconds to orient himself.

Philip picked up the phone and removed the earplugs he used on occasion. Who could have guessed that someone as feminine as Dorothy would snore like a longshoreman? The phone stopped her snoring for a few seconds, but he knew she could sleep through almost anything.

Rubbing his eyes, Philip said, "Hello."

"Dr. Sarkis, this is Lieutenant Detweiler. I got a message last night that you and Dick Deaver wanted to speak with me?"

"Yes," said Philip, trying to keep his voice down while he walked into the adjoining bathroom. "We think it would be a good idea to catch you up on what we've found out so far."

"Your father-in-law didn't sound happy on the voice message he left me, and I just talked to him yesterday."

"Dick isn't my father-in-law, at least not yet." Philip stopped short. This was one of the rare times he implied that he and Dorothy might tie the knot someday. "There's a lot more detail to discuss, and we thought it might be better to do it in person."

"When would you like to meet?"

"How about this morning?"

"Is that an invitation to breakfast?"

Philip hesitated. Dorothy liked to be prepared for company, but he wanted Detweiler's feedback as soon as possible. "Sure," he said finally. "Come on over and we'll make sure you have a nice mountain breakfast."

Detweiler happily accepted. "I should be there in an hour. And I'm not picky. I take my eggs any way you want to cook them."

"Right," Philip said half-heartedly. Finding eggs in Dorothy's kitchen was about as likely as discovering scruples in a politician. "I'll see what I can scare up."

After he rang off, Philip went to his changing closet, threw on jeans and a T-shirt, and quickly left the bedroom before the dogs noticed. He smelled the coffee immediately and knew that Dick was up and about. Dick was sitting at the kitchen table, elbows propped on the table with a coffee cup in both hands while he watched CNN on the miniature TV on the counter.

"You're up early, Dick," Philip said cheerfully.

"The older I get, the earlier I wake up. I used to lie there and try to go back to sleep, but my mind would just run crazy. So now I push myself out of bed, put on some coffee, and do something productive while my mind is fresh. By nighttime, I'm fairly worthless."

"When I worked at GMH, I did the same thing," Philip observed. "Up here, I sleep a lot more, but I'm not sure that's necessarily a better thing."

"It probably means you're relaxed. How bad can that be?"

"It ain't easy trying to be at ease with all of the crap going on."

"It's affected Dorothy, hasn't it? I haven't seen her this concerned in a long time. It usually takes a lot to rattle that girl."

"I feel bad about that," Philip said sheepishly. "I guess you could say I brought the virus home."

"You sure did." Dick refused to let Philip off the hook. "Not that you weren't warned. And I thought you would have learned your lesson from the Hamlin case."

"That was different, Dick," Philip almost whined. "I had skin in that game, and I had no choice but to get Dorothy involved."

"Maybe," Dick conceded. "You were screwed in that case for sure. But you were on the sidelines in this one and you didn't have to put your butts in jeopardy. And the bad guys here are not some dumb ass and his ditsy girlfriend. These guys are certifiable crazies on a mission."

"But you should also consider that Hugh and Bonnie killed just two people—maybe three if you count Bonnie's ex. The nut cases up here have offed... well, we really don't have any idea how many they have murdered, do we? Dozens at least. So don't you think my reaction was justified?"

Dick rose from the table and poured himself more coffee. "Get yourself a cup and stop being sanctimonious. How can you be so profound this early in the morning?"

"Damn it, Dick, Dorothy means as much to me as she does to you. It makes me sick to think I've put her in harm's way."

"Well, it's done and you can't go back. The priority now is to just let the authorities do their thing. Which is pretty much what we have to tell Detweiler."

"You're going to get your chance. Detweiler is on his way over here and he's under the impression he's getting breakfast."

"Who's coming for breakfast?" Dorothy was standing in the kitchen doorway, rubbing her eyes and yawning. It didn't take long for Mitten and Buffy to scurry in behind her, wagging their tails and begging for attention.

"They always act like they haven't seen me for days," Philip laughed as he squatted down to pet the dogs.

Dorothy frowned. "I'm still waiting for an answer."

"Oh. Detweiler is coming by soon."

"What's on his agenda so early in the morning?" Dorothy asked, shaken a bit by the impending visit by a murder detective.

"It's more like our agenda," Philip replied. "Your dad thinks, and I agree, that it's time to turn this baby over to the coppers."

"What a relief," Dorothy replied. "I have had my fill of skinheads and their extremism. What I really want is to be able to sleep soundly at night."

"Sounded like you were snoozing pretty good last night. But I understand. Any weird sound outside puts me on edge, too."

"This is no way to live," Dick agreed. "People hire me to put an end to such nonsense for them. All you guys have to do is say 'uncle' when Detweiler gets here."

The three split up for bed making, food preparation, dressing, and dog feeding. Detweiler's car pulled into the driveway about an hour later. He was greeted by the dogs that raced out the front door to meet their guest. Detweiler extended his leg to keep the dogs away. Philip remembered that Mark Twain had suggested that a person who didn't bend over or squat to pet a dog probably wasn't worth spending time with. Was this a reason not to trust this guy?

After shaking hands all around, they gathered at the dining room table where Dorothy had laid out breakfast, eggs not included. Detweiler removed his jacket and sat down before the others chose a seat.

"Mighty nice of you to make something to eat. I usually end up at Dunkin' Donuts this time of day. And I know that isn't good for me at all."

While they passed around orange juice, fruit, and bagels, there was the usual useless small talk but with little enthusiasm. Each waited for someone to get to the point.

Detweiler finally broke the ice. "Dr. Sarkis, your message implied that the three of you had reached some kind of closure on this case. Is that true?"

"Closure is an interesting way to put it, Lieutenant. I wouldn't go that far. I think it would be fair to say we've taken this project about as far as we can."

Dick cut in. "Lieutenant, as we discussed yesterday, we think you can make a strong case against Adolphus, Brenda Straub, and her henchmen."

"Right, that's what I gathered."

"And," Dick continued, "We have a real fear that these rats feel cornered and are going to continue lashing out. That turnpike accident was no accident."

"I understand, but the State Police have told me they haven't found anything new. They had to list it as a hit and run."

"You don't suspect Adolphus?"

"Sure I do. But the basic question is whether or not all this circumstantial evidence reaches some kind of threshold."

"And does it, Lieutenant?" Philip asked, perhaps a little too eagerly.

"What I think doesn't matter, Dr. Sarkis. It's what my superiors have to say that's important."

"We are literally on the edge of our seats, Lieutenant," Dorothy offered sarcastically.

"It's complicated. My captain and I took this to the highest levels, believe me."

"I think I know what's coming," Philip said, grimacing.

"Actually, we got a lot of traction from almost everyone in the department. Most thought the case at least merited a grand jury review."

"But…"

"We hit a wall with the big brass. Bill Hoffman, one of the senior ADAs, was adamant that the case was too fragile and wouldn't stand up to any kind of intense scrutiny."

"And he is single-handedly going to freeze the deal?" Philip asked incredulously.

"I'm afraid so. The system is actually very pyramidal. The DA delegates a tremendous amount of authority to his assistants and rarely overrules them."

"I sense a political agenda here," Dick said.

"I don't know how we'd be able to rule that out," Detweiler conceded. "I do know that this would be an enormous problem even if mere allegations got out. The economy up here ain't exactly robust, if you know what I mean, so making our hospitals look bad wouldn't be terribly popular."

"And it was a just a bunch of old guys who were killed, so who cares?" Dorothy spit out.

"Ms. Deaver, my job is to protect our citizens no matter how old or sick. This thing makes me queasy, too, but we're stuck for the time being."

"How do we get unstuck?" Dick looked perplexed.

"I'm not sure, Mr. Deaver. I don't have any easy answers."

"You realize these two have put together as much of a case as amateurs can," Dick said, pointing his fork at Detweiler. "Surely you don't expect them to do a whole lot more. They've already put themselves, and me, in some serious jeopardy."

"No, it's clearly our job now. I've been told to back off from making arrests, but there's nothing to stop me from keeping the file open, and my captain agrees with that approach."

Dorothy's voice rose a couple of decibels. "Lieutenant, at this point, we need physical evidence. That means search warrants and interrogation of suspects. You're telling us you aren't going to do any of that?"

"No. I can't defy my superiors. I know this disappoints you, but it is what it is. I do have a suggestion. Could you and Dr. Sarkis put together a brief summary of what you have found to this point, including your case review and interviews? That would be very helpful to us as we continue to pressure our superiors."

"That isn't a problem, Lieutenant," Philip replied quickly. "I started doing that just last evening."

"But they won't be putting their name on it or signing anything, damn it," Dick interjected. "For obvious reasons, you need to keep them on the sidelines."

"I understand that. I just want to be able to refer back to the facts of the case, if necessary."

"How about posting some policemen out here in the middle of nowhere for a while like you promised? I didn't see any patrol cars last night, and I was up to the bathroom a few times," Dick said.

Before Detweiler could answer, Dorothy piped up. "That's not necessary. I don't want police guards hanging all over the place."

"Maybe we can strike a compromise," Detweiler said in a conciliatory tone, "I'll arrange to have a few patrol cars drive by during the night just to make sure there aren't any suspicious characters parked in front checking out the place. Would that arrangement be acceptable, Ms. Deaver?"

"I guess so. I don't want to sound ungrateful, Lieutenant, but our lives have been miserably interrupted already, and I don't want things to get worse."

"Gotcha. Why don't we just end it here?" Detweiler said rising stiffly from his chair. "I'll continue to lobby internally, and you folks can chew on things a bit more. If anything else occurs to you, let me know."

As he walked to the door, donning his jacket, he turned and said sternly, "It goes without saying that you need to steer clear of the bad guys. No more 'interviews' with Ms. Straub, if you please."

"Roger that, Lieutenant," Dick said as Detweiler closed the door behind him and headed out to the black sedan parked in the driveway.

"That was pretty frustrating," Dorothy said, plopping down in a chair.

"But not unexpected," Dick replied. "This is a hot potato politically, and everybody in the DA's office knows it. They aren't going to call the world down on Wilkes-Barre and Scranton based on what they have so far."

"So you think they're just going to let the criminals go on with their work?"

"No, I suspect they're banking on the idea that the skinheads will cease and desist, now that they've been fingered."

"And how will they know that?" Dorothy asked.

"Detweiler won't divulge his surveillance techniques, but I suspect they have something in mind."

"And they aren't going to warn the hospitals?"

"Never happened," Philip cut in. He had his elbows on the table, head in hands, looking dejected. "It's political dynamite. And hospitals are notorious rumor mills. If this ever got out, it would spread like wildfire and be in the press in a New York minute."

"Cheer up," Dick teased. "At least you're not dead—but you might be if you don't take Detweiler at his word. Stay clear of those jokers and put it away, please."

They cleared the few breakfast dishes and Dick pulled out a cheap murder mystery and parked himself on the sofa, where he would remain for the next few days. Dorothy and Philip spent the afternoon trying to appease Buffy and Mitten, who had been ignored for far too long.

Later in the afternoon, Philip and Dorothy decided on a long walk through the woods to the far side of their lake where the dogs loved to frolic, chasing sticks in exchange for treats. The day was picture perfect, clear blue skies with just a hint of a breeze, and the promise of a peaceful twilight. As they watched their pups hurl themselves in and out of the water, they discussed the case and where it had brought them.

"Philip," Dorothy observed, "We really have to get back to normal."

"I thought I had some idea what that was after we moved up here, but now I am not sure what 'normal' is supposed to be."

"It means doing our jobs, putting money in the bank for our retirement, spending time with your kids and our dogs, eating healthy and exercising, and sleeping through the night without worrying about somebody trying to kill us."

"Sounds too simple."

"It is simple, damn it. It's amazing how we lose sight of

how easy most people live, especially up here. We don't need the stress and the strife, Philip. Look at this beautiful weather and this wonderful place. We need to concentrate on enjoying our time up here and stop worrying about things we can't possibly control."

Philip nodded and smiled. He grabbed Dorothy's hands and faced her, leaning forward to kiss her on the forehead. "If I were smart, I would remember that you are indeed my compass and that I should let you direct our lives. You have good sense, Dorothy Deaver, and I love you for that."

They turned to face the lake, and laughed together as Buffy chased her tail in the water, and looked up with a face full of water, growl laughing with the joy of the moment. Listen to Dorothy, Philip thought, and simplify, knowing, almost at the same moment, that it would never happen.

Chapter Eighteen

Gradually and inexorably, Philip's and Dorothy's lives slid back to their familiar routine. Dorothy returned to her neglected case files, and Philip did his regular shifts in the clinic. Mitten and Buffy were happy to get more attention, including walks in the woods and lake shenanigans. They cherished their canoe rides, which gave them a chance to see their neighbors and bark at the ducks that floated past them carelessly, oblivious to their canine temper tantrums.

Philip continued to comb listlessly through the files in his office, usually early in the morning when there were no distractions. He spent more time staring out at the lake and talking to his dogs than concentrating on the material. Dorothy saw the change and encouraged Philip's diversion by finding things for the two of them to do together.

Once a lonely backwater, the Poconos came to offer more to see and do, in response to the influx of the sophisticated New York community. Restaurants were more plentiful, with a wider range of cuisine and wine selections. And although Philip and Dorothy had not welcomed the arrival of gambling houses, the casinos engaged famous entertainers for shows that Philip and Dorothy enjoyed. Avoiding the casino game rooms was no problem. Philip was so opposed to legalized gambling that he started to twitch when he saw the blackjack tables and roulette wheels.

At one of their casual dinners, Dorothy summoned the courage to discuss the case one last time with Philip. They had finished a hearty meal and were enjoying dessert and coffee at the Powerhouse Eatery. This restaurant was one of their favorite places. It was a renovated plant that had supplied electrical power to one of the many tuberculosis sanitariums that sprang up in the Poconos in the mid-twentieth century. The sanitariums were so completely and intentionally isolated from the surrounding villages that each had to produce its own electricity and heat.

The restaurant was an amazing facility that preserved much of the equipment that had been used when the plant was in full operation. After chatting with the owner one evening, Philip did some Internet research that had uncovered an interesting link between the Mt. Laurel sanitarium and the case in Philadelphia that had ruined his academic career. Adalina Romano, the mother-in-law of Bonnie Romano, had spent two years at Mt. Laurel. Philip smiled wryly as he remembered that Bonnie, his patient's murderess, had herself died in the back of a submerged limousine just two days after having her murder case dismissed in Philadelphia court.

"Have you come across anything new in your research of the Adolphus case?" Dorothy asked, sipping her coffee. She hoped for the desultory reply she received.

"Nah, just more of the same. I am impressed, though, by how carefully Adolphus picked their cases. Every one of the guys they targeted had some cardiovascular risk."

"So when they developed an arrhythmia, nobody was surprised."

"Right. And in most cases, the family had little or no medical background to challenge what was going on. They could only sit there and watch their husband or father or grandfather die."

"So, are you ready to put the case aside and leave it to Detweiler?"

"I guess so. I'm embarrassed to say that I am losing momentum. I'm not as personally invested in this case as I was in the Hamlin murder."

"I understand," Dorothy agreed. "The magnitude of this case is staggering, but it is just so dangerous. Brenda Straub is a scary person."

"She must be if she intimidated your dad."

They went on to rationalize their position and to convince each other that they didn't need to pursue the case further. They both felt as if they were abandoning a number of innocent people who had been ruthlessly victimized. Good Catholic upbringing had taught them how to feel guilt, even when they weren't at fault.

Over the next weeks, the case rarely came up in conversation. The files were pushed to the back of Philip's office as well as his mind, and Dorothy was pleased not to have to worry about starting her car in the morning. The police eased up gradually on their neighborhood patrols, and strange sounds at night no longer had Philip vaulting out of bed to investigate.

And then one midweek morning, Philip was again awakened by a telephone call in the early hours. The sun was not yet up, and Philip had a tough time focusing his eyes to read the clock that told him this was not going to be a routine telemarketer interruption. Unless it was a wrong number, this wasn't good news.

"Hi, Phil. Is that you?" asked the anxious voice on the other end of the line.

"Yes, this is Philip. Who's calling?" Philip didn't recognize the voice but he did recognize the urgency.

"It's your cousin, Donny. Donny Russell? From Collegeville."

Philip shook out the cobwebs while he walked into the kitchen. He tried to visualize the person on the other end of the connection. He was having a hard time because he hadn't seen Donny since he was a student. That was when Philip's parents had invited the Russells to their house for a family picnic, and Philip had played basketball with all three of the Russell boys. Donny was the youngest, as Philip remembered.

"Geez, Donny, it's been a while. I didn't even recognize your voice. I'm sorry."

"I know, Phil, and I'm also sorry we haven't seen each

other for so long. I heard about your troubles and kept meaning to call. But, you know, things get so busy with the kids."

Donny's voice trailed off after his guilty admission. It had been a long time. Philip figured it was at least twenty years, during which time Philip had morphed quite a bit. He wondered if Donny had as well. Still and all, Philip had been bitterly disappointed that not one of his relatives, aunts, uncles, or cousins, had made an effort to help him when he had been down and out. He tried not to be resentful and to understand how difficult it would have been for the family he didn't know well to get involved, but it was a hard thing to put aside.

"Not your fault, Donny," Philip lied. "Things have been a little hectic for all of us the last few years, I bet."

"You can say that again, Phil."

Philip winced. He hated it when people called him Phil. It was his nickname as a kid, and he had tried to ditch it when he went to medical school. He thought Philip was more sophisticated. Relax, Philip thought. Donny was using the only name he knew.

"So, what can I help you with, Donny?" Philip asked, barely refraining from making a sarcastic remark about the time of day.

"Well, I'm not sure you can help us, but I promised Gail I would call for advice."

"Sure." Philip wasn't in the mood for twenty questions and hoped Donny would get to the point soon. He wasn't disappointed.

"Do you remember Gail's father, Mr. Lasordi?

Philip did remember the old guy. In fact, he had known Nicholas Lasordi years before Donny met and married Gail, his third daughter. The Lasordi family lived in Bridgeport, near where Philip had grown up.

"He was the barber on our street, right?" Philip asked.

"Yep, he gave a lot of kids in our family their first haircut."

"Including me," Philip piped up.

But that wasn't all he remembered about the gentle man his neighbors called Nick. Mr. Lasordi was an excellent athlete and loved to play ball with the kids in the old neighborhood.

"Do you like baseball, young man?" Nick asked Philip one day while he spun him around in the barbershop chair. Philip was about to get his annual crew cut, which his parents preferred for the summer months.

"Yes, sir," Philip replied enthusiastically. Nick smiled, and the next time Philip came in to the shop, Mr. Lasordi presented him with a baseball mitt.

"Wow," Philip gushed. "This is a first baseman's mitt. I always wanted one of these." He put it on his left hand and tried to make it look like it fit—it was only twice as big as his hand.

"It isn't just any old first baseman's mitt, Phil. I got it from Eddie Lopatan. Do you know who he is?"

Philip was a rabid Phillies fan and knew exactly who Lopatan was. "He was the starting first baseman for the Phillies last year. What happened to him?"

Nick didn't have the heart to tell Philip that Lopatan was doing some hard time for a little misunderstanding about the age of a young woman who had solicited him outside of the clubhouse one sultry evening after a game. Or that Lopatan had given Nick the glove in exchange for free haircuts at the prison that Nick serviced on a regular basis.

"He got injured," Nick said, winking at Philip's father. "He'll be back next year for sure. In the meantime, what do you say we break that baby in this evening? Have your dad bring you over to my place and we'll have a catch."

Philip was excited that an adult was willing to play catch with him. Fortunately, Philip had grown up in an era when the attention that an older man paid to a young boy was not immediately assumed to be diabolical. Philip's parents were happy that their son had a new friend. Philip's father knew nothing about sports and had no interest in learning, so a baseball mentor was a godsend.

Philip and Nick had so much fun that evening that the catch became a regular thing. Whenever Nick could spare the time, Philip would go to his backyard and practice taking grounders and pop-ups while pretending he was stationed at first base at

Connie Mack Stadium. Nick got tickets to games a few times a year, and would take Philip and other neighborhood kids. They talked nothing but baseball, reviewing the status of multiple players they each liked to follow, with most of the Phillies leading the list, of course.

A privately owned and operated barber shop was a flourishing enterprise in the 1950s and 1960s, but when Philip was a freshman in college, Mr. Lasordi and his family were forced to close up. He had been pushed out of business by a couple of large haircutting franchises that offered short waits, cheap haircuts, and sexy women barbers. So what if they didn't do an impeccable job? Most men didn't know the difference or care, especially if there was some cleavage to gawk at.

The Lasordis moved to the Scranton area, where Nick worked for one of the few barbershop chains that was willing to hire senior men. He was shipped around the area according to the needs of the day. He managed to hold on for a few years, until he was finally forced out by the management, who thought he took too long to cut hair and talked to the customers too much.

Nick regretted losing his neighborhood connection and sense of community. To preserve some of that, the Lasordis would journey back to Bridgeport to visit regularly, and it was during one of those trips that his daughter Gail had met Donny. They were married soon thereafter and started a family, settling in the Collegeville area outside Philadelphia.

"The last time I spoke to Gail, she told me that her father was doing well," Philip said. "But that must have been at least ten years ago."

"He was doing well. Believe it or not, he still cuts hair. Part time, of course. He put a little shop in his basement and services a few close friends and their families. He gets a big kick out of it."

"But you said, *was* doing well," Philip interjected.

"Until yesterday. It was a pretty warm day up there, and he had been on his feet for a few hours cutting hair for some little kids in the neighborhood when he got real weak and dizzy."

"Did he pass out?" Philip asked.

"Gail said no, he sat down and started feeling better, but everybody was concerned. He's had some heart problems and takes medication, so they decided to take him to Memorial in Scranton and have him checked out. You know we're living down here in Philly, so Gail drove up right away to make sure he was OK."

"What did they find at the hospital?"

"Gail said that the tests came out fine. His blood pressure was a little low. They had been giving him a water pill for high blood pressure, and the ER doctor up there thought he had become a little dehydrated. Sometimes when the old dude is working he loses track of eating and drinking."

"So they gave him some fluids, and sent him home, I hope."

"They were going to do that, but by the time they got all his tests back and figured out what was going on, it was late in the day. The ER doctor decided to keep him in the hospital—he said Dad's electrolytes were a little screwed up, and they should be corrected before he went home."

"They could have done that as an outpatient."

"Yeah, but Mom died last year and Dad lives alone up there, so everybody felt better about having him watched overnight. Who knew things would go bad?"

"What happened?'

"We aren't sure. Gail's sister Becky lives up there in Scranton, so Gail had decided to drive back down to Philly after she saw her dad. Becky said that shortly after the old guy got to his room, his heart went out of rhythm. Gail turned right around and went back up there. When she arrived, the floor nurse told her that Nick was in trouble and that the doctors were going to move him to the ICU to figure out what to do."

Philip was so upset he could barely speak. "Donny, this is a big problem."

"I know, Phil; that's why I called you. Can you give us the name of a good cardiologist up there who can help us out?"

"No, Donny. It's a long story, but trust me, this is not a routine problem and there is no doctor up there who'll know what to do with this."

"Nobody? Come on, Phil." Donny remembered Phil as being a little full of himself, but he really didn't expect such an egotistical attitude.

"I don't have time to explain, Donny. I'm going to drive to the hospital myself right now, and talk to the physicians up there. In the meantime, you need to call Gail and tell her to tell the doctors to consider digoxin toxicity. Do you have that?"

"Digoxin toxicity. How do you spell that?"

"D-I-G-O-X-I-N poisoning," Philip answered, trying to keep the growing panic out of his voice.

"What is that, Phil? I don't remember Dad taking a medicine called digoxin. And what do you mean by poisoning?"

"I know he hasn't taken it himself. Tell Gail that somebody may have slipped him the drug to try to hurt him. She needs to convince the doctors to consider the possibility. If they don't, Nick will die. I'll get there to help just as soon as I can get dressed and out the door."

"OK, Phil, if that's what you think, I'll call her right away. It just seems awfully strange that somebody would try to hurt Nick."

"Donny, call Gail and do it now before it's too late. I've got to get going."

Philip hung up abruptly. He couldn't afford to give Donny any more opportunity to whine about the bizarre message he had to relay to his wife.

By the time Philip got off of the phone, Buffy and Mitten were wide-awake and pacing around the bedroom. They assumed that Philip was making another one of his early morning starts, and they expected to be let out for their constitutional. Dorothy was barely conscious, mumbling something about Philip making too much noise.

Philip didn't have time to deal with any of his bedroom mates or to brief Dorothy. He mumbled something about Nick Lasordi being in some trouble and told her and the dogs to go back to sleep. He ran into his small changing room, threw on a pair of jeans and T-shirt and headed out the door to the garage. He fired up his old Toyota and was on the road on the way to Scranton in a blink.

Philip was speeding and he knew he had to be careful. At this hour, the local police were known to be on the prowl for drunks and stupid kids in violation of curfew. Once he made it to the turnpike, he turned it up another notch, figuring this was as close to a life and death emergency as one could get.

Scranton Memorial Hospital was a pitiful throwback to the Fifties. Most of the building was brick, discolored from years of pollution. The wooden window frames hadn't been painted since Reagan, and the driveway was a mass of potholes from years of disrepair and neglect.

He quickly found a spot in the visitor's lot and ran through the front door. The information booth was deserted, but a security guard was standing nearby. He was an elderly African American, slight of build and with a wisp of a moustache. The old guy wore his cop cap at just a bit of a jaunty angle. Philip tried to run past him, but the guard stepped in front of him, ready to take a charge if necessary.

"Sorry, young man. Visiting hours don't start until 10:00 A.M."

"I'm a doctor from another hospital. I need to get to your cardiac ICU to see a patient as quickly as possible. Can you direct me?"

"I'll have to see some identification, Doctor."

Philip hated it when people spat out the word *doctor*. It reminded him of how lawyers used the word to belittle physicians in the courtroom. "Can you tell me how you came to be such an incompetent idiot, *doctor*?" He was getting ready to fire back at the rent-a-cop but realized with a start that he had forgotten his wallet. "I don't have identification on me. I need to get up there right now. This is an emergency."

"Which is why we have good doctors who stay in the hospital all night—so they can take care of emergencies."

"This is a special case. The house doctors won't know what

222

to do because they don't know what's causing the problem."

"And you do, of course. Doctor, I'm sorry, but I can't let the public into the hospital except during visiting hours."

"OK, do me a favor, and at least let me talk to one of the doctors up in the unit."

"Any of them, or is there one in particular."

"Is there a cardiologist in the house?"

"Might be. Lemme see." The guard pulled out his on-call list and scanned down the page.

Philip was about to jump out of his skin. "You have to hurry! A patient up there is going to die!"

"Keep your shirt on." The guard found a name. "The cardiologist in the house tonight is Dr. Van Gelder. Nice lady. Let's see if I can get her for you."

The guard picked up the house phone at the desk and called the operator. "Jean, honey, I wonder if you could page Dr. Van G to this number for me. I have someone here who wants to speak to her."

The guard hung up and suggested to Philip that he try to be patient. "Dr. Van G is usually pretty good about answering her pages promptly."

Except this time. It took nearly ten long minutes for the phone to ring while Philip paced back and forth like a caged animal.

"Dr. Van G, I have a man down here who says he is a doctor and is desperate to speak with you about a patient in the ICU. Do you have a minute?"

Philip grabbed the phone without waiting for an answer. "Doctor, are you taking care of a patient named Nicholas Lasordi tonight?"

There was a momentary silence. "Why do you ask?"

"Please. I'm a cardiologist *and* a relative," Philip lied.

"As a matter of fact, I *have* been coding a Mr. Lasordi. That's why I couldn't answer my page immediately."

"Please, please tell this guard to let me come up there now. I know why he's coding, and I can help you resuscitate him."

"I didn't get your name."

"Philip Sarkis."

"You gave grand rounds up here a few years ago, didn't you? Aren't you an arrhythmia expert?"

"*Was* an arrhythmia expert. Just let me up there."

"OK. Put the guard back on."

The guard grunted once or twice while Van Gelder gave instructions, then he hung up. "OK, Doctor," the guard said. "Follow me and we'll have you at the bedside in no time."

The single ancient elevator took a few more minutes to transport Philip and the guard to the ICU floor. Philip wanted to streak into the unit but had to wait for his much slower companion to show the way. As they passed the waiting area, Philip saw Gail, seated on a sofa crying softly, flanked by a couple of nurses who had their arms around her. Philip decided to avoid Gail and keep going into the unit with the guard. They found the door to Mr. Lasordi's cubicle closed, and the monitor off. He went to the nurses' station and asked a tall blonde woman in a white coat, scrubs, and clogs if she could find Dr. Van Gelder.

"Dr. Sarkis, it's a pleasure to meet you."

"Dr. Van Gelder? What happened to Mr. Lasordi?"

"You didn't give me a chance to tell you on the phone, but I declared him dead just after my beeper went off."

"No!" Philip wailed so loud that the entire ICU staff turned to look at him.

"He started having VT storms about an hour ago. We tried everything, including IV amiodarone, lidocaine, magnesium, the works."

"How about digoxin antibodies?"

"Why on earth would I have tried that?"

"Because that's what killed him."

"Killed him?" She was incredulous.

"It's complicated. Do you happen to know who the nurse was who was looking after him this shift?"

"Funny you should mention it. It was a male agency nurse. I hadn't worked with him before, but he was really competent. I even told him how much I appreciated his assistance with the resuscitation."

"I bet he was supposed to go off duty right afterward."

"Yes, as a matter of fact. He stayed overtime just to help with Mr. Lasordi. He looked really dragged out. I told him to go home and get some sleep."

Philip wondered if there was any point in getting the nurse's name. It would be impossible to prove he had done anything wrong. He looked at the EKG strips that Van Gelder showed him. There was little question as to what had happened.

Philip sat in a desk chair in the nurses' station and buried his face in his hands. Tears refused to flow, but the significance of the event was not lost on him. The last prerequisite to get him more involved with the case had been fulfilled. Without knowing it, Brenda Straub and Adolphus had just made the case personal, real fucking personal.

Chapter Nineteen

Dorothy had not been able to get back to sleep after Philip left the house. The few snippets she heard from his conversation had been disturbing. Who was Lasordi and what had happened to him that had Philip in such a yank? Why had he run out of the house without telling her what was going on, or taking care of the dogs? Had he mentioned something about digoxin, or was that a dream? She tossed and turned for a few hours and then realized that Mitten and Buffy were awake again, and anxious to do their business. Once they made up their mind, there was little recourse.

Dorothy got out of bed, shivering from the cold. No matter the season, mornings in the Poconos demanded a sweater or a sweatshirt right out of the gate. It was another one of the things they loved about the place—rarely hot, and surely no need for air conditioning. It looked like a sunny day, so it would warm up soon enough.

Buffy and Mitten were already at the back slider, pawing at the glass. She scooted them out and turned her attention to the Tassimo—she needed strong coffee, and badly. While the coffee dripped, she tried to reach Philip on his cell for a status report, but was sent to voicemail. Philip frequently ignored his phone. Things she had found alluring during their courtship were becoming pains in the neck. In her infatuation stage, she had thought it attractively quirky that Philip hated cell phones. Not picking up his phone now, especially when Dorothy thought she had a good reason to speak with him, was not so cute—just annoying.

Listlessly, Dorothy continued through her morning routine, starting with a breakfast of cereal and fruit, a glance at the paper, a snippet of TV news and weather, and a hot shower finished off with a long blow dry. She checked her morning schedule on her Blackberry to discover a few meetings that made her frown.

To start with, Dorothy strongly suspected that the family she would see at 10:30 was lying to extract money from an insurance company. Sure, the husband had been on a municipal bus when it rammed a trash truck on Washington Street in Scranton, but the doctors Dorothy used to examine the victim hadn't found evidence of an injury severe enough to cause intractable back pain. She was sorry to have agreed to represent them before a thorough background check and medical examination. Now she was stuck. If she bailed out, they would certainly not be able to sustain their claim and their entire family, including some little kids, would be out on the street in no time. If she continued, she had a good chance of pulverizing the dolt who represented the city and coming out of the case with a big verdict or settlement that her clients didn't deserve. Once you stepped in dog dirt…

That case conference would be followed by a dreary succession of business meetings, as the law firm partners tried to determine how to keep solvent a practice that charged comparatively little and consistently strove to do the right thing. Maybe Dorothy and her colleagues should try to turn the crank and take on more cases that could generate real revenue, as had so many of the scummy law practices in the area. Maybe they should advertise on television. More off-the-street business might improve the chances of keeping the place open and their staff employed. Dorothy had never enjoyed the business end of law practice and had avoided most of it. But things were in crisis, so this little confab was a must-show.

Dorothy rolled these things over in her mind as she prepared food for the dogs. After Buffy and Mitten were fed and situated in the backyard, Dorothy grabbed her briefcase and headed for the front door. Her car, though far nicer than

Philip's, rarely had the benefit of being indoors. Philip's bomb occupied half the garage, while junk accumulated in the other bay. They had resolved to clean the garage out so many times that Dorothy had lost count. At least at this time of year there was no need for de-icing or snow shoveling that had become such a fun part of her winter morning routine.

Dorothy eased her car out of the driveway and onto Lakeview Drive. The first few minutes of her commute were the best. The small roads around the lake provided inspiring views of the early morning sky. This morning it was blue and cloudless, a perfect backdrop for some spectacular foliage. Admiring the day, she turned slowly onto Woodland Avenue, a severe downhill that would take her directly past the end of the lake itself.

As she came gently over the hill and started her descent, Dorothy tapped the brake pedal. It felt soft, and the car began to accelerate down the grade. She pumped the brake pedal repeatedly with no response. Finally all tension in the pedal was lost, and it dropped uselessly to the floorboard. Panic set in as Dorothy realized her brakes had failed. The road would take a severe bend in just a few yards, and at her current pace she knew that her car would skid uncontrollably into the water. She had to make a quick choice: strike an obstacle to stop her car before it gathered even more momentum, or find herself submerged in the lake.

The decision was reflexive. Dorothy pulled hard on the wheel of her SUV and slammed into the base of a large tree. She felt herself thrown forward just as the airbags inflated and prevented a vault over the steering wheel into the windshield. Dorothy was stunned but awake enough to realize that the front of her beautiful car was pulverized, and that she had not been injured severely.

Fortunately, there were several people on the roads near the lake at that time of morning, exercising before heading off to work. The noise of the collision shattered the still morning air, so in just seconds, a couple of bikers and joggers were yanking on Dorothy's door. Though it was banged up, the door opened with a creak, and the bystanders were able to pull Dorothy out of her seat and lower her to the ground. She kept repeating, "My brakes failed, my brakes failed. I thought I was going to die."

It didn't take long for the police and ambulance crew to arrive at the scene, summoned by a neighbor who had witnessed the accident and had the wherewithal to call for help. A quick examination by the ambulance crew reassured them that Dorothy had no major injuries, but the police recommended a trip to Pocono Hospital for a more in-depth evaluation.

"I'm really OK," Dorothy protested to the policemen. "I have an important appointment and I really need to get to my office."

"I know, ma'am, but our policy is that passengers involved in a nasty crash have to go to the emergency room for an evaluation." It was clear they were not prepared to accept responsibility for what might happen to her if she had an undiscovered serious injury. The taller and more handsome of the two officers tried to reassure Dorothy.

"Miss, I don't think you're going to be at the hospital very long, but you *are* going to have to get checked out. I am sure the people at your office will understand."

"All right," Dorothy conceded, trying to figure out if she was an old miss or a young ma'am. "I guess there's no point arguing about it."

As the ambulance crew got Dorothy onto a stretcher and loaded her into the vehicle, the policemen asked a few general questions about the accident. It became clear that she was in no condition to supply any detail and that the interview would have to wait.

"Tell you what," the tall officer suggested just before the ambulance door closed. "I'll call your husband and tell him what happened. We'll get things settled here and then come over to the hospital. After you're cleared, we can review what happened and see if we can piece it all together."

"There isn't a whole lot to tell you, but that sounds like a reasonable plan," Dorothy agreed. "By the way, the person you're going to call isn't my husband—at least not yet. We live together, and he'll definitely want to hear the details. Can you also ask him to call my secretary so she knows what's going on?"

As the ambulance pulled away, the patrolman went back to his car and asked dispatch to put a call through to Ms. Deaver's boyfriend. Philip had just left the hospital and was in his car, stopped at a traffic light, on his way home. Although he hated talking on his cell, the origination of this call piqued his interest, so he hit the receive button on his Blackberry.

"Hello?"

"Mr. Sarkis? This is Patrolman Andy Pigorsky. I'm a policeman here in Tobyhanna Township. Dorothy Deaver asked us to call you."

"Is she OK?"

Andy anticipated the question. He knew it was important to put the good news up front in a call such as this—if there was any good news to give. "Yes, she's fine. She had a car accident this morning near your home. She didn't have any major injuries, but she's pretty shook up. The car was badly damaged. She's on her way to the Pocono Hospital emergency room. She wanted us to let you know and to have you call her office so they are aware…"

Before Andy could continue, Philip interrupted. "I'm on my way."

"Mr. Sarkis, there's no need to rush. Please don't drive recklessly. The ambulance crew who picked her up told us she's completely stable and in no danger. We sent her to the hospital as a precaution."

"It's Dr. Sarkis, officer. And I know how good ambulance crews are at making clinical assessments in the middle of nowhere. I won't break any laws, but I'll be there very soon. Can you give me the details about the accident when I get there?"

"Of course. We also want to ask Ms. Deaver some more questions so we can get this sorted out. So far, we really don't know what actually happened."

Philip hung up and then did exactly what he said he wouldn't, driving at warp speed down Interstate 380, hoping that the State Police were on a coffee break. He parked his car in one of the visitor spots outside the ER and ran into the lobby where a triage secretary who looked pretty surly greeted him.

"Can I help you?"

"I'm here to see Dorothy Deaver. I was told she was brought here after a traffic accident."

The secretary, a strikingly obese middle-aged woman with long greasy hair and no make-up, made a frown, as if to imply that a name would have sufficed. "Yes, she's in room 12. May I ask who you are?"

Philip hated that question because he didn't know how to answer. "Husband" would be a lie but would be the answer to get him in to see Dorothy the quickest. "Boyfriend" sounded juvenile and he knew the secretary would tell him to take a seat until Dorothy's family arrived. "Fiancé" might work, but judging from the scowl, this woman most likely wouldn't be persuaded by romance. He finally decided to try a different gambit.

"I'm a very close friend and her physician. She called and asked me to see her."

The fat woman hardly looked up from her computer screen. "ID, please."

Philip was getting tired of having his identity challenged by hospital drones, but this time, he was prepared. He had rifled through his glove compartment and found a medical identification card from his practice. The receptionist glanced at the card and it seemed to satisfy her, even though Philip had not bothered to get it re-validated and the expiration date was months previously. "Bed 12 is straight back on your left. I'll let her nurse know you're on your way."

"Can I also talk to the physician on duty?"

"That would be Dr. Reddy. She's back there too, but we're pretty busy right now. It might take a while for her to get to you."

Philip went through the double doors. Indeed, most of the

bays were occupied with the usual assortment of ER patients. Some had bandages, while others were lying quietly on gurneys waiting to go off for tests. Philip paid little attention; he wanted to eyeball Dorothy as soon as possible and satisfy himself that she really was OK.

And as soon as he saw her, he smiled. She was sitting up in bed, holding a cup of coffee, chatting with the nurse, obviously feeling no pain. "Look at me, Ma—nary a scratch," she said to Philip with tears in her eyes as he walked over to the stretcher to embrace her awkwardly.

"Thank goodness," Philip sighed. "The patrolman told me it was a pretty bad accident. What happened?"

"I don't have the slightest idea. I was coming down Woodland to go around the lake. I hit the brakes, and they completely failed. So I turned into a tree to keep from going into the water, but by the time I did, the car was going pretty fast. I suspect that was the end of my Lexus."

"The car is not the issue," Philip said dismissively. He stopped, obviously lost in thought. "Have you had any problems with the car recently?"

"No, it's been fine. I just had it in for service about three weeks ago."

Philip didn't tell her why he asked. He stared at Dorothy for a few seconds and then turned to the nurse.

"So you're happy with her status?"

"Yes, there aren't any apparent internal injuries—just a few bumps and bruises, mostly from the air bag. Her vitals are stable, and her heart rate and blood pressure are coming down nicely. They were pretty high when she came in. No surprise there."

"I would like to speak with Dr. Reddy, if possible," Philip requested.

"Dorothy told me you're a physician?"

"Yes, I am. I know Dr. Reddy is busy, but I just need a word."

The nurse nodded. "Let me see what I can do."

In a few minutes Dr. Reddy appeared. An attractive Indian

woman, Dr. Reddy wore her white coat over traditional ethnic attire, which Philip thought incongruous. She shook hands with Philip and gave a brief synopsis of her evaluation, confirming the nurse's observations, and then asked Philip if he had any specific questions.

"Dr. Reddy, do you mind if I speak to you privately?"

"Certainly," replied Dr. Reddy who led Philip out into the hallway.

"Is there any chance that Dorothy passed out before she lost control of her car?" Philip began.

"I didn't find anything on neurological examination to suggest that."

"No amnesia?"

"No. She was able to give a clear history. I think it really was a car malfunction from her description. Why do you ask?"

"I'm sure the insurance company will want to know," Philip said, while trying to avoid eye contact. "I appreciate your help Dr. Reddy. Thanks for taking good care of her."

"You are most welcome. We do have to take care of our own, don't we, Dr. Sarkis?"

"You know who I am?"

"I do. You gave a grand rounds lecture up here a few years ago that I attended. It was one of the best I have ever heard. I still use some of the things I learned to take care of patients who come in here with cardiac arrhythmias."

Philip blushed and smiled. This was the second person this morning who knew his name. Maybe he wasn't washed up after all.

"I'm very happy to hear that, Dr. Reddy. In fact, you have no idea how pleased that makes me."

"In any case, we should be ready to let Dorothy go in a little while. Keep an eye on her the next few hours and bring her back please if she starts having any neurological symptoms."

As efficient as Dr. Reddy tried to be, "a little while" in the hospital usually translates into a few hours. Philip sat with Dorothy and tried to soothe her, even while he ruminated about the cause of the accident. Was it just a mechanical problem, or had someone tampered with her car? Was there a reason to tell the police about the Adolphus case, or should he keep his mouth shut?

When Officer Andy and his partner arrived in the ER, Dorothy was asleep and Philip intercepted them.

"Officers, Dorothy is really not feeling well." He had decided to play dumb and tell them nothing of his suspicions of foul play. He wanted to check on a few things, and his first priority was getting Dorothy home and settled in what he presumed was a safe environment. The police took a few notes and promised to follow-up later. Philip was grateful that Detweiler had apparently not entered information about the Adolphus case that was recoverable on the police computer system. As far as they were concerned, this was just another auto mechanical failure.

Neither Philip nor Dorothy spoke much during their ride home. They didn't really have to. Both of them understood the implications of the car accident. Finally, as if they had been communicating telepathically, Dorothy turned to Philip and asked, "Should we call Detweiler when we get home and tell him that my car brakes failed?"

Philip stroked his chin and shook his head. "That's a tough call. We can't prove that someone tampered with your brakes yet. Are you sure you just didn't hit an oil patch or something and then swerve into the tree?"

"I'm positive," Dorothy answered with an edge. "I was coming down the hill perfectly carefully, and when I tapped my brakes, it was like they just gave way. Fortunately, the first part of that incline is pretty gradual, so I had a chance to react."

"The officers gave me the name of the repair shop where they were taking the car. I called the guy who runs the place while I was waiting for you to get ready to come home. He told me he was going to go over the car this afternoon so he could give a report to the insurance company. Let's see what they find before we jump to conclusions."

"Did he say anything about fixing it?" Dorothy asked. "I

really like that car."

"No, he hadn't even seen it yet, but from what the officer said, you'll be getting a new car for sure."

"Can we afford a new car?"

"We might have to settle for a used one—the new Lexus models are pretty expensive. We'll see. In the meantime, we will have to get a rental." Philip didn't want to upset Dorothy any more than she already was, but the Lexus was one of the last few semblances of their former affluent life, and unlikely to be replaced.

They pulled into their stone driveway, and Dorothy, hearing barking from the backyard, made a beeline to check on the dogs. Philip waited until she was out of sight, and then crouched down and poked around the area where Dorothy had parked her car the night before. He thought his mind was playing tricks, but he could swear that the stones had been pushed toward the spot where the car would have been standing. He began to doubt himself until he saw small pieces of silver cable sitting on top of the stones, clearly visible and obviously out of place. Philip put his head in his hands, as he squatted there, trying to come to grips when he heard Dorothy calling for Buffy.

They met on the side of the house and Dorothy was frantic. "I can't find Buffy, and Mitten is acting strange. She's running all around the yard looking for her sister. I don't like the way she's barking."

"Huh?"

"Dogs communicate with their bark. Come on, you have to know this."

"Sorry, you lost me."

"Mitten is worried about Buffy! And you know very well that Buffy wouldn't run off, especially not by herself."

They toured the periphery of the property checking the integrity of the fence, and then they walked around the neighborhood. Philip talked Dorothy out of using his car to expand the search. His own auto tour of the area yielded nothing, and he was just about to turn for home when his cell phone beeped indicating a text message from a strange number. At first he thought it was a mistake; people rarely texted him. But on his screen was an address on a street about two miles away. When it finally dawned on him what it meant, he gunned his old Toyota and almost annihilated several small critters that dared to cross his path.

As he careened down the street in question, the first thing he saw was Buffy's long white paws stretched out on the side of the road. Philip was convinced she was dead in the gutter, but as he got closer, Buffy jumped up and tried to run to meet him. A length of rope tied to the mailbox on the property snapped tight and she was pulled to the ground, whimpering. Philip skidded to a stop, jumped out of his car, and ran over to Buffy, reassuring her that everything was OK, even though he wasn't so sure. Philip unknotted the rope, put Buffy in the car, and took a quick look around. He knocked on the door of the house but nobody answered.

Philip returned to his car and called Dorothy to let her know he had found their pup. Dorothy was relieved but not terribly surprised. "I had a feeling you were going to find her, and I have some news for you when you get back."

Philip drove home almost as fast, anxious to hear the next sound bite from Dorothy. This had turned into an eventful day, all before lunch. What next?

Dorothy was standing in the driveway as Philip arrived. She pulled the car door open and gave Buffy a big hug and kiss. Buffy responded with a lick to the chops, while Mitten practically burst through the front door to see her sister. "I wish these two could tell us what happened here this morning," Philip said.

"They don't have to tell us," Dorothy offered. "I know exactly what's going on."

"Really? Would you like to share it with me?"

"Let's talk inside."

They took a couple of seats at the kitchen table, Dorothy finishing the tea she had brewed after she learned that Buffy was recovered.

"So what's your theory?" Philip asked, fairly sure that Dorothy had arrived at the same conclusion as he.

"It's intimidation, pure and simple."

"Who's intimidating who?" Philip asked, trying to sound naïve.

"Don't play Perry Mason with me, Philip. You know perfectly well this is Adolphus' doing. The other piece of news I have for you is that the auto shop called and said my brake cables were broken. And then Buffy is taken from our yard and deposited two miles from here, unharmed. It has to be foul play."

"But why did they tell me where to find her?"

"For the same reason they disabled my brakes here, near the lake. The chances of killing me with that little trick were pretty small. Much more likely that I would just crash the car and walk away from it. It would have been a different story if the brakes had gone out on the Interstate. They didn't want to kill me or our precious dog."

"They just wanted to frighten us? But why now? We haven't been on their case for weeks."

"Philip, are you not processing because of sleep deprivation? Where did you go early this morning? And what did you find?"

"You mean my visit to the hospital for the Lasordi case?"

"Yes, you dolt. Adolphus now knows this thing has turned personal for you. You have a real stake in it. They couldn't have been aware you had anything to do with old Mr. Lasordi until you showed up. The nurse who killed Lasordi must have called Brenda. She realized that you and I, more than anyone, can tie them to this latest murder and she freaked."

"So the best way to keep that from happening is to…"

"To scare the shit out of us, but cause no permanent damage. If they killed me, that would just piss you and my father off and make you go after them harder. And I'm sure they know about the Hamlin case."

"I didn't kill the Hamlins."

"Save it, Philip. We both know what you did and I'm get-

ting really fucking tired of hearing you pretend you're innocent. In this case, the possibility that you know how to murder
people or have them murdered may have saved my life—and
Buffy's. Anyway, they put us on notice."

"So it's up to us to make the right decision about going to
the police?"

"That doesn't matter as much to them. The law doesn't intimidate them. Detweiler made it clear why the authorities are
ineffectual. They've been getting away with murder around
here for quite some time."

"So they think we're their main danger?"

"In many ways we're the wild card. The next move is ours.
I suspect if we stop snooping around and don't go after them,
they'll leave us alone."

"And it will get uglier if we don't?"

"Let's put it this way: the next time they take one of our
dogs, I wouldn't expect to find her tied to a mailbox post."

Philip bit his lower lip—not a good sign at all, in Dorothy's
experience.

Chapter Twenty

Philip and Dorothy figured that Detweiler would get wind of the day's events from the police, so they decided to call him themselves that afternoon, to give him their perspective on what had happened over the last twenty-four hours. Philip put him on the speakerphone so they could give him their tag-team version of Lasordi's demise and Dorothy's near-death experience.

The lieutenant grunted a lot during the conversation, and asked a few questions for clarity, but didn't volunteer anything. Philip couldn't decide if he was thick or in denial. He seemed completely uninterested in Buffy's kidnapping, cutting Philip off in mid-sentence.

"Dr. Sarkis, what exactly did you want me to do about any of this? I presume the patrolmen have looked into it and will find an explanation for your dog's disappearance."

"Lieutenant, Dorothy and I are pretty convinced that Adolphus is behind her accident and Buffy's kidnapping."

"You think they're trying to frighten you?"

"Destroying someone's brakes probably goes a little beyond bullying, don't you think?"

"It's going to be difficult to prove that Adolphus is responsible, Dr. Sarkis. I'll talk to the policemen who investigated the accident, but it doesn't sound like they have physical evidence at this point."

For Dorothy's benefit, Philip silently mouthed a few choice epithets before replying. "There won't be any evidence, Lieutenant, unless your department chooses to look for it. When I spoke to the patrolmen yesterday, it was pretty clear that the Adolphus case is not on anyone's radar screen. They didn't even mention it."

"We haven't put it in the general file because we don't have enough evidence yet. I thought that was what you preferred based on our last conversation."

"I didn't intend to have you completely call off the dogs. I was sort of hoping you guys would at least keep an open file for your own use. Obviously you haven't," Philip said with an obvious edge.

Detweiler paused to gather himself. Dorothy figured he was trying not to get into a pissing contest with a know-it-all doctor.

"Like I said to you last time, Doctor, my superiors are not interested in pursuing this case right now. They want to see more evidence before they'll go after anybody. But I'm glad you called. I'll check with the patrolmen and get back to you soon."

"And what about Lasordi's death?"

"What about it?" Detweiler hissed.

"You should be able to get the name of the nurse who was looking after him before he coded."

"And what proof do we have that he was killed?"

"As much as we have in any of the cases we've unearthed so far."

"I'll look into it, *Doctor*. Goodbye."

There was that word again. Philip hit the disconnect button angrily. He hunched over the island counter where Dorothy was starting to get dinner ready.

"That was the usual police gibberish, wasn't it? He wants to talk to the officers who responded to your accident and see if there's any physical evidence they can come up with before talking to his superiors or doing anything. And it's just too bad about Lasordi. Just another WOP thrown into the meat grinder."

Dorothy shook her head. "You'd think that sliced brake cables would be adequate proof that someone had murder on their mind. I should be scared, but I think I've convinced myself that we've been warned."

"I wish I were as confident."

"Trust me on this one, Philip. I think if we don't provoke these people, they'll be more than happy to leave us and our animals alone."

"Maybe, but I don't think we should leave the dogs outside when we go out. At least not for a while."

"And what precaution do you want to take for me? Or haven't you gotten that far?" Dorothy asked.

"You know it's always all about the dogs," Philip replied, trying to be funny. Dorothy didn't grin. "Seriously, we'll just have to think about things more carefully—like putting your car in the garage at night."

"What car? That's something else I have to deal with tomorrow—new wheels."

Dorothy had found a used car on the Internet, the same make and model she had before, but with considerably more mileage. She knew that losing her car was another consequence of living with Philip the nutcase. Maybe all of this was punishment for their adultery years before. Now there was a good Catholic girl's guilty conclusion, Dorothy thought cynically.

For the next several weeks, their routines didn't change but still, they slept lightly, aware of every random noise. Philip was careful to illuminate the property when the dogs ventured out at night. He watched them from the porch, glancing nervously about until they returned to the bedroom. The dogs went back to sleep quickly after snapping up a treat; Philip was rarely that lucky.

They decided not to tell Dick about what had happened, at least not right away. His ill-conceived visit to Brenda Straub only served to make matters more dangerous, and they were both worried about the consequences of another Dick Deaver temper tantrum.

Dorothy noticed a distinct change in Philip's demeanor. For years, Philip was known to have abrupt mood swings that would challenge a full-blown manic-depressive. So at first, Dorothy didn't make much of it. But as the days went on, Philip grew quieter and darker. Dorothy had a difficult time engaging him in any kind of conversation, and he spent the bulk of his evenings, surfing TV channels, and staring blankly at mindless programs that he ordinarily avoided.

After giving him a few days to straighten out, Dorothy decided to call Philip's brother, Brian, to see if he could help. Philip and Brian had been close as kids. Philip was nine years older than Brian, and there wasn't a lot of sibling rivalry. Philip was more of a parental figure who had helped raise his baby brother.

Philip hadn't seen much of Brian after he left for college, but they had remained good friends, if not confidants. Each had worked with their father in the family business, vowing to find a way to do something different with their lives. While Philip decided on medicine, Brian pursued business.

After a degree in chemistry, Brian earned an MBA. He was staggered when he couldn't find a job after graduation, and had been forced to drive the family truck for a few more years than he had expected. When a sales job opened up at a local utility company, Brian jumped at it and hadn't looked back. He took on menial projects at the firm with cheerfulness and enthusiasm. His bosses liked his attitude, and when they realized he had a good brain, he rose like a rocket. Besides becoming the firm's youngest senior vice-president, Brian brought in bushels of new business. His latest big problem was sorting through the dozens of job offers he had begun to receive, hoping to latch onto the right CEO position to cap what was already a remarkable career.

Brian and his wife Bernadette lived near Philadelphia but had purchased a vacation home not far from Philip and Dorothy's place in the Poconos. Their proximity provided an opportunity for Philip's and Brian's families to see each other on weekends and holidays. Philip made a point to pick up his kids from his ex-wife Nancy on these occasions so they could play with their cousins.

Dorothy hoped that getting everybody together for dinner in the Poconos would be therapeutic for Philip. When she called Brian to invite his family over, she briefed him on the latest events. Brian was dumbfounded.

"How come he never told me about any of this? I thought he was finished with playing amateur detective after that thing with the Hamlins."

"Me too. I will take some of the blame for this. When he first told me what was going on with the malpractice case he was reviewing, I should have shut it down, but I didn't. Before I knew it, I was sitting in some murderer's office impersonating an applicant and pumping her for information. What a dope I was."

"Don't be too hard on yourself, Dorothy. You were brought up and trained to do that kind of thing. My idiot brother was not. He should have stuck to medicine."

"He tried to, Brian, and he got screwed. The Hamlin case really got to him, and I think I underestimated how much. This new case just compounded the problem. The doctor Philip was trying to help settled the case and retired. So many people up here have lost loved ones, and the police have just sat there and done nothing. Ever since the episodes with my car and Buffy, he's been terribly introverted and sullen."

"I suspect he's worried about you. He doesn't like to be out of control," Brian said, remembering his brother's maniacal need to direct everything around him, including the young Brian. "He feels like he's at the mercy of some bad people, and I bet he's trying to figure out a way to get out from under."

"I wish he would talk to me about it. It's frustrating not to be able to share our feelings and solve the problem together."

"I'll see what I can find out when we come over," Brian offered. "He doesn't open up easily, but maybe he'll be a little more forthcoming after a few drinks on the dock."

The dinner started out auspiciously enough. They convened

on the lake on a balmy Saturday evening. Dorothy mixed up a pitcher of frozen margaritas. Philip made small talk with the grown-ups while the kids took the canoe for a lap around the lake.

Dorothy was always amazed how little the brothers resembled each other. Brian had softer features, and wasn't as dark as Philip. Even more striking was the difference in their personalities. Brian was more introspective and thoughtful, needing to be prodded to give his opinion, quite a contrast with his bombastic brother. The family was so struck by the differences in the brothers that they used to kid around about the Irish milkman who had taken a shine to their mother. Was that why a good Lebanese boy had such a decidedly Gaelic first name?

"Dorothy told me about what happened to Donny's father-in-law," Brian observed, trying to steer the conversation, hoping that the alcohol would loosen Philip's tongue a bit.

"Yeah, it was real bad. I guess she also told you about her accident and Buffy's disappearance?"

"Yep. Sounds like someone was gunning for you guys?"

"Maybe so. The police are supposedly on it. We'll have to wait and see."

Philip walked away from the group, and yelled out to the kids to stay close by where he could watch them. Before Brian knew it, Philip managed to change the subject to sports, weather, and other trivialities.

As the evening went on, Philip progressively withdrew, so by the time the steaks were cooked and served, he was nearly mute. Brian tried several times to talk about the case, but Philip found ways to change the subject or didn't answer at all. Dorothy suspected that Brian was used to this rude behavior since he easily moved on to other topics, including his own work and politics. Bernie and Dorothy cast anxious glances at one another across the dinner table, waiting to see if Philip would open up.

They would be disappointed. After dinner, Philip jumped up before everyone was finished, began to clear the table, and then excused himself. He stomped into the TV room, put on a baseball game, and collapsed into his recliner. Brian followed him but couldn't engage Philip beyond the casual expletive when one of the Phillies struck out.

The evening was clearly ruined. Dessert never happened. Brian and Bernie made an excuse about needing to drive back to Philly early the next morning, which meant getting the kids into bed as soon as possible. Brian whispered an apology to Dorothy as he gave her his best brotherly hug and headed for the door. Philip called goodbye from the TV room. Brian and Bernie ushered their children to their car seats—they couldn't wait to get on the road.

After Brian and Bernie pulled away, Dorothy stormed into the den and unloaded. "Philip, what the hell was that all about?"

Philip played dumb, staring at the TV screen, head propped on hand. "What on earth are you talking about?" he muttered.

"You can't possibly be that dense? You just trashed a perfectly nice evening with your brother's family."

"I did?"

"You stopped talking. And don't pretend you don't know what you were doing. It was pretty obvious."

"Honestly, I didn't realize. I'm terribly sorry."

"Brian tried to talk to you about the case and offer some support, and every time he did, you just clammed up and walked away. You were really obnoxious."

"The case is none of his damn business. He shouldn't stick his nose where it doesn't belong. And you shouldn't encourage him to do that, either."

"He's your brother, for Christ's sake. He's worried about you like the rest of us. I told him you were in a funk—it was his idea to speak with you."

"There's no need to worry about me, and I know how to take care of my family," Philip grunted.

"What the hell does that mean?"

"Nothing you need to be concerned with."

Dorothy clasped her hands on her head, obviously completely exasperated. "Philip, I'm getting extremely tired of your attitude and your stupid excuses. I worked hard to organize tonight. I wanted you to have some time with your brother. The food was good, we had some nice wines, and you finished things off by ignoring everybody. What the fuck is your problem?"

"I don't have a problem."

"Good, so it shouldn't take long for you to fix it. Because I'm simply not going to put up with it anymore."

"What does that mean, Dorothy?"

"Stop playing stupid, Philip. Either you come out of your shell and work with me on this problem, or I am out of here."

"You don't mean that."

"I can put up with a lot of stress—of which there has been plenty around here lately. But I am not sure I know why I should swallow all your crap. I thought we cared for each other, but I'm not sure about that anymore."

"Are you saying you don't love me?" Philip asked, finally looking at her.

"I'm afraid it's the other way around, Philip. If you loved me, you wouldn't make my life even more miserable than Adolphus has. You know how scared I am of those people and what they might do to us. I need your support, not your surly moods."

"I'll do better."

"Talk is cheap, Philip. Change or I am not hanging around. Now, I'm going to bed."

Dorothy stormed into their bedroom, leaving Philip with his ball game to contemplate the future of their relationship. Philip glanced over at Mitten who had been asleep on the sofa. Mitten now had her head up and was looking at Philip disapprovingly.

"I guess she means it, girl," Philip observed. Mitten jumped off the sofa, nudged Buffy to wake her up, and then the two of them trudged into the bedroom. And their tails were not wagging. Philip sat brooding, watching the Phillies beat up on the Mets. By the time he joined the three ladies in the bedroom, the light was out and they were fast asleep, heads turned to each other and away from Philip's side of the bed.

Chapter Twenty-One

Over the next few days, Philip and Dorothy didn't see much of each other. Philip had drawn several twelve-hour evening shifts at the clinic, and Dorothy was working late at the office routinely while preparing for a big court case. Dorothy was relieved to have some time away from Philip, and hoped that the respite would change his demeanor, or at least mitigate her angry response to it.

She returned from work late one evening to find flowers in a vase on the dining room table with a note from Philip. "I decided to go to a cardiology conference in Philly. It's a retread course for gomer docs like me who have been out of the academic mainstream for a while. I leave tomorrow morning after my night shift so I probably won't see you. I'll be home Saturday afternoon. I'm sorry I've been such a pill recently. I promise to refresh at the meeting and come home a new man."

Dorothy could hardly believe what she was reading. First of all, Philip hated going to medical meetings. He looked for every excuse to avoid them. He got most of his continuing education credits online, stating clearly that he hated airplanes, hotel rooms, and stale coffee, not to mention the mindless conversations with ignorant strangers at meals that were hardly palatable.

Dorothy had convinced herself that Philip was angry with the medical establishment for taking away his career. After all, Philip used to be on the faculty and lectured at many of the meetings that he now despised. And he had been very good at it. In his heyday, he had received hundreds of invitations every year to give talks and seminars. She was sure that sitting through a talk given by someone he regarded as an inferior intellect would be unacceptable, and that was why he shunned the meetings.

So why was he going now? Maybe the fact that the meeting was in Philadelphia had something to do with it. Philip still had a few friends there. Maybe he was planning to see some of them. The decision had been abrupt, but perhaps it was a good idea.

"I don't get it," Dorothy said to her father on the phone that evening. She had just finished lying to Dick about her car accident, and had no intention of telling him about the dog-napping. She did want to commiserate with her father about Philip's behavior. "First he withdraws and hardly speaks with me, then he acts like a jerk with his family, and now, out of the blue, he decides to go off to the kind of medical meeting that he usually avoids like the plague."

"Dorothy, you know I never liked this guy much, but if you're going to stay with him, you have to cut him some slack. He was a minor whacko to begin with, but the stuff that happened to him in the Hamlin case screwed up his head real bad."

"I thought he was finally getting over it, Dad."

"Look at it this way, Dorothy. Some of us are used to dealing with scumbags like the Hamlins and Straub. It was why I wanted you to work with me at the agency before you went to law school. I hoped it would desensitize you like it did me. Philip was a virgin when he walked into that mess, and a know-it-all to boot."

"I guess you have a point."

"Not only did he get sued and lose everything in his life, but then he had to watch the people who put him in the oven get off scot-free."

"I can't help believing that Philip knew about the Romanos' plans to kill the Hamlins and he just made sure we had an alibi." Dorothy mused. "Now, this Adolphus thing, it's practically all we talk about anymore."

"Philip is naïve, but he isn't stupid. Getting into bed with the Romanos would have been suicidal. I think you can put that possibility out of your mind. Besides, didn't you ask Vincente Romano that specific question?"

"And you think I could believe what that monster answered?"

"Look, you're getting all wound up about this, and it ain't going to help. How about if I give Philip a call and have dinner with him while he's down here at the meeting? Maybe I can convince him to forget about this Adolphus crap so you two can get on with your lives."

"Dad, I would really appreciate that. And maybe if I'm not around, he'll tell you what's really on his mind."

"I'm not going to be his friggin' shrink, little girl, but I'll hear him out and let you know how it goes."

Philip was away for four days. He called Dorothy every night to catch up on the day's activities. He told her that most of the meeting was as boring as he had anticipated, but he was happy he had attended. Some of the seminars were valuable, especially those about medical malpractice.

"I had no idea how complicated this area is."

"Yeah, really fascinating."

Philip could hear the sarcasm right through the telephone. "You don't agree?"

"I guess I've been a lawyer for too long. I agree that malpractice litigation is complicated, and you don't meet the nicest people."

"You mean the docs or the lawyers?" Philip asked.

"The lawyers I expect to be scumbags. What surprises me is how many physicians milk the system."

"I know. Almost every doctor I talked to at that seminar does expert work nearly full time."

"So I guess you can't really say they're physician peers?"

"Most have had extensive practice experience at some point in their careers, but then they go over to the dark side. A lot of them are retired and some just got fed up with the practice scene. I can see why they're seduced. The work isn't very hard."

"Let me guess why else," Dorothy posed. "Could it be green with photos of historical figures from the 18th century?"

"That has to be a big part of it—but not all. I think they also get a charge out of playing the big shot for a captive audience. In front of a jury, even an average joe has to look brilliant. And they get off on being called an expert when they are anything but."

"So what else did you learn from the seminar?"

"They talked about how to advertise your services."

"You aren't thinking about doing that, are you?"

"No, I haven't sunk that low yet. I still have a scrap of credibility I would like to protect. The session on file review and report preparation was a little helpful but the real interesting part was how to answer questions at deposition and trial."

"I bet they spent a lot of time on that."

"Yep, and they brought in some guys who did demonstrations for us. It was pretty interesting how they dissected the questions and constructed the answers. It looked like a damn chess game."

"Yes, it is. It has little to do with getting to the truth. It is much more about outmaneuvering your opponent."

"And putting the doc on the spot. Experts may be dirt bags, but the good ones have to be smart. You need to know the case details cold. The attorneys like nothing better than making an expert look stupid when he or she can't answer a fact question."

Dorothy wanted to change the subject. She heard enough of this stuff at work every day. "So did my dad call you?"

"Yeah, he left a message on my cell phone. He wants to have dinner."

"Right. He told me he was going to call. Get him to take you down to one of his favorite Italian places in South Philly."

"He's a step ahead of us. He has a reservation at The Saloon for this evening."

"Great, order the gnocchi. It's homemade and outrageous

with braciole or sausage. Make sure you put a lot of parmesan cheese on it, too."

"Sounds like you know the place pretty well."

"I used to take out-of-town clients there when I lived in the city. It's what visitors want and South Philly Italian never disappoints."

"I'm pretty surprised that he invited me to dinner. He hasn't seemed inclined to become my best bud."

"I think it's finally dawned on Dad that you're in it for the long haul and he might as well get on your good side."

"If he wants to see you frequently, that is," Philip finished her thought, pleased with Dorothy's attitude about their relationship.

"Yes, it's always a competition for the affection of the darling daughter, don't you know? Dad likes to see me and maybe now he realizes that he'll accomplish that easier with you as an ally and not an enemy. Use it for all it's worth, Philip."

Philip laughed. "So who's manipulating whom?"

"I wouldn't worry about that a whole bunch. Just go out and have a nice dinner with my father, and we'll see where it all goes."

Dorothy hung up feeling better about things. Philip had been upbeat on the phone, and her father was likely to be helpful in his own tough way. She went back to her work and looked forward to Philip's return on Saturday.

Dorothy decided to work at her office on Saturday morning. She had a few trials lined up in the next few months and she liked to get all of her deposition questions outlined far in advance. That meant poring through the background material her staff had accumulated on each of the witnesses. Dorothy had learned long ago that the more personal information she had in her possession when she sat across from a witness, the better the chance she would find something she didn't know but could be valuable at trial. It was a lot of work, but it never failed to pay dividends.

Dorothy left Scranton before lunch and pulled into the driveway to see Philip unloading his car. He gave her a big smile and hug at the doorway.

"I brought some hoagies home for lunch. I was going to get cheese steaks but they'd be cold before I got up here."

"Dalessandro's?" Dorothy surmised.

"You bet. Had to drive a little out of my way but it will be worth it."

The hoagie shop had been one of their favorites when they lived in the city. A dumpy little place in a blue-collar part of town called Roxborough. But if you didn't call ahead and order your sandwiches, especially at lunchtime, you could look forward to waiting in a line that usually stretched out the door and up the street. A lot of people thought that a Dalessandro's sandwich was worth almost any wait.

"I love the woman behind the counter," Philip recounted as he pulled lunch from the back seat. "Remember her? Always had a cigarette hanging out of her mouth? Well, she's still there, and bitchy as ever. Anyhow, she remembered me and that I like a ton of hot peppers on my hoagie."

"She might be irascible but nobody can call her dumb," Dorothy agreed. "She also knew what toppings we liked on our pizza, so when she saw our number on the caller ID, she would just ask if we wanted the usual."

They got the car unloaded and the dogs settled before sitting down with their sandwiches topped off with a bag of Herr's barbecue flavored potato chips. Given the calorie load, it was almost funny to chase everything down with Diet Cokes.

Philip was obviously in a good mood. "After I spoke with you the other night, the meeting picked up."

"That's good."

"Yep, I learned a lot in the last couple of days. I had some major questions that I think I finally got answered."

"Great. How did dinner with my father go?"

Philip hesitated a beat before he answered. "Terrific. We had a great time. We actually ran into a few of his pals who joined us for dinner."

"Business associates?"

"You could say that. People he's known for years who he helped out on a few cases."

"I hope they didn't bore you with shop talk."

"Oh no, I was very interested in everything they had to say. The cases they discussed were really fascinating."

"So did you get any one-on-one time with my dad?"

"Oh yeah, his friends left right after coffee, and we decided to walk back to my hotel. We had a nice chat about things and then a nightcap at the hotel bar. Your dad knew every cocktail waitress in the place."

"I bet he knew them better than you think," Dorothy laughed.

As interested as she was in what her men had talked about, Dorothy was reluctant to probe much further for fear of giving away the evening's intent. Philip didn't let her twist.

"Dorothy, I know why your father called to have dinner. You wanted him to talk to me to see if he could straighten me out. I resented your interference at first, but as it turned out, it was a real good idea. Your father and I had a productive conversation, and I definitely feel better about things."

"You do?"

"Yes. You were right. I've been moody, and I think it's because I've been worried about you."

"You have a funny way of showing your concern."

"I know, and I apologize. That evening with my brother was brutal. I knew I was being a dick but I couldn't help myself." Philip took Dorothy's hand. "Thanks for setting things up with your dad. It was a great idea, and getting away to the meeting definitely helped."

"It did?" Dorothy realized she was being monosyllabic but she could hardly believe her ears.

"I promise to do better," Philip pledged.

Dorothy was relieved. She choked up and tearfully replied, "Philip, you have to remember that we're in this together. When you withdraw, it scares me even more because I don't know what you're thinking, and I can't rely on you."

"I think I'm clear on that now, and I'll be more forthcoming. Spending more time with your dad might help, too. It'll help both of us."

"That sounds great. Now why don't we clean up, take these poor and ignored doggies for a romp in the woods, and get on with our weekend?"

"Sounds perfect. I could use some fresh air."

Later, as they strolled down a hiking trail near their house, Philip had another suggestion for Dorothy.

"While I was in Philly, I scouted out some new restaurants. I found this great little Lebanese place called Cedars. It's a block off of South Street near Penn's Landing. What do you say we meet your father there for dinner on Friday evening?"

"You mean, just go down for dinner and come back?"

"Or we could stay over."

"I don't have my Blackberry with me, but I think I have a pretty busy day on Friday, with a deposition in the afternoon that could turn into a marathon. Why don't we go down on Saturday?"

As soon as the words were out of her mouth, Dorothy could sense the tension build between them.

"That won't work," Philip said through clenched teeth.

"Why not?"

"First of all, I don't think your dad can make it on Saturday. I already asked him for Friday. And they have belly dancers on Friday night. He and I thought it would be fun to see a little live entertainment."

"Can I let you know later in the week?"

"Reservations are really tough to get there. It's just a little place with a few tables and homemade food. Can't you start the deposition earlier or move it to another day? Lawyers pull that trick with docs all the time."

Dorothy knew that Philip wasn't going to back off. It was either change her office schedule or risk the return of Mr. Hyde. That thought made the choice easy for Dorothy.

"OK, Philip, I'll see what I can do when I get back to the office on Monday. My secretary should be able to juggle things so we can leave Friday afternoon. This place had better be worth it."

"Thanks. Yes, it'll be a blast, I promise."

Oh yeah, Dorothy thought, it could be great fun—depending on which Philip Sarkis showed up for dinner.

Chapter Twenty-Two

Dorothy's heavy caseload routinely kept her at work much later than she would have liked. Philip was on the day shift, but they still didn't have much time to share. Dorothy was frustrated—she had taken this job expecting a lighter schedule. After a few high-profile wins, referrals picked up considerably and now she was inundated. On the other hand, the law firm's other partners were delighted and promised to hire more people to support her, but they weren't serious. They needed the revenue to keep the firm afloat, so helping Dorothy attain a better lifestyle was not on their immediate agenda. They justified their decisions by pointing out that the cases would require Dorothy's direct supervision no matter how many minions she had. And so her file count and her work hours just kept growing.

Philip and Dorothy usually emailed frequently during the day to stay in touch. On this particular Friday, Philip sent Dorothy his plans for their junket to Philadelphia. He suggested in his first message that they leave around 4:00 P.M., pick up her father at his condo at 6:00 and arrive for dinner by 6:30. Dorothy agreed.

"Should we get a hotel or drive home?" his next message asked.

"I'm glad you finally asked me," Dorothy chided. "I volunteer not to drink much and be the designated driver so we can return Friday night and have an entire weekend at home for a change."

"Done," Philip replied in his last message. Dorothy was relieved. She didn't want to get into more of a hassle about the trip, and she didn't want to pay a fortune for a hotel room *and* an overnight dog sitter. Having a neighbor come in to check on Mitten and Buffy once or twice was a lot less costly, and easier to arrange. Besides, the hounds loved Dana, the person next door who played with them even when Philip and Dorothy were home and would gladly check to make sure they were OK.

By the middle of the afternoon, Dorothy was glad Philip had insisted on an early departure. She was eager to leave her office. The summer weather was perfect, and the forecast called for a beautiful weekend. She had been mired down at work and finally realized how desperately she needed a break.

With little traffic, she sped home, met Philip, settled Mitten and Buffy for the evening, wrote out some instructions for Dana, and changed into jeans and a polo shirt. The drive to Philly was easy—all the cars were traveling in the other direction, north to the Pocono Mountains. Philip was in a good mood, chatting about work, his kids, and whatever else popped into his mind. Dorothy flicked through the radio stations and enjoyed the scenery, nodding once in a while but not paying much attention to Philip's chatter. Philip didn't mind. He seemed perfectly happy to hold forth with minimal response from his daydreaming companion.

Dick Deaver was waiting for them in the lobby of his condominium building. Condos in Philadelphia were a hot item. Many empty nesters were selling their large houses in the suburbs and moving into the city. Dick lived in one of the priciest. He loved the convenience of walking to work, shops, and restaurants. And his "pad," as he called it, was a cool place to take the women he met while barhopping.

"I think *I'm* the most interesting man in the world, not that dorko on the beer commercials," Dick liked to point out to his daughter. Dorothy laughed but had to admit he had an argument. He did interesting things, had a million great stories to tell, and, with his neatly trimmed graying beard, he even looked a lot like the guy on television. He certainly knew how to "stay thirsty."

It was a short drive from Dick's place to Cedars, and they even found a parking spot right in front of the restaurant. Philip had called ahead for the reservation, and when they arrived, he was greeted like an old friend.

"Mr. Philip Sarkis, we are so glad you can join us. I am Thomas Chamoun, the owner. We so much enjoy welcoming our Lebanese brothers to our humble restaurant. We have been looking forward to seeing you again."

Philip look confused. "Thomas, it is nice to have such a warm greeting but this is the first time I've been here."

Now it was the owner's turn to be nonplussed. "You and your family were here a few months ago. I remember it well."

"Philip, don't you have cousins in the area?" Dorothy interjected.

"You're right. I think you must have met my cousins, Mr. Chamoun."

It was a story Philip's father loved to tell and one Philip, in turn, had related to Dorothy. After the Second World War, the Sarkis family immigrated from a small village in northern Lebanon to the United States, and they arrived piecemeal over the course of several months. They did so intentionally because they didn't want to attract attention at a time when America was beginning to impose immigration quotas. Almost all of them entered through New York before dispersing to areas around the country where relatives had already established toeholds. Philip's family had decided on Philadelphia. His father was thoroughly impressed with the Liberty Bell and thought that any city that had preserved such an amazing symbol of freedom would certainly smile on new immigrants and allow them to prosper.

Based on reports from friends and relatives who had preceded them, they were certain the clerks at the immigration stations would butcher their Lebanese names. They wanted to preserve the family's identity so they decided to take the name of their village as their new last name. Philip's family came from a small farming village north of Beirut called Sarkis. They also agreed to use English first names, and combed through books at the local library before their trip and asked any westerners they met for suggestions.

Unfortunately, the extended family didn't confer about which first names they would use at the immigration desk. One of Philip's uncles, who came into the country just ahead of Philip's parents, chose the same names for his children as Butrus Sarkis. Since that part of the family settled in the Allentown/Bethlehem area north of Philadelphia, Philip's parents lost touch with them, and when they eventually discovered the duplication, it was too late to change. Philip liked to imagine there was someone not too far away who was living a mirror-image life. And every once in a while, their paths came tantalizingly close, and the name issue led to mistaken identities.

"So the Philip Sarkis you met a few months ago was my cousin," Philip explained to Mr. Chamoun.

"I can assure you, there is a strong family resemblance, Mr. Sarkis."

Philip hadn't seen his cousins in many years, but he remembered that they had similar features. In Lebanon, as in many other Middle Eastern countries, families in small villages had intermarried over several centuries. Philip suspected this was why inheritable diseases like diabetes were so prevalent among his uncles and aunts.

Philip introduced Dick and Dorothy to Mr. Chamoun, who had saved a prime table for his countryman. Thomas looked surprised as he shook Dick and Dorothy's hands. He hadn't expected that some of his countryman's guests would look anything but Semitic.

After a round of Lebanese beer, Philip ordered all of the food for the table. They started with a full spectrum of appetizers with plenty of pita bread to mop up the glorious hummus, babaganoush, and tabouli. Next came grape leaves, kibbi, lamb kabob, and rice. The portions were monstrous. Philip wondered if they were usual size or loaded up for "homeys." Philip ordered round after round of beer for Dick and himself, while Dorothy was content nursing a glass of Chardonnay.

Toward the end of dinner, while baklava and espresso were served, the belly dancers made their first appearance. Dorothy was immediately struck by how non-Arab the dancers looked. "I think these are people who took a belly dancing class at the Y to stay in shape," she observed to Philip.

"They aren't natives, that's for sure," Philip agreed. "Maybe you're just jealous of those great bodies."

Dorothy spun around, surprised by Philip's observation. Philip must have had a lot to drink—he rarely ogled women or commented on their anatomy. "They are amazing, I have to admit," Dorothy finally answered. "And they dance up a storm."

She didn't need to point any of this out to her father, who was mesmerized by the show. To Dick's delight, the women danced around the tables, inviting the customers to place tips in their outfits. Philip was clearly embarrassed, and he reluctantly obliged. Dick, on the other hand, took out a wad of tens and twenties and began to stuff them into whatever part of the costumes he could access. He was the life of the party, calling the waiters over to order drinks for the owners and the other customers.

"Philip, this is a great place. How come you never took us here before?" Dick asked during one of the breaks in the show.

"I didn't know much about the place. One of the endocrinologists at the hospital told me about it a few years ago, but I just never got around to looking it up. When I was in town last week, I decided to come down to South Street to do a little exploring, and I stumbled on it."

"South Street is great," Dick agreed. "They have so many great shops and restaurants down here, it's hard to keep track."

After another dance set, they decided to take advantage of the sultry summer evening and sample the street. Philip paid the bill, and they said goodbye to Mr. Chamoun and his family after complimenting them on a splendid dining experience, and promising to come back soon. As they came out of the restaurant, they were immediately engulfed in the South Street crowd.

"This is amazing," Dorothy practically screamed to be heard. "The place is really alive."

"It's Friday night. What better way to start the weekend?" Dick observed.

The street was teeming with people, young and old. Cars clogged the narrow streets as drivers trolled for parking spaces. The three enjoyed the people watching as much as the window-shopping. After a few blocks, Dorothy suggested they call it a night.

"I'm pretty tired, and since I'm the chauffer for the evening, I get to decide when we hit the road."

"Party pooper," Dick teased. "No, you're right. It is a long drive back for you."

"We won't hit much traffic in town," Philip agreed. "But you never know what the old turnpike will be like."

Dick stopped and frowned. Philip had meant construction and accidents but he had hit a nerve and realized it immediately.

"Damn it, Philip, did you have to say that? I worry every time you guys come down that road."

"Sorry, Dick. I was thinking about the traffic delays, not about bad people."

"I think I'll just take a cab back to my place. You guys go ahead and get on the road home. Dorothy, text me when you arrive, will you?"

Before they had time to argue with him, Dick hailed a cab and was climbing in.

The drive home was uneventful after all. By the time they tended to the dogs, checked for messages, and got ready for bed, it was 2:00 A.M. Philip was unconscious in moments, while Dorothy had to read a little to settle her brain. She eventually got to sleep despite the cacophony of snoring coming not only from Philip, but also from Mitten and Buffy.

Philip was still asleep when Dorothy awoke the next morning. She could hardly believe she had slept until 10:00 A.M. The dogs had been restless, and she had heard Philip get up with them at least twice during the night. Still, it was unusual for their day to start so late.

Dorothy shuffled out the front door to get the *Pocono Record* at the end of the driveway. It wasn't the big city paper she had always favored, but they had agreed that getting the local news was a good idea. The paper usually came early and scanning it was now part of Dorothy's early morning routine.

She sat sleepily at the kitchen table, sipping her coffee and trying to wake up as she took off the plastic cover and unfolded the front page. The banner headline on the front page nearly knocked her off the chair: "FIRE KILLS THIRTY AGENCY NURSES." The caption under the headline identified the victims as employees of the Adolphus Nursing Agency in Wilkes-Barre.

Dorothy quickly read through the first few sentences. "Thirty members of the Adolphus Nursing Agency perished in a flash fire at their headquarters building in Wilkes-Barre on Friday evening. The names of the nurses are being withheld pending notification of the families.

"The fire appears to have started in the building's heating system and spread rapidly to the first floor, where the nurses were holding their monthly business meeting. Thirty of the agency's fifty nurses were in attendance; most of the others were working their customary shifts. Adolphus supplies nurses to intensive care and intermediate care units for several area hospitals. Agency officials could not be reached for comment."

Dorothy shook her head. Was she still asleep and dreaming? No, even she couldn't conjure this one up; it had to be real. There were a few other facts about the agency and about the fire investigation in the story. She recognized what was left of the building in the post-blaze photo.

Philip had to see this—now. She burst into the bedroom, roused Philip and waved the front page in his face. Philip opened his eyes, focused on the paper, read for a minute or two, and then looked up at Dorothy.

"Gosh, that's incredible," Philip said, yawning and rubbing his eyes.

"That's all you have to say?"

"What do you want me to say?"

"Are you kidding me? You just found out that thirty Adolphus nurses died in a fire. I expected a little more shock and dismay, maybe?"

"I *am* very surprised. Like I said, it's incredible," Philip said, climbing out of bed.

"Were you going to ask if there were any details in the article?"

"Sure, what were the details?"

"It's too early for details," Dorothy sneered. "It happened just last night. And they said that agency officials were not available for comment. That's most likely because Brenda was killed in the fire. They said it occurred during a business meeting, so she was probably running it."

Philip shook his head and looked over at the dogs that had jumped into the bed to take their place on the warm covers. He was scratching his head now, and his ennui just made Dorothy angrier.

"This whole thing just keeps getting crazier," Dorothy ranted on. "First we find out these people are killing old guys, then the police refuse to go after them, then they nearly murder me, and now over half of them are dead. Philip, this is freaking me out!"

"Let me get some coffee, and I'll read the whole article."

Dorothy walked back into the dining room to wait for Philip, but before he came out of the bathroom, the phone rang. Dorothy picked it up, and when she heard who was on the other end, her heart sank.

"Ms. Deaver, this is Lieutenant Detweiler."

"Good morning, Lieutenant," Dorothy managed. Her throat

felt like sand.

"I don't expect you've seen the news this morning?"

"Yes, Lieutenant, we have."

"Pretty incredible stuff, wouldn't you say?"

"To say the least, Lieutenant." Dorothy was not enjoying the sparring, and the word "incredible" was beginning to really piss her off.

"Is there some reason you called, other than delivering bad news?" Dorothy asked.

"I'd like to come over and ask you and Dr. Sarkis a few questions, if that's OK."

"Certainly, Lieutenant." There was no point in objecting; he was coming over with or without permission. "What time did you have in mind?"

"How about now? I can be there in thirty minutes."

"That would be fine, Lieutenant. You'll excuse us if we don't have breakfast for you this time."

"No, Ms. Deaver, I've already had breakfast and coffee, so that won't be necessary. We'll try to keep this as brief as possible, and we'll try to avoid a trip to the station."

"A trip to the station? What does that mean, Lieutenant?"

"I'll explain when I get there, Ms. Deaver. And please make sure Dr. Sarkis is present as well, so we can get this over with."

Dorothy hung up, relieved that she hadn't lost it during the conversation. She knew exactly what Detweiler wanted to talk about and it wasn't going to be pleasant.

Philip finally stumbled out of the bathroom and made a beeline for the coffee. Dorothy always had a difficult time reading his thoughts, and this situation was no exception. His face was expressionless as he scanned the front page, seated at the counter, sipping from his favorite mug. Finally, he looked up, shrugged and asked, "So, who was on the phone?"

"I thought you'd never ask," Dorothy answered, with obvious irritation. "It was our new best friend, Lieutenant Detweiler."

"Really! And what did the good Lieutenant want?"

"What the hell do you think he wanted, Philip? He's coming over to talk to us about what happened to those nurses last night, and I wouldn't anticipate a lovely chat."

Dorothy couldn't stand to look at Philip and his dead-pan expression one second longer. She started for the bedroom, and spoke over her shoulder. "I'm going to put some clothes on, and I suggest you do the same, Philip. Real clothes. Who knows, we may get a chance to take a ride in the back of a police car."

As she turned to close the bedroom door, Philip was scratching his groin, hunched over the newspaper, sipping coffee and looking as oblivious as could be.

Chapter Twenty-Three

When Dorothy returned to the kitchen, Philip seemed to have snapped to after three cups of coffee. While pulling on her jeans, Dorothy had thought about prepping Philip, but realized they didn't have time to adequately preview Detweiler's questions. She quickly straightened up the house while Philip showered and dressed. Mitten and Buffy found a comfortable spot next to the slider that went out to the deck and sunned themselves while Philip and Dorothy crisscrossed the house, exchanging sound bites as they passed each other in the rooms and hallways.

Dorothy: "Do you think he believes we had something to do with this?"

Philip: "I'm getting tired of seeing this guy."

Dorothy: "Maybe if the police had spent more time making a case against those nurses, this wouldn't have happened."

Philip: "We have to find out if they think the fire was set or it was an accident."

Dorothy: "Thank goodness we were away last night or that dork would think we set it ourselves."

Philip: "Did he say if any of the nurses in the building survived?"

Dorothy: "If the families up here found out those nurses were killing their relatives, Detweiler would have plenty of suspects."

It went on like this until they had finally readied themselves and heard Detweiler's car rumble over the stones in their driveway. When the detective entered, they could tell immediately he was in a much different frame of mind than the last time he visited.

Detweiler took off his coat and gave it to Dorothy; Philip led him to the sofa in the living room. "Are you sure you don't want coffee or tea," Dorothy felt obliged to ask as she seated herself on an armchair across from the Lieutenant.

"No thank you, Ms. Deaver." Detweiler didn't want to waste time on small talk.

"I'll tell you what I know, and then I'd like to ask you both a few questions."

"That's fine, Lieutenant," Dorothy answered.

"First of all, let me stipulate that neither of you are official suspects..."

Dorothy cut in, "Do you mean 'yet,' Lieutenant?"

"Not at this point, Ms. Deaver. And so this is an informal interrogation. But if you want an attorney present, that would be your prerogative."

"Why don't you just read us our Miranda rights, Lieutenant?"

"Now, Ms. Deaver, you know that isn't necessary. You haven't been charged with anything."

Philip was uncomfortable with the confrontation between Dorothy and Detweiler and tried to intercede. "As you know, Dorothy is an attorney, Lieutenant, so I think we are OK with going ahead."

"I'd like to tape this conversation so I don't have to take notes—is that OK with you?" Detweiler asked.

"We have nothing to hide, Lieutenant," Dorothy answered faster than Philip expected, and with each reply, her tone was edgier.

Detweiler took out a mini-tape recorder, turned it on, and

set it up on the table. After a brief introduction about whom he was interviewing, where, when, and why, he began the session.

"Let me start by giving you some of the facts as I know them, and then I'll have a few pertinent questions for you. At about 9:00 P.M. last evening, a fire broke out at the Adolphus Agency building outside of Wilkes-Barre. Are you familiar with the building?"

"I've driven by there," Dorothy answered without missing a beat. She managed a sideway glance at Philip, clearly warning him to keep his mouth shut.

"Good. So you know it's set back off the road a few hundred feet and that there are no other buildings close by. It was frame construction, but pretty sturdy and well maintained. Anyhow, according to the secretary who arranged the meeting, the nurses were having their regular business discussion in the conference room. They had dinner brought in by a caterer. She said they had a long agenda so she thought the meeting would have gone until at least 10."

"Who called the fire department?" Dorothy asked.

"Nobody. They had a smoke alarm system that went directly into the local fire company. They were there within minutes."

"So the place burned that quickly?" Philip asked.

"You can say that again. It was an inferno by the time the fire trucks arrived."

"Did anybody get out?"

"Nope. All of them were in the conference room. The Fire Marshall suspects that they were overwhelmed by smoke so quickly that they couldn't get to the doors or windows."

"So maybe they didn't suffer too much," Dorothy surmised.

"I think that is a little dismissive, Ms. Deaver. They were all burned to a crisp, and it was pretty gory. It's going to take a long time to identify the bodies. The only way we've been able to get an idea about who was actually in there has been from the license plates of the cars in the parking lot."

Dorothy asked the obvious question. "Was Brenda Straub

present?"

"So you know who the directress was, Ms. Deaver?"

Dorothy blushed, realizing that she had given Detweiler a reason to be even more suspicious. "Was, Lieutenant?"

"The secretary told us she was running the meeting, and her Subaru was in the first parking spot," Detweiler concluded.

"Oh my God, this is terrible," Dorothy gasped.

Philip noted that Detweiler was sizing up Dorothy's reaction, trying to see how authentic it was. It looked pretty good to Philip at least.

"Have the fire officials come up with a cause for the fire?" Philip asked.

"It's probably better if I don't divulge that information now, and it's too early to be certain. They were surprised at how fast the place burned and how much smoke it produced."

"So you think somebody may have used an incendiary?"

"That's what the fire chief thinks, but I really can't get into particulars."

Detweiler had a lot of other information he wasn't going to divulge, especially not to these two jokers. From the pattern of the blaze, the fire inspectors were fairly certain that a flammable substance had been planted in the basement ceiling, right below the conference room floor and around the outside walls of the building. In that case, the fire would have burned upward into the walls of the conference room very quickly, in effect cutting off escape in any direction. If the inspectors confirmed all of this, the killers would have been pretty sophisticated and knew exactly what they were doing. Not only was their plan perfectly executed, but apparently no one had smelled anything before the fire was actually set.

"Who could have wanted to set the fire?" Philip asked in an innocent tone. Dorothy almost choked on her coffee. Even Detweiler couldn't conceal his astonishment. It took him a few seconds to recover.

"Are you toying with me, Doctor?"

"This is not a joking matter, Lieutenant. I'm serious."

"If the story you brought me about the agency's mission to

kill World War II veterans is true, we have the potential for an army of suspects, excuse the pun. I know that my people didn't divulge the identity of the nursing agency to the victims' families. Did either of you, by any chance?"

"No," Philip answered haughtily. "We were very careful not to mention Adolphus or Brenda Straub to any of the families. When we requested records, we made up a story about a hospital audit."

"If word got out that those nurses were neo-Nazis, as your father's detectives suggested, there'd be a lot of other people who might want to see them dead."

"My father assured me that the investigative files were sealed."

"I'm inclined to believe that, knowing your father's business. And if this were planned, it wasn't some bleeding heart liberals merely trying to teach skinheads a lesson."

"How do you know that, Lieutenant?" Philip asked.

Detweiler looked down at his clasped hands. There was more information from his investigation that wasn't for public consumption. The police learned from the secretarial staff at Adolphus, none of whom attended the fateful business meeting, that a new service company had visited the agency building the day of the fire. Reliable Heating and Cooling showed up unannounced to do "routine maintenance" on their furnace and air conditioning units. They told the staff they had bought the contract from Kessler's, the company that had been servicing the facility since it was built.

According to the daytime security crew, they wore uniforms, had valid credentials, and went about their business professionally. They were down in the basement, where the climate control systems were kept, for almost two hours. None of the security people had bothered to go down to see what they were up to except for Jake, the rookie on the crew. And Jake hadn't bothered to report back to the security desk or clock out before he left for the day. After hearing that story, Detweiler wasn't surprised when Jake didn't answer his phone and was not at his apartment. The on-site detective was pretty sure he was going to need Jake's dental records, and Detweiler had agreed.

Not surprisingly, there was no company called Reliable Heating and Cooling in the phone book or anywhere else, and Kessler denied being replaced by another provider. They had recently renewed their contract with Adolphus and had no plans to go out of business.

Detweiler wasn't about to tell Philip and Dorothy any of those details. It wasn't their business, and he didn't want to help them hide what they had done—if in fact they were involved.

"Suffice it to say that we have good reason to believe that whoever did this knew how to plan a complicated job, and had the resources to pull it off," Detweiler answered finally and in a carefully crafted understatement.

Dorothy was becoming progressively uncomfortable with the conversation. She finally let it out. "Lieutenant, can we be straight with each other? You didn't come over here to brief us. You said you had some questions for us, and that's why your tape recorder is running. So what are they?"

"The most obvious, Ms. Deaver, is your whereabouts yesterday?"

"We were both at work most of the day," Philip chimed in. "About 4:00 P.M. we drove down to Philly to have dinner with Dorothy's father at Cedars on South Street."

"I assume you can tell me who might have seen you there, and when?"

"No problem," Dorothy said, sounding very confident. "My father can tell you, but we also talked to the owner of the restaurant when we arrived and when we left at about 9:00 P.M. There were some dancers there who will surely remember us, especially my father."

"We can check on all of that," Detweiler said. "Since this job was most likely for hire, your alibi doesn't get you completely off the hook, but it will help a good deal."

"If you wish, Lieutenant, we can give you access to our bank account records. I think you'll agree when you see our finances that bankrolling a job like you described is as much in our price range as paying for a trip to the moon."

"Thanks for the offer," Detweiler deadpanned. "We will probably want to take you up on that as well, although most killers don't make out checks to their accomplices."

"Lieutenant, do you really think we would try to kill all of those nurses?" Dorothy asked, tears welling up.

"Maybe you didn't mean to kill all of them. In fact, if you did, you missed twenty or so who were working at the time. Maybe you just wanted to get Brenda Straub and the others were collateral damage. But I know people can get pretty angry when their loved ones are put in jeopardy."

"Right, Lieutenant. Going after Dorothy was bad enough, but when they screwed around with my dog..."

"Philip, stop that!" Dorothy cut him off.

"I couldn't help myself."

Detweiler brushed off Philip's sarcasm. "I know this is wearing on both of you, Dr. Sarkis, and I wish I could leave you alone. But under the circumstances, I wouldn't be doing my job, would I? You have to be on the list of candidates for this murder, if not suspects, and we just have to go a little further to get you cleared."

"What do you have in mind, Lieutenant?"

"I was going to suggest a lie detector test."

Dorothy put her hand to her mouth. She didn't want Detweiler to see her reaction. He'd expect her to be pleased to have the chance to prove their innocence. She was anything but.

"What would that prove beyond what you already know?" she asked trying to be as matter of fact as possible. "We have an alibi, and we didn't have the means to pay somebody else to do it."

"Let's be frank, Ms. Deaver. If this were anybody else, I would check your alibi, look at your recent bank transactions, and call it a day. But as you'll recall, two people in Philadelphia were x'ed out a few years ago in a professional hit. It just so happened that Dr. Sarkis had a good motive, but jeez, what a coincidence, he had an instant alibi that involved fun time with you at the Jersey shore."

"I had nothing to do with those murders, Lieutenant. That book was closed a long time ago," Philip said indignantly.

"As well it should have been, based on the evidence available at the time," Detweiler agreed. "But here we are again. Murderers not brought to justice but guilty in your opinion, found dead after a professional hit. Come on, Doctor, you can't expect me to let this go as a coincidence. So are you up to the challenge?"

Dorothy didn't let Philip answer. "Absolutely not. I don't trust the technology, and we aren't going to place ourselves in jeopardy just to help you with your investigation or to satisfy your curiosity."

"Lieutenant, you have my word that I had nothing to do with this," Philip continued. "That's going to have to be good enough for now."

Detweiler turned off the recorder, put it in his pocket and rose to leave. He grabbed the jacket that had been folded over a dining room chair. "I understand, but I strongly suggest that neither of you leaves the area until we check up on a few things and develop the case a little further. And think long and hard about the lie detector test. It ain't so bad, and it would get you off the hook completely."

"We'll ponder that, Lieutenant, and we weren't planning on going anywhere for a while," Dorothy answered.

"Good, and if anything else comes to mind, please give me a call. I'll be working the case myself for a while. The boys upstairs have finally started paying attention."

"What do you think will happen to the Adolphus Agency?" Dorothy asked.

"I can't imagine it will survive this tragedy. From what I heard, Brenda Straub was the heart and soul. I suspect the rest of the nurses will move on."

"That's a big blow to the local hospitals."

"I suspect it is. But things will get back to normal eventually. They always do."

Detweiler walked out the front door, got into his car, and pulled away. Dorothy and Philip closed the door and went back to their Saturday chores. But they both knew that the Adolphus incident would remain a hot topic for a long time to come.

Chapter Twenty-Four

As anyone could have anticipated, the media had a field day with the Adolphus tragedy. The story had all of the elements of a great tearjerker. Here were thirty people who had served their country in the armed forces. After putting their lives in jeopardy to treat and heal our valiant troops, they returned to their native land to care for sick and dying hospital patients. Not only that, but they had chosen the unglamorous and much maligned coal mining region of Pennsylvania to carry out their life-saving work. They and their wonderful families had become part of the fabric of the community and, most notably, brought cutting-edge nursing care to the region. To have perished in a fire at their agency was mind-boggling. Their deaths were a tragedy at so many levels, not the least of which was the loss of the skillful care they rendered to thousands of local residents. To the many who would feel their loss, the community expressed its deepest sympathy, most importantly, to the families of the wonderful nurses.

Philip and Dorothy followed the stories because they had no choice. Every radio and television station carried regular reports including interviews with assorted people who had even the slightest relationship to the fallen heroes. "This stuff makes me want to gag," Philip finally admitted. "I've never heard so much hyperbole and schmaltz in all my life."

Dorothy's reaction was much less visceral. "I wonder how many of the nurses' families knew what their relatives were really up to? Or maybe some of them were in on the mercy killings themselves."

Despite their cynicism, Philip and Dorothy understood why most people weren't able to divert their attention from the tragedy. News people and paparazzi took full advantage, staking out the homes of the grieving neighbors and friends, struggling to get an interview or at least a few shots of sorrowful relatives.

But true to Detweiler's word, very little information had been given to the media about what exactly had happened. The reporters uniformly stated that the cause of the fire was under investigation, and none specifically mentioned arson. Detweiler himself continued to pursue a murder theory, but only his secretary and his chief knew all of the facts about what the Adolphus agency may have been and the potential reasons for the suspicious fire. Though Dorothy and Philip expected to see Detweiler's mug in front of the cameras, he seemed content to stay out of the limelight.

And, despite their alleged research prowess, no news agency had yet discovered that Adolphus was the front for a neo-Nazi organization. "What a lollapalooza of a story that would make," Philip observed one evening as he sat in front of the television watching the local news. "If the truth got out, the media circus would go three-ring real quick. Detweiler wouldn't be able to walk out of his office to use the men's room, let alone do fact finding to make his case."

The nurses who came from the area were buried by their families in a series of emotional ceremonies that gave the newspapers and TV stations great photo opportunities. The region, for which "big" was a 4-H show, saw itself on the national news several evenings in a row. Even the Vice President, who had roots in the area, made a trip to Wilkes-Barre and Scranton to meet with the mourning widows, children, and parents of the dead nurses. How ironic, Dorothy and Philip thought, that the villains who had killed war veterans were being themselves lionized as heroes and patriots.

The hype went on for several days until it was time for the mass media to move on to other carnage, this time a multiple homicide on a western university campus. That was followed soon thereafter by coverage of an oil spill that threatened to wipe out half the world's sea life. Finally Scranton/Wilkes-Barre was left in the dust. In his most cynical tone, Philip observed, "There's nothing like a natural disaster to keep the viewers engaged and to jack the price of commercial time."

Meanwhile, Detweiler was accumulating information. So far, the preliminary opinions of the fire officials were holding up: someone had planted a combustible in the basement in large quantity, and had concentrated on the walls surrounding the conference room. The fire had clearly started in or near the heating unit in the basement and quickly ignited the floors and walls of the conference room. It was still not clear what the murderous substance was, but it didn't stink and produced immense amounts of smoke early in the fire. Not only did the intense smoke impair the victims' vision, but it also started coughing fits that made organized escape much less likely. Judging from the few cases in which autopsies were possible, the coroner believed that the smoke had mercifully knocked out at least a few of the nurses before they were incinerated.

Detweiler conferred with the Scranton crime-scene team that had been dispatched as soon as the fire officials suspected foul play. He wasn't expecting too much. The team was hardly the real-life equivalent of the crew that roamed Las Vegas on TV every week. After a cursory examination of the property, to Detweiler's chagrin, they had ultimately filed a sloppy report stating they believed that the fire had been set, but, because of the extent of the damage, it was unlikely they'd be able to identify the arsonists or the material that had been used.

Detweiler was furious as he sat combing through their comments. In their desultory two-page preliminary filing, they mentioned in passing that they had collected a few dozen nails on the floor of what was left of the conference room. The report gave no details as to where the nails had been and what they were used for, but Detweiler's attention was piqued immediately.

Detweiler had been wrestling with the question of why the nurses had not simply opened the windows and jumped to the ground. The meeting room was on the first floor. The glass itself was shatterproof, so only if the frames had somehow been sealed would escape have been impossible. Because the building was fully air conditioned and centrally heated, the windows were rarely opened. But that didn't mean they couldn't have been used to exit in an emergency. Why hadn't the nurses escaped?

Detweiler used his computer to comb through the photographs of the scene taken before anything had been disturbed. He matched the photos to diagrams of the structure, which he had obtained from county records. He then magnified the areas where the windows should have been, and filtered the images looking for metallic reflections. He wasn't particularly surprised to see several gleaming nails scattered in clumps just under the few identifiable windows. The only question was how long before the fire had the windows been nailed shut and the trap prepared?

Detweiler also personally supervised the search for the Reliable truck. It had not been seen by anyone in the area before or after its visit to Adolphus, which was not surprising because the agency building was in a pretty isolated area. The only break came from the turnpike guys, who had a photo of the truck going through the E-Z Pass lanes illegally about an hour before it would have arrived at the agency. At first, Detweiler was surprised that the murderers would have made such an amateurish mistake, not paying a measly toll, until he found out that the plates had been snatched from a rig that had been reported stolen in South Philadelphia. Although the name "Reliable" was visible on the turnpike photo, the resolution and lighting didn't permit a look at the passengers, even after the crime-scene people played with the images for hours.

Detweiler concluded that the murder was a well-planned execution by an out-of-town crew. This was not particularly surprising; South Philly was a den for professional wiseguys who knew the Poconos. They liked to dump their marks in the mountain wilderness, almost as much as the New York hoodlums favored the Jersey wetlands for corpse disposal.

But a contract to kill thirty people at one time, and to make it look like an accident, would have been extremely expensive, a premium job even by hit man standards. After checking Philip and Dorothy's bank records, it was clear they didn't have much cash. There had been one withdrawal from Philip's account of 3500 dollars a few months before the murders, but Detweiler doubted that would cover a fraction of the cost of such an ambitious scheme. It also didn't take him long to find out that their alibi was airtight. The owner and the belly dancers at Cedars remembered Philip and Dorothy and the "dirty old man" who had accompanied them.

In fact, Philip and Dorothy's alibi was almost too good. They had chosen a place with a lot of people, but intimate enough so that the owners and patrons easily remembered them. Detweiler suspected that one or both of them knew about the hit before it happened. Nonetheless, proving they were complicit and then finding out who had actually killed the nurses was going to be quite difficult.

Over the next several days, Philip and Dorothy gradually returned to their routines. They didn't talk much about the incident, although one evening Dorothy confided to Philip that she was still anxious about being home alone or driving her car. What if the remaining skinheads came to the same conclusion as Detweiler, namely that Philip and Dorothy had somehow arranged to kill their colleagues? What if they decided to exact their revenge? Were they as organized a group without Brenda Straub? Or with the head cut off, would the monster just fall dead?

Philip tried to reassure Dorothy that things would get back to normal soon. His confidence confused her, and she found nothing soothing about his attitude or opinions. As she had so many times before, Dorothy tried very hard to put the episode behind her and move on.

A few weeks after the fire, Dorothy awoke on a bright Saturday morning and prepared to run errands. Philip had worked the 4–to-12 shift the night before and, as she dressed to leave, he was sleeping soundly, surrounded by the hounds, out cold and snoring louder than Philip. Dorothy shook her head. They had agreed to try to get the dogs off the bed at night. Everything they read said it wasn't healthy for either of them. But neither had the heart to kick the mutts off. Mitten and Buffy were so possessive of the covers that it sometimes seemed to Dorothy that the humans actually slept in the dogs' bed.

Her work schedule had been tough lately, so she had a million things on her to-do list, and, of course, Philip had added a few more, including stopping at the cleaners for his shirts and picking up his skis after their off-season tune-up.

The *Pennsylvania Almanac*, that always-reliable prognosticator of weather and natural disasters, had predicted a lot of winter snow, so Philip was anticipating a good ski season. "I want our equipment in top shape," he advised Dorothy. She merely shrugged. The summer was just starting, and whistling down a ski run, several months from now, was about the last thing on her list these days. But getting Philip to do something other than work on his stupid legal case seemed like a good idea.

She was almost out the door when she realized she didn't have her cell phone, and, even worse, had forgotten to charge it the night before. She scooped up Philip's BlackBerry; chances were good he'd sleep until she returned and wouldn't miss it. Dorothy left him a note so he'd know how to reach her.

After a few local stops, she decided to call the shop in Wilkes-Barre to make sure the skis were ready. It was a long ride and the guys at the store were usually more concerned about planning their own winter ski adventures than satisfying the customers. She didn't have the store number and was about to Google it when she made the fateful decision to check Philip's address book. Sure enough, he had saved the number for Romanelli Ski Shop. She was about to click on it when her eyes caught a familiar name next on the alphabetical list. Was this a new number or a leftover from bygone days? She went to Philip's call log. Since he rarely used his phone, she was able to see calls from more than a month ago. To her chagrin, she found that same familiar name attached to a call made when Philip was at his medical conference in Philadelphia.

Still unwilling to believe what she was seeing, and beginning to doubt her own sanity, Dorothy decided impetuously to call the number. After three rings, the phone was answered by a man with a voice that she'd never forget. "Hello, this is Vincente. Can I help you?"

Dorothy hung up immediately, realizing she had made a foolish mistake. She deleted the phone call from Philip's log, but Romano would be alerted to a call from Philip's cell phone and might phone Philip later to find out what he wanted. Hopefully Philip would assume that he had made an accidental "butt call" and leave it at that. But if he didn't...

Dorothy's head was also spinning because her suspicions about Philip were being substantiated. Philip had clearly called Vincente Romano shortly before the fire that had killed the nurses. Did that mean Philip had set them up, or did he have other business with a famous mafia family?

Dorothy was in a dilemma. If she confronted Philip, she knew he'd deny everything. "No, Dorothy, I was just getting a price on a new dishwasher," she could hear him say sardonically. After all, the Romano family did operate a legitimate appliance business in Philadelphia. But she didn't need any more bullshit from Philip. She wasn't prepared to believe anything he told her about the case. She wanted the truth, even if it meant visiting the two men in the world who frightened her more than anybody.

She decided against calling the Romanos directly, but to schedule an appointment through their business office. This would allow the brothers a chance to decide what they were willing to tell her, and would also give her some time to settle down before facing them. She finished her errands and resolved to set up a meeting in Philadelphia the following week.

Dorothy went out of her way not to get into prolonged conversations with Philip over the subsequent weekend. He seemed to be in a good mood, and Dorothy didn't want her suspicions to ruin what was supposed to be a relaxing couple of days.

Philip occupied himself cleaning up the beach, taking a few more boats down to the dock, and raking up the debris that had accumulated on the property during the long, cold winter. Philip was clearly enjoying the nesting behavior and working up a good sweat. They took the dogs for walks, had drinks on the dock, and grilled fish on the back porch. The weather was perfect, the nights cool, and the sleeping enjoyable. Somehow, Dorothy was able to put the Romanos out of her mind, and to concentrate on being a "normal person" for a change.

But she was back at it on Monday morning. She called Romano Appliances from her office. "Hello, my name is Dorothy Deaver. I'd like to schedule an appointment with Vincente and Giancarlo Romano this week, if I might."

"Can I tell them what this is regarding?" the receptionist asked in a most cordial tone. "Is it about an appliance you purchased here? If so, I can transfer you to customer service."

"No, I'm an attorney working on a case they might be interested in. I just want to ask them a few background questions."

"And they'll know the case you're referring to?"

This person was well trained, Dorothy observed. What did you expect, she mused, a South Philly bimbo who didn't know her ass from her elbow? The movies tended to preserve inaccurate stereotypes of organized crime figures. In fact, these people were enormously successful, and they didn't get that way by hiring incompetents.

"Yes, they'll know the case, I can assure you. You can tell

them it's a pretty recent case in the Wilkes-Barre/Scranton area."

"Well, I'll have to clear this with them, but assuming it's acceptable, I can give you 10:00 A.M. tomorrow morning, here at the store on Broad Street."

"That would be fine. Will you please call me later today at my office to confirm? And your name is?"

"Rose Marie, but people here call me Roe. Yes, I'll call you this afternoon and leave a message if you aren't available."

"Thanks, Roe," Dorothy said. "You've been very helpful."

Dorothy had to work hard to focus herself for the rest of the day's work. She couldn't stop thinking about the case. She knew that Detweiler had held back some salient facts, but even so, it was likely that the fire had been set by professionals, and the Romanos certainly had the wherewithal to supply the talent. Not only did she believe that, but at this point she also didn't particularly care who did it. The murders had saved the state thousands if not millions of dollars it would have spent prosecuting the Adolphus murderers, that is if they ever got around to it. The neo-Nazi thing likely extended into the upper echelons of the local government, maybe even into the DA's office, which would explain the profound lack of prosecutory enthusiasm. Maybe the fire truly was the only just alternative.

She didn't expect the Romanos to tell her everything either. No, what she really wanted to get from the Romanos was their word (for whatever that was worth) that Philip had nothing to do with the murders of the Adolphus nurses, specifically, that he hadn't known about it or at least that he hadn't set them up.

Dorothy rehearsed her questions during the ride down the turnpike. She had to show respect for the old men, but she couldn't afford to let them intimidate her like they did during the Hamlin case. She had bad memories of wilting when they confronted her in their office and on the courthouse steps. How could such cute and polite old guys cause her palms to erupt in sweat and her heart to beat like a drum?

Vincente and Giancarlo had to be in their eighties now, but that didn't mean they'd be any easier to interview. This was going to be hard, but she had to look them in the eye and ask them the important questions. Had they decided to go after the Adolphus nurses, and, if so, why? And if Philip hadn't been the person who alerted them to what the nurses had done, who did? And what did the Romanos stand to gain from what happened?

She had to get clear in her own mind that she wasn't trying to get to the truth of what happened to the agency nurses. She had to meet with the Romanos because it was the only way she'd be able to salvage a relationship with the man she loved.

Chapter Twenty-Five

The Romano Appliance store on South Broad Street was a Philadelphia landmark, almost as familiar as William Penn standing imperiously atop City Hall. For more than forty years, the Romano family had sold the most modern appliances to the Italian community in South Philadelphia. They made their reputation on low prices, impeccable customer service, and community involvement. They gave to every charity, bought tons of Girl Scout cookies, attended civic association meetings, and helped whoever came to their door. They almost never refused an accommodation, particularly if it came from a member of the neighborhood they loved so much.

And it was not just about the Italian community. The Romanos were happy to assist any organization as long as they were good citizens and neighbors. The politicians tripped over themselves to win over Romano support in any election. Their endorsement had enough weight to carry many a borderline candidate into office. Without their help, even strong candidates were doomed. Once in power, officials found that the Romanos didn't ask for many favors, but when they did, a prompt and positive response was mandatory.

For example, the Romanos fought hard to keep minorities

out of their neighborhood. They did not believe that non-whites, the "jungle bunnies," "spics," and "slopes" who had infiltrated most of the Philadelphia communities, were worthy of living in their part of South Philadelphia. Consequently, unlike other wards in the city, political representation from their area remained as purely white as it had been for decades, without much hope for change as long as the Romanos had anything to say about it. Individuals who had the audacity to complain experienced a tragedy that quickly slackened their enthusiasm for change.

Vincente Romano founded the store shortly after his arrival from Italy after World War II. He had never wed. Giancarlo joined him two years later, married the beautiful Adalina Sicaronza and had two adopted children. Mary, his daughter, lived in the area and had given Giancarlo three gorgeous and devoted grandchildren. John, his childless son, died suddenly and under mysterious circumstances.

A few years later, John's widow, Bonnie, was found submerged in a limousine in the Schuylkill River with her second husband, Hugh. Their murders occurred shortly after they were found not guilty of killing Hugh's first wife, Moira. Rumors abounded, suggesting that John Romano and Moira Hamlin's deaths were somehow related, and that the Romanos had been involved in the "assassination" of Hugh and Bonnie Hamlin. The Romanos quietly but consistently denied the accusations, and the local authorities were only too happy to accept their attestations of innocence.

Despite their advanced years, each of the men was vigorous. They worked at the store every day, and although they didn't put in as many hours as they used to, and had ceded some of the decision making to Giancarlo's son-in-law, they kept a high profile that kept the business flowing. "We are the rainmakers," Vincente liked to tell his friends and family, and he was right. No one could imagine the business without the affable brothers, sipping cappuccinos at a table outside the front door of their store, or chatting with the mailman or a ward leader about sports, the weather, and current events. And no one else could muster the political muscle that had been necessary to preserve the South Philly culture in which their business flourished.

Vincente was the extrovert, and always the gentleman; Giancarlo, reserved and thoughtful. Some thought he was still grieving the death of his beloved child. John had been all that Giancarlo had hoped for in a son, not only a successful obstetrician, but also an expert in infertility. Ironic, since it was his mother Adalina's post-tuberculosis infertility that had led to John and Mary's adoption.

John's untimely and sudden death had shocked Giancarlo, who regarded the episode as one of the few times the local authorities had failed him. After a standard but careful evaluation by the police and the medical examiner, the conclusion was that John had died naturally.

The brothers didn't believe it. John had been the picture of health. They pursued the case for years. After their inquiries had drawn a blank, Dorothy Deaver had arrived at their door. In the course of her investigation of the death of Moira Hamlin, Dorothy uncovered circumstantial evidence that his wife, Bonnie, may have murdered John.

Though years had elapsed between John's death and this revelation, the brothers were happy to finally receive information to confirm their suspicions. Bonnie had not been a good daughter-in-law to the Romanos, and even before John died, they had seen little of her. A prenuptial agreement between Bonnie and John had ensured that she'd receive almost nothing if they divorced but she would be the sole inheritor of his estate upon his death. So not only did they lose their son, they also saw their hated daughter-in-law abscond with millions of dollars, money they had worked hard to accumulate for their family.

They believed that Bonnie's greed was too much of a motive to ignore. They were able to use Dorothy's facts to launch another round of inquiries that eventually convinced them that their suspicions about Bonnie had been correct. What they did next was only logical and expected.

Dorothy herself still had nightmares about her first meeting with the Romanos. Part was just plain fear of men who were so closely tied to organized crime in Philadelphia. She was also ashamed of the fact that she had inadvertently provided them with their first real clue regarding John Romano's death. Had the information she gave them caused the murders of Hugh and Bonnie Hamlin? After thinking about it for years, she arrived at the conclusion that she had been an unwitting accomplice in the grisly killings. Even worse, she feared that her discoveries had led Philip to conspire with the Romanos to kill the Hamlins in revenge for the ruination of his cardiology career.

These thoughts and memories churned in Dorothy's mind during her drive to Philadelphia, and she was so consumed by them that she hardly noticed the brutal traffic on the heavily traveled roads. She recited and memorized her questions. Notes would be confiscated on arrival during the dreaded body search for wires the Romanos would order as a condition of the interview.

Dorothy remembered Vincente's faint Italian accent. It had been so pleasant to listen to that she feared she would lose her concentration. She was going to have to work hard to sound knowledgeable, stay on point, and get answers to all of her questions.

Dorothy managed to find a parking space on Broad Street, not an easy task on that busy thoroughfare, where double and triple parking was an urban survival skill. A handsome salesman, decked out as if he were going to a wedding, sporting a designer suit, tie, and cufflinks, greeted her at the store. He directed her to the company's offices on the second floor.

Roe greeted her there, and was not the person Dorothy expected. Roe looked like a fresh-faced Irish kid from the suburbs. She was dressed conservatively, had a disarming smile and pleasant manner, and looked authentically happy to see Dorothy.

"Ms. Deaver, I'm so glad to meet you. The Romanos are

looking forward to your visit."

"Really?" Dorothy replied, surprised to be so well received. "I'm pleased they remember me."

"Oh, they remember you very well. I didn't work here the first time you visited, but you apparently made a fine impression on both of them. Can I offer you some coffee or tea?"

"No, I'm fine, but thanks."

"I do have just one unpleasant request."

"I think I know what it is, so let's just get it over with."

"I'm so sorry to put you through this, but I'm afraid that it is fairly standard procedure around here. Recording devices are so small and easy to hide these days."

The search, conducted in a large restroom adjacent to the office lobby, was thorough but somehow polite and quick. Dorothy took advantage of the opportunity to use the toilet after her long ride in the car. She wanted to be as comfortable and composed as possible during her interview.

Roe ushered Dorothy into Vincente's office. It was just as Dorothy remembered it in her dreams, remarkably modest, with a small desk in front of which sat two armchairs for guests, one of which was occupied by Giancarlo. Vincente rose from his seat behind the desk when he saw Dorothy and came around with a smile, extending a well-manicured hand to greet her. He was dressed casually, with an open white shirt and a beautiful violet cashmere sweater that matched perfectly with cuffed blue slacks that rested perfectly on soft black Gucci leather loafers.

"Ms. Deaver, we are happy to see you again. You look as beautiful as always."

Dorothy blushed despite herself as she shook hands with Vincente and then with Giancarlo, who also stood in greeting. Giancarlo was as quiet as ever in a buttoned suit and plain tie, nodding politely as he gestured for her to sit in the other armchair.

"Mr. Romano, the pleasure's mine," Dorothy finally managed as she seated herself. "I want to thank both of you for taking the time to meet with me today."

"How could we refuse? You're a good friend, and we are happy to help our friends whenever they need us." Vincente smiled as he took a seat behind his desk.

Dorothy wondered if the double entendre was intended. Were they acknowledging that they already knew about and had intervened in the case that brought her to their office?

"Roe offered you coffee, I'm sure. She never misses a detail."

"She was very nice," Dorothy said as she sat down next to Giancarlo. "I had coffee before I got here, and I'm trying to limit my caffeine."

"A very good idea. We've been trying to do the same thing. Coffee is like a lot of things in life—a little is very good, but large amounts can be harmful."

Dorothy smiled nervously while she chastised herself. She had to stop trying to find hidden meaning in everything the Romanos had to say. Maybe gangsters engage in small talk just like everybody else.

"We want to apologize again for the inconvenience of the search. We know it's demeaning, and we don't want you to think we distrust you. Maybe we have been watching too many episodes of *The Sopranos* on television," Vincente laughed. Even Giancarlo cracked a smile.

"I understand," Dorothy lied. "One can never be too careful."

"In exchange, Ms. Deaver, we promise to answer your questions as fully as we can," Giancarlo added. "We only ask that you preserve confidentiality."

"Disclosures lead to grave consequences, in our experience, Ms. Deaver," Vincente said. "But enough of these gloomy thoughts, eh? What can we help you with today?"

"I'm sure you've seen reports in the papers about the terrible fire in Wilkes-Barre that killed thirty nurses," Dorothy began.

"Yes, the Adolphus fire," Vincente replied matter of factly.

"Exactly. So you've heard about it already."

"It has been all over the news, and Giancarlo and I like to

keep up with current events."

"Of course," Dorothy stammered. I must sound like a total idiot, Dorothy thought.

"Why are you concerned about that tragedy, Ms. Deaver?" Vincente asked.

Before she could answer, Giancarlo cut in. "Vincente, perhaps it would be best if we put our cards on the table." Giancarlo's monotone made Dorothy suspect that the remark had been planned. Before Vincente could answer his brother, Dorothy decided to speak up.

"Yes, I'd greatly prefer that you tell me what you know about the fire and the things that led up to it. It would make things much easier for all of us."

"Very well," Vincente said, leaning back in his desk chair, hands behind his head. "Here is what we found out. Several German and Italian Americans died of an unanticipated cardiac disorder at several hospitals in the Scranton and Wilkes-Barre area over the last several months."

"How did you find out?" Dorothy interrupted. She was desperate to discover what had put the Romanos on the trail. Vincente didn't hold back.

"Several of the Italian families contacted us after you visited them, Ms. Deaver. You told them that the cases were "under investigation." They talked among themselves, put two and two together, and wanted us to find out if there was foul play. It was logical for them to do that, don't you agree?"

Oh yeah, Dorothy thought. After someone visits your house asking questions, you should immediately suspect that your loved one has been killed. And then, it would only be logical to call your regional Cosa Nostra. Standard operating procedure, as far as she could tell.

"Why did they come to your family, Mr. Romano? Aren't there people in that area who might be as interested and helpful?"

"Good question, Ms. Deaver," Vincente replied. "We do have associates over a very large area of the state, so the inquiry was broadcast pretty widely. You'll have to admit that coming to us with such an inquiry is better than going on Google."

Again, chuckles from the brothers. Dorothy thought, I should have suspected as much. This is a highly successful organization with long tentacles. I bet the feds would just love to know how extensive the network really is.

"So you conducted an investigation?"

"Yes, we certainly did. Let's just say we took a personal interest in the case."

"And what did you discover, if I may ask?"

"That a neo-Nazi organization, comprised of nurses who had worked in the US military, were massacring old men who had fought against their 'homeland' in World War II."

Dorothy didn't try to look surprised. "I guess that didn't make you happy."

"Let me be honest," Vincente replied. "If they had restricted themselves to the German pigs, we would have given them a medal. But they went too far."

"Ms. Deaver," Giancarlo rejoined, "they saddened and aggrieved hundreds of our kin by what they did. We had no choice but to handle the problem with a minimum of fuss."

"Ms. Deaver, are you aware of the fact that Al Romanzo was a distant relative?" Vincente asked.

Dorothy had to struggle to remember that Romanzo had been the victim in the malpractice case that Philip had reviewed. "No, I didn't know that."

"Well, he was," Vincente continued. "That branch of the family kept the 'z' in their name. Alfonzo worked with us after he got out of the Army and college. He left us to start his own store in Scranton, but we kept up with him through the years. His children, those scum, abandoned him to that nursing home but Giancarlo and I went up to see him once in a while. We were very sad to hear of his passing, but amazed to learn that it wasn't a natural death."

"I assume you didn't consider going through channels and working with the police?"

"Are you joking? The police department, and every other

governmental agency up there, is rife with corruption. We were able to ascertain that several of the people who were supposedly investigating the case were either bribed by Adolphus or were part of the conspiracy. And it went from low to high in the organizations."

Dorothy could only shake her head. It is precisely what Philip and her father had surmised. And it certainly explained why the police investigation had been inadequate from the start. "Anybody in particular I might know?"

"We can't divulge names. That might place our people in jeopardy. Suffice it to say, Ms. Deaver, that some of the folks most involved in the murder investigation have interesting military service backgrounds that you really should have known about."

Dorothy's head began to spin. Were Detweiler and the people in the District Attorney's office a party to the Adolphus conspiracy? Her father would be embarrassed to admit that he hadn't done a background check on the men, even when the jerks had stubbornly refused to pursue the investigation. How had the Romanos come to suspect them? She'd love to get the answer to that question, but she needed to keep her eye on the prize.

"So you took matters into your own hands."

"That is far too literal, Ms. Deaver," Vincente replied. "Let's just say we have access to a wide variety of people who possess certain unique skills, and they were as cooperative as always."

"Did you have to kill so many and in such a brutal way?"

"Ms. Deaver, we specialize in providing protection for our people. Believe me, the decision to go forward with the plan was not made in haste. We carefully considered all of our alternatives, including punishing the corrupt law enforcement people up there."

"Wouldn't that have been a better solution for the long term?"

"Corrupt politicians are like serpents with many heads. You can cut one or several off, but they grow back with a vengeance. To fix the political system in any jurisdiction requires fundamental changes in the laws and in the way the system operates."

"That is a little beyond even our capabilities, Ms. Deaver, don't you agree?" Giancarlo added with a smirk.

"So we decided to do the best we could to stop the murders permanently," Vincente continued. "And to be honest, we had yet another motivation. Health care in that region has not been excellent. But in the last few years, we have seen a dramatic improvement. If it ever got out that patients were being systematically murdered in hospitals in Wilkes-Barre and Scranton, those institutions would be harmed and our friends would suffer even more, and for many years to come. It may have been another reason why the authorities dragged their feet on the case, but it certainly motivated us to take action. As you can see, the true scandal never made it to the media."

"And we thought the best way to accomplish our purpose was to take out a very large number in one stroke," Giancarlo insisted. "The meeting was our best opportunity to have a majority of them in one place. Given the nature of their business, we knew that eliminating all of them would be impossible. We wanted to make sure the others wouldn't summon up the courage to carry on. The more messy their deaths the better, in that respect."

"Remember, our friends up there were absolutely furious when they learned the truth about their loved ones' deaths," Giancarlo continued. "We were worried that some of them might pursue their own justice. Amateurs can be sloppy and cause difficulties for themselves and everybody else if they aren't careful. As it turned out, they were more than satisfied with our solution."

"Ms. Deaver, I have to admit that we were also concerned by your mishap," Vincente added in a soft voice.

"You knew about my car accident?"

"Accident, Ms. Deaver? You're not that naïve, are you?"

"Ms. Deaver," Giancarlo continued, "was it a coincidence that while you were investigating Adolphus you were almost killed?"

Dorothy didn't answer. She was trying to decide if she should feel guilty about the murders or relieved that she had guardian angels watching over her.

As if he were reading her mind, Vincente posited, "And have you taken note that since the fire, no one has come anywhere near you, your home, or your beloved dogs?"

"How did you know about Buffy?"

"Giancarlo and I love dogs, Ms. Deaver," Vincente smiled as he deftly sidestepped Dorothy's question. "I'm embarrassed to say that we may have been as upset about your dog's kidnapping as we were about the murders. Such matters shouldn't affect poor dumb animals. It confirms what amateurs those evil people really were."

"We thought that they were only trying to intimidate us."

"Ms. Deaver, we care very much about you. Assuming that bad people will stop with intimidation is very much like expecting Democrats to balance the budget and cut taxes. It could happen but why take the chance?"

"So, as with the Hamlin murders, there were multiple agendas?"

"Yes. That is a good analogy, Ms. Deaver. The Hamlin case was also complicated and personal, of course, but it did solve a problem for multiple constituencies, don't you agree?"

Dorothy steeled herself for the most important query. "Did Philip have anything to do with the fire?"

"Do you mean did he have a hand in it or did he know about it beforehand?" Vincente asked.

"Yes."

Vincente came around the desk, and stood over Dorothy. He took her hand, just as he had years before after the Hamlin murders, looked her in the eye, and said, "Ms. Deaver, I can assure you that neither Dr. Sarkis nor your father participated in or had any knowledge of the murders."

Dorothy was so relieved that she nearly cried. "I was so worried. When I found out Philip had called you a few days before the fire, I was worried he was involved."

"He did call here, Ms. Deaver," Vincente answered, looking deeply into her eyes. "He wanted to know if we had learned about the crime and if we had any insight. We denied any knowledge, of course. He was on the phone, and wiretaps are everywhere. Besides, we like Dr. Sarkis, and we didn't want him to have to lie under oath if there was any suspicion."

Dorothy composed herself. "You don't have any idea how much this means to me, Mr. Romano."

"I wish you would call us Vincente and Giancarlo. If I may, Dorothy, we are very fond of you. You're a nice person and well intentioned. Giancarlo and I think of you as one of our family. I hope you appreciate that."

Dorothy was even more frightened to think that these men accepted her as one of them. But she nodded and said some nice things while preparing to leave.

Giancarlo had one last admonition. "Remember Ms. Deaver, we have denied everything you asked about today, and we will do so again if asked by anyone else. I strongly suggest you share this with no one, aside from Dr. Sarkis, of course. Your safety and ours depends on your discretion."

Giancarlo and Vincente escorted Dorothy to Roe's desk and said their good-byes. In a few more seconds, Dorothy was back on the street. The interview that seemed like hours had only lasted twenty-five minutes. Lost in thought, she climbed into her car and began the long drive home, grateful for the opportunity to replay and process the events of the last several months without having to envision Philip as a key player in the incredible drama.

Chapter Twenty-Six

After her meeting with the Romanos, Dorothy felt better. Her most important questions had been answered succinctly and openly. She wasn't going to hazard adverbs like *honestly* or *truthfully*. She might be naïve about some matters, but she was savvy enough to know whom she was dealing with. The Romanos made their living using lies and deception. Just because they were nice to her didn't mean they weren't laughing now about how easy it had been to manipulate a naïve lady attorney who practiced law in the sticks.

Dorothy decided to stop at a rest station on the Pennsylvania Turnpike to fill her tank. She hadn't done that in years, usually driving straight through from the Poconos to Philadelphia to shop or see her dad. She was surprised to see that the political hacks who sat on the Turnpike Commission had finally figured out that there was profit to be made from the captive customers who used the toll road. In addition to paying a lot of money to drive on an antiquated and poorly maintained highway, now if you wanted food, you could get an upscale meal or snack that had some chance of tasting good. Her rumbling stomach reminded Dorothy that a bite was in order. She bought a croissant and a cup of tea from a bakery counter, and settled into a booth for a minute before resuming her journey.

It gave her some more time to think quietly, a luxury she didn't enjoy very often.

Dorothy's father had taught her to consider all possibilities. For any situation, there were always many potential explanations. She tried to conjure up all of the ways that Philip could have participated in the assassination of the Adolphus nurses. First, Philip could have set the fire. No way in hell, Dorothy thought. He was intimidated by lighting the grill on their back porch. He backpedaled when he threw in the match and a flame leapt up. The central figures in the assassination were professionals who knew how to get on the property without suspicion, plant the incendiaries, and ignite the fire remotely. Philip had an exactly zero chance of pulling that off.

Second, Philip could have paid for the hit. Once again, this was unlikely. In his prime, Philip made a lot of money giving lectures, consulting, serving as an expert witness, and running clinical trials. Those days were gone. Philip was salaried by the clinic. He was asked to do a few small-time lectures here and there, but nothing that would net him enough money to pay for a complicated mass murder. Dorothy didn't know the going rate, but she imagined that it would cost several thousand dollars to compensate a team of people to burn nurses to death in their own building. Philip didn't have that kind of juice. Nancy had taken most of the jointly held assets that had been salvaged from the malpractice verdict, and he had child-care payments. He still owed money to the Hamlin estate, and the lawyers had been very careful to make sure he didn't have assets squirreled away somewhere.

Third, Philip could have gone to the Romanos and encouraged them to assassinate the Adolphus nurses. Philip certainly had the motive and the opportunity. She had proof he had spoken to the Romanos shortly before the incident. The Romanos, however, didn't strike Dorothy as the kind of people who would take murder requests like a DJ at a radio station. There had to be a strong personal reason to do a big job like that, or the person making the request had to be perceived as a "member of the family" who had somehow made a large contribution to the good of their organization. What had Philip done for the Romanos to motivate them to go out on a limb just for him? Admittedly, he may have set up the Hamlins for them those many years ago, but more likely Dorothy had done that herself, albeit unwittingly.

Finally, the Romanos could have been informed about the situation by the families of the victims, as they claimed, and merely advised Philip to look for cover. It would explain the hurriedly arranged trip to Philadelphia for dinner with her father, and Philip's insisting to go to Cedars on Friday rather than Saturday.

Her father! Dorothy realized with a start that the Romanos had specifically included Dick Deaver while absolving Philip. What the hell did that mean? Dorothy hadn't mentioned her father to the Romanos, though she was sure they knew who he was and what he did for a living.

She remembered Dick's reaction to her accident. He had been concerned, but he wasn't exactly enraged. In retrospect, how strange it was for Dick not to have extracted revenge for Alex and Chris' murders. He had warned Brenda Straub not to put his family in jeopardy, and he had read the riot act to Detweiler, that snake. Had Philip disobeyed her and told Dick about her accident and Buffy's kidnapping?

If so, the Dick Deaver she knew would not have let bygones be bygones. Was that why Dick had dinner with Philip in Philadelphia during the medical meeting? During their dinner at Cedars, Dick hadn't said a word about the "low lifes" at Adolphus. Was he satisfied that the fix was in and that his hands would be clean?

And why had Philip invited her father along to dinner at Cedars? Twenty-dollar bills for the belly dancers? What better way to etch yourself in someone's memory than by grossly over tipping and making a drunken fool of yourself?

As pissed off as she was at her father and Philip for their duplicity, she had to admit it would have been the smart thing to do. If the Romanos had it right, Detweiler was either part of the Nazi gang, or he had been motivated or cowed into letting them get away with murder. What better way to stymie an investigation than by planting a sympathizer right in the middle of it? And if Detweiler was a member of the merry men, he played it perfectly. Enlist a couple of amateurs who might lay bare some of the facts, but never enough to bring an indictment or stop the perps. Intimidate them and even kill them if necessary, but use them as an excuse to stall the investigation and keep your brothers from getting caught. And was it just a coincidence that his boss' name was Hoffman?

Detweiler must have been as shocked as anyone by the fire that cooked his cronies. But he was a smart guy and probably very grateful he wasn't among the dead. So he made damn sure the fire investigation focused on Philip and Dorothy as persons of interest, not wanting to play hardball with the people he knew were the real culprits. He'd never be able to bring the Romanos to justice, and if he tried, he'd be the next rotisserie offering.

Playing by the rules got Philip and her father precisely nowhere, so when presented with the opportunity, Dick had to figure he could get the retribution he desired with no cost, minimal risk, and impeccable results. Philip already knew the Romanos—Dick just had to use Philip to make the contact and stand back and watch the fireworks. It sure beat finding a horse's head in your own bed.

Her thoughts naturally turned from her father to the other man in her life. If her assumptions were correct, Philip's transformation had been remarkable: from an innocent, well-intentioned, newly minted nerdy cardiologist to a cold, calculating accomplice to multiple murders.

She had fallen madly in love with that idealistic, driven physician who had aspirations to rid the world of heart disease. He had been off to a good start until he stepped on the Hamlin land mine. The malpractice suit took his life away and devastated him, but Dorothy had been so proud of his resurrection, and ultimate redemption. If only the inane legal system had punished Moira's killers. When it failed, Philip was transformed once again, this time into a demon.

She had tried hard to believe him when he pleaded his innocence to the Hamlin murders. He had been convincing—a performance worthy of an Oscar. In fact, his profession of innocence was reminiscent of Michael Corleone's words to his wife in *The Godfather.* " Just this once, Kate." And "No, I didn't have Carlos killed. Do you think I would make my sister a widow?" Had Philip watched the movie to get his lines straight? Had she believed him so readily because she so desperately wanted to?

This time the case started out much less ominously. The perpetrators were very bad people, but it wasn't personal. Quickly, the stakes were raised. Before she knew it, they were embroiled in a case with themselves as potential targets. Philip suffered the loss of a dear old friend, and then the wackos at Adolphus went after Buffy and her. She dared not wonder which insult pricked him more. The final straw had to be Mr. Lasordi, Philip's hero barber growing up. The nutcases killed the old guy right under Philip's nose. As convincing as Vincente had been, after considering the entire case and Philip's frame of mind, Dorothy couldn't help but believe that he and her father had taken an active role.

These thoughts swirled around in Dorothy's mind as she left the rest stop and navigated her way back up the Pennsylvania Turnpike and then across Route 940 to their home. The sun was just beginning to set as she parked her car and opened the front door and saw Philip in the kitchen. He had worked the night before, had napped, and was standing at the counter, smiling and mixing vodka tonics for their "docktails."

"Great timing," Philip chirped happily. "Just getting our drinks ready, and I have some salmon to throw on the grill. How was your trip to Philly? Did you get all your business done?"

Dorothy quickly tried to remember which lie she had told Philip that morning when she had informed him she'd be on the road. With just a momentary hesitation, she answered, "Yeah, I met with the plaintiff's counsel, and she appeared to be ready to settle the case. We have some negotiating to do, of course, to get the amount right."

"Greedy lawyers," Philip said smiling. "Well, you were paid well for your time at least?"

"You bet," Dorothy agreed. "And mileage, of course."

Dorothy quickly changed into jeans and a long-sleeved T-shirt, and they walked down the stone path to the lakefront. Four chairs were already perched on the dock so both dogs would have a place to rest as well. Philip pulled four cushions out of the storage locker, and they all made themselves comfortable. They loved watching the ducks and beavers swim by. The sun was beginning to sink behind the hill across from their house. There were just enough clouds to make the sky turn pink and purple.

"What a beautiful sunset," Philip observed. "I can't say that I've ever been more at peace with things."

Dorothy just smiled. When Philip was in this kind of mood, she knew he'd carry the conversation. A good thing, since she wasn't in the mood to make a lot of small talk.

"The kids will be up this weekend," Philip continued. "I was thinking we could take them to Camel Beach."

Oh great, thought Dorothy, a hot weekend day at the local water park with a bunch of screaming kids and obnoxious New York parents who have nothing better to do than push and shove their way to the front of the line. She loved Philip's kids, but they weren't hers. And the more that she felt distanced from him, the more that time with the kids became a chore. "That would be fun," she lied.

"Maybe your father would like to come up, too, and spend some time with us. He is always complaining about not having grandchildren. Maybe he can adopt my kids."

"Is my father your new best friend?" Dorothy asked.

"I enjoy seeing him, and we obviously have some common interests."

You can say that again, Dorothy mused. There's nothing like a good murder conspiracy to keep the home hearth warm. "We can ask him," she answered. "I wouldn't be surprised if he had plans."

"I hope he can make it. He is good with kids. Dick has some fine family values."

You bet, Dorothy thought. And so do some gentlemen in Philadelphia you've gotten familiar with. "No doubt about that. He's very protective of his family; a lot like you," she said.

"What makes you say that?" Philip turned to ask.

This was her opening, an opportunity to confront Philip with what she had learned from the Romanos that day, and to let him deny his involvement, exactly as he had after the Hamlin murder. If she demurred and didn't try to find the truth, in her eyes he'd no longer be the serious physician-scientist trying to do the best thing for his patients. Rather, she might come to perceive him as a vindictive, cunning accessory to murder. And as a bonus, one who managed to drag her impulsive and well-meaning father into the morass.

"How about another vodka tonic?" was all Dorothy could manage.

"It would be my considerable pleasure. I could use a fresh one myself."

Philip rose stiffly from his chair, grabbed the glasses, and started up the walkway. After he was in the house and out of earshot, Dorothy turned to Mitten and Buffy, as Philip frequently did when in a quandary. According to Philip, the dogs were good at giving advice and answering tough questions. They opined with their bark, their eyes, and their tails. People who think dogs have nothing to "say," just don't know what to look for. It was a matter of paying attention to the subtleties.

"Well, girls, what do you think? Did your dad go over the line and have those agency nurses killed, or am I making a mountain out of a molehill? Should I be worried, or should I just get on with things?"

Buffy had nothing to say on the matter, according to Dorothy's interpretation. Her chin was propped on the left arm of her lounge chair, her eyes closed, and her tail still. Dorothy thought, she's deferring to Mitten.

Mitten was the senior of the two and clearly the intellectual. She rarely acted impulsively, and pondered things for a long time before expressing an opinion, especially in matters of such gravity. Mitten clearly heard Dorothy's question, and looked up the path, lost in thought about her master, Philip. After a minute, she jumped off of her chair, ambled over to Dorothy, put her paw on Dorothy's lap, looked her in the eye, and raised both ears, higher than Dorothy had ever observed.

"You're surprised, old girl, that I would make such an accusation. You have faith in your dad, don't you?"

Mitten began to pant, and her ears went down. "Exactly," was her response, "how could we think less of that silly guy?"

Dorothy smiled. "All right girls, I'll take your lead. I won't ask him the question, at least not now. We will give this thing a little more time."

The evening turned into a pleasant one for all four creatures. After another vodka tonic, a fine dinner of salmon that the dogs shared with their kibble, and a brandy for the humans, Philip and Dorothy made love and fell asleep in each other's arms.

Dorothy awoke in the middle of the night to find both dogs at the foot of their bed, sleeping peacefully. She looked over at the dozing Philip and realized how much she truly loved the guy despite his quirks. I like this life, she thought. But am I ignoring too much to keep it like it is?

Dorothy lay back on her pillow contemplating this, the most important and fundamental issue of her life. It was going to be a tough question to answer, one that even the magnificent Mitten would have to ponder long and hard.

PETER R KOWEY MD

Dr. Kowey is an internationally respected expert in heart rhythm disorders. After college at St. Joseph's University in Philadelphia, he attended medical school at the University of Pennsylvania and trained in cardiology at Harvard. For the past thirty-one years, he has developed a large referral practice in the Philadelphia region, caring for thousands of patients with various cardiac rhythm problems while teaching and mentoring countless medical students, residents, fellows, and physicians in practice.

Dr. Kowey's research has led to the development of dozens of new drugs and devices for treating a wide range of cardiac diseases. He authored hundreds of scientific articles and textbooks chapters before embarking on his first work of fiction, the widely praised *Lethal Rhythm*, published in 2010.

Dr. Kowey and his wife, Dorothy, have three daughters and six grandchildren. Their permanent residence is in Bryn Mawr, Pennsylvania, but they spend time throughout the year with their Portuguese water dogs at their lake house in the Pocono Mountains.

Deadly Rhythm

Peter R. Kowey